I took information on the Yanomami from the *Times* and on Rome from *National Geographic Traveler*. I would like to thank Janet Buck's ladies for their information (they know who they are), Bernadette Forcey for the joke and Pamela Norris for her constant support. Also deep gratitude is owed to the brilliant Clare Ferraro and Pamela Dorman and their team at Penguin Putnam, and to Louise Moore and her team at Viking Penguin, plus my agent, Mark Lucas. This is not to forget my family and other friends.

Living well is the best revenge

Old Spanish proverb

Praise for *Revenge of the Middle-Aged Woman*

"Wise and wonderful. The 'revenge' in the title has little to do with getting back at people. Rather, Buchan celebrates the patience and wisdom that only age brings." —*USA Today*

"Revenge may be sweet, but *Revenge* is not, thank goodness." —*The Wall Street Journal*

"Middle-aged or not, readers will find this book funny and sad, serious and light. Bottom line: Get *Revenge*." —*People* (Page-Turner of the Week)

"Buchan's writing has the elegant understatement and wry wit that Americans so cherish in the British." —*Chicago Tribune*

"Warm and insightful." —*The Dallas Morning News*

"In the end, *Revenge of the Middle-Aged Woman* is not about revenge as much as it is about change. Thought-provoking in its restraint; this is a novel that is about a three-dimensional woman, not a stereotype, and she's a character that grows on the reader while she grows into a new stage of her life." —*The Denver Post*

"A sophisticated and satisfying novel . . . Buchan opts for a more believable examination of one intelligent woman's coming-of-age." —*Publishers Weekly* (starred review)

"Elizabeth Buchan takes a familiar story and reinvigorates it with honesty, humor, warmth, and wisdom. What a *satisfying* book. I couldn't put it down." —Patricia Gaffney

"Brilliant, deliciously sensual, exquisitely crafted [with] intelligent restraint. Bravo to Buchan's witty, wise, and wonderfully readable novel." —Wendy Holden

"What a terrific book! *Revenge of the Middle-Aged Woman*—from that wry, powerful title to its final paragraph—is so beautifully executed that it becomes new, fresh, and interesting." —Fay Weldon

"Wise, melancholy, funny and sophisticated." —*The Times* (London)

"What a good writer Buchan is." —*Daily Telegraph* (London)

"Here is proof that pain can serve as a catalyst for a glorious rebirth. What I like best about this novel is everything." —Elizabeth Berg

ABOUT THE AUTHOR

A frequent reviewer for *The Times, Sunday Times,* and *Daily Mail,* Elizabeth Buchan has also been a judge for the Whitbread and Betty Trask awards. Her book *Revenge of the Middle-Aged Woman* has been optioned as a feature film, and her next novel, *The Good Wife Strikes Back,* is newly published by Viking. Elizabeth Buchan lives in London with her husband and children.

Revenge *of the* Middle-Aged Woman

Elizabeth Buchan

PENGUIN BOOKS

For Lindy

PENGUIN BOOKS

Published by the Penguin Group

Penguin Group (USA) Inc., 375 Hudson Street, New York, New York 10014, U.S.A.

Penguin Books Ltd, 80 Strand, London WC2R 0RL, England

Penguin Books Australia Ltd, 250 Camberwell Road, Camberwell, Victoria 3124, Australia

Penguin Books Canada Ltd, 10 Alcorn Avenue, Toronto, Ontario, Canada M4V 3B2

Penguin Books India (P) Ltd, 11 Community Centre,

Panchsheel Park, New Delhi – 110 017, India

Penguin Books (N.Z.) Ltd, Cnr Rosedale and Airborne Roads, Albany, Auckland, New Zealand

Penguin Books (South Africa) (Pty) Ltd, 24 Sturdee Avenue,

Rosebank, Johannesburg 2196, South Africa

Penguin Books Ltd, Registered Offices: 80 Strand, London WC2R 0RL, England

First published in Great Britain by Penguin Books Ltd 2002
First published in the United States of America by Viking Penguin,
a member of Penguin Putnam Inc. 2003
Published in Penguin Books 2004

9 10 8

Grateful acknowledgment is made for permission to reprint an excerpt from
"Ash Wednesday"from *Collected Poems 1909–1962* by T. S. Eliot. Copyright 1930
and renewed 1958 by T. S. Eliot. Reprinted by permission of Harcourt, Inc.

PUBLISHER'S NOTE

This is a work of fiction. Names, characters, places, and incidents either are the product
of the author's imagination or are used fictitiously, and any resemblance to actual persons,
living or dead, business establishments, events, or locales is entirely coincidental.

THE LIBRARY OF CONGRESS HAS CATALOGED THE
AMERICAN HARDCOVER EDITION AS FOLLOWS:
Buchan, Elizabeth.
Revenge of the middle-aged woman / by Elizabeth Buchan.
p. cm.
ISBN 0-670-03206-9 (hc.)
ISBN 0 14 20.0372 7 (pbk.)
1. Middle aged women—Fiction. 2. Life change events—Fiction.
3. Married women—Fiction. 4. Adultery—Fiction. 5. England—Fiction. I. Title.
PR6052.U214 R4 2003
823'.914—dc21   2002074060

Printed in the United States of America
Set in Bembo • Designed by Erin Benach

Chapter 1

"Here," said Minty, my deputy, with one of her breathy laughs, "the review has just come in. It's hilariously vindictive." She pushed toward me a book entitled *A Thousand Olive Trees* by Hal Thorne with the review tucked into it.

For some reason, I picked up the book. Normally I avoided anything to do with Hal but I did not think it mattered this once. I was settled, busy, different, and I had made my choice a long time ago.

When we first discussed my working on the books pages, Nathan argued that, if I ever achieved my ambition to become the books editor, I would end up hating books. Familiarity bred contempt. But I said that Mark Twain had got it better when he said that familiarity breeds not so much contempt but children, and wasn't Nathan's comment a reflection on his own feelings about his own job? Nathan replied, "Nonsense, have I ever been happier?" and "You wait and see." (The latter was said with one of his ironic, strongman I know-better-than-you smiles, which I always enjoyed.) So far, he had been wrong.

For me, books remained full of promise, and contained a sense of possibility, any possibility. In rocky times, they were saviors and lifebelts, and when I was younger they provided chapter and verse when I had to make decisions. Over the years of working with them, it had become second nature to categorize them by touch. Thick, rough, cheaper paper denoted a paperback novel. Poetry hovered on the weightless and was decorated with wide white margins. Biographies were heavy with photographs and the secrets of their subjects' life.

A Thousand Olive Trees was slim and compact, a typical travelog whose cover photograph was of a hard, blue sky and a rocky, isolated shoreline beneath. It looked hot and dry, the kind of terrain where feet slithered over scree, and bruises sprouted between the toes.

Minty was watching my reaction. She had a trick of fixing her dark, slightly slanting eyes on whoever, and of appearing not to blink. The effect was of rapt, sympathetic attention, which fascinated people and also, I think, comforted them. That dark, intent gaze had certainly comforted me many times during the three years we had worked together in the office.

" 'This man is a fraud,' " she cited from the review. " 'And his book is worse . . . ' "

"What do you suppose he's done to deserve the vitriol?" I murmured.

"Sold lots of copies," Minty shot back.

I handed her *A Thousand Olive Trees*. "You deal. Ring up Dan Thomas, and see if he'll do a quickie."

"Not up to it, Rose?" She spoke slowly and thoughtfully, but with an edge I did not quite recognize. "Don't you think you should be by now?"

I smiled at her. I liked to think that Minty had become a friend, and because she always spoke her mind I trusted her. "No. It's not a test. I just don't wish to handle Hal Thorne's books."

"Fine." She picked her way round the boxes on the floor, which was packed with them, and sat down. "Like you said, I know how to deal." I am not sure she approved. Neither did I, for it was not professional behavior to ignore a book, certainly not one that would receive a lot of coverage.

My attention was diverted by the internal phone. It was Steven from production. "Rose, I'm very sorry but we are going to have to cut a page from Books for the twenty-ninth."

"Steven!"

"Sorry, Rose. Can you do it by this afternoon?"

"Twice running, Steve. Can't someone else be the sacrificial lamb? Cookery? Travel?"

"No."

Steven was harassed and impatient. In our business—getting an issue out—time dictated our decisions and our reactions. After a while, it became second nature, and we spoke to each other in a shorthand. There was never time for the normal give and take of argument. I glanced at Minty. She was typing away studiously, but she was, I knew, listening in. I said reluctantly, "I could manage it by tomorrow morning."

"No later." Steven rang off.

"Bad luck." Minty typed away. "How much?"

"A page." I sat back to consider the problem, and my eye fell on the photograph of Nathan and the children, which had a permanent place on my desk. It had been taken on a bucket-and-spade holiday in Cornwall when the children were ten and eight. They were on the beach, with their backs to a gray, ruffled sea. Nathan had one arm round Sam, who stood quietly in its shelter, while the other restrained a squirming, joyous Poppy. Our children were as different as chalk and cheese. I had just mentioned that a famous novelist had also taken a house in Trebethan Bay for six months to finish a novel. "Good heavens." Nathan had made one of his faces. "I had no idea he was such a slow reader." I had seized the camera and caught Poppy howling with laughter at this latest example of his terrible jokes. Nathan was laughing, too, with pleasure and satisfaction. See? he was saying to the camera. We are a happy family.

I leaned over and touched Nathan's face in the photograph. Clever, loving Nathan. He considered that the job of fatherhood was to keep his children so amused that they did not notice the unpleasant side of life until they were old enough to cope, but he also loved to make them laugh for the pleasure of it. Sometimes, at mealtimes, I had been driven to put my foot down: at best, Sam and Poppy's appetites were as slight as their bodies and I worried about them. "Mrs. Worry, do you not know that people who eat less are healthier and live longer?" demanded Nathan who, typically, had gone to some pains to find out this fact to soothe my fears.

Back to the problem. As always with the paper, there were political factors, none significant in isolation but taken together, they could add up. I said to Minty, "I think I'd better go and fight. Otherwise Timon might get into the habit of paring down Books. Don't you think?" The "don't you think" was cosmetic for I had made up my mind, but I had fallen into the habit of treating Minty (just a little) in the way I had treated the children. I thought it was important to involve them on all levels.

Timon was the editor of the weekend Digest in the Vistemax Group for which we worked and his word was law.

Minty had her back to me and was searching for Dan Thomas's telephone number in her contacts book. "If you say so."

"Do I hear cheers of support?"

Minty still did not look round. "Perhaps better to leave it, Rose. We might need our ammunition."

When it was a question of territorial battles, Minty was as defensive as I was. This made me suspicious. "Do you know something that I don't, Minty?" *Not* a silly question. People and events in the group changed all the time, which made it a rather dangerous place to work, and one had to become rather protean, undercover and dangerous to survive.

"No. No, of course not."

"But . . . ?"

Minty's phone rang and she snatched it up. "Books."

I waited a moment or two longer. Minty scribbled on a piece of paper, "An ego here bigger than your bottom," and slid it toward me.

This implied that she would be on the phone for several minutes, so I left her to it and walked out into the open-plan space that was called the office. The management reminded its employees, frequently and cheerily, that it had been designed with humans in mind, but the humans repaid this thoughtfulness with ingratitude and dislike: if it was light and airy, it was also unprivate and, funnily enough, despite the hum of conversation and the underlying whine of the computers, it gave an impression of glaucous silence.

Maeve Otley from the subs' desk maintained, with a deep sense of grievance, that it was a voyeur's paradise. It was true: there was nowhere for staff to shake themselves back into their skins, or to hide their griefs and despairs, only the fishbowl where the owners had not bothered to put in a rock or two. I grumbled with Maeve, who was another friend, against the imposition, the terrorism of our employers, but mostly, like everyone else, I had adapted and grown used to it.

On the floor below, Steven was surrounded by piles of computer printout and flat plans, and looked frantic. A half-eaten chicken sandwich was resting in its container beside him with several small plastic bottles of mineral water. When he saw me bearing down on him, he raised a hand to ward me off. "Don't, Rose. It's not kind."

"It's not kind to Books."

He looked longingly at his sandwich. "Who cares, as long as I can get it done and dusted and into bed? You, Rose, are expendable."

"If I make a fuss with Timon?"

"You won't get diddly . . ."

No headway there. "What *is* so important that it thieves my space? A shepherd's pie?"

"A nasty demolition job on a cabinet minister. I can't tell you who." Steven looked important. "The usual story. A mistress with exotic tastes, cronyism, undeclared interests. Apparently, his family don't know what's coming, and it's top secret."

I felt a shudder brush through me, of distaste and worry. In the early days, I used to feel plain, unadorned guilt for the suffering that these exposés caused. Lately, my reaction had dulled. Familiarity had made it commonplace, and it had lost its capacity to disturb me. Yet I hated to think of what exposure did to the families. How would I cope if I woke up one morning to discover that my everyday life had been built on a falsehood? Would I break into pieces? The effect on the children of these stories of deceit and betrayal did not bear too much thought either. But I accepted there was little I could do, except resign my job in protest. "And are you going to do that?" asked Nathan, quite properly. *"No."* So my private doubts and occasional flashes of guilt remained private.

"I feel sorry for them," I said to Steven. All the same, I ran through a list of possible candidates in my head. I was human.

"Don't. He probably deserves it."

Steven took a bite of his sandwich. "Are you going to let me get on?"

By chance, Nathan stepped out of the lift with Peter Shaker, his managing editor, as I was going in. "Hallo, darling," I murmured. Nathan was preoccupied, and the two men conferred in an undertone. It always gave me a shock, a pleasurable one, to see Nathan operating. It was the chance to witness a different, disengaged aspect of the man I knew at home, and it held an erotic charge. It reminded me that he had a separate, distinct existence. And that I did, too.

"Nathan," I touched his arm. "I was going to ring. We're due at the restaurant at eight."

He started. "Rose. I was thinking of something else. Sorry. I'll—I'll see you later."

"Sure." I waved at him and Peter as the doors closed. He did not wave back.

I thought nothing of it. As deputy editor of a daily paper published by the Vistemax Group, Nathan was a busy man. Friday was a day packed with meetings and, more often than not, he stumbled back to Lakey Street wrung out and exhausted. Then it was my business to soothe him and to listen. If the look on his face was anything to go by, and after twenty-five years of marriage I knew Nathan, this was a bad Friday.

The lift bore me upward. Jobs and spouses held things in common. With luck, you found the right one at the right time. You fell in love with a person, or a job, tied the knot and settled down to the muddle and routine that suited you. I admit it was not entirely an accident that Nathan and I worked for the same company—an electronics giant which also published several newspapers and magazines under its corporate umbrella—but I liked to think that I had won my job on my own merits. Or, if that was not precisely true, that I kept on my own merits.

Poppy hated what Nathan and I did. Now twenty-two, she had stopped laughing and believed that lives should be useful and lived for the greater good, or she did at the last time of asking. "Why contribute to a vast, wasteful process like a newspaper?" she wanted to know. "An excuse to cut down trees and print hurtful rubbish." Poppy had always fought hard, harder than Sam, and her growing up had been like a glove being turned inside out, finger by finger. If you were lucky, it happened gently, the growing-up part, and Poppy had not fared too badly, but I worried that she had her wounds.

When I returned to the office, Minty was talking on the phone but when she saw me she ended the conversation. "I'll talk to you later. Bye." She resumed typing with a heightened color.

I sat down at my desk and dialed Nathan's private line. "I know you're about to go into the meeting, but are you all right?"

"Yes, of course I am."

"It's just . . . well, you looked worried."

"No more or less than usual. Anyway, why the touching concern all of a sudden?"

"I just wanted to make sure nothing had happened."

"You mean you wanted to be first with the gossip."

"*Nathan!*" But he had put down the phone. "Sometimes," I addressed the photograph, "he is impossible."

Normally Minty would have said something like: "Men? who needs them?" Or: "I am your unpaid therapist, talk to me about it." And the dark, slanted eyes would have glinted at the comic spectacle of men and women and their battlegrounds. Instead, she took me by surprise and said sharply, "Nathan is a very nice man."

Knocked off guard, I took a second or two to answer. "Nice people can be impossible."

"They can also be taken for granted."

There was a short, uncomfortable silence, not because I had taken offence but because what she said held an element of truth. Nathan and I were busy people, Nathan increasingly so. Like damp in a basement, too much busyness can erode foundations. After a moment, I tried to smooth it over. "We're losing a page because there's a demolition job going in."

"Bad luck to them." Minty stared out of the window with a *sauve qui peut* expression. "So, it goes on."

Again, it was unlike Minty not to demand, "Who—*who?*" and I tried again. "Are you going shopping this evening?" I smiled. "Bond Street?"

She made a visible effort. "I may be getting too fat."

Private joke. Bond Street catered for size eight. Since Minty possessed fawnlike slender limbs, a tiny waist and no bosom, this was fine. No assistant fainted at the size of her arms. But I was forced to shop in Oxford Street where the stores grudgingly accepted that size fourteen did exist. Ergo, together we formulated the Law of Retail Therapy: the larger your size, the further from the city center a woman is forced to forage. (Anyone requiring the largest sizes presumably had to head for the M25 and beyond.) Apart from that, Minty and I suffered—and, in our narrow retail culture, I *mean* suffered—from big feet, and the question of where to find shoes for women who had not taken a life's vow to ignore fashion was a source of happy, fruitful speculation.

The conversation limped on. "Are you doing anything else this weekend?"

"Look, Rose," Minty shut her desk drawer with a snap, "I don't know."

"Right."

I said no more. After all, even in an office, privacy was a basic right.

I had to make a decision between two reviews because one had to be sacrificed. The latest, and brilliant, book on brain activity? In it, the author argued that every seven years our brain cells were renewed and replenished, and we became different people. This seemed a quietly revolutionary idea, which would have clerics and psychotherapists shuddering as they contemplated being put out of business. Yet it also offered hope and a chance to cut chains that bound someone to a difficult life or personality. However, if I published the piece, I would have to drop the review of the latest novel by Anna West, who was going to sell in cartloads anyway. Either the book that readers *should* know about, or the one that they *wanted* to know about.

I rang Features. Carol answered and I asked her if they were running a feature on Anna West.

Carol was happy to give out the information. "Actually, we are. This issue. Big piece. Have you got a problem?"

"I might have to spike our review so I wanted to make sure there was coverage in publication week."

"Leave it to us," said Carol, delighted that Features would have the advantage over Books. I smiled, for I had learned, the hard way, that a sense of proportion was required on a newspaper, and if one had a habit of bearing grudges, it was wise to lose it.

I worked quickly to rearrange the two remaining pages, allocating top placing to the seven-year brain-cycle theory. Ianthe, my mother, would not see its point: she preferred things uncomplicated and settled.

As the afternoon wore on, the telephone rang less and less, which was perfectly normal. Minty dealt with her pile of books and transferred them to the post basket. At five o'clock, she made us both a mug of tea and we drank it in a silence that I considered companionable.

On my way home, I slipped into St. Benedicta's. I felt in need of peace, a moment of stillness.

It was a modern, unremarkable church, with no pretensions to elegance or architectural excitement. The original St. Benedicta's had been blown up in an IRA terrorist campaign thirty years ago. Its replacement was as downbeat and inexpensive as a place of worship should be in an age that was uneasy about where the Church fitted.

As usual, on the table by the glass entrance doors, there was a muddle of hymnbooks and pamphlets, the majority advertising services that had taken place the previous week. A lingering trace of incense mixed with the smell of orange squash, which came from an industrial-sized bottle stored in the corner— presumably kept for Sunday school. The pews were sensible but someone, or several people, had embroidered kneelers that were a riot of color and pattern. I often wondered who they were, the anonymous needle-women, and what had driven them to harness the reds, blues, circles and swirls. Relief from a drab existence? A sense of order in transferring the symbols of an old and powerful legend onto canvas?

St. Benedicta's was not my church, and I was not even religious, but I was drawn to it, not only when I was troubled but when I was happy, too. Here it was possible to slip out from under the skin of oneself, breathe in and relish a second or two of being no one in particular.

I walked down the central aisle and turned left into the tiny Lady Chapel where a statue of the Madonna with an unusually deep blue cloak had been placed beside the altar. She was a rough, crude creation, but oddly touching. Her too-pink plaster hands were raised in blessing over a circular candle stand in which a solitary candle burned. A Madonna with a special dedication to the victims of violence, those plaster hands embraced the maimed and wounded in Ireland and Rwanda, the lost souls of South America and those we know nothing about, and reminded us that she was the mother of all mothers, whose duty was to protect and tend.

Sometimes I sat in front of her and experienced the content and peace of a settled woman. But at other times I wondered if being settled and peaceful had been bought at the price of smugness.

Fresh candles were stacked on a tray nearby. I dropped a couple of pounds into the box and extracted three from the pile. One for the children and Nathan, one for Ianthe, one to keep the house—*our house*—warm, filled and our place of our refuge.

I picked up my book bag, had a second thought, put it down again and hunted in my purse for another pound. The fourth candle was for the erring minister's wife, and my dulled conscience.

On the way out, I stopped and tidied the pamphlets on the table.

Even though it was dark, I continued home by the park, prudently choosing the path that ran alongside the river.

Nobody could argue that it was anything but a city park, ringed as it was by traffic, pockmarked with patches of mud and dispirited trees, but I liked its determination to provide a breathing space. Anyway, if you took the trouble to look, it contained all sorts of unobtrusive delights. A tiny corona of snowdrops under a tree, offering cheer in the depths of winter. A flying spark of a robin redbreast spotted by the dank holly bushes. Rows of tulips in spring, with tufts of primula and primrose garnishing their bases.

So far, winter had been a mild, dampish interlude. Earlier in the day, there had been halfhearted spatters of rain but now it was almost warm. It was too early to be sure, only February, but there was a definite promise of spring shaping up, things growing. I stopped to shift my book bag from one shoulder to the other, feeling the stretch and exhilaration of my life pulse through me.

I was late. I must hurry. I must always hurry.

Five minutes later, I walked up the tiled front path of number seven Lakey Street. Twenty years ago, Nathan and I had talked of restoring a silk weaver's house in Spitalfields, or discovering the perfect-priced Georgian family house on four floors, which—unaccountably—no one else had spotted. Lakey Street fitted between our small flat in Hackney and any wilder speculations. One day, we promised ourselves, we would upgrade, but we settled promptly into the Victorian terrace that comfortably encompassed our family and forgot about doing any such thing.

The streetlights were lit, and the fresh white paint on the window frames was washed with a neon tint. The bay tree dripped onto me as I passed and, for the thousandth time, I told myself it was far too big, planted in the wrong place, and would have to go. For the thousandth time, I reprieved it.

Chapter 2

Six hours later we were in bed, and Nathan laid his hand on my breast in the old familiar way. There was no trouble and no barrier. It was as easy as silk sliding over silk, and I wrapped my arms and legs around him and drew him down. Afterwards, he murmured, "That was nice," and drifted into sleep.

I should have dropped off, too, for we had been out late at a company dinner, but I was too tired for sleep—a hangover from the days of having small children. Recollections of the evening threaded through my mind, cobwebby, not important, but there.

"The works," Nathan had ordered, as he plunged barelegged around the bedroom in his socks. He gave off an air of I-have-too-much-to-think-about, and I fetched his shirt for him. "Best bib, Rosie, and glam. Otherwise these damn politicians think that all we're capable of is rolled-up sleeves and eyeshades."

Occasionally, Nathan's fixed ambition nettled me: it was so

set, so immutable, so . . . predictable, and I had lived with it for a long time. Selling your soul was one thing; having the greater portion of your home life dictated by a newspaper was another. Then I reminded myself that, in my own way, I was as committed to my job, and the irritation never lasted long. I helped him on with the shirt and did up the top button. "Darling, that's only in Hollywood."

Only Nathan called me Rosie—I would not allow anyone else to muddle around with diminutives. "That's because roses are too beautiful and important," Ianthe had once told me. "Roses are the only flowers that have never had a nickname. No heartsease or Dutchman's breeches for the *rose.*" She was holding me tight after an adolescent wobble in confidence. "Roses rustle in the wind and smell of heaven. They are tokens of love, as well as grief. Think of that." Goodness knows what she based this on, but her words flowed through me, gelled, and prescribed the manner in which I perceived my name and, I suppose, myself.

Nathan was different. He could call me what he wished.

I had put on a sleeveless black sheath, which was a little too tight, and high heels. My hair needed cutting but I had had no time recently to get to the hairdresser so I bundled it up into a chignon—not the most flattering style but it would do.

With Nathan's hand tucked under my elbow, we walked into the smart restaurant, the kind featured in magazines that existed to make their readers miserable because their own lives were so far removed from the fantasies on the pages. It was awash with silver and glass and exquisitely colored blush ranunculus in white vases.

Peter Shaker and his wife, Carolyne, were already there with a young rising star called George from the financial department and his pregnant wife, Jackie, who both looked nervous. They were hammering into the champagne. Although we were not intimates, we knew Peter and Carolyne quite well: Carolyne was also in a black shift and high heels, but she is tiny and dark while I am tall with chestnut hair so the effect was different.

Carolyne kissed me, more or less affectionately. Over the years we had seen a lot of each other at company dos, but that was all. In the beginning Carolyne, who did not have a job and was an *über*-wife, asked me to accompany her to several afternoon charity functions, which I always had to decline, and therefore, too, the possibility of friendship. Since then, whenever we met, I could not help feeling that Carolyne, whose home was immaculate, whose two daughters won scholarships to their secondary schools *and* made their own clothes, was making a point about our respective choices. In the nicest possible way, of course. She was, she implied, a Good Wife. Women are as competitive as men but their subversions are better hidden and sometimes their competitiveness is, curiously, a sign of affection.

While we waited for our guests—a couple of politicians and Monty Chavet, an author who specialized in insider exposés of Westminster—we drank more champagne and exchanged company gossip.

"Have you seen this week's figures, Nathan?" inquired Peter. He stood boldly in front of Nathan, legs a little akimbo. When he was younger, Peter had been painfully thin but, with the growth in his confidence, he had put on weight, which suited him.

Nathan frowned. "We'll have to talk about last week's dip—"

Before the numbers game could begin in earnest, the other guests arrived and I found myself sitting next to a junior health minister, whose name was Neil Skinner. He was pale-skinned and red-haired, with the sort of lips that cracked easily in the cold, which could not have been good for winter television appearances. I found myself pitying him: his ambitions were so transparent, and health such a difficult portfolio—only for political suicides. We plodded through the highways and byways of his career, and then he asked, "What do you do?"

"I'm the books editor for the weekend Digest." *Oh, books, said people I met at social events, you're so lucky. Have you met Salman Rushdie?*

"And a very good one," Monty cut in. He was talking to Carolyne but listening to our conversation at the same time. It was how he found his material, he had once told me. "Best pages in town."

"Oh dear," Neil Skinner frowned, "you must think I'm very stupid."

My lips twitched and I wondered who suffered from the worst inferiority complex: the politician or the journalist? Out of the corner of my eye, I watched Nathan being his most charming with the second and more senior politician who, rumor had it, might make the cabinet in the next reshuffle. As usual, he was utterly focused and alert. "Not at all," I replied. "Why would I?"

Neil tapped his glass with a finger that I could swear had been professionally manicured. "Isn't it difficult working for an outfit that can do such damage to people?"

I looked into the pale eyes and replied truthfully. "Sometimes."

He leaned forward and refilled my glass. "But you do it?"

"Yes, but I believe in my bit and I think you have to hang on to that."

"Well," he said, "we have something in common."

A sixth sense told me now that Nathan was not asleep, he was too still, and I flipped over to face him. He was lying stiff and straight under the duvet, not in his usual akimbo style. I laid my palm on his chest. "Are you worrying about something?"

There was a silence. Then he shifted on to his side so that he was turned away from me. "Of course not. Go to sleep."

"Nathan?" Our pillow talk was usually conducted face-to-face and this was when we exchanged snippets that we were supposed to keep secret. "We've got a nasty exposé coming. A minister, actually."

There was a grunt. "I know. Timon warned me. It's Charles Madder. They've been working on it for months. Had a whole team on the case."

That meant at least six people had gone through whatever material they could lay their hands on, dustbins, past records, that sort of thing, and probably kept a watch. "Neil Skinner asked me if I minded working for an outfit that could do so much damage to people."

"You could ask the same question of politicians."

"True." I shifted closer to him and slid my arm round his waist. "Even so, I don't like to think about what's going to hap-pen to that home." I kissed his shoulder, the bit where it begins to curve down into the arm. "Death is supposed to be the worst thing to happen, the event that tears out your heart, but it must be far crueler to be made a fool of by the person you loved and trusted. At least if someone dies you can shape them up nicely in your memory."

"If you can't stand the heat, Rose, you know what to do."

I pinched the edge of his pajama top between my fingers. "Hey, there's no need for the Gordon Gekko act. We're in the privacy of our own home."

I was expecting a laugh. Instead, Nathan repeated, "Go to sleep," and edged away.

I drifted and dreamed, moving in and out of memories,

drowsing in scenes of past family life, for things had changed at Lakey Street. The children's growing up and leaving home had left a space in our married life. Or rather, it had hauled up an anchor and sometimes I worried that it had left Nathan and me curiously untethered. It was not surprising that from time to time we were taken by surprise at having to make adjustments.

Which was different from the early days, when we had expected a challenge.

When I climbed the steps onto the plane in Brazil, I was so weak that my legs shook. I had lost a lot of blood and the doctor warned me snappishly that it would take time, *given my foolishness.*

The cabin smelled of plastic with an underlay of sunburned flesh and businessmen's aftershave, and was artificially cool. As it was high summer, it was full of families with screeching children and backpackers who had drunk too much beer, heading home to grown-up life. It was going to be a long, trying journey to London.

I found my seat by a window, and dropped into it. There was a smear of dust on the pane and I rubbed it away with my finger. A bus disgorged yet more passengers who filed up the steps. Quite a few were elderly, kept back, I supposed, so that they could take their time in getting on.

My finger traced a pattern on the window. Old people did not feel so acutely, did they? The prick and burn of guilt and longing had dulled, their nerve endings had worn away. I wished that I had left behind the years of feeling, stepped over them and gone on to the next stage.

Figures darted to and fro on the liquefying Tarmac outside. Inside I was liquefying, too. I could not remember ever crying as I was now—the tears seemed unstoppable. I stared out of the window, and they dripped down my cheeks, along my chin and made a right angle down to my neck where they pooled on my sodden collar. My nose streamed.

Goodbye, sweet.

The Brazilian sky, which had been hidden from us in the jungle, had never seemed so blue. When it grew dark in the jungle, fireflies gathered on the branches in glowing necklaces that wove in and out of the leaf canopy.

"Look," said a male voice in the next seat, "you're probably trying to hide it, but I can see that you're crying and in need of a handkerchief. Please take mine and I promise not to notice."

Something was placed in my lap and my fingers encountered a square of cotton, so soft it must have been washed a hundred times. It felt so civilized, so clean and domestic. I grabbed it. By the time the aircraft rolled out of its berth, it, too, was sodden.

We had been airborne for half an hour or so when, eventually, I was sufficiently in control to thank my rescuer. He was a little older than I, and neatly turned out in a linen shirt and pressed trousers, but painfully sunburned on his neck and hands. He had a briefcase, supple and beautifully sewn, which looked expensive. He was reading a paperback with careful attention. I knew this was intended to reassure me that he would not force his company on me.

"You have been very kind," I said.

He glanced down at the wet ball in my hand. "Please keep the handkerchief."

"I'm so sorry I've disturbed you."

His smile almost suggested that he welcomed the idea of a female weeping over him. I noticed, too, that he smiled properly, with his eyes as well as his lips. "If it's any comfort, I've encountered far worse. So carry on, if you want to."

I took him at his word, and continued to cry sporadically for most of the flight while he read his book on South American politics, scribbled in the margins then ate his meal and mine.

After the trays had been cleared away, he asked, "Would you like my shoulder sleep on?"

Feeling rather foolish, but too exhausted to argue, I accepted and soon slipped out of my anguish. When I woke, we had flown into the night and my companion was asleep, too, his shoulder still supporting me.

As the aircraft began its descent into Heathrow, the shockingly dull brown and green patchwork of Middlesex framed itself in the plane window. He adjusted his seat into the upright position. "It is, of course, perfectly possible that you're upset over the state of South American politics—don't look so surprised, some people are. I am, and I would be happy to tell you about it sometime. Or, having murdered a tax inspector, you're going home to face prison. Or perhaps you have had to say goodbye to a member of the family and you will never see them again, but I think it's more likely that it has something to do with a love affair." I said nothing. "He must be a rat," he remarked. "I'd never give up a woman with hair like yours." There was nothing to be said to that either.

The runway roared up beneath us, and the plane touched down, bounced and taxied toward the terminal. "Would you like to share a taxi with me into London?" he asked. "Don't worry about the cost, I'm on expenses."

Too tired to care about anything, I accepted. "I'll try not to cry." I looked out at a gray, sodden sky. "Do you always deface your books?"

"Only if the contents aren't up to it."

"Poor book." It was how I felt, too. Failure tasted and felt terrible.

"My name is Nathan Lloyd." He held out his hand. "What's yours?"

I told him.

At seven-thirty we were woken by the phone. Nathan groaned and reached out. "Yes," he said blearily, then snapped to attention. "Okay, Peter."

I slid out of bed. I knew the form. There was a crisis and Nathan was required in the office. War had been declared, a royal had misbehaved, a libel writ had been slapped on his desk. We had lived through them all several times. The curious thing about human behavior was that it went on happening, despite everyone knowing better.

I pulled on my dressing gown and padded down the stairs to the kitchen, stopping on the landing to take a look in the mirror that hung there and smooth my hair behind my ears. I remembered the cartoon joke where the woman looks into a mirror and exclaims, *"Hang on, there's some mistake. I'm much younger than this."*

The years had nibbled away the clear-cut contours and it was a high-risk strategy to get straight out of bed and count on looking fine. No, more than that: it was impossible. Although I liked faces that were blurring into softness in exchange for the willow sheen of youth—Ianthe, for example, was much more interesting to look at now than she had been at forty—it took a bit of getting used to. I had not reckoned on being more self-conscious at forty-seven than I had been twenty years earlier: I had always imagined that in that respect being older was liberating. But it was not, and it went without saying that it was not a subject I discussed with Nathan.

In the kitchen, I snapped up the blinds, and the room was

swathed in a weak sunlight. I drew a deep breath. It was going to be a day of pottering in the shed, getting through tasks that never got done if the weather was too cold.

I set a couple of rashers of bacon in a pan to fry, laid the table, squeezed fresh orange juice and made the coffee. I loved my kitchen. It was my locus in which I took endless pleasure, and I filled it with cream and white objects, jugs, bowls, china, which I had chosen carefully over the years. My dressing gown flapped against my legs as I moved around tidying, putting dirty mugs into the dishwasher, folding unironed laundry into a pile.

When the bacon was crisp, I heated milk in a saucepan, catching up the skin in a spoon, then called Nathan. He came winging into the kitchen in his dress-down office trousers and jacket. Already his mind was fixed on business. The transition of Nathan, the junior political correspondent whom I had met on the plane, to deputy editor, had been hard-fought. Once, when I asked him if he minded that he no longer foraged for stories in the field, no longer wrote the articles, he replied that as he could not remember what it had been like he could not miss it. That had made sense.

I poured him coffee and sat down opposite him. "Wish you didn't have to go."

He shrugged. "We all know the form. Shouldn't take all day, but I'll let you know." There was a pause. "Where will you be?"

I glanced up at the window. "I'll do some chores, then if the weather holds I'll be in the garden." The garden was mine, and I spent any spare time in it. Nathan hated anything to do with soil: his role was to sit in a deck chair and make comments.

He finished his bacon and reached for the toast. "The garden will bankrupt us," he said.

"It's going to be wonderful this year. You wait. I've done marvels."

"That's what you always say."

"And it's true."

A faint early-morning smile crossed his face. "Yes, it is."

Nathan and I rowed over me tramping through the house with bags of mushroom compost and manure—and yes, I did make a mess. We rowed over the money I spent on plants, and we rowed because I refused to take a holiday when the *Paeonia suffruticosa* shook out its skirts to reveal its secret, bloody stains.

He did not like it when I read gardening books into the night, keeping him awake, and he complained bitterly when I ordered a tiny fountain to be constructed in the garden. That had been a Pyrrhic victory, for the fountain was a source of end-less trouble, requiring regular maintenance and cleaning.

Yet they were good rows, the kind that people who live to-gether should share. They raised the whirlwind, shook the furni-ture and vanished, leaving calm. Nathan and I were happy to occupy opposite sides of the garden fence over which we could shout at each other.

The hot milk had grown a second skin so I fetched the strainer then refilled Nathan's cup. "Have you phoned Poppy yet?"

In May she would take her finals at Nottingham University, and neither of us was convinced that she was doing any work. Nathan had resolved to give her a lecture, although I had argued that, at twenty-two, Poppy was free to choose what she did with her life, and Nathan had argued back that, in that case, she choose between my position and his.

"I haven't but I will," he said irritably. "This evening. Don't go on about it."

"I'm not going on about it. I'm just reminding you."

I poured myself some coffee and Nathan went upstairs to do

his teeth. A little later he came clattering downstairs, shouted goodbye and the front door closed.

Another Saturday.

I looked at my coffee. Flat platelets of skin were floating on its surface, leaving a trail of fatty bubbles in a gray liquid. I threw it away.

Chapter 3

When I rang, Poppy was asleep. "I just wanted to see how you are," I said.

She was cross. "Mum, what time *is* this?"

"Sorry. I just wanted to talk to you."

"Talk to me at a decent time." She sniffed. "How's Dad?"

"At work. A crisis."

"He enjoys those," said his daughter. "Makes him feel needed."

"He'll be ringing you. I thought I'd get a word in first."

Poppy's sigh gusted down the phone. "Look, I know what you're going to say . . . but there's no need. I deal with my own life . . ."

There was a lot more in this fashion. Poppy was warning me politely to stay within the limits and, after a while, I gave up. She promised that she would come home soon, that she was well and happy, and that was that.

I fed Parsley her biscuits for elderly cats, and she drowsed on the shelf above the radiator. Parsley was sixteen, which I tried my best to ignore. She held my heart in her killer tawny paw and, as far as I was concerned, she must live forever.

I stacked the breakfast things in the dishwasher, as I listened to the radio news. Another serial murderer in America, civil war threatening in Indonesia. A desperate British couple had traveled to South America to adopt a baby, only to find they had been duped.

I made myself listen. By the skin of my teeth, I had got away with it. My life had been filled with children and Nathan and work, which had given me happiness. I had drunk greedily of that happiness, knowing that others were denied it.

"Is it *possible* to be happy when somewhere in the world someone is dying because they do not have enough food, or have been born with scrambled genes, or their very breath is a political problem?" I asked Nathan as we sat at the table in the kitchen, soon after we had moved into Lakey Street. I was twenty-two, pregnant with Sam, dreamy and apprehensive. Before the babies arrived, there was still time for conversations such as this one. "Shouldn't they overshadow us, those with dreadful lives, unconsciously perhaps?"

Nathan poured wine for himself, milk for me. "If you're talking about the Freudian idea of 'the other' for which we unconsciously seek, then no, you're applying it too loosely. Anyway, it's just a theory and humans are far more selfish than you suggest."

The reference to Freud floored me and reminded me that there was much I did not know about Nathan. Yet. "I've no idea about the Freud, I was just speculating," I said. "I hope *we* can be happy."

There was a dreadful silence and I wished I'd kept my

mouth shut. "Rosie, look at me. *Of course* we can be happy," he said vehemently, troubled at the way the conversation had turned. I got up and kissed him until he forgot.

Luckily that was all in the past, just a ruffle in the surface of an infant marriage.

If there was benefit in the children leaving home, it was my rediscovery of delight in domesticity, which had been pushed to one side. Some women hated it, but I loved the business of cleaning—the ritual of sweetening and cleansing a house was as old as time and I liked the idea that I was one in a long line of women to perform it. Nathan loved my buffing and polishing, too, and confessed that sometimes, at work or traveling, he thought of me wielding a feather duster in a polished, gleaming setting. It was an intimacy no one else shared. He added, with a grin, that I was free to use the feather duster on him anytime. I promised I would.

Today the table required its weekly polish. It was made from French walnut and unsuitable for use in the kitchen, but since we ate there, I had wanted a table at which we could celebrate our family life. Anyway, it was beautiful. I had seen that instantly when I came across it, bruised and battered, in a junk shop in Norfolk, and set about saving it.

The cleaning materials were kept in a room that opened off the kitchen. The estate agent who sold us Lakey Street, whose imaginative abilities could not have been faulted, referred to it as "the original game larder" but it was more likely to have been the privy or washhouse. It was a tiny room and I piled into it all the objects I could not bear to discard—an old stroller (might come in useful), Sam's discarded Meccano (ditto) and Poppy's foldaway pink Wendy house (a reminder of Poppy's fantasy life). On the shelves stood my collection of vases, also liberated from junk shops—overdecorated china flutes, cheap glass that tried to look like crystal, and imitation art deco. I was touched by their makers' ambition.

The polish spread milky clouds over the table surface, and I buffed away at it until I was satisfied that the satiny wood was protected for another week. Then I stood back and surveyed my work.

Since we had moved in, only a year after we were married, number seven Lakey Street had enshrined most of Nathan's and my life together. Someone once told me that, if you knew your stuff, old walls could be read like books. The contents of houses were no less intimate and fascinating. If you were interested, it took only a glance at a room to tell who was fussy, who had given up, who despaired.

Lakey Street had been in a bad state of repair when we bought it and, consequently, cheap. We went into battle with the damp, the mice and the structural wobbles. Building it up had been like applying coats of lacquer: slow. Mistakes had been made—the unfortunate terra-cotta paint in the dining room, which we had never got round to changing, the bathroom put in in just the wrong place, the uncomfortable and ugly sofa in what had been the au pair's room. When I chose it I had thought it smart. The less said about the ruffled blinds on the landing, the better. ("Tart's knickers" was Vee's verdict when she first saw them. "Do you have a past, Rose?") They were so old now that they were fraying.

Nathan and I had promised each other that when the children were off our hands we would do something about the house. We never had. We were too comfortable in it as it was.

I spent that Saturday morning peacefully in the kitchen sorting, tidying and making shopping lists. The radio was playing a

Mahler symphony, full of despair and lament for the composer's unfaithful wife. Every so often, the music forced me to stop and listen. Mahler's anguish was our gain. The fresh, starchy smell of ironed clothes, mixed with beeswax polish and the faintest reminder of coffee, drifted through the room. Occasionally, Parsley got up and stretched.

I left the kitchen to carry the ironing upstairs to the airing cupboard in the spare room. A spare room was a luxury and, for that reason, I kept it immaculate. It had white cotton quilts on the two beds, a faint pink wash of toile de Jouy as curtains and, on the wall, a painting of white roses against a dark background, which had been a birthday present from Nathan. "It's for our bedroom," he had said when he gave it to me. "The artist is Russian, quite young still, and his work is smuggled over. It's a rather complicated arrangement, but I had a tip-off. When I saw it, I knew it was for you."

Nathan often received tip-offs. He pretended they just came along, but I suspected he encouraged them because it flattered him to be in the thick of what was happening.

"I adore it, Nathan," I told him truthfully. "It's beautiful."

He was pleased. "I'm so glad I've got you something you like." He was less confident when talking about the arts, which I found touching. "I like the way he paints in the older European tradition. Modernism doesn't seem to have affected him," he added carefully.

"No," I agreed.

The combination of realism with beauty, religiosity with diligent truth, melancholy and depth told me a lot about the unknown painter, and I was not surprised that Nathan had fallen for it. Arranged in a pewter vase, with a rosary thrown beside it, the roses were painted from many tints, grey, chalk, sludge, but the effect was of radiance, a sensual ruffle of blossoms, even though the artist had included a scattering of blown, brittle petals. The dark background masked other dramas, but I would never know what they were.

"They remind me of you and the garden," Nathan said. We were standing looking at it together, and our reflections glimmered faintly on that dark background.

We never did agree on a place for it in our bedroom. Besides, I felt the painting was set off perfectly in the spare room.

I stacked the laundry in the cupboard, double sheets in one pile, pillow cases in another, shook out a couple of lavender bags to release their scent and left the room.

Sam was in London for the weekend and dropped in for Sunday lunch. Without Alice.

Sam was beautiful and fine but, to his credit, did not know it. He worked for a scientific research company in an old pig factory on the outskirts of Bath. He was considered a young turk, and had the salary and lifestyle to prove it. He had a long, strong finger on the pulse of genetic probabilities and anticipated the dawning of a world where human genes would be manipulated for everyone's comfort and health. He truly believed that things would get better and I loved him passionately for himself and his beliefs.

He did not, however, hold a long, strong finger down on his emotional life.

As I got lunch under way, he wandered into the kitchen and took up a post by the window. I fluffed up the parboiled potatoes in the colander. "Why do you do that?" he asked.

I spooned them into a tray of hot fat. "Makes them crisper."

"I must tell Alice. We're both learning to cook."

I pushed the tray into the oven. Sam should have known by

now that Alice was not the sort of woman to appreciate cookery tips. What was more, her immaculate good looks and naked ambition made older women uncomfortable. "How is she?" I avoided his eye.

"Fine." A pause. "I think."

"You think?"

"She went skiing in Austria." Sam dug his hands into his pockets, which made him look just like his father. "An all-party girl."

Alice hurt Sam regularly. He was admirably reticent about it but Nathan and I did not require chapter and verse. One fine day, he had met the golden-haired Alice at a conference and, far too quickly for warnings, had fallen in love. There was nothing to be done, except sit it out.

To go with the chicken, I had planned tarragon gravy and tiny carrots, peas and broad beans. The carrots were fiddly and I had to concentrate on scraping them. "Lay off, Mother," Poppy would say—but there was no point in having children and not involving yourself in their lives. It was as natural as breathing.

"I asked her to marry me, you know."

The peeler caught my nail and I sucked my finger. Alice's answer was reflected in Sam's stiff attitude. I knew I should be the Samaritan, the wise counsellor, but Sam's hurt and disappointment distressed me so much that I was at a loss. "Sam, why don't you open a bottle of wine?"

"It's okay. I can talk about it."

"So . . . ?"

"She doesn't feel there's any point in getting married. She has a fantastic job and a fantastic salary. A fantastic flat. A fantastic car. The works. Why spoil a good thing?" His eyes were dark with longing. "But I want to start something."

"Have you explained this to her?"

He shrugged. "Sure. Alice feels that people do unspeakable things to each other when they get married. She thinks it's wrong to base your life on the idea of love. Women don't buy that any more. As an organizational principle, love has flaws."

"Will you give up?"

"I don't know."

"Oh, Sam . . ." I took his hand and stroked it, willing his hurt on to me—which is what mothers do.

When the chicken was ready Nathan carved a couple of pieces of breast and arranged them in a fan on Mr. Sears's plate. I added the roast potatoes and vegetables, and a separately made portion of gravy: Mr. Sears had an aversion to herbs. "I'll only be a couple of minutes," I said, and left Nathan stirring the gravy and Sam laying the table.

Mr. Sears lived on his own next door and was bedridden. I went down the stone steps to the basement of number nine. During the war, Lakey Street had been the random target of a bomb flung out of a plane on its way home to Germany, which had destroyed three houses. During the fifties, the council had nipped in and built three neither beautiful nor appalling replacements.

"Who's that?" Mr. Sears called at my knock.

"Rose." I was never the person he wanted, which was Betty, his daughter who, long ago, had packed her bags and done a bunk. Betty got in touch with her father once a year, and then only grudgingly.

I let myself into his sitting room where he had been eased into his chair, surrounded by newspapers and full ashtrays. "I've brought your Sunday lunch."

It was important to remind Mr. Sears of what day it was be-cause it was difficult for him to remember. Time no longer functioned for him in the conventional manner and calendars were of no use to him; he never looked at them. "That's nice," he said, looking surprised. "What made you do that?" Off and on, I had been bringing him Sunday lunch for the last five years.

I fetched a tray from the kitchenette, and settled it on his knees. "Chicken. Your favorite. Unless you've changed your mind."

He poked at a carrot and I knew he would need encouraging.

"Thought you might like to know, Mr. Sears, they're taking off the Routemasters on the eighty-eight and putting in pay-the-driver buses."

"Are they now?"

"Everybody's grumbling about it. There's a protest meeting being organized."

This information excited Mr. Sears so much that he took his first mouthful and I relaxed.

Ours was a carefully developed friendship, which had taken years to mature. Before he had become housebound, Mr. Sears had spent his days riding the buses. They were his passion and he had mastered the network of interconnecting routes, a king of the city. What he did not know about timetables, tickets and bus territory nobody knew. So, in a small way, I had made buses my business, too. I told him about breakdowns, the latest adverts I had seen pasted onto their sides, and sometimes swung by the depot in Stockwell to give him an update.

Mr. Sears's other great passion was Parsley, who treated number nine as her second home. If the subject of buses ran out, we talked about her and Ginger, the cat Mr. Sears had once had.

I checked up on the rota to see which of his home-care

nurses would put him to bed. "Marilyn's coming this evening, Mr. Sears. She's the one you like." I heard that falsely cheerful note creep into my voice. It made me wince.

Mr. Sears shot me a look.

"I hope you enjoy your lunch," I said.

"Chicken gives me a headache," he said, to punish me.

Immediately after we had eaten, Sam left Lakey Street, and I insisted that Nathan and I take our coffee out into the garden. "See?" I said, flinging open the French windows. "Perfect."

The first growth of the Buff Beauty was struggling for space through the bullying *Solanum jasminoides*. The Marie Boisselot clematis had already put out a few leaf buds and the Rambling Rector rose was readying itself to dust, later, in the spring, its tiny creamy buds—like Poppy's baby fist—along the fence. In fact, all the plants were poised to shake out their plumage for their annual show. *Lavendula* "Nana alba," *Artemisia nutans* "Silver Queen"—my lovely, tender children. I almost forgot the olive tree in the stone pot. That, too, had a silvery gleam in the thin light.

During the winter, moss had edged over the stones and colonized the bench. They required dousing and scrubbing with disinfectant and I fetched a bucket. Nathan scuffed the patio with his shoe, revealing grubby streaks of the stone underneath.

"You've been very quiet, Nathan." I scrubbed at the bench and wiped it over with a cloth. He watched me.

"It's far too cold." He sat down but did not look at me and I wondered if he was angry with me.

I tried again. "I think I saved the clematis."

"I don't know why you're obsessed with white. Can't we ever have a bit of color to liven things up?"

It had crossed my mind more than once that Nathan was

jealous of the garden. "I don't know. I love white—but maybe as a change I could go for red."

Now Nathan said something that struck me as strange. "I don't think I've ever understood you, Rosie."

It was too serious a statement not to treat it as a joke. "You don't have to." I leaned over and kissed him. "That's part of my mystery."

"Don't be silly."

Why did I love white in a garden? No doubt some of the books that passed over my desk offered explanations of the white period in a gardener's history. Picasso had had a blue one, and plenty of print had been devoted to analyzing it. Perhaps white gardens revealed an unconscious yearning for purity. More likely, the fat, innocent buds butting their way through chocolate earth, the tender, reliable goodness of a garden, provided a direct contrast to what took place in the world. Yet any fool can tell you that it is not the answers which are significant, but the garden itself. My white beauties traced pathways over rotting fences and spread their cool canopies over tired city soil. It may be true that I was gripped by the longing for clarity and resolution that white suggests, which I could not explain to Nathan, but it was the visible beauty that was the real point.

Nathan stood up. "I'm going indoors."

"Would you like to go for a walk? I can do this another time."

"No. I know you want to tackle the moss. I might take myself off for a stroll."

"Fine."

I refilled the bucket at the outside tap, poured in disinfectant then got down on my hands and knees and began to scrub. The disinfectant was astringent and clean-smelling and made my skin tingle. Nathan moved about inside the house. He washed something up, made a phone call, and then I heard the bang of the front door.

The scrubbing brush was new and bit hard into the moss. A swathe of freshly minted stone flag appeared. A cheap substitute for limestone, this stone had been imported from India, hewed from hot, dusty plains. It was old and some of the flags had fossils imprinted on them. A foamy leaf. A fish bone of fern.

I traced the fern with a wet finger. Nature produces her enormous variety from only ten basic patterns: the whorl, the spiral, the crystal, the branch, etc. I learned that while I was a student at Oxford. I loved that piece of information. I found nature's strictness reassuring—and I was the woman who still cherished a silver medal engraved ROSE UTTLEY: FOR TIDINESS AND NOT BEING LATE. FORM 3 I liked the notion of such order, such simplicity. It was one of the reasons I had married Nathan. Etc., etc.

I finished the patio and embarked on the garden furniture. It was hard work and I grew pleasantly warm. Every so often I looked up—just for the pleasure of looking—at the green and brown of the waiting garden. When we had moved in, forty-five feet of bleak, leached London clay, tangled with briars and rubbish—the same imaginative estate agent had called it "a mature prospect"—had greeted me. "Try me," I fancied it was saying. "I dare you."

The fountain was situated at the bottom and the water fell out of a pitcher, held by a woman in drapery, into a brick pool into which I had piled stones collected with Sam and Poppy on Hastings beach. I saw in it an amorphous, eternal quality. Things changed, but they also remained the same.

My eyes traveled over the lilac, which was old and woody.

Yet it had that pregnant look about it—so, too, did the roses, the leaf clumps from which the black and white poppies would emerge, and my treasured tawny verbascum. Everything, in fact. Spring *was* coming. Once again, the cycle had traveled back to the beginning, ready to start again.

Chapter 4

On Monday, the group reverberated with the Charles Madder scandal. All over the building phones rang, lawyers were consulted and journalists chewed over evidence. The atmosphere was shrill and rancorous and, I suppose, we were, too.

The smell of bad coffee from the vending machines was particularly offensive. Someone had spilled a cup over the red carpet just outside my area. It left a dark stain, like blood, over which I had to tread.

By Tuesday, the furor was less intense. It was reported that Charles Madder had resigned as a minister to spend more time in cherishing his constituency. The consensus among his constituents was that he had had it coming. Only one person was reported as saying that he was a good and decent man. The ship sailed on, leaving polluted water, and the ex-minister's wife, Flora Madder, drowning in shock and distress. "Don't be woolly," said Minty, when we queued for lunch in the canteen and I expressed sympathy for her. "A wife must know if her husband is straying. As for the undeclared interests, it's collusion, surely. She's in it up to her neck, too." She checked herself. "Don't look like that, Rose. You know as well as I do that sometimes the nice explanation will not do."

I was used to Minty's cynicism, but it was not like her to be quite so harsh. "If you mean human beings are never straightforward, well, yes," I said.

She flushed and it was then I realized that she must be having an affair with a married man. I felt a stab of . . . what? Complicity? Not exactly—more curiosity, but not, I think, envy. Relief, too, that her choice was not my business. Mine had been made.

I looked at her hard. Her heightened color made her look young and hopeful. "And what are you up to, Minty?"

She grabbed a fat-free yogurt. "Nothing."

Long ago, I had settled on what I wanted. Put crudely, my ambitions were to be a good mother, a Good Wife (to Nathan, of course), and have my career. I wanted others in my life to nurture. Not very grand, certainly not earth-shattering, some might say boring. Convenient? Yes and no. We have to choose something, opt for some species of shelter—and I found those ambitions immensely absorbing, ever changing.

As she often reminded me, Minty was different. She was bold and, to Ianthe, shocking in her outspokenness—her gender was not a problem. She was courageous and upfront—"I want to go places." She had no family to speak of—"Who wants one?"—and hated the idea of children: "Why put a millstone round your neck?" She chose her role models from Hollywood and television. She did not take drugs but reckoned you had to be good-looking to get on. She liked sex, and rated presentation and PR. It was a generation thing, she argued, a mentality thing.

Sometimes Minty seemed as old as time. Sometimes she was the child in a sweet shop, desperate to try out all the sticky humbugs and gobstoppers. And why not? She had flown in from another planet and she fascinated me. At twenty-nine, smart, sharp, glossy, free-ranging, she was as different from me at that age as it was possible to be.

"I hate my bust." This was the first of several intimacies she had dropped during our first lunch together after she joined the office. "It's the kind that promises much, but delivers little. But I use it all the same."

"I see." Any shortfall in Minty's breasts would be made up for by her mixture of honesty and greed. "Men are easily led," she said also, and her dark eyes flashed subversive knowledge. "Easy, easy. Especially if you tell them there are no ties."

"But where are they led to?" I asked.

She fixed me with that unblinking, comforting gaze.

By Wednesday, Charles Madder was regulated to page five, it was on, on with the news, and the atmosphere had changed to shock and *something must be done:* the daily paper now focused on a medical scandal. As a result of acute lack of funding a hospital porter with no medical qualifications had been acting as the triage nurse in a Cornish hospital's A&E department. A woman had died as a result of his ignorance. The journalists shed their rancor and became the nation's social conscience, the exposers of society's ills.

On Thursday . . .

On Thursday, Minty arrived—unusually—more than an hour and a half late. She was wearing a floaty skirt, a tight Lycra top and kitten heels in glacé pink. She looked dewy and flushed but, also, curiously determined. "Apologies, Rose."

It was copy day, time was extra tight and the phone had not stopped ringing, mostly with authors and publishers complaining about unfair treatment. They all had to be placated. "You might have phoned."

"I said I was sorry."

I was not angry often, but when I was, I was. "Go and check with Steven that the pages are okay this week."

"I don't think that's a good idea." Minty hung up her jacket.

"What?"

She sat down at her desk and switched on her terminal. "We should hold our firepower."

This was the first time that we had openly disagreed on policy, and I was puzzled. "Minty, I don't know what is going on in your private life but you could do as I ask and not treat me to the fallout. If you feel differently, we can discuss it later."

"Fallout?" she queried.

I glanced at my watch. "I don't care what we call it, just get on with it. Please go and talk to Steven."

Phones rang, computers whined, the post trolley, pushed by Charlie, swayed through the desks. The walls of the building shut out goodness knew what weather. Scowling, Minty got to her feet—she reminded me of Poppy when she had been out-flanked. My lips twitched. "We've got off to a bad start. Let's be friends and then thrash out the policy. Or, rather, get the pages to bed."

She thought for a moment. "That's the trouble with you, Rose. You bring things down to the personal. It's very female."

"So do you."

"Not like you."

It was a truce. Of sorts.

At the end of the day, Minty got up from her desk, put on

her jacket and said goodnight. She did not look back as she clattered out on the glacé kitten heels.

By Friday, a royal had been photographed in a compromising position and a row was ding-donging over privacy. How far? How much? Whose?

The news desk in the goldfish bowl seethed and hummed. When I arrived, dead on nine o'clock, Maeve Otley was hunched over her desk, white and speechless. A bad rheumatism day. I made her a cup of tea and took it over but it was not the moment to commiserate. Charlie delivered a stack of post and a couple of boxes of books.

Minty rang. "I can't come in. I've got a . . . migraine."

This was unlike her. "Shall I phone later to check if you're okay?"

"No." She sounded choked. "Don't do that. No need."

"I hope you feel better."

But Minty had put down the phone.

In planning terms, summer was on the doorstep, and I spent the day teasing out ideas for the June pages. Ringing the changes was almost impossible on the familiar categories of "travel" and "holiday reading," but I was toying with the idea of a section on books "to be read for a second time."

Meanwhile, for this week's travel slot, we had covered books on India, Thailand, Greece, Hal Thorne's *A Thousand Olive Trees,* of course, and a thick, illustrated travelog devoted to Rome.

Long ago, when I had been Rose-the-traveler, I had gone to Rome.

The sun shone on my bare arms and boiled the sweat on my back. My feet spread damply inside my cheap sandals and I knew I would get blisters. I did not care. I was sixteen, in Rome, and in love for the first time—with being there, out of England. Rome was noisy, filled with smells—coffee, exhaust, sweat, hot buildings—and its flux of life, noise and sensation flowed through me, intensely, luxuriously felt.

I was in Rome. I was intoxicated.

Life, wrote Virginia Woolf, was a luminous halo, a semitransparent envelope. Oh, no, it was not. Not for some. Some of us lived in a plain brown envelope. It took the trip to Rome to see the luminous halo, the semitransparent one.

Ianthe nearly talked me out of it: I did not have any proper summer clothes or shoes, and my underwear was not good enough, she said, unless I wanted to wear my gym knickers and plimsolls.

A godmother had taken pity on Ianthe's penniless widowhood, not to mention her hungry, sensation-starved daughter (who had read her E. M. Forster and reflected seriously on Lucy Honeychurch's experiences) and paid for a place on the school expedition. Ianthe clicked her tongue and did her I-am-a-Yorkshire-woman-I-am-not-a-cause-for-people-to-patronize-and-lighten-their-consciences bit. I had been forced to abandon Lucy Honeychurch and to adopt Jane Eyre: "Please, please, Mother . . . 'Do you think, because I am poor, obscure, plain, and little, I am soulless and heartless?' " before she ungraciously allowed my godmother to get out her checkbook.

Perhaps it was really my lack of wardrobe that bothered Ianthe but it was unlikely: Ianthe, in make-do-and-mend mode, could fashion a dress from a sack. I sought a better explanation. I knew from my reading that mothers found it hard to let go of their adored children. They dreaded the end of their womanly role and death beckoning, the logical finale. This left me with a moral quandary. Should I sacrifice my yearning to give back my mother her role?

I calculated she could manage without it for a week. In return, I decided to pay three pounds into the charity box, which was then a considerable sum and, therefore, a conscience appeaser.

Lips tight, Ianthe set about preparing my wardrobe between working and running the house. Scrupulous as ever, she washed all my clothes by hand and dried them over the clothes-horse in the kitchen.

The day before I left, she set up the ironing-board. A ham bone boiled on the stove, and the kitchen grew steamy with starch and stock. The radio played softly. Every so often, she dipped her hand into a jug of water, and shook drops over the ironing board. The iron bit into the material with a hiss. When she had finished, she folded each garment with exquisite neatness.

I watched dreamily. She was wearing her everyday flat shoes, polished to within an inch of their lives, and there was a careful darn in her stocking, but her hair had escaped its coil and a frown puckered her forehead. Every so often, she glanced up at me, the movement emphasizing her extreme thinness. I knew what she was thinking. *She will get ideas above her station.* My mother had been so careful not to raise my expectations.

"Rose," she cut sharply into my reverie, "don't just sit there, let down that dress. And don't look like that."

She was not taking her defeat lightly, nor did I expect her to, and my victory was too precarious to jeopardize. I pulled out the sewing box and set about the dress, which had already been rehemmed twice. I cut and snipped and eventually the remaining spare inch of material, which was of a much darker color, had been tacked into place. I held up the dress. "It'll look awful."

"Beggars can't be choosers." Ianthe was at her most maddening, but her eyes were cloudy with distress. This was final proof, if she needed it, that I was growing beyond her reach.

So, there I was: a creature in a seersucker dress with an obviously let-down hem, from a cool, wet island, without a history of my own, bewitched by a city that had almost too much.

There they were: the great *fontana* of the Trevi and the Barcaccia, or the more playful ones, like the Fontana delle Tartarughe with its bronze tortoises, which I found tucked behind the ghetto, and at street corners the intimate *fontanella*. Plump women reclined with their breasts displayed, sea gods grasped tridents, nymphs crouching at their feet, while dolphins, seahorses, lions and amphorae emerged from bronze and stone. Creatures of myth and legend had been summoned from the four quarters of the world.

Those sleek, gleaming men, women and animals had nothing to do but ensure that water was tossed from shell and mouth, and how happy they seemed to me as they guarded the arcs of water in the sun. But I also figured, with a little help from Keats, that they were happy because nothing ever happened to them.

Our hotel was in the via Elisabetta, on a corner, and its top story almost collided with its opposite neighbor's. It was a simple place, with hard beds, white cotton covers and a tiny niche in each bedroom that housed a plastic statue of the Virgin, which we had been warned not to touch. "I dare you, I dare you," cried Marty, my roommate. Marty was going to be beautiful. She came from a better-off family and her wardrobe was extensive. She was contemptuous of me and, because I feared her, I accepted her dare and hung the door key off the Virgin's plaster hand.

Later that night, I lay and listened to the traffic snarl past and waited for Marty to go to sleep. When I was sure that she had, I slid from under the rough sheets, crept over to the Virgin and removed the key. *Mother of God, forgive me. I knew not what I did.* Where had I read that? In the half-light, jeering Marty slept, almost like an angel.

The via Elisabetta ran through the Trastevere district from San Pietro in Montorio, past the piazza Santa Maria and down to the river. The Trasterine reputedly have loud, hoarse voices, drink lots of coffee, eat *maritozzi* for breakfast and *spaghetti cacio e pepe* for supper. (I had done my research.) It was an area that traditionally had absorbed foreigners and nonconformists. From ancient times, it had understood diversity and the quirks of different peoples.

Ecco.

It was a serpentine street, coiling down to the river Tiber but, by the end of the second day, if you had blindfolded me, I could have led you to the laundry, or to the shop that sold pictures of Christ, heart exposed, surrounded by roses, lilies and flowers of the field. I puzzled over the cards, which seemed to me intemperately vulgar, and as to why Christ had appeared to have had open-heart surgery.

Walking south from San Pietro, the first stop had to be for a *café ristretto* at Nono's to brace you for the walk to the river. (In penance, Marty treated me to one.) Long before you saw the water, you sensed its flow and heard its ancient sounds, but before it came into sight, the via Elisabetta widened and flared into a modest square, flanked by the pinky terra-cotta-colored buildings. In the center of the square was a fountain: a stone youth with a drawn sword guarded a woman in flowing robes, who wore a crown and balanced a pot on her shoulder from which the water gushed. The pot had a pattern of bees engraved into it.

Here, I discovered the Café Nannini, run by the family. In the morning, Signora Nannini presided over a magical machine that produced an elixir called coffee, which was nothing like the coffee I knew but was topped by foam over which lay a drift of chocolate. In the afternoon, Signor Nannini took over. In halting Italian, I asked him about the fountain in the middle of the square, which seemed rather ornate for such a modest square. "Why the bees?"

"Barberini bees. A Barberini gave the money for the fountain to be built. A long time ago."

"E la donna?"

"She is the wife of the king of the gods. A woman who suffered because her husband liked the pretty girls."

I remembered the frozen stone face. "Wasn't being wife to the king of the gods enough?"

"It is nature."

Lucy Honeychurch and Jane Eyre did not help me in this matter. Hoping for enlightenment, I inspected the face again, but I did not find any.

"Rosie," said Nathan, as I dumped my book bag on the sofa in the sitting room that evening. It fell over, spilling its contents. "Rosie, we must talk."

He had his back to me and was gazing out of the French windows into the garden. He had not changed out of his office suit, his third favorite one in dark gray with the faintest red stripe running through the material. The cut flattered him, and I urged him to wear it more often.

Nathan sometimes issued imperatives. They meant nothing. I was late, tired, my feet were wet and it had been a trying day.

"Sorry I'm late. Minty was ill and I had to cope. I expect you're hungry. I'll just change my shoes."

"Now . . ." He sounded strained, my energetic, thrusting, ambitious husband.

I went over to him, slid my arms around him and laid my cheek on his shoulder. "All right. Go on."

Then, he turned round and pushed me away. He looked me straight in the eye. *At least he did that.* His were alight with an excitement and dread I could not place. "This is not a good talk."

Chapter 5

I couldn't explain it—I never could when he did it: Nathan went absent. He simply folded his mind into a secret place and disappeared inside himself. It was a habit of his, and it was particularly noticeable when he was nerving himself for a confrontation at work.

"Not one of the children?" I demanded, with the flash of fear that always lay waiting.

"No, nothing to do with them." Nathan appeared to be in need of something to do with his hands, and he stuffed them into his pockets. It was the gesture he had used when he demanded that I marry him. Then, his pockets had practically disintegrated from tension and imperatives—"Say *yes*. Now."

He began to speak, thought better of it, and tried again. "Rosie, we've been happy, haven't we?"

Words can be spoken, they can be written in Gothic script,

they can be sung, and we all agree to agree on what they mean. Yet their real meaning is in *how* they are said.

"Haven't we?" With astonishment, I realized that Nathan had pronounced those words with finality. Alarm and bewilderment began to grate in my stomach. I replied. "Yes, we have."

"First of all, I want to say that I have been happy with you. Very, very happy. Despite my not being your first choice, so to speak."

"Nathan . . ."

"Let's establish it, I have been happy. Despite . . . everything," he muttered.

"What are you talking about?" I stared at him, and comprehension crept in. "You're not on about that again? I can't believe you're still going on about a love affair that . . . Everyone has a love affair before they get married. You can't possibly imagine . . . or think . . ."

"Only because you do."

"I don't. I promise I don't."

"Oh, come on, Rosie. We know each other well enough. The truth?"

I swallowed. "I suppose I do, very occasionally, think about Hal, in a remote way, but only to remind me of how happy I am and how much I love you. Occasionally, I think, what if, but only if we've had a row. It's harmless, foolish stuff. Why are you bringing this up? What's happened?"

He grabbed my arm, and his fingers bit into the flesh. "No regrets?"

I smiled up at him, tender and committed. "You know there are not. You silly," I added. "You know how grateful I am, what you mean to me. The children, the house. Our life. Us." I touched his lips with a finger, outlining their shape, gently, softly. "Why don't you go and have a bath, Nathan, and I'll get supper?"

It was not quite true about the regrets. No life, or decision, is possible without a few, at least I don't think so. But I kept mine private, those memories of being careless and ignorant—not even Vee or Mazarine knew about them. Certainly not Nathan. Regrets are a tool that should be used only as a last resort. Anyway, they bore people.

Nathan's fingers dug deeper into me.

"Do you think you could let go my arm, or at least not hold it so tightly?" I asked.

He released me at once. "There's no easy way to say this, Rosie, so I'll say it straight."

But he did not. The words drizzled into silence, and he swung back to his contemplation of the garden in which he took no interest. At last, he drew an audible breath and said, "I've found someone else."

The shock hit me like a hammer. "What?" I groped for the sanctuary of the blue armchair. "What did you say?"

"I've found someone else, and I've fallen in love with her." Nathan turned to face me. "I'm sorry. I'm very, very sorry."

I said the first stupid thing that came into my mind. "You can't have done. I would have known." He shrugged. I tried again. "I don't believe you."

He shook his head as if to say, "Don't. Don't make it worse."

I struggled to concentrate. Affairs happened to other people, not to Nathan and me, a happily married couple. I plucked at a thread trailing from the arm of the chair. I always insisted on sitting in the sun by the window and the original bright delft blue of the chair cover had faded over the years to the softest powder.

"Listen to me." Nathan sat down opposite me and hunched

over his knees. "I have found someone else, and we need to talk about it."

I looked down at my hands. I have been told they're nice, with long fingers, and that the simplicity of a heavy gold wedding ring sets them off to advantage. "I don't know what to say."

"Look at me, Rosie."

I did so, but I was concentrating on my chest where my heart was banging in an unfamiliar fashion. "I don't understand," I whispered. He gave me a long, pitying look, and the blood drained from my cheeks. "You seemed perfectly happy, Nathan."

His silence told me another story, the real story. He had been happy because of someone else. I returned to the observation of my hands, which suddenly seemed thin, worn and breakable, the tiny lump on the ring finger joint more noticeable. I made an effort to pull myself together. "Why are you telling me all this?"

Nathan climbed wearily to his feet. "Isn't it obvious?"

"No, it isn't. Should I be cracking open the champagne or something?"

"Rosie . . ."

The sensation in my chest crescendoed, and I felt sick. I leaped up and fumbled my way to the bathroom where I hung over the basin and stared at the taps. Nathan was never unkind. Careless and preoccupied sometimes, yes. A man who craved much from his work, and went to pains to obtain it, yes. Determined. Predictable. That was what I loved about him, and needed from him. But he was never cruel.

Little by little, I was forced to face the conclusion: if those judgments were correct, Nathan must mean what he said.

After a few minutes I felt steadier. I drank some water from the tooth mug, which tasted of mint, wiped my face and braced myself to confront Nathan, who was hovering in the doorway.

"Are you all right?"

"What do you think?" His question was crass, and made me angry, which was the easiest to deal with of the many feelings that surged through me. Disbelief, hotly pursued by terror, then, stalking through dark, unmapped thickets, rank humiliation.

Nathan placed a hand on my shoulder, and inspected my face. He gave a faint, guilty smile. "I thought for a moment you might do something stupid. But you mustn't, you know, not over me."

"I thought that was the point, Nathan. If you love someone you're prepared to do something stupid."

"We have to talk. Properly." He took my hand and led me along the landing and down the stairs. I tried to snatch it away but he held on tight. I was dragged behind him, my feet slipping on the treads. "You're telling me that you're having an affair and you want me to go over the fine print with you? Would you like advice on what underwear to buy her?"

"Shut up, Rosie."

We blundered back into the sitting room where Nathan tore off his suit jacket and flung it down. He grasped the back of the sofa, took a breath—the speech pose. *We should discuss the paper's circulation.* Nathan often practiced on me when he required advice and input. *Don't patronize. Be clear.*

I said, desperately, "Nathan, we could forget this conversation. We need not go on."

He was taken aback and muttered, "I prayed it wouldn't come to this."

"Obviously not hard enough." I heard a sharp voice, and it was mine, and I hated it.

"The stupid thing is, I need help and I can't ask you."

I sat down in the blue chair and plucked at the stray thread. Blue was the color of life: the lapis used by the master painters I had seen in Rome, the cerulean of hot skies, the metallic gleam of a duck's wing, a vein twitching under skin. "No, you can't ask me for help."

That had been a rule in our marriage. We never talked about it, but we understood: if one was in trouble, the other came to help. He helped me. I helped him. We helped each other.

Again there was a silence. Eventually Nathan cleared his throat. "You have every right to be angry."

Angry? Bitterly so, that Nathan had been so stupid to tell me. Married people did fall in love with others, and out again. The trick was to be very clever and very secret about such a predicament, and I would have expected Nathan to be very clever and very secret and to have starved his love until it died from lack of nourishment. "Why have you told me? It w-wasn't necessary."

"Rosie, you haven't understood."

"No, I haven't." But then I did. I forced myself to raise my eyes. "You want to leave home? You want to leave me? You can't. There are the children to consider."

"The children are twenty-two and twenty-four. They can handle it. Lots do."

"It doesn't matter what age they are."

He shrugged with unfamiliar emphasis, and I noticed a feather of gray hair above his ears. Nathan would have noticed it, too, for he kept a rigorous tally on the signs of decay.

"But why do you want to leave? Surely we can get over this . . . episode. I wish—I wish you hadn't told me but I'm not blind, I know these things happen. Things happen under the surface all the time, every day. Nathan, trust me. We can get over it."

It was true. I was not stupid. Love had many forms, and assumed different shapes at different times, sometimes glorious, sometimes terrible, always necessary. It was a question of believing in it, and fighting for it, and the necessary bit sometimes meant sacrifice, precisely because everything could change. Just like that. With a couple of sentences. Yes, Nathan and I could find a box, pile in any lies or deceit, shut the lid and go on. The act of will was the crucial thing, the factor that pulls the messy tendrils and mistakes back into order.

He paced up to the French windows and back again. "For some time now I have been thinking about milestones and of how we're getting older."

"Nathan, you're only fifty-one. Anyway, it isn't the point."

But it was the point.

He stopped in his tracks. "It is and it isn't. I need freedom, space. We build cages for ourselves, Rosie, in all sorts of ways. Work, family, habit. I've realized that I feel imprisoned by the walls I've built around myself."

In all our marriage, I had never heard such words leave Nathan's lips. It was a new language for us both and I didn't think he spoke it fluently or even well. I groped at my unruly chest. "Imprisoned? But you wanted to be. You spent . . . energy, time doing it. You wanted a family and the career. You've had them, and enjoyed them, and you can't just discard a family because you feel a bit bored."

"You don't want to live with someone who feels like I do, do you?"

"Isn't that for me to decide?"

"I'd better be completely honest with you, Rosie." I quivered at the thought of Nathan's complete honesty. "The other I could have dealt with but this person . . . She gives me . . . what I think I must be looking for. She admits new possibilities?"

"Or do you mean sex?" I flashed.

We glared at each other and I was sorry I had allowed myself to say something so obvious, so revealing. Then again, it was obvious.

"Don't be silly," said Nathan, but the gleam in his eye told me otherwise. I thought of the other night, when it had been so easy, so affectionate, and I felt black outrage. Back went Nathan's hands into his pockets. "When we married, we agreed that we would always give each other space. I've been a good husband, yes?"

"Yes, you have." I spoke as calmly as I could.

"I've done everything you could ask?" I nodded. "Well, I'm asking now for my space."

I wondered what could possibly help me. A drink? A blow to the head? "How long has this . . . Nathan? *Who?*"

"About a year."

"Oh, God," I said. "So long. We've been living a lie so long." So long that it took in last Christmas. ("Nathan, what do you think—Christmas lunch or Christmas dinner?") The autumn holiday in Scotland where rain fell as soft as bottled water and we found wild bilberries on the hill. Nathan's birthday party in August (forty people came and toasted him), and the familiar cycle of Monday and Friday, the suppers we had shared, the bottles of wine, the intimacies . . . They had all been different from what I had supposed them to be.

Nathan looked sick and stricken. "Not a lie, Rosie, because it didn't start out serious."

"Nathan, have you had affairs before?"

"No. Never." He took my hand. "I promise." He dropped it.

In a way, that made it worse. "Nathan, have you been pushed into this by whoever it is? You really, really mean what you say?"

"I must have change. I must have some air. I can't stay where I am any longer."

I dropped my head into my hands. "For God's sake, Nathan, *don't*. Spare me. Please don't dress an affair into some great plea for freedom. I can't bear it."

"If that's the way you want it."

"But who is it?"

Nathan took his hands out of his pockets and smoothed down his hair. The transition from the successful newspaper executive into a troubled, middle-aged man shocked me. "I can't believe I'm doing this . . ."

Head bowed, like a victim, I waited. "Who, Nathan?"

He swallowed. "It's Minty."

After Nathan had shoveled a few things into a bag and departed, I walked through the house. I did not know what else to do. I went up the stairs and along the landing. Outside the main bedroom, our bedroom, I came to a halt for I could not bring myself to enter it.

It's Minty.

No, I choked, backing away from Nathan. It's not possible. Minty would not do that.

But she had.

I grasped at the banister for support. Did hearts stop beating with grief and shock? Mine was thrashing around like a wild thing, and I was shivering uncontrollably.

Down the stairs I went, clumsy and frantic, into the sitting room and, with hands that felt as if they did not belong to me, I emptied my book bag onto the floor: papers, a novel, a cookery manual, a biography of Gladstone.

Why had I done that?

I abandoned them there, a frozen torrent on the floor, and went to inspect the invitations propped up on the mantelpiece. Only a day ago, I had scrawled an A on both and entered the dates in the family diary. I turned them face down—how silly, how convenient, I had not wished to go to either. As I did so, my wedding ring caught my eye. I stared at it, heavy on my finger with the weight of the years. It did not belong there any more. *It did not belong there.* It scraped at my flesh as I tugged it over my knuckle—ripped at the weight of those years—and dropped it beside the invitations.

The catch at the French windows was stiff and always stuck. I had to pull hard before the doors opened. Cold evening air streamed into the sitting room. I sat down in the blue chair and shivered.

Eventually, when the interminable evening had worn away, I went up to the spare room, to the toile de Jouy curtains and the white roses, and lay face down on the bed, my arms stretched out in my personal Calvary.

Some time during the night I woke, frightened by the unfamiliarity of the bed and unsure where I was. I was still lying face down and the pillow under my face was wet.

I remembered. I got up, went to my own room and climbed between the sheets, inhaling a faint smell of Nathan. It was dark, but no darker than the darkness in my mind.

How had I not seen?

How had I not sensed?

You have been a fool, Rose.

I had married Nathan because he understood. He, too, had wanted to step inside the house and shut the door against the world. Within the closed intimacy, the unity of us two, we had loved each other with gentleness, tenderness and gratitude, and we had told each other that we might try to build a Garden of Eden together.

I suppose we both forgot that everything is finite and everything decays.

Last June Minty had come to Lakey Street for supper, *just spaghetti and a glass of wine,* over which we had planned to discuss various projects. You don't mind? I asked Nathan. She won't stay late. As long as she doesn't, he replied. I'm tired.

Because I was behind with the food, I spent quite a lot of time in the kitchen, cooking the tomatoes into pulp then sieving them.

"Oh, Nathan," I heard Minty exclaim, and then her breathy laugh. They were sitting in the garden, making inroads into a bottle of wine. I fried an onion until it was beautifully transparent, added a little grated carrot and stirred it into the ragú. Leaf by leaf, I washed a lettuce, dried it and set a pan to boil for the pasta. Let them talk, I thought to myself. It will do Nathan good.

I was hot and tired, but the kitchen was untidy and I took time to wash and dry the used utensils, then put them away. It was nine o'clock before I carried the supper into the garden and the wine bottle was empty.

Nathan was talking and gesticulating, and Minty was watching him through slanting dark eyes. I set down the tray. "What are you talking about?"

"Loyalty," said Minty. "We were discussing how you are loyal to people you have known for a long time."

"How do you mean?"

Nathan got up, opened another bottle and poured more wine. "Whether you lose sight of the original reasons for your loyalty and end up being loyal simply because you have known someone a long time." His hand poised over my glass. "Don't you agree, Rosie?" He was smiling but I sensed that he was angry, too.

Puzzled, I looked up at him. "I suppose I do."

"I think you do."

Holding her glass to her chest, Minty sat back in her chair. "I've no idea. I expect I'll find out . . ." A wing of shiny hair fell across her face and she brushed it back. "When I'm older, I suppose."

Later in the conversation when we were discussing holidays, Nathan astonished me by saying, "Rose has this secret lust for adventure, although she hides it because I prefer to keep going back to the same place. She traveled a bit before she met me."

"Nathan's teasing, Minty," I interjected lightly. "He's also quite wrong. I gave all that up when I married him. It was no sacrifice. Being on the move isn't always what it's cracked up to be."

Minty's dark eyes, resting on Nathan, were shiny with sympathy. "Oh, yes," she said. "Rose told me she used to go traveling with Hal Thorne."

I cried out into the silence of the bedroom. Once. Twice. Cries of pain and disbelief.

A long time later, the darkness in my mind merged with the darkness in the room and I must have slept.

Chapter 6

The phone by the bed woke me abruptly. With an effort, I turned my head and the clock informed me that it was six o'clock. The possibility that either Sam or Poppy was in trouble pierced my torpor, and I snatched up the receiver.

"Rose?" It was Nathan and, for a second, I imagined he was ringing to tell me that he had been kept overnight in the office—*big story breaking, Rosie*—and that he was on his way home. "I wanted to check you were okay." It was the calm, sensible, negotiating tone. "Are you?"

It had taken me a few years to understand the art of negotiation with Nathan. It was a question of returning a question with a question. "What do you think?" My hand crept across the space in the bed that he should have been occupying.

There was a quick intake of breath and the public voice vanished. "I couldn't bear to leave you like you were . . ."

He went on to say a lot of things about not wishing to hurt me and how his decision had been made after careful thought— "Not so careful," I flashed back—and how he would not have done it unless he considered it was necessary for his happiness . . . and, even, mine.

Etc., etc.

"Keep my happiness out of it," I said. "You're muddling us up."

"Sorry. That was stupid. But I just need to know you're okay."

"That's very touching, Nathan."

Supposedly the past is a foreign country of which we should beware. That was not true: it was oneself that was the foreign country, the unexplored, possibly dangerous side. The woman who clutched the telephone with whitening knuckles and wished to inflict as savage a hurt on her husband as he had inflicted on her was unknown to me. I did not recognize her and, although I was interested in, even intrigued by, this strange woman, I was also repelled by her. "I thought the point was that you did not care about my welfare any more. That's why you have left. You care about s . . . someone else's."

"Of course I care."

"Oh, Nathan."

"You don't have to live with someone to care about them."

"This is a pointless conversation."

"I know," he conceded miserably. Then his voice hardened. "I did try to explain yesterday."

I saw this image of us both on skates, veering round a rink, neither of us reaching the point where we faced each other. I began to shiver again, but I managed to say, "I can't talk any more."

"Wait . . . wait, Rose. We must discuss details. Money and things . . . You'll need some."

Nathan was neither mercenary nor ungenerous, but money always had to be dealt with first. That was how he was. Once that was done and discussed, he was free to deal with subtler considerations. Over the years I had worked out strategies to deal with it—one of the most successful being, if I was desperate, to ignore him. "Where are you at the moment?"

"At Zeffano's."

It was the hotel used by the paper's journalists when they had worked too late to go home.

"Why aren't you at . . . Minty's?"

There was a short, pregnant silence. Parsley stalked into the bedroom, jumped onto my feet and treated me to one of her stares.

"Minty isn't quite ready to have her space invaded."

More new language from Nathan. *Really?*

"I respect her for that."

I had the advantage over Nathan, for I was familiar with Minty's vocabulary. She talked about freedom, space, noncommitment and sex-for-pleasure-not-love, in the way that Ianthe talked to me about duty and restraint.

Where had they been together? How often? Was it in the afternoons? Or that shadowy moment between work and home, what Mazarine would call the cinq à sept? The hours set aside for married lovers.

The questions choked me. How? Why? When? I wanted to know the details. I wanted chapter and verse, to feast on it like an insect on rotten fruit. But I did not wish Nathan to witness my need, or grant him the power to refuse to answer.

Instead, I said, "Nathan, the company won't foot the bill for your love affairs."

"I know."

I thought of our years together: Nathan, encouraging and committed, ambitious, sometimes bad-tempered, mostly sweet; myself, eager to be settled, flustered by the arrival of children, perhaps a little unquestioning in the latter part of the marriage, a little too ready to accept that life had settled into a particular shape. All of that could change. In the breathing space that the departure of the children had left, all of that could—should have been examined. "Nathan, have you been so very unhappy? If you have I'm sorry, so sorry." The words were dragged from me. "I thought I made you happy."

"Oh, Rosie," he said, "you know how I loved you. From the moment I saw you on the plane."

"Then why?"

He said sadly, "You never loved me in the same way."

"That's not true, you know it isn't. Yes, I loved Hal but I loved you, too. In the end much more, with a real love based on a real life. Remember all the things—*all* the things—twenty-five years . . . Nathan, listen to me, you've let your imaginings get in the way. We know each other too well to throw it away. I know romance dies. I know I'm not twenty-nine any more, and Minty is lovely. I understand . . ." I made a huge effort. "It's not too late."

"Look," Nathan cut me off, "about money. I won't let you down."

I believed that without question, but I clung to my pride. "I have a perfectly good job. If I have to, I can manage."

He said, patiently, stubbornly, "For the time being I will contribute my half of the bills. I don't want you worrying."

I could not bear to hear any more. I knew I should be clever and search for a better, more sensible, resolution. *Think again. For the children's sake. For my sake. You will get over this, and I will forgive you. Maybe I should be asking, What have I done to you? Maybe I should be begging, Nathan, you must forgive me.*

But the voice that usually issued from me—the one in which wives and mothers cajoled, bossed, teased, wooed, which might be snippy, tender and powerful—failed. It had fallen silent.

I dropped the receiver into the cradle and slumped back on the pillows. Sensing her opportunity, Parsley slid closer. I dropped my face into my hands. *Talk money.* Nathan's kindness was unbearable. I had much, much rather that he had been cruel and angry. It was difficult enough, almost impossible, to absorb what had happened, let alone consider a salvage operation. But Nathan had. He had been working covertly and underground, his miner's lamp shining on a rich, new seam.

I thought of Poppy, and of a glove being turned inside out, finger by finger.

At eight-thirty I rang Vee, conscious that it was Saturday and the worst time of the day for her. Along with Mazarine, Vee was my oldest friend and all three of us had been at university together. "It's Rose, Vee. I'm sorry to ring at this hour, but I had to talk to someone."

"Oh, Rose. Goodness. It's ages since you've been in touch. Yes, of course. What's wrong?"

"Nathan has left me. He's gone to live with my assistant."

The cries of Annabel, seven, and Mark, five, were loud in the background. Vee's voice veered into a shocked upper register: "You're joking. When?"

"Last night." A child's wail punctuated this exchange and Vee shouted at it to be quiet, that Mummy was coming. "I'm sorry, Vee, this is the wrong time."

"Look," she said, "I can't talk. There's a taxi at the door for Luc and me, and the children are playing up. I'll ring when I can."

The exchange had exhausted me and I pulled the sheet over my head. If I was going to suffer—that is, more than I was at the moment, and there was no doubt that I would—I might as well do it properly and give myself up to grand and august pain.

But thoughts like tiny white-sailed boats skidded inconsequentially over the waters. I had to put out a note for the milkman. The gas bill was overdue. My passport needed renewing. I should ring the children—but I did not want to face them with the earthquake that had shaken their parents' marriage. It was children who came to parents for help and advice, not the other way round.

I flipped back the sheet and struggled upright.

Poor Mum, he's left her for a younger woman.

I began to weep, wildly, convulsed from head to foot, and went on until I retched with exhaustion. Eventually I crept into the bathroom, propped myself against the basin, and ran a bath. The toothpaste had been squeezed last by Nathan. As usual, he had not put the top back on.

Like a convalescent, shaky and unsure, I lowered myself into the water. I lay and looked at the shelf above me. Bath oil. Mouthwash. Surgical spirit. A spare soap—the pick 'n' mix of family life.

I looked down at my partially submerged body. What did I expect to see? The gleaming bronze of a fountain nymph, whose lines flowed untouched and unmarked? My body had swelled in gestation. It had been stretched, ripped, sewn up. It had carried children, cradled them and, when the time had come, pushed them gently away. It had learned to be endlessly busy, to snatch at repose, to guard its silences in the hot, crowded demands of the family. How could all this activity not be written into the flesh?

"That's what women are put on earth for." Ianthe was clear on the point. "There's no more to be said. Take it or leave it, Rose." I remembered that she had been peeling away the brown, waxy skin from a boiled ham. "If you do what's right, you won't go wrong." Taking up the knife, she scored the fat, which had gone transparent with boiling, then stuck in cloves to make diamond patterns. "Raising children and keeping the family going brings its own reward."

My skin was beginning to wrinkle. "Mum is a prune, Mum is a prune . . ." That was Poppy, who used to climb into the hot, soapy baths in which I took refuge. There would be a scrabble of thin limbs, a displacement of water, and a wet, bony little form attached itself to me. Sometimes Sam appeared, too, and asked, "Can I come in?" And we ended up in a heap of wet bodies and giggles. Unless I was tired and snapped at them.

As I got dressed in a pair of old jeans and a jumper, I noticed that my hands were shaking. Stop it, Rose, I admonished myself. You must think. You must be strong. I went downstairs to pull back the curtains, write the note to the milkman, begin the business of living through today, tomorrow, the next day and the one after that.

Later in the morning, I went out into the garden. During the winter, the roof of the shed had yielded to frost and its age, though I secretly suspected the squirrels, and had sprung a leak. Inside there was a scum of moisture from the previous day's rain. I hoicked out the fork and secateurs and carried them over to the lilac tree. Lilac is greedy: it drains every drop of moisture from the soil, the garden dipsomaniac, but mine got away with it because of the pleasure I took in its scent and heavy, erotic flowers, but the patch under it remained the one place where I struggled to make any plant thrive, however often I got down on my knees and coaxed.

A solution was to cut a rain tunnel into its branches now before the new growth was too thick or the tiny infant blossoms had appeared, when I could not bear to cut them away.

Deadwood is easy enough to target: it takes only a snip here and there and the dry, brittle spikes fall away. But last year's growth was strong, sappy and lubricated with coming spring. It resisted my invasion: it did not understand the need for a rain tunnel. For half an hour or more, I fought with it, and my secateurs bit deep into pulpy flesh, leaving scars that would weep into the rain.

Anyway, I needed Nathan on the stepladder to finish the job properly. My sense of balance had never been good, and he had never let me up the stepladder. "I want you alive," he said. "How would I manage without you?"

I began to cry again.

I seized the fork and drove it into the earth. At best, digging was a calming activity; at worst, it induced exhaustion. I did not care which. This many-times-performed ordinary task must help me: it would provide reassurance that energy continued to flow over obstacles, and that digging and weeding would always be required. Even if a wife was not.

Despite applications of mulch, the earth remained stubborn and fractious, clagging the tines. The handle whipped out of my hands. Again, I lifted the fork and sank it into the dry, lumpen clay. This time, it struck a root mass and refused to budge.

"Go on, damn you," I muttered. "Please." But it was no good: the fork was stuck. I wiped my face with the back of my hand.

A click sounded in my head. Almost immediately, there was an alteration in my vision of the merest fraction, but what I saw was wider and larger, less exclusive. It was like cutting into a piecrust to discover that underneath was rotten meat. It was like peering at my picture of the roses to see not only the ruffle of the petals and tender green calyx, but the canker, the sulphurous weal, burning on the bud.

How had I missed the rot on the Iceberg rose? Or the woodlice and wireworms snaking through the meager patch I had turned over. Or the spume of stones, the shard of orange plastic and a ring pull from a can. Woven, too, around these underground citizens and invaders were the lusty, ubiquitous roots of bindweed.

"I can't believe it," said Vee, when she rang later that evening. "Did you have any idea? I haven't talked to you properly for so long, Rose, that I don't know what's been going on."

Once upon a time, we would have known exactly what was happening in each other's lives, but recently, not so much. Our once close, interconnecting friendship had been the victim of our busy lives. Vee was the books editor on a rival newspaper— "Rivals make the *best* of friends"—she was on her second marriage and a late-starter mother, while I had been caught up in my job. There was no room in the spaces between these intense, life-building activities to cram in any more.

Vee sounded tired and I felt guilty that I had bothered her. "No, I didn't but I wasn't looking. He didn't buy new underwear, or put on aftershave, or read poetry. Vee, I'm sorry I bothered you, but I couldn't think of who else to turn to."

"Of course you should have rung me. But I was on the way to my ex-nanny's wedding. The last thing I wanted to do on a precious Saturday but all in a good cause. I wanted to make sure that the current one realized how solid and friendly our relationship could be."

I understood the subterfuges to which a working mother descended. They were justified on the grounds that no moral scruple was greater than ensuring the care and comfort of children—which left pretty much a blank sheet where behavior was concerned.

"Look, would you like to come over here? I could fix some supper."

I was having difficulty focusing on anything, and the idea of leaving the house made me panic. "No, no, it's fine. Just talking to you is enough."

"Have you told the children?"

"I can't bear to. Not just for the moment." Sam would go silent with shock; Poppy's red mouth would pale and tremble.

"Rose, I know how you're feeling, believe me. You must call me, day or night."

"Thank you."

There was nothing more to add.

I went on the hunt for Nathan's whiskey and found it in his study. An empty glass with a thumbnail of peaty residue in the bottom stood beside the bottle. No doubt he had drunk it while he waited for me to come home and planned his escape from our marriage. I disliked whiskey but I poured myself a slug and it obliged me by punching into my empty stomach.

I thought of Minty shaking her shiny head, the soft whoop of her laughter, and Nathan joining in. I supposed some of their amusement had been directed at me.

I had the strangest sensation that my body had become a foreign entity to which I held no key; neither did I possess a map to its arrangement of skin, bones and blood. I held out a hand.

Would my fingers flex? Would I manage to swallow? Would the air in the tiny alveoli in my lungs perform its chemical exchange? A pain pulsed above my left eye, and my throat was sore from crying. Shock, of course: my body had raced ahead of my mind. Although I had listened to Nathan, heard the front door snap behind him, and I had inhabited an empty house for a day and a night, a part of me did not believe that he had gone.

Nathan loved his study. The notice on the door said, KEEP OUT, and he had insisted on installing two phone lines and purred when they rang at the same time. His study had been the dry run for the office, and in it he reflected on weighty office matters. He had taken pains also to set up systems to deal with bills, insurance and family finance.

I sat down at the desk, opened a drawer and was confronted by his neat arrangement of Scotch tape, pens and screwdriver. On the notepad by the phone was written, "Ring accountant."

It was a fair bet that he had—before quitting the study to sack his wife. Nathan always worked methodically through the tasks he set himself.

A long time ago Vee had accused Nathan of being unimaginative, but I argued that he was the opposite. It was precisely because he could imagine only too well the disasters that might overtake his family that he took such pains to anticipate them.

Hanging above the desk, at the point where it would have caught his eye each time he raised his head, was a framed photograph of Nathan and his colleagues at last year's Christmas dinner. The men—they were all men—were in dinner jackets, which conferred clubbable conformity and suggested that the occasion, which was about eating and drinking, was important. I had teased Nathan about that.

He was seated between the chairman and the editor, and

when he first produced it, the photograph had given me pleasure, for he looked so toned and relaxed. It read differently now:
shining in Nathan's expression was not the natural pleasure of a
man at ease with his work and home but rather, the excitement
of a man who had embarked on a different course entirely.

Chapter 7

Early on Sunday morning, I fumbled into consciousness. I had been woken by the sound of footsteps in the hall and someone mounted the stairs.

It was Nathan coming up with the breakfast. As he always did on Sundays. "This is our time," he said, when the children were big enough to make their own breakfast and then so big that breakfast had become a vague memory. "Just you and me." Sometimes, he did not wait for me to finish but took away the tray. "Our time." Lately, conscious of my early-morning face, I had retreated under the sheets and he had found me there.

The air in the bedroom felt sour and despairing, and I no less so. I lay without moving, without curiosity, even, fear absent. If it was the mad axman about whom Poppy had had nightmares my death at his hands would be easy. No more than a gentle sigh of acceptance and a plea to do it quickly.

"Mum?" Sam peered round the door.

Briefly happiness streaked through me and I struggled upright. "Sam . . . you've come."

"Of course." He advanced into the room, bent over and kissed me. "I couldn't let you be on your own. Dad phoned me last night and told me of his extraordinary decision. I couldn't think what else to do. Except something stupid, like bringing you flowers." He looked down at me bleakly. "I had no idea."

"Join the club."

He reached over and took one of my hands. I clung to him. "You must have got up at the crack of dawn to get here," I said.

Sam would have set the alarm in his bachelor bedroom in his elegant town flat, slid out from beside the sleeping Alice, dressed so quietly that she did not stir. Perhaps he had not even told her where he was going. Perhaps Alice had not been there.

Sam was never at his best with high emotion, and he patted my leg awkwardly. "You look awful. When did you last eat?"

"I don't know. It must have been yesterday, but I attacked Dad's whiskey . . . okay," I admitted, "not good, but it won't become a habit. And I felt entitled to a glass too many."

He sighed. "I'd better get you breakfast." Parsley head-butted her way into the bedroom. Sam picked her up and placed her in my arms. "Here, take your dysfunctional cat." He moved round the room, pulling back the curtains and piling my clothes onto the chair—uncharacteristically I had scattered them on the floor. Damn them, I had thought, fighting with my jeans and sweater, which I had seemed unable to remove last night. Maybe clothes have a point of view, too—maybe they're protesting at my fate.

It was not a good idea to think too much about the previous evening, and I buried my face in Parsley's warm fur and battled with a heaving stomach. "Sam, don't make me any coffee."

"You drink far too much of it anyway." He went out and closed the door.

Parsley rebelled at the straitjacket, and I released her. Her green eyes questioned my trustworthiness before she settled down beside me.

Sam returned, bearing tea and toast on a tray. The tea had slopped into the saucer and the toast was spread with the thinnest scraping of butter but my heart melted.

"Eat *now*," he commanded.

The toast fragmented on my tongue. I thought briefly of other breakfasts—thick, white toast, lashings of butter and an icing of bitter marmalade—which I had shared with Nathan. Already, they seemed to have taken place way back in another life. "Was Dad all right when you spoke to him?" I asked.

Sam's brows snapped together. "Not too bad." He was trying to shield me from anything that might cause me additional misery. At the same time he did not want to hear any fierce, hot words against his father.

I shut my eyes and tried to summon the perfect loyalty to Nathan that only yesterday had been so easy, so automatic. I did not want Sam to shield Nathan. Greedily, I wanted to claim all of my children's loyalty and affection. Circles of light slid across my vision, and my breath sounded harsh and labored in my ears.

"Mum," he said, "please don't look like that."

I pulled myself together. "Sam, c-could I have some more tea?"

After I had got dressed, I made my way downstairs and went into the kitchen. Sam was flicking through the *Sunday Times,* keeping half an eye on the bacon he was grilling. Sam liked a cooked breakfast. So did Nathan. Except on Sundays, of course. A little dizzy, I leaned on the doorpost and observed Sam for a moment or two. A turn of the head, the flicker of a muscle, and he looked just like his father.

Sensing my presence, he swung round. "I didn't have time to eat." He hooked out a chair from under the table with his foot. "Come and sit down."

I sat and watched him as he demolished bacon and toast, then put down his fork. "I just want to say that I don't know what Dad's doing, but please don't think of him too badly."

That was just like Sam. From the word go he had been such a fair, modest person, with an innate sense of natural justice. Even when Poppy had been born and displaced him so thoroughly, Sam had got on with his little life and quietly accepted that he was no longer the prime focus of attention.

"I don't know what to think, Sam. Or rather, there's too much to think about and I can't take it in yet. For one thing, I feel shamingly foolish. Stupid, even."

"You really had no idea?"

I shook my head.

"It could be that he's woken up this morning and realized he's made a monumental mistake."

"Your father told me that he wanted some freedom, and he meant before it was too late. Of course, it's perfectly natural to have thoughts like that but—" My voice broke. Sam frowned and I realized that, at this time in his life, Nathan's ambitions made no sense to him and he would not understand. I bit my lip. "It's going to take a bit of forgiving."

"That suggests you think he might come back." I shrugged and Sam asked earnestly, "Would you like me to talk to him?"

I shook my head.

Sam shoved away his plate. "You'll have to deal with Minty."

"I've thought of that."

He smiled grimly. "I wouldn't like to be in her shoes." He got up and slid an arm round my shoulders. "I'm pretty sure Dad's going to find out that he's made a mistake."

Sam's championship reminded that there were important, unchanging things amid this mess to which I could cling. I had been lucky. Some families did not have that glue of memory.

"Give me Poppy." Nathan steadied himself on the path that led precipitously to the beach. "I'll take her." He handed me the picnic basket and swung Poppy into his arms. She gave a little cry of excitement and flopped against him. "Stay still, wriggler." He kissed her neck, and began a careful descent.

The path was treacherous. I bent over Sam: "Keep close to Dad." Clutching his spade and bucket, Sam padded behind Nathan, placing one sandal carefully in front of the other, negotiating the loosened stones and potholes. I flung the rug over my shoulder like a plaid—a Jacobite soldier off to war, said Sam— and brought up the rear, with the thermoses rattling in the picnic basket.

"I'm in front," yelled Poppy.

The weather had been dry and hot, and in places the path had crumbled away. Tufts of thrift and wild marjoram pooled across the slopes on either side and, high above, the swifts called to each other. We edged down until we reached the stony lip of beach. At the last minute the path vanished, and we had to jump.

"Go on, then." Nathan swung Poppy to the ground and, a sprite in yellow shorts, she raced across the stones toward the sea, which glittered in the summer sun. Sam jumped and looked back at me to make sure I had witnessed his prowess.

"Rosie?" Nathan turned back. I had been about to launch myself at the beach but he caught me and swung me down. In that brief moment of contact, I heard the thud of a steady heartbeat. My own raced with exertion. "Light as a feather," lied Nathan.

The heat pulsed off the rocks, too much so for comfort, and we chose to sit by one draped with cool, insulating ropes of seaweed. Nathan spread the rug and I anchored it with stones. Poppy's skinny white limbs waved like an insect's as I pulled off her T-shirt and shorts. She escaped me and, stark naked, hopped around trying to insert a leg into her swimsuit. I captured my giggling daughter and covered her with kisses. Over by an adjacent rock, Sam had made a base camp for his possessions and he came over to request that they were not touched. I assured him that they would be safe.

From here, the view was of uninterrupted water and the cliffs hid the sprawl of bungalows and houses that crept over the wildness. There was no one else on the beach. The sun made our eyes water, and the coconut scent of the suntan lotion on our hot skin was whipped away by a salty breeze.

The children raced off, thought better of it as the stones bit their bare feet, and skipped their way to the edge of the water, squealing as the water splashed over their toes. Nathan sat down on the rug and stripped off his shirt. "They're growing up, aren't they?"

At six and four, this was overstating the case a little. "Way to go," I said.

Nathan always got burned unless I took action. He was not someone who thrived in hot climates. I opened the suntan lotion, tipped a pool into my cupped hand and rubbed it into his back. "More," he demanded, "just there," as my fingers explored the area by his neck that was knotted and painful with tension.

After a bit he got up and joined the children. I pulled out

my book, lay on my stomach and read. Every so often I looked up and watched my family failing to outwit the sea. The book palled and I dropped my head onto my arms. I could hear the sea vibrating, the tiny hiss of displaced sand and the click of stones. If I lay still and quiet enough, I thought, I could melt into this elemental world of sun, water and wide, open horizon.

Sam ran back with a fistful of shells to show me before transferring them to his base. "Poppy won't get them there," he said.

I sat up and put my arms around his shoulders that felt so childish, so vulnerable. "Poppy doesn't get everything," I reassured him.

He gave me one of his challenging stares. "Yes, she does."

My fingers must have pressed too hard at the junction of his shoulder and arm, just where the nerves flowed under the skin, and he flinched. "No, Poppy doesn't," I promised. "Wait and see."

He pulled himself free.

"Why don't you help me get the picnic ready, Sam?"

He laid the rug with four different-colored plastic plates and distributed the individual sandwich parcels I had made and labeled: on Sam's I had drawn a smiling face, on Poppy's a big teddy bear, on Nathan's a pair of sunglasses. On mine, I had written, "Sleep." Then he put out matching plastic mugs, carefully matching the colors to the plates.

We ate cheese and cucumber sandwiches, and drank orange juice. Poppy refused to eat either the cucumber or the cheese and gave them to me. For pudding we opened a packet of bourbon biscuits and a bag of apples.

I edged up beside Nathan so that our thighs touched. Hard, taut muscle alongside softer, sand-dusted flesh. Large though my feet were, Nathan's were bigger, and the comparison always made me feel ridiculously feminine and cherished. "Happy?" I asked.

He leaned over and rubbed his nose gently on mine. "Never happier."

I sighed with contentment. Nathan straightened and rubbed at his reddening forearms. "Can't ask for much more," he said. "Can we?"

"I'll have to get back," said Sam. He clasped his hands on the tabletop, and his thumbs knitted together. "I think you and Dad need to get together."

He was hoping to leave with some hope, and it was a relief to have to think about his needs. "I'll make you some sandwiches."

I cut bread, and buttered it, noting with surprise how competent my movements were. I took care to slice the Cheddar thinly. Tiny parings fell onto the table; I brushed them away.

Sam watched me and accepted the neat foil packet. "You didn't need to do that."

"Oh, yes, I did. You don't know how much. Thank you for letting me."

"I was just wondering," he said, "if you and Dad aren't sorted out, maybe you'd like to come to Greece in July with Alice and me?"

I launched myself in his direction, caught him round the waist and kissed him. "Certainly not, but you're the most wonderful son for even considering it."

He held me tightly. "Thought I should ask."

"A sacrifice too far."

"Have you talked to Poppy?"

"Not yet, but I will."

"She'll take it badly."

"I know."

When Sam left, number seven Lakey Street returned to silence. I switched on the radio but it was playing a violin concerto. Each sweet, perfect note cut into me like a knife slicing my flesh. I gasped, gagged, lunged forward, snapped it off and fled from the kitchen.

My study was on the first-floor landing, a space kidnapped from the turn in the stairs. Its window overlooked the garden and fitted badly. I kept a rug on the chair to wrap round myself on cold days when I sat at the desk I had squeezed into the space. The family scoffed at the term "study," and at the idea that I needed one. For years, the children had had their own way of making their disapproval felt: they made a point of thumping up and down the stairs as noisily as they dared—"Shush, Mummy's working in her study," they told each other, in whispers guaranteed to penetrate the Tower of Babel. I sat there now, so cold that I had wrapped the rug round me twice.

I picked up the phone and rang Poppy. "Darling, are you all right?"

"Mum, will you stop fussing over me? I'm fine." Her voice softened. "But it's nice to hear you."

"Dad didn't ring you last night?"

"Out until the wee small hours, Mum."

"Darling, I have to tell you something. I'm afraid . . . I'm afraid Dad has found . . ." That sounded so bald and I thought Nathan deserved better. "He has fallen in love with someone else and has left home."

Poppy's cry of disbelief echoed down the phone. "Who? Which woman?"

"Minty."

There was a long, long silence. When Poppy spoke, she

sounded different—quite old, in fact, and as if a joyous element in her had shriveled and died. "The old goat. Dad's turned into an old goat."

"Please. Don't say that about him."

"But it's *true*."

"It's a bit more complicated. Obviously, he had come to a point where he felt he must have a change."

"I don't want to hear," Poppy shrieked. "I wish you'd never phoned. Mum, I can't talk about it. I'll have to talk to you later."

"Of course."

At that Poppy calmed down. "I should be comforting you— and I will, I promise I will, Mum, but I'll have to get over the shock first."

Next, I dialed Timon's private number.

Timon's wife, Mary, bitterly resented intrusions at weekends. We had discussed this sometimes at office parties and she told me that one of her tactics was to freeze people out. When she answered the phone I got the freezing treatment. I explained that I would not have dreamed of ringing on a Sunday morning unless it was necessary. "Oh, well, then," she said, caught perhaps by curiosity, "but we do have guests." She handed the phone to Timon.

"Rose, has something happened?"

A food processor sprang into life in the background, accompanied by a meaningful clash of saucepans. "I thought I should explain that I shall have to sack Minty on Monday."

"I see," said Timon. "Listen, can you hang on? I'm going to change phones." When he came back on the line the noises had stopped. "Could you give me the details?" So I did.

"Nathan has left you for Minty." Timon gave a short laugh that meant, "Who would have thought there was life in the old dog?" that made me angry on Nathan's behalf. "This certainly presents complications," he said.

"I can't have her in the office. You do understand?"

"Hang on." Timon became formal. "There are rules and regulations, Rose. *You* can't sack people just like that. I think you must leave this to me."

I swallowed. "All right. But I won't have her sitting in my office. She will have to go somewhere else."

Timon cleared his throat. "Under the circumstances, you might like to take a day off, Rose. That would be perfectly all right. Take the week."

"No," I said, "you don't understand. The work is important to me, and I wouldn't dream of abandoning it."

"As you wish." He considered further. "Leave it with me, and see me at eleven-thirty on Monday."

I finished that conversation feeling better. At least I had done something. Made a stand over Minty.

Huddled into the rug, I sat and thought about deceit. How was it possible to live for long periods of time without letting clues slip? In a peculiar way, I felt nothing but admiration for Nathan and Minty because I didn't think I would have had the wit and style to carry off such a secret. How did Minty square taking such an interest in my clothes, my ideas, my family, which I knew was genuine, with the knowledge that she was taking my husband to bed?

How, for example, did Nathan manage to insist that I sit down with him and review our pension situation when he knew he was not going to be around? Perhaps the effects of harboring a deep, fearful secret were so debilitating that an autopilot took over the normal, humdrum bits of your life and permitted you to act normally.

Perhaps we all lived on several levels and juggled them without thinking about it. Perhaps one grew so attached to everyday habits and questions—they were so bred into the blood and the bone—that one could not bear to give them up, even though one knew that, by any law of justice, one should do so.

Chapter 8

On Monday morning I prepared myself to go into work. I sat down at the dressing table, and smoothed layer after layer of cream into my face. It was dry and sore from weeping, and the skin under my fingertips felt like cracked tissue paper.

The sunlight in the bedroom spared me nothing: a startlingly blue vein on my leg, the dark, troubled circles under my eyes, a toe that had once been unblemished. *Hang on. This is not the right woman in the mirror. The right one is the young, happy one.*

I chose a sea-island T-shirt, a linen trouser suit and flat black pumps. I put on mascara, a slash of red lipstick and brushed my hair into shiny obedience. Then, with Parsley colonizing my lap, I painted my nails bright battle red. This was my armory, the best I could summon, but when I levered myself to my feet, and Parsley slid protesting to the floor, I discovered cat hairs trapped in the wet varnish. "You wretch, Parsley."

The green eyes turned in my direction. *You fool, Rose.*

I picked the cat hair off my nails and went downstairs to the kitchen. I tapped the coffee pot, but decided against it and tried to eat a banana, but abandoned it.

Outside, it looked as though it was going to be fine again and, concierge and custodian, I went from room to room, drawing back curtains, plumping up a cushion, wiping away a smear of dust, seeking comfort from the intimacies and familiarities of my routines. The clock's tick in the sitting room seemed abnormally loud in the still, silent air.

The contents of my book bag remained where I had left them. I checked them over. A piece I should have edited. A couple of memos I should have read. The novel, the cookery book and the biography, which, in the normal course, I would have dipped into before sending them out for review.

Bag over my shoulder, I closed the door on the house, the cool sitting room and its ticking clock, on the garden, and the drift of a light rain on the grass, on the double bedroom where, deep in the past, Nathan had whispered to me that he was so lucky, *so lucky,* to have me and, in reply, I had breathed thankfulness into the night.

The strap of my bag had made a groove in my finger—I was clasping it so hard—by the time I stepped out of the lift at the office. Jenny from human resources was waiting to get in. When she saw me, her expression turned to mild panic and I thought, So soon. Not that I had imagined Nathan and I would be immune from gossip. To give Jenny a chance to collect her wits, I made a play of swapping my heavy bag from hand to hand. "Morning, Jenny."

"Look," she muttered, "I want you to know . . ."

It was the cruel office joke that, despite being a paper expert on human resources, Jenny was no good at them in the flesh, and she could not finish whatever she wanted to say. Instead, she bolted for the lift. The doors clacked shut.

It was not a good start, and as I made for my desk, I summoned every ounce of the control and wit I would need to negotiate the long hours. Then, with a shock, I realized I was not very interested in getting through the long hours. Feeling sick and shaky, I sank into my chair and the photograph caught my eye.

Nathan's face smiled out at me, and I tried to think of something else. Ianthe maintained we were on this earth to be tested. I always laughed when she said this, and told her she was being old-fashioned, New Testament-ish. I said it even though I knew she was right.

The coffee machine clicked and gushed. The photocopier disgorged hot, acrid shanks of paper. The clack and bustle of office life closed in, insulating the occupants of the building with thick, polystyrene walls of habit.

The phone rang. It was an author whose novel had received a bad review. I listened politely to an outpouring of rage, which finished, "You were out to get me."

"No, not at all. The piece made the point that you would sell magnificently. I'm sorry my reviewer did not like it."

He snapped back, "You don't *like* the fact that I've made a lot of money."

"How very nice for you."

Out of the corner of my eye, I caught a glimpse of Nathan . . . in his gray suit, heading for Timon's office and disappearing inside. He looked neither to right nor left. Caught off-guard, I dropped the phone and buried my face in my hands.

"Rose," Maeve Otley limped over, "you don't look so good. I've brought you a cup of tea." She edged it onto my desk with her lumpy, painful hands. "Put some sugar in it. Go on, you'll need it."

Maeve was far shrewder than she ever let on. She touched my shoulder briefly. Her sympathy was easy, but I had never imagined it would be so hard to accept. "Thank you," I managed.

Maeve favored long sleeves to hide her hands, and she fussed with the cuffs of her purple dress. I think she was making a judgment about how much I could, or could not, take on board. "Don't let them beat you," she said at last, and returned to her desk.

I had neither the energy nor the focus to consider what she might have meant, and I reached for something, anything, from the nearest basket on the desk. As it happened, it was the discarded review of Hal's book. "This man is a fraud . . ." wrote the critic happily. I held it between fingers that had grown cold with the shock of seeing Nathan. Hal was too good and too stringent a writer to have an easy ride. Anyway, he always maintained that a gene had been implanted in the English that triggered the worst. Quality and brilliance reacted with envy to produce acid.

My rule had been never to look at Hal's books and I had kept to it religiously. But now I picked up *A Thousand Olive Trees* from the June pile. Once upon a time, I had imagined that Hal's face would remain in my memory forever. It had not. The details and sharp outlines had faded, leaving an impression, the blurred recollection—like all the other so-called ineradicable memories. Like old stone weathering and fading. Like sand shifting in dunes. I turned to the back flap of the jacket, and there he was, leaner, older, fair hair bleached and battered by the sun, looking much as I would have expected.

Nathan was carving the chicken. The kitchen was steamy and fragrant with cooking and herbs; the radio played in the background. I chopped carrots into matchsticks. Having been dragged out of bed at midday, the seventeen-year-old Sam and fifteen-year-old Poppy were in their rooms, reluctantly getting dressed. Sartorially they were at the stage of toned-down anarchic punk. Sam offered us a variety of spray-painted T-shirts, incorporating the word "kill." Poppy favored jeans with the waistbands cut off.

"The book of the week," said the announcer, "is an account of a journey through the North African desert. *Desert and Go* by Hal Thorne will begin on Monday at nine forty-five . . ."

In the saucepan the water hissed and foamed as the carrots hit its surface. "Lunch will be in a moment," I said. "Can you chivvy the children?" Since Nathan did not move I went and shouted to them up the stairs. "Thanks," I snapped at him on my return.

"Have you read it?" Nathan carved a slice of moist white flesh.

The question had been sprung with the quiet of the hunter. "No."

"Why not?"

"Because . . ." I moved over to the sink and tipped the carrots into a colander. The steam batted me in the face.

"Because," Nathan finished the carving, and arranged the chicken on an oval plate, "he is still with you. Or the idea of him."

"This is the one o'clock news," interposed the newscaster.

I transferred the carrots to a dish and put it in the oven to keep warm. Nathan and I had being going through a bad patch, but nothing too significant. We were tired and far too busy, that was all. The truth was that Nathan's job was getting in the way of our family life, which was changing anyway, and my job was pretty demanding, but I reckoned we could weather the irritants. Even so, I did not consider the subject of Hal a good one to pursue. I said lightly, "That's not true, Nathan. I don't read his books because they don't interest me."

"But it's your business to read what you don't necessarily like."

I busied myself with chopping parsley. "Not always."

"Oh, Rosie, you're such a bad liar."

No, I'm not, I thought. I'm a brilliant, accomplished liar. But I have always lied for a good cause, the best of reasons. When Nathan moved toward me in the bed and I, having twisted and turned through a day of children's cries, work's demands and husband soothing, thought, Sleep, sleep, peace. And he said something like, It's been a long time, Rose. And I replied, still aching for sleep, Far, far too long. That was one of my best lies.

"Why are you bringing all this up now, Nathan? It's gone, finished. I married you, remember? We're happy." I moved back to the stove and gave the gravy a quick whisk. "I couldn't be happier."

Nathan continued, as if I had not said anything, "Weren't you going to travel through the desert with him?"

"There was talk of it at one point, but it came to nothing. It was a very long time ago. Please, go and call the children again or lunch will get cold."

Nathan dropped the carving knife and fork with a clatter that cut through the mutter of the radio. "Call them yourself." He swung on his heel and left the kitchen.

I knew where to find him: in his study. Hands folded in his lap, he was sitting at the desk, staring at the neat pile of bills and family documents. There were tears in his eyes, tears that were almost certainly my fault but I did not know what they were for.

I stood with my hands on my hips. "Nathan, you're making more of Hal than I ever have. It's become a habit, an excuse. You know perfectly well that as a subject Hal could not be more dead."

Nathan shrugged. It was a gesture that begged for the balm of reassurance and comfort. I knelt beside him, took his hands in mine and kissed them. "Nathan, you could not be more wrong."

A sixth sense prompted me to look up. Minty was walking toward me, as purposefully as her kitten heels would permit. She came to a halt by my chair.

At first, I refused to look at her. Then I did.

She was sleek with triumph and secret pleasure, or so it seemed to me, the Rose with new vision. Cowering was not Minty's style, and I had always admired her courage. That, and the slender body under the white tank top and tiny black skirt. Her beauty and promise were handled . . . how? With the confidence of a woman whose generation did not understand why feminism had been necessary.

"Please leave," I said. "I've asked for you to be transferred, if not sacked. Didn't Timon phone you?"

"Yes, he did." She moved across to her desk and flipped on the screen. "I considered not showing, but I thought I owed it to you to face you, and you can call me any name you like. So now I have, and I'm getting out for the time being, but just before I quit the battlefield, I'll check my e-mails." Cool and efficient, she typed in her password.

"Why?" I asked her. "We were friends."

"Of course." She executed a couple of commands, peered at the screen, then signed off.

"I gave you your break."

"And I've thanked you for it, Rose, more than once. Do I have to be grateful for the rest of my life?" She opened her drawer and took out her contacts book and diary, which she dropped into her bag. "Why don't we talk about the real subject of this conversation? Nathan was there for the taking, Rose. Ask him."

"Nathan was perfectly happy."

Her dark eyes did not blink. "He says not. He says he needs some attention. I give it to him."

Suddenly I was fearful for Minty. "And you believed him? I thought you were so sharp."

Minty got to her feet. "You can say what you like, Rose, but it won't change anything."

I wanted the words to cease, and craved the mercy of silence. I wanted to give in to despair, to crawl away, lie down and die, like a diseased pie-dog in the sun. But if I did that, I would be yielding every advantage to Minty. It was not as if Nathan and I had grown miles apart and there was nothing left. It was not like that at all. I had memories, joyous and nourishing, of a good, happy family that Nathan and I had built brick by brick. Good, strong achievements, for which it was worth fighting.

I pushed myself upright wearily. "You're interfering in something you don't understand. You don't know the truth about our marriage, whatever Nathan may have told you." Minty leaned back on the desk and transcribed a circle on the carpet with a slender foot. It infuriated and terrified me. I added, "He only says that for the obvious reason."

"He could get that anyway. No lies necessary."

"Oh, God." I dropped back into the chair.

The hope that this episode was a minor one, through which Nathan and I would struggle, vanished and with it the flare of hope that I could mastermind this . . . test. If Nathan had lied through his teeth to gain occupancy of Minty's body then I would have wept, burned and forgiven him. But this. *No lies necessary.*

"Was it you . . . or him?" I looked down at my naked hand. "Who?"

She understood. "It was me, Rose. I've always liked Nathan. He's a nice man, a wonderful man, a pussycat, who happens to be rather powerful. It was a fling at first, nothing for you to worry about and I wasn't ever going to let you know. Then it became more . . . complicated and I'm afraid you had to be told."

"He is wonderful," I said.

"What a pity you didn't tell him," Minty reflected. "But I shall."

Her arrogance was astonishing. I concentrated on the one aspect of this cold little history with which I felt I could cope. "And you carried on working with me?"

"It never does to mix things up. It's a bad habit." She checked the contents of her bag and picked it up. "For what it's worth, Rose, I'm sorry it was you. I wish it had been anybody else."

At eleven-thirty sharp I knocked on Timon's door—editors were allowed doors—and was told to enter.

Timon watched me cross the carpet toward his oversized desk. "You don't look well, Rose." He brushed aside my apologies for ringing him on a Sunday and told me to sit down.

"Nathan came to see you. How was he?" I asked.

Timon rearranged his papers, which, on the vast desktop, appeared like postage stamps. "It's not easy for anyone. However, I have now had a chance to appraise the situation."

"I'm sure you agree that I cannot work with Minty."

Timon picked up a pen and drew a large circle on a notepad with a bright pink cover. "I want to get this sorted out quickly."

"Okay." I was riveted by the bright color, which fragmented in front of my tired eyes.

Timon drew a second, less perfect circle. "I am sorry you have run against rocks in your private life. Believe me, we have all been there." He looked up, and his scrutiny was modulated neither by pity nor understanding. "The fact is, we have been taking a good, hard look at the books pages. They need a re-vamp. As you know, if I had my way we would probably dump them as they have no advertising pull."

This was not the conversation for which I had nerved myself, but if that was what Timon wanted, I would summon my energy and play ball. I had facts and figures at my fingertips and I launched into them, but Timon cut me off: "I don't think you get the point. Change is happening faster than ever and we must harness all our energies to keep up. No," he held up a finger, "not to keep up but to be ahead."

It was the rhetoric spouted all over the industrialized world and I was used to responding to it. "Fine."

Timon was not listening. "The pages need to be sharper, sexier. More celebrities. We need radical change."

"I can do that. Tell me the budgets."

"Of course you can do it. But the fact is I want someone else to take an absolutely fresh approach, which means that we're letting you go, Rose. Ten years . . . it's a long time in one job. Jenny in human resources is cobbling together a package. We'll treat you properly. No need to call on our learned friends, Rose." He drew a third and final circle. "You must clear your desk, of course, but I would like you out by lunchtime."

"I don't think you can do that."

His expression did not alter. "Have you checked your contract lately?"

I held my voice steady. "I'm not going to abandon the pages while we're getting everything ready for press, Timon."

"Sure, sure, admirable, but Minty will deal with them."

"I don't wish her to do so."

Timon rose heavily to his feet. "Believe me, this is not an easy decision, but the change in your circumstances decided me. I called Nathan in this morning to tell him what was going to happen. I'm afraid I've asked Minty to take over your job."

I cornered Nathan in his office. "Give me five minutes." I muttered to Jean, his secretary, as I went past. "Private."

Ashen-faced, Nathan got to his feet as I wrenched open his door and walked in. "Did you know?" I asked.

He went over and shut the door. "No, I didn't. You can't imagine that I wouldn't have told you if I knew anything. I wouldn't do that to you, Rose."

No, he wouldn't, but rage streamed through me and I grasped at it with relief. Rage was better than anguish. "Oh, you wouldn't sack me at work, but you've sacked me at home."

He flinched and said, "I'm sorry, I didn't mean that."

There was a silence as my rage cooled and I struggled to put things right, to untangle the snarled strands of this situation. I said tiredly, "Why didn't you tell me that you were so unhappy? We could have done something about it. Talked. Gone to see someone. Something. Even, even——" I beat my fist on his desk "——you could have had your affair, if you had to, Nathan, if you absolutely had to, and come back."

"It doesn't work like that."

"It does. It can. If you make up your mind. A good marriage is flexible. Why didn't you come to me and say, 'Rose, I don't think I'm getting what I need from you.' Or 'Rose, you've taken me too much for granted, can we change this?' Or . . ."

"Or 'I've been measured against another man for a long, long time . . .'"

This was a Nathan who had folded himself up and traveled a long, long way away. "*Please* don't give me that excuse again, Nathan. It's tired, and not the real one. You're using it as a convenience for something else."

Nathan shook his head and did not reply.

Surprise winded me——that clever, thoughtful Nathan could make such decision on so little evidence. And so deceive himself. "All that was such a long time ago, Nathan. I thought we were over it. Do I ever go on about your love affairs in this way? No, of course not. I thought I'd persuaded you. Don't our years together mean anything in the way of proof?" I placed my hands on the desk and leaned toward him. "Is the real reason that you . . . don't find me attractive any more and you're trying to spare me by dressing it up?"

Had we shared the bathroom once too often, eaten in silence once too often, heard the other repeat a favorite gripe once too often?

There was no response and I tried again: "Is it because as we grow older we grow less confident? More nervous that we're horrible to look at, too set in our ways? And we need to reestablish ourselves all over again? Is that it, Nathan? Because if I know one thing, it cannot be your vague anxiety over a long-ago affair that has brought this about. It's something, perhaps, that you can't describe or understand, but at least be honest and say so."

Either this was too near the bone for Nathan, or he did not understand what I had said, but it was clear that I would get nothing more out of him. "I'm tired, Rose. I want a fresh start. I've fallen in love with Minty. The children are old enough to take it."

I walked over to the window and looked out. Traffic clotted the street, and the shop windows were bright with neon light and spring fashions. I followed the progress of a police vehicle weaving in and out of the queues. Suddenly I realized what had happened. How a shadow had become substance. And an excuse. A convenient mental lay-by. "Hal means more to you than he does to me," I said slowly. "He's become a fantasy."

Behind me, Nathan shuffled papers. My anger stirred, ignited, flamed. I swiveled round to face him. "Do you know what made Timon decide to sack me? Apparently, it was you and Minty deciding to set up house that gave him the out."

"Don't," he said, and looked quite gray.

"I'm sure you didn't mean it to happen but it has."

"Rose . . . if you want help on the details, the package . . ."

I looked at him helplessly. "The only details I want to go over with you, Nathan, are *our* details, the ones we should be discussing."

For a second he stared at me with the old tenderness, and there was a hint that we were making progress, that we were going to talk. Properly. Painfully. Honestly.

"Nathan, please, let *us* think again—"

Jean opened the door and cut us off. "Nathan, red alert in the boardroom. Now."

Nathan's eyes did not leave my face. "Five minutes, Jean."

She shook her highlighted blond head. "Now. The minister's wife has killed herself."

Chapter 9

The journey, which we knew like the backs of our hands, had been hard-fought down the conveyor belt of traffic stretching from London to Cornwall, but now the packed car nosed round the headland. Since Launceston, Nathan had been humming off and on under his breath and persisted in saying, "Yip, sirree," when I asked a question. Sam, twenty, and Poppy, eighteen, who had both been at all-night parties and had not been to bed, woke up. Poppy put on her glasses and punched Sam lightly on the arm. "You owe me a beer."

The car bore its hungry, thirsty pilgrims down the unmade road. *Yes, yes, there it was, windows glinting in the sun.* Sited in a dip overlooking the sea, which sheltered it, the cottage possessed a privacy that, in our family, went beyond its physical location.

By now, we were experts in the light and weather that swept over the coastline: gray storms, pink and gold sun-drenched evenings, meditative blue on calm clear days. Sometimes a mist layered the coast and hid the beach. Quite often clouds were pasted over the horizon, which had the curious effect of bringing it closer. Sometimes I imagined myself walking across the water and climbing on to it. If it was blue, we went fishing. If it rained we went in search of fish and chips or hiked over the headline to the village where we ate Mrs. Tresco's cream and treacle, "thunder and lightning" teas and drank beer in the pub.

"Yip, sirree. Nice and blue." Nathan stopped the car. "I'm going straight out."

I folded my hands in my lap and asked sweetly, "What about the unpacking?"

He came round to my side of the car and opened the door. "Sod the unpacking. The children can do it. You're coming, too."

"Sod the unpacking." I abandoned the car and its mess of suitcases, papers, empty drink cartons and boxes of food.

Sam sighed. "What's it worth?"

"Quite a lot," I said. "We'll fix the exchange rate later."

Nathan picked up his fishing bag and grabbed my hand. I had time only to snatch up my sweater. Down, down to the beach we went, like the excited children we had once shepherded so carefully. My feet in their plimsolls sped over the turf, sprang over the stones, dug into dry white sand.

Johnny the Sail had towed the boat down to the beach and left it in its usual place, with the outboard oiled and ready. Nathan unhooked the tarpaulin, wrestled with the stiff, damp awkwardness, stowed it, then threw in his bag. I joined him and we pushed the trailer to the water's edge.

Nathan swung over the side and primed the motor. I pulled the trailer back up the beach, and waded through silky ruffles of water toward the boat.

"Come on." Nathan held out his hand. "Are you going to be all day?"

Proud of the deftness acquired over years, I slotted the oars into the rowlocks. They dipped into the water, and I began the measured, steady pull, feeling the muscles tighten in my back and arms and the tide working against me. I quickened the pace and, pretty soon, I stopped shivering.

The wind sharpened at Fiddler's Rock and I took care to skirt a field of flat, rank-smelling seaweed, which hid rocks with sharp pointy teeth that liked boats for breakfast. "Okay," said Nathan, and I stopped rowing. Instantly there was hush, except for the water slapping against the clinker side of the boat. Nathan pulled at the string, the motor spluttered, roared and settled down. He took the tiller and we rode the waves out toward the place where the mackerel cruised.

I busied myself sorting out the line. However carefully it was stowed at the end of the season, it always twisted in storage and I had to concentrate so that the hooks did not catch my fingers. Nathan cut the engine and primed it again, ready for a quick start if necessary. "You go first."

I threw the line overboard, watching the bright bait feathers swell as they touched the water. The sun beat down on my bare arms, warming flesh that had been hidden in the city. I looked up. Nathan was watching me. "We'll have time together this year," he said, "won't we?"

The line tugged in my hands, the water flip-flopped against the boat and the light was dazzling. I found myself astonished and shaken by joy. It was the joy of being alive, of being part of the mystery of existence, the more simple joy of Nathan's love.

An hour or so later, we clambered back up the path to Beach Cottage. I carried the fishing bag, and Nathan carried our supper. Three mackerel: the best ever for a first day's catch.

At the top of the path, Sam was scanning the cliff, one hand shielding his eyes. When he spotted us, he started down the path toward us. Lazily, I imagined what he might say. *All done. Beds made. Food stowed. Pay up.*

Instead, when he arrived, panting, at the ledge where we had stopped to look at the sea and Nathan had slipped his arm around my shoulders, he said, "Dad, there's been a phone call. They want you back in London."

Why hadn't I put my foot down then, I thought, and at all the other times? Why didn't I now?

"I'm sorry," said Jean. "I know you and Nathan had things to talk about, but it was impossible not to interrupt." She looked pained, and I knew that she knew.

"It was ever thus, Jean."

"I know," she said sadly.

The minister's wife had been only thirty-seven. Judging by her picture on the television screen in the office, which beamed in a constant stream of news, she looked pretty, and very English in a fair, large-boned way. In the photograph, she was dressed in a pair of trousers and a polo-neck sweater, the neat, unthreatening clothes of a Good Wife. There were two teenage children, the younger of whom had discovered her hanging from the banisters.

Good Wives kill themselves as thoroughly as anyone else.

Her face was vignetted in the top right-hand corner of the screen as commentators were wheeled in to discuss her death. Accompanied by their modulated tones, I emptied my desk and packed my bag, arranged the piles of books in publication order and deleted files from the computer. I rang Steven to warn him of late pages.

"Leave it for Minty to sort out." Maeve was clearly furious. The bush telegraph had been at work and she came over to supervise my career demise—and to learn the details. Her penciled-in eyebrows snapped together. "I don't know what Timon thinks he's doing. It's an outrage." But her indignation was tinged with unease. "It'll be me next, no doubt, as I'm no spring chicken." She leaned over and urged, "Go to a tribunal. Fight for the older woman because that's what it's about."

I was shaking with fury and shock, but I continued to sort out the piles of books. "I don't think it's as simple as that, Maeve."

"Wake up, Rose." She prised a couple of books out of my hand. "Stop it. Don't waste one more minute on them than you have to. You don't owe them anything."

The television commentator stood outside the minister's house, which was under siege, and reported on the charitable and constituency activities of the minister's wife, the reaction of appalled friends, and of how the children had gone into hiding.

With the grief of the minister's children in mind, and the woman's death, I could not bring myself to make the gesture of leaving those last unnecessary tasks unfinished. Together, Maeve and I packed up a box with my stationery and pens, my files— the photograph—and left it for delivery to Lakey Street.

Maeve glanced at the screen where the minister's solicitor was now making a plea for the family's privacy. "What fools," she said fiercely, and surprisingly. "Letting themselves get like that."

I kissed Maeve, promised to keep in touch, and gave her my mug, which had I IS EDIKACATED printed on it, and went to see Jenny in human resources. Neither of us enjoyed the fifteen minutes I spent in her office, and I emerged with a portfolio of documents I had refused to sign until I had consulted my solicitor. "Timon won't like that," Jenny said, flustered, and I toyed with the idea of telling her that she was in the wrong job.

At the front desk, I surrendered my pass to Charlie. "I'm sorry about this, Rose," he said, as he canceled it. He had signed my forty-fifth birthday card, which had been organized by Jean— over forty signatures spidered over it, promoting in-house jokes (would I remember what they meant?) and wishing me long life.

"I enjoyed working with you," I told him, but Charlie had transferred his attention to a messenger.

I walked out of the building and came to a halt. Only once before in my life had I had no idea what to do, or where to go next. Only once before had I felt as exposed and crushed by the weight of grief and despair.

I breathed in traffic fumes, a whiff of rotting litter, and the knowledge that, for the moment, I was lost. The book bag hung limply over my shoulder, a symbol of my emptiness.

A woman bumped into me and hurried on. A mother wheeled a baby past in a buggy. A man in a black overcoat shouted at a bus.

My feet moved forward. The air was pulled in and out of my chest. I continued down the street, but I watched that woman walking along with her empty bag from a great height. I felt an enormous detachment, and a curious desire to laugh. *Look on the bright side, Rose. You won't have to worry about people at work knowing about Nathan.*

Outside the gym, I stopped. Anyone who was anyone knew that this was the place to be. The gossip and deals of the women's changing room outflanked those of the office canteen. It was private, intimate, naked—the bone of a matter was always reached quickly and thoroughly: the smoothies at the bar, which machines did what to the anatomy and, especially, the air quality were avidly discussed. Some days the air was fine, on others it was dense with sweat sucked up from laboring bodies. At other times, diseases were said to lurk in the pipes.

It was precisely the sort of place that Minty would choose to make her second home.

The thick engraved-glass door swung open and shut, open and shut, revealing a receptionist in a tight, acid green T-shirt. A posse of women carrying sports bags streamed in, chattering to each other. The door closed silently, reinforcing the gym's exclusivity.

From the outside, I looked in.

Eventually I pushed open the thick, dividing door and went inside.

Minty was not in the bar, or in the spa, or on a machine. I tracked her down in the changing room. Hunched on a bench, she was naked, absorbed, oblivious, drying between her toes. Then she stood up and rubbed lotion into her hard, confident body, which she tended so well.

Pink, white, ivory and black, tumbling hair, long legs, firm stomachs: the room was heaving with feminine flesh. Women padded between the lockers and the showers, hair dryers hummed, a locker door slammed. They were all still young. Their bodies were not yet slackening and disobedient, and the gap between their desires and what was returned had not yet widened to be impossible. Perhaps that was what Nathan was trying to redeem, and felt he could not tell me.

Minty continued to stroke and perfect the body he preferred. With a shaking hand, I wiped away the damp that, in the heat, had flowered on my upper lip. I should face Minty and call her to account. But, trembling and afraid, I fled.

When I got back to Lakey Street there was a rucksack in the hall. Poppy flew out of the kitchen as I stepped into the house. "Mum, I'm here."

I drew my daughter into my arms. She nestled into me and

the relief at having her there was like a burst of sun. I thought, This is what matters. Eventually, she drew away, slid her arm round my waist and led me into the kitchen.

"You look awful, Mum." She took off her glasses and polished them on her muslin skirt, her eyes widened with the effort of focusing. Poppy was extremely short-sighted, hated her glasses and was never comfortable with them, but hated more the idea of contact lenses.

I tried to smile, failed, then explained that I had lost my job to Minty.

The full red mouth tightened with fury and distress. At the best of times, Poppy did not find life easy and had not, as yet, had time to develop a sense of irony that would protect her. The pitfalls ahead of her were different from those that confronted Sam, but both were capable of being terribly wounded. That kept me awake at night, too.

"Dad can't possibly want to live with someone who's done that." She struggled to get the words out, and her bewilderment was like a stake driven into my heart. "Can he?"

I tried to explain that Nathan had not meant any of this to happen, and that connections between events do not necessarily exist even if they appear to. "It was coincidental, Timon's decision. Dad didn't know. I'd been there a long time, Poppy, and they wanted a different approach."

"Like hell." Poppy's eyes filled and overflowed. "Timon wouldn't have done it unless Dad had left you. He wouldn't have dared. Oh, God," she wiped away the tears with the edge of her skirt. "I feel so miserable."

"Bet you haven't eaten." I took refuge in being predictable and motherly.

Poppy went over to stroke Parsley, who was sitting in her customary place. "Parsley looks older," she said.

"Parsley is an old lady," I said quickly. "Look, I'll make you an omelette." I was already reaching for the eggs and the cheese.

"I'll go and phone Richard."

Fifteen minutes later, I went in search of Poppy and discovered her fast asleep on the sofa in the sitting room, her mobile phone clutched in one outstretched hand. The tearstains were still on her cheek. When I kissed her awake, she turned to me in the old way and I caught my breath.

Halfway through the omelette, she put down her fork. "There's nothing Sam and I can do, is there?"

"I don't think so. It's between your father and me."

Poppy tried to digest this. "How *could* he have left you?"

My knees went weak with the effort to concentrate. How could I devise rules quickly for a situation of which I had no experience? I sat down, facing Poppy, and struggled to be dispassionate and fair. "We'll try to make it as civilized as possible. We won't treat you and Sam to scenes."

"Why not? You don't feel civilized, do you?"

I sometimes forgot how shrewd Poppy could be. There was a cloudy patch on the walnut surface and I rubbed at it. "No, I don't. I feel as if a limb has been cut off."

"I can't believe it."

The kitchen was very quiet. "Neither can I."

With no evident enthusiasm, Poppy tackled the remainder of the omelette. "Dad's behavior is many things, *and* it's embarrassing. Who does he think he is, going after a younger woman? It's such . . . such a cliché."

Her vehemence made me anxious. "I'm sure he'll talk to you about his feelings. You must go and see him."

She gave an impatient click of her tongue. "I'm not sure I want to see him. He's ruined our family. He's let us down."

"Poppy, you're an adult now and he's still your father."

She brushed me aside. "How will you live? Where will you live? Which one of you is home?" Poppy put her hands up to her face and covered her eyes. "Lakey Street will be sold. Picture it, Mum. One weekend with you, one with Dad. Awful meetings at weddings and funerals . . ." She went quite still. "It's broken. Our life. The picture of our life."

If it curves too grandly a river will take a short cut, or so I had learned in geography, which creates an ox-bow lake of drenched grasses, watercress and busy, secret life. Poppy had the same way of cutting across loops and corners as the river and I puzzled as to where she had got this stubborn, leapfrogging bit of her—the bit that also ignored rules, and inconvenient things like exams and the necessity of earning a living.

"Let her—the child—tell you her needs," wrote one pundit, in whom we had initially believed. Nathan read from the book as I paced up and down with a squalling three-month-old Poppy, who had given notice that sleep was boring. It was a sentiment so thoroughly in tune with a society that wanted to reshape itself and rethink its women. By the time we discovered what the pundit *really* meant, that "We should bloody allow our children to stamp all over us," as Nathan put it (after a clash), Sam and Poppy were well advanced.

I stacked Poppy's plate in the dishwasher and put an apple in front of her. "Here, eat this."

She looked up at me. "It wasn't anything Sam and I did, was it? I used to think we were such a drain on you that you didn't have any time left for Dad. Then there was your work." She took off her glasses and placed them on the table in front of her. "It couldn't be that, could it?"

"No."

She pushed the glasses away. "Promise?"

"Promise."

Poppy bit into the apple. She seemed more relaxed and reassured. "I gave Dad what-for on the phone. I made him angry, actually."

I did not want to look into those puzzled, short-sighted eyes so I busied myself at the sink. "Poppy, one day . . . everything will be more normal and we'll have to build bridges. Do you see? Do you understand?"

"Sure." Poppy picked up her mobile, which was never far away, and fiddled with the buttons. "Message from Richard. He loves me." She giggled. "I love him. He's so full of life. So adventurous. So generous. I don't think Richard could ever be a drag. By the way, we're off east the minute finals are over."

"I thought you and Jilly were going to do something." Jilly was Poppy's closest friend. They had met at university and fallen instantly into that absorbing intimacy that is only possible before real life begins.

"Jilly is off to New Zealand to see an aunt or something."

Poppy spoke carelessly but I could tell she felt a little betrayed. I wiped down the sink and hung the dishcloth over the tap. My chest felt tight, as it had when Sam announced that he was going to Mozambique to teach in his gap year. It was partly the danger, but more that the nestlings were shaking their wings and flying. "Where will you go? And on what?"

Typically, Poppy ignored the last bit of the question. "India, I think. Perhaps Thailand. I don't know yet. It's the last fling, Mum, before we become boring and serious. You mustn't worry. Richard will look after me."

This was not reassuring. The last time Nathan and I had seen Richard, he had hair flowing over his shoulders, was dressed in a *shalwar kameez* and treated us to a lecture on the wickedness of Western economic imperialism when he used expressions such as "way cool" and "oppressors." To this day, I was not sure if he was teasing or in earnest.

I knew perfectly well what I should not say, and said it. "What about job-hunting?"

Color had crept back into Poppy's mouth. "I don't want to get all tied up and desperate a minute before I have to, Mum. Like you did."

"What do Richard's parents think?" They lived in Northumberland and were, as far we could make out, a fairly shadowy presence. "Has Richard thought about the future?"

Boredom was registered in every line of Poppy's body. "I have no idea. Possibly." She turned her head and looked out of the window. "Everyone insists on talking to me about the future—well, anyone who's over twenty-five, which seems to be the age when brain degeneration seriously sets in. It's like a disease. They can't wait to get me sorted into a category they can understand. 'It's so exciting,' they say. If only they knew what they sounded like."

I looked round the kitchen, alive with murmurs from the past. "Remember the red shoes?"

Poppy chased an apple around the plate. "That old story."

For her seventh birthday, Nathan, Ianthe, Sam and I had taken Poppy to purchase the exact pair of red shoes that the advertisements promised would turn her into a princess. The royal status failing to materialize (also the ballgown), Poppy's cries had cleared the shop. "But they promised, and it's not true," she sobbed. "They promised."

"It was one of the rare times Dad said, 'Here, you take her.' He was usually the one who could calm you down."

Poppy's face crumpled. "Oh, Mum," she choked, "it's so awful. Everything's changed. I thought the one thing that would never change is you and Dad. And it's so awful that I'm not taking it better."

Poppy stayed for three days, pretending to work and refusing to see Nathan. She would not even to talk to him. That must have hurt him.

"My dad," Poppy was overheard confiding to a friend at her ninth birthday party, "doesn't get cross with me." But he got cross with Sam, of whom he expected different, sterner things. Other than the garden, it was one of the few things about which Nathan and I rowed. Sam's gravity settled over him when he tumbled to the idea that life was intrinsically unfair. In successfully claiming a monopoly on Nathan's heart, with witchery, a pair of large eyes and sulky red lips, Poppy had early taught her brother a brutal, useful lesson.

Laden with food and vitamin pills, she took the coach back to Nottingham. I offered to pay her train fare but she was not having it. "I *like* all this sort of studenty thing." Stubborn and insistent. "After this one I have only one more term left."

Chapter 10

Since half of me was my mother, it was natural that I shared some of her habits.

When it became intolerable, my thoughts too black and too weary to bear, I found myself pacing from room to room, as Ianthe had after my father died. Up to my study, an aimless rattle through the papers on the desk, along to the spare room, back down the stairs into the kitchen.

It was a reflex I must have learned from her—a way of making sure that the body still functioned, of dealing with great loss.

The days dragged into night, night into day.

A man from Gleeson's rang me. "Is that Mrs. Lloyd? I have the new vacuum cleaner you ordered. Will someone be in the house on Wednesday?"

"I don't know," I replied.

"Mrs. Lloyd?"

"Yes, yes, they will be."

I was frightened by my responses. Overnight I had lost the ability to decide the simplest matter. I spent hours working out what I would say to Nathan—a whole architecture of new beginnings and promises, and as many hours deciding not to see him at all, ever.

If I closed my eyes, I was confronted by pictures of myself hurling violent abuse at Minty. If I dismissed them, equally vivid ones of *hurting* her took their place.

I went through all the dreary how-could-you-do-this-to-me-Nathan routines. I pointed out that I had been a Good Wife, I had loved him, produced his children, contributed financially. I had been faithful. Was this not a rotten return on that emotional investment?

And what about my lost job? How could *that* have happened? Where was the natural justice there?

Thus I yo-yoed. From job to marriage. Marriage to job. One was greater than the other, yet they were bound together.

I could not eat and, by the end of the week, I was shaky from lack of food.

I tried to read, but books failed me.

Music was worse.

When it grew dark, I lay on the bed with hot, burning eyes and begged for sleep.

From time to time, I was lucky, fell into a doze and dreamed, always, of a sun-washed garden: of the felty leaves of the olive tree, of smelling spring, fresh, light and sweet, of driving my fingers into the soil and letting it sift through them. In those dreams, a voice sounded across those gentle canvases: the garden anchors you, it suggested. Its complications and subtleties are never treacherous. Yet when I wrestled impatiently with the catch of the French windows and went out, I could not see it.

The fug of traffic smothered its sharp, spicy fragrance, the soil was clogged and sour, the plants sullen. The garden was dead to me, and I to it. More often than not, I returned inside.

So I drank Nathan's whiskey and, as my mother had before me, I paced through the house.

"He was so upset by the Suez affair," Ianthe told me, when I was old enough to understand what Suez was. "That was the killer."

I think she was right. Suez cut to the quick of my father's old-fashioned honor, rattled what we knew too late was his damaged heart muscle.

"He was so angry," she said. "And humiliated by the botch-up. He said we were supposed to lead the world but we had turned out to be Hitlers. He was never the same afterward."

It froze hard and deep that January, the week of my eleventh birthday. The cold killed, cemeteries were overflowing and the council issued a notice forbidding people to die within the parish boundaries of Yelland. If there was the least likelihood of anyone doing so, they were to be conveyed to the next parish. My father had a good belly laugh over that one. "There's nowt like a council that thinks it's God."

I'm glad he found something to laugh about, and even gladder that he could not possibly have seen the irony.

The cold flayed fingertips and cracked lips. On the morning of my father's death, I pushed open my bedroom window and peered out. More snow had fallen during the night and cleared the sky. The moor was white and sparkling, and the wind had traced patterns on the beautiful snow plains. My breath vaporized into fog and my cheeks burned. I leaned on the casement and imagined that outside was a giant birthday cake, just for me.

Downstairs, in his chair by the stove, my father toasted bread on a fork, drank his tea, and went through the daily pantomime of finding his glasses. Then he buttoned his tweed coat, and put on his flat cap. "I'll fetch the shovel," he said to my mother, "and clear the path."

He never returned.

It was Ianthe who found him, still holding the shovel in his rapidly cooling hands. A heart attack. The manner of his death was so commonplace that it was unremarkable as, indeed, was his omitting to have made a will, which resulted in even more muddle and anguish. It is possible that my father believed doctors could heal themselves. More likely, though, he ignored his condition. If he had suspected his heart was so fragile, I am sure he would have tried to pay off his debts, incurred from having run his country practice on the basis that need came before profit.

I remember being so frightened by my mother's face: it was tight, contained, dead-looking.

Only at night when she paced through the cottage did she give way. Lying freezing and anguished in my bed, I knew exactly which stair would creak, which door was heavy with damp, and which floorboard shifted outside my bedroom when she halted outside to check my breathing.

All the remaining winter and into a cruel spring, the wind rattled and snow crept into the oddest corners. It was a wet, dispiriting summer, too, and a dank autumn, and one day a van stopped outside Medlars Cottage.

"These nice men are coming to take our furniture," a red-eyed and now wraithlike Ianthe announced. "We don't need it, Rose, and we will have a little extra money for a new home. We're going to a new home. Isn't that a lovely surprise? Don't worry, it will be fun." She held my hand tight as the men tip-tupped our possessions over their shoulders and carried them out to the van.

Tears streamed down her face and every line of her body shouted protest. Yet . . . "Rose," she proclaimed, through those tears in her trained way, "isn't it lucky we have a new home to go to? We have lots to be grateful for."

I looked from my mother to the rapidly emptying room. I had not realized that the skirting-board sagged, that the paint-work was so shabby, or that the floorboard under the window was rotten.

Why had I not realized, either, that Ianthe told lies?

How's my little chickaninny? I heard my father murmur, deep in my head. I wanted him to be there, I wanted Medlars Cottage to remain ours, even with the cracks, and space, and emptiness. "But there's nothing to be grateful for," I cried.

"Shush." Ianthe drew me close to her body. I felt her hip bones press into me, smelled clean cotton and soap. "Shush, now."

But fathers came and went, homes were emptied, mothers were duplicitous. Despite the council's best endeavors, death could not be ordered into obedience and the bright, scrubbed surfaces of my home hid secret catches of snow and ice.

For the first week, books, sent by publishers hoping to bypass the system, continued to arrive. I did not bother to open the pack-ages for I could guess what they were. The heavy biography. The large illustrated cookery book. A manuscript.

By the second week news had got round. The packages dwindled and, soon, the postman no longer rang the bell.

Minty wrote me a letter.

Dear Rose,

You won't believe me when I tell you that I did not know what
Timon planned until very recently. However, presented with the idea,
I was not going to turn it down. I reasoned that you had had your
turn, had your day in the sun, and now it was someone else's, mine,
and there was a natural justice in that. I know that natural justice
is a concept you believe in and I hope one day that you will acknowl-
edge that I made the right choice for me. But the purpose of this let-
ter is to tell you that Nathan did not know. I miss our conversations.
Minty

I read and reread that letter, with its so-called honesty, its specious explanation and breathtaking assumptions, which were a mask for Minty's hungers. Rotten fruit and rotten meat: she disgusted me and I rejoiced in my disgust.

I could not put off any longer telling Ianthe and I rang her up, got into the car and drove over to Kingston.

"Cheap and cheerful, Rose, just what we need," had been Ianthe's masterly verdict, delivered with typical Mrs. Miniver good cheer, on Pankhurst Parade. Number fourteen was sited in one of several identical roads in the housing estate outside the town. Why Kingston? The reasons for Ianthe's uprooting both of us from Yelland to down south were too complicated for either of us to attempt to disentangle at the time. Cheap it had been, cheerful, no.

Today, dressed in a Viyella shirt and wool skirt, she was sitting in her chair with her hands folded. This was Ianthe's waiting pose. You see it in paintings: a female form—it is more often than not female—composed on a chair, or a bench, or a sofa, waiting for orders, or for life to begin or be over.

For such a busy woman, Ianthe had an extraordinary gift for it—waiting for me, waiting for a meal to cook, waiting for God in church in a hat and a tweed coat, waiting for events to right themselves, providing she observed the rules. *Patience is as patience does, she said.*

Unusually, she was pale and unmade-up, hair not properly seen to. "Tell me what's wrong, Rose."

I bent over to kiss her, sat down and took her hands in mine. "I'm in trouble."

"I thought as much." Ianthe's fingers dug into my hands. "Not the children?"

"No." I had to force myself to go on. "It's Nathan. He's decided to leave me for another woman. Actually for Minty, my assistant." I swallowed. "And I've lost my job . . . also to Minty."

Ianthe shook her head. "I think you'll have to tell me again."

"Nathan w-wants his freedom. He thinks that Minty will give it to him."

She struggled to absorb the news, and tried to equate it with the image of the son-in-law she cherished.

It was a family joke that Nathan and Ianthe defied every mother-in-law cliché, for they loved each other. On holiday Nathan sent her extra-sized postcards, brought home presents of chunky jewelery and honey in china pots with overweight bees embossed on them. He fussed over her pension, arranged her tax and insisted on paying for medical insurance, of which she disapproved. "I don't want to be a nuisance, and I don't like private doctors," she told me. "I don't like their hands. Too manicured."

She dabbed at the wisps of hair at her neck. "You were always so busy, Rose. Never any time. Always on the run."

I concede that we can only see events from our own point of view, but her reaction stung. "Is that all you can say?"

"This is terrible." Ianthe leaned back in the chair. She looked hurt and, suddenly, worn out by expectations that had turned out to be increasingly cruel in their disappointments. I got up and stood by the window. "That awful girl."

That did not surprise me. On the one occasion Minty and Ianthe had met at a Sunday lunch, Minty had been unable to deal with Ianthe. "I don't do older people," I overheard her explaining to a friend on the office phone. "I don't get them." And Ianthe had displayed a surprising blind spot. "People like her make such a *point* of being youthful, which is very selfish. It makes the rest of us feel so redundant."

"Rose, you have talked to Nathan, tried to sort it out?"

"Nathan did not give me much choice."

Her tone sharpened. "Marriages don't end just like that. You'll see. Men are such funny creatures. They need a lot of looking after."

"That's bad luck on Nathan, then, Mum. Minty's only interested in number one."

"Perhaps Nathan needs reminding of how much he means to you. He's had a little rush of blood to the head and, at the moment, he can't see straight."

"Hardly to the head, Mum."

"You know what I mean."

I did. Ianthe had been taught her views by her mother, who had been taught by her mother before her, women who had scrubbed their doorsteps, made their own bread, had their babies at home. She had bowed her head and made it her life's work to obey their strictures.

The doorbell rang and I went to answer it. With surprising speed, Ianthe got to her feet and nipped into the downstairs cloakroom where she kept her emergency supplies of lipstick and powder, emerging half a minute later with smoothed hair and orange-pink lips.

Charlie Potter was delivering the bridge timetable. I observed my mother flirt gently and declare that, yes, she would be on time and she was planning to make a plate of his favorite egg sandwiches.

While they talked, I went upstairs to my old room, which remained unchanged but had a trick of growing smaller each time I went into it. At this rate, it would not be long before the white candlewick bedspread and the lamp with the pink shade dwindled to the size of doll's-house furniture.

Downstairs Charlie Potter gave a belly laugh and my mother accompanied it with a discreet chuckle. It was a nice sound, Ianthe's innocent flirting.

My childhood seemed very far away and I needed to grab something of it, anything. I opened the cupboard in which Ianthe stored my childish, but not discarded, objects. Dust filmed the boxes and there was a dry, musty scent of decayed lavender. Propped up at the back was a collage of newspaper cuttings and pictures from magazines and portraits of favored authors pasted onto hardboard. It had occupied me for years and colonized the room. Ianthe hated it, but it had been my way of marking who I was and the interminably slow passage of growing up. I begged, salvaged, hoarded and squirreled away cuttings, photographs, postcards, and from these images I built kingdoms. One of the earliest was a picture of an ordinary family having a picnic by the sea: Mum, Dad and two little girls.

I had studied that picture for clues as to what I was missing: smiles, a gingham tablecloth, potted-meat sandwiches, a father with his arm around his eldest, a mother busy with the picnic. How I had wanted to be that family. How I had wanted my father back, and to see my mother pat her hair into place when she heard his step in the evening. How I wanted him sitting at the table.

A family.

When I became a teenager the collage changed. My chosen images breathed of escape. Here was the picture of the oxbow lake, and an aerial view of a Patagonian wilderness, pink, blue and gray-green, stolen from the *National Geographic* magazine. The glue had made its corners curl like apple peel. Here were the deserts, jungles and strange locations to which I ascribed magical powers to transform and enchant. Only step into them, and the girl in a cheap blue school uniform would become powerful and knowing. The more different and alien from Kingston they appeared, the stronger their fascination and the more I dreamed over them.

"I'll see you tonight, Charlie," called Ianthe downstairs.

I touched the postcards of Jane Austen and the Brontë sisters, part of a picture sequence of writers, which formed the other side of the collage. The cards were brittle and darkened from age and handling, and thumbtacks had punctured the corners, but the pinched, intelligent faces of the women remained unchanged. *They knew the secrets of men and women, and how they behaved,* and I imagined, too, that I was going to help myself to their knowledge and that pinched intelligence.

After I came back from Brazil, I took Nathan to meet Ianthe for the first time and, wonderfully, they fell for each other on the spot. In the kitchen Ianthe served up beef stew and carrots with mashed potato. She arranged a careful spoonful of the latter on Nathan's plate, and said with a shy, awkward tilt of her head, "You'll think I'm silly because I've got no brains. I'm not like that lot up on Rose's collage."

Nathan leaned over the table. "I don't go for bonnets either. Never could get the hang of them."

Ianthe had smiled, and dished out a plate of stew for me.

Now, sneezing, I went downstairs.

"Such a nice man . . ." Ianthe watched Charlie Potter's retreating back. "Such a terrible wife."

We sat and drank tea from a tray laid with a starched cloth, china and a plate of digestive biscuits arranged in a fan. Ianthe snapped off a tiny piece of one and ate it. "Do you think you helped Nathan enough? Do you think that he wanted more help from you?"

This was a reasonable question from the woman who yielded up all claims to a teaching career when she married and my father gained, in one clean economical pincer movement, an unpaid secretary, counselor and cleaner to help run his practice.

"We helped each other." I was careful to make the point. "Both of us did. But I'll have to get another job. As soon as I've sorted my severance package."

"Oh, work." Ianthe raised her shoulders in a dismissive gesture.

"Mum, I have to earn my living. It won't be easy—I can't not work."

Ianthe regarded her tea thoughtfully. "That's what I mean," she said finally, the ace barrister wrapping up her case.

To keep me, Ianthe had been employed for fifteen years in a travel agent's in Kingston, issuing tickets and timetables. ("And I'll have none of your snobbishness about that," she said, more than once. "It does me fine.") She looked at me sadly. "I worked because I had to take on your father's role. You didn't have to."

My ringless hand, which held the cup, felt odd, weightless, unfamiliar.

Ianthe warmed to the attack and bore down on me, as she always had. "Nathan loves you. I know he does. You married each other and that has not changed. There are the children to consider. They suffer, too, you know, even in their twenties.

Look at me, Rose. A woman must think about others." With an angry gesture, she refilled her cup and added the milk, a widow who bore the scourge of her conviction, a sense of duty and her decades of waiting with an unsettling grace. "Go home, ring Nathan and make him come to his senses."

As always, I ignored Ianthe's command but fretted about doing so. She had that effect. Instead I rang Mazarine in Paris.

"Oh, the stranger," she said, coldly. "I've been waiting for some sign of life. Vee and I were just saying the other day how little we hear from you."

"I wanted to ring you, but I've been busy."

"Too busy for your oldest friend?"

"Yes."

"Well, you need to look at your life."

A ball bounced back across the court. Fifteen years ago I had told Mazarine something similar when she was in danger of losing Xavier, the man she eventually married. "Mazarine, listen. Nathan has left me."

There was a silence. "I didn't mean *that* much of a change."

"Will you listen?"

"You know I will."

I was so tired that I faltered over my French—we always talked in French—and Mazarine corrected it as patiently as was possible for someone as rigorous as she. She was as quick to take a point of view. "You mustn't be too hysterical, Rose. This is only an interlude. Nathan will come back."

"Would I want him back?"

"Whatever happens, you will adapt."

"What do I do?"

"Do? You look for a job and wait for Nathan to find out that he has made a fool of himself. Rose, you must smooth this over. Be practical and wise, it's our role in a crazy world. An affair is not such a huge thing, you know. *Of course* you know, and Nathan is bound to you. He just doesn't see it that way at the moment. What have you eaten today?"

"A biscuit. I think."

"Don't be so conventional. It's exactly what every aban- doned woman does. Be different and eat a proper meal."

Mazarine could not see the wry smile on my lips. This was the woman who, incoherent with shock, called me after Xavier, who had been eating foie gras, had dropped dead of a heart at- tack in a restaurant. ("So serve him right," said Poppy. "Foie gras.") I had caught the next train to Paris and fed her soup, coaxing spoonful after spoonful into her unwilling mouth.

"I'll try."

"You will do more than try, and you will come and see me. By the way, I thought Vee was looking a bit dowdy last time I saw her."

"Vee is happy and she's lost her sense of style. It happens."

"In that case, there must be an awful lot of happy English women."

I laughed until I was forced by lack of breath to stop, and I thought how odd it was to be laughing when my life was in ruins.

Chapter 11

A silence between Nathan and me stretched for well over a month—and the frost of anger, incomprehension and unforgiveness crept into the crack and forced it wider. During that time, I was advised by my solicitor to accept my severance package, and the features editor of Vee's paper rang me to ask if, in the context of the suicide of the minister's wife, I might like to contribute a short, touchy-feely piece on being abandoned?

This polite request contained various pieces of trickery, not least the chance to expose the marital mishaps of an executive on a rival paper. When I said no, but I was happy to research and write a piece on the difficulties of being a political wife, the features editor's interest disappeared. "Yes . . ." He sounded vague. "We have our regular journalists to do that sort of thing."

Then, one evening, Nathan turned up on the doorstep carrying a brand-new suitcase. With a stranger's formality, he asked, "Can I come in?"

The mixture of hope and despair in my breast was unbearable. "Of course."

He stepped into the hall and put down the case. It was clear that it was empty. "I need my things, so I thought I'd pack them up."

My hopes took a realistic turn, and I said coldly, "Do as you wish."

"Fine."

He went up the stairs to our bedroom and I went into the kitchen, where I could hear him moving around. Drawers were opened and shut, shoes hit the floor, a chair scraped. After a while I could not bear to hear those sounds. I scooped up Parsley, bore her into the sitting room, sat down in the blue chair and held her tight.

I tried to see events through Nathan's eyes. I really tried to see what had changed, what had recast his philosophy—apart from the obvious excitement of sex.

On our twentieth wedding anniversary he took me out to La Sensa. ("My God," exclaimed Vee. "He must have been taken out a second mortgage.") He fussed over the choice of champagne, which was so dry that my mouth tingled. He picked up his glass. "I want to thank you, my darling Rose."

It seemed to me that the boot was on the other foot. "I should be thanking you. You came to the rescue."

It was not the right thing to say—but it was not so very heinous a slip.

Immediately Nathan frowned, and I rushed on, "You came to the rescue and taught me about real, proper love."

"Ah," he said, with the soft, private expression that belonged to me and the children. "I see what you mean."

My relief that we had got over the misunderstandings that litter any marriage and had reached this point was overwhelming. "I love you, Nathan. You know that."

He reached over, took my hand and kissed it, the seal on our bargain.

Eventually, there was the slither and clump of a suitcase being manhandled down the stairs and Nathan reappeared. "Rose, if you let me know when you won't be here, I'll arrange for the rest of the stuff I need to be collected."

Parsley used me as a springboard into the garden. I rubbed at the pinprick of blood on my thigh left by her claws. "I take it you're being let into Minty's personal space."

"As it happens, yes."

I took the opportunity to study my husband. The gleam that freshened his skin and straightened his shoulders was different. I closed my eyes and asked the question that I needed to ask more than once. "Have I become so undesirable, Nathan?"

"I don't know what you mean."

I opened my eyes. "You do."

"No." His were kindly, and I was terrified that he was lying. "You are still . . . very lovely." He gave a strained smile. "Your hair is still the same, too. Still honey chestnut."

"Then why?"

He shoved his hands into his pockets. "I'm as astonished as you are. I never imagined that I would leave you."

"Then *why*, Nathan? Your reasons are usually so clear and thought-out."

"I know."

I looked down at my hands, at the whorl of the fingerprint, at the heart-line, the life-line. Perhaps I had never known

Nathan properly. Perhaps he had kept hidden from me a part secret to him. Probably. If I was truthful, there were the deep, dark spaces in myself of which he knew nothing. "*Please* think again." Nathan did not answer and I tried once more. "Was it when I started working?"

Those times when he came home and found me still in my office clothes, thin, exhausted, dervishlike, giving supper to one child, supervising the homework of another. Then he was pulled away from contemplation of his own day and forced to consider mine. Had he been panicked by this dull, dun, harassed creature? More than once he must have wondered if all women, all *mothers,* lose their sexual luminosity and turn into wild, anguished figures, and why the transformation should be so unfair to both parties.

On one of the worst days, when I was weeping from the battery and assault made on me by my children and by the work that Nathan had been against me doing anyway, he took me in his arms and stroked my hair. "Shush," he said. "We're in this together."

Now I said, "Ianthe thinks I didn't help you enough. Is she right?"

Nathan shrugged. "God knows, Rose. There were times, yes, when I could have done with you more on my side but I am sure it was the same with you."

We were back on skates, veering round the rink, neither of us reaching the heart of the matter. Automatically, I rubbed my shoulder, which plagued me with stiffness, an on-going condition from too much typing.

"Is it hurting?"

"Yes."

"Badly?"

"Actually, yes. I must have slept on it awkwardly."

Automatically, Nathan moved toward me. *If I rub here, is it better? Or here?* At the last moment, he turned away. "Rose, I don't know what to say about the job."

"Timon took a risk firing a group executive's wife and replacing her with his mistress."

"They took a risk in taking you on in the first place."

This was true. "They will pay me reasonably, if I go quietly and agree not to take on a similar job for six months. The usual thing. I will probably accept."

He nodded. "Timon is anxious to push for extra numbers. There has been a lot of discussion and strategy meetings."

Circulation, policy, revenues . . . Nathan and I were used to talking to each other on those subjects, and on those subjects Nathan trusted me. They sounded prosaic, but they were not. Revenue and circulation figures can be just as much of a glue as poetry and passionate sex.

People are rude about habit. It is supposed to suggest sloppiness and laziness, but I don't think they have thought about it properly. Habit is useful and comforting: it rides over the bumpy bits, it is the track that cuts across hills and valleys and carries passengers safely through.

"How are the figures?" I asked, grown cunning and devious.

Quick as a flash, he replied, "I haven't seen Wednesday's but judging by . . ." The sentence remained unfinished for Nathan suspected, rightly, that the old conversations might entangle us.

"Nathan, Minty knew she would probably take over from me and she didn't tell you."

As cool as if he was negotiating, he had his answer ready: "Minty was protecting me. Chinese wall . . ."

"Nevertheless, it was Timon who told you, not Minty."

The implications were obvious, and Nathan flushed a harsh

red. "The situation was tricky and Timon had to think carefully how to play it. It was impossible for Minty to say anything."

I drew an obscure and shameful comfort from this admission. Early on, Nathan and I had made a pact to tell each other everything.

"Look on the bright side, then," I said, and hated what I was saying. "At least you didn't have to worry about split loyalties between Minty and me."

We stared at each other. In a low voice, Nathan admitted, "Minty's secrecy should make a difference, I know, but it doesn't."

It was this extraordinary exchange that finally convinced me Nathan was serious. He loved Minty enough to be honest, so honest about her ambition and duplicity that he could not, would not, grant me the grace of a little verbal deceit.

I gave a shaky laugh. "And I had been preparing to forgive and forget." I went over to the French windows and looked out. Despite my efforts to dig it out the bindweed was back in force under the lilac tree and I wondered why, until now, I had failed to notice how invasive it had become. "I hope they don't sack you, too, Nathan."

"Anything's possible."

"Be honest, Nathan. Tell me what's wrong." I wrapped my arms across my chest, ready to ward off the worst.

Nathan began to speak. "I can't get over how much Minty reminds me of you when I first met you. You were so young, so hurt, but so determined that what you had done was right."

I cried, "Minty is nothing, *nothing* like me," and my shoulders shook with the effort of not weeping. Nathan came up behind me and placed his hands on them.

"Minty reminds me of how you were before . . . I don't know, before we all changed. Became middle-aged, I suppose."

"But that's not fair," I cried out passionately. "How could I not change? I *am* older. I can't avoid that. Neither can you. I couldn't avoid being changed by having children. Neither could you." Nathan removed his hands from my shoulders. "What have you been telling her?" I asked. "What have you made up to convince her that you are so misunderstood? Or so she tells me."

Nathan sat down in the blue chair. "Are you sure you want me to go into this?"

I turned round and faced him. "You might as well."

"If you must know, I told her that living in a crowded marriage is worse than being in a cruel one, and she looked at me with her great steady-as-you-go eyes. 'But Rose is devoted to you,' she replied."

"She could not have said otherwise," I interjected. "She listened to me often enough." I turned my head away. "How could you have said it was 'crowded'? I don't understand."

Nathan's face darkened. "Whenever there was trouble between us, when one of the black periods that descend on all marriages descended on ours, I just could not get out of my head that you were taking refuge in an old love story and it was his image that comforted you. Minty said she was sure you didn't know you were doing it."

"Nathan, I can't believe you allowed it to matter. To be so afraid. To not trust me. At this stage, I'm far more likely to fantasize about a face-lift or writing a seriously good book than to hark back to an old love affair . . . however much it meant to me once. We don't think like that any more." I swiveled on my heels to face him. "It's a cheap excuse, and I can't bear it."

Nathan paid no attention. "I knew when that man bootlegged his way back."

"You are too clever for fantasy, Nathan."

An obstinate look settled over Nathan. "I was up against a fantasy."

"Nathan, I had left Hal for good when I met you. I had made a choice."

"So I thought. And I had just got it settled in my mind. Then . . . why did you tell Minty about it?"

"Girls' gossip. Not something you usually concern yourself with."

"Minty says I should. She thinks it's good for my emotional health."

"And what else does Minty say? How else does she manipulate you? For that's what she's been doing."

"She told me that she has had a good time in the past, but it would not come with her."

"And that makes everything all right? That gives you clearance? Oh, Nathan, what a fool you are."

"Enough." Nathan got to his feet. "I'll be going now."

I kept my arms wrapped tight across my chest. "I see."

Nathan picked up the suitcase. Then he put it down again. "This is dreadful. You won't believe this, Rosie, but I love you very much, and I can't believe how I'm making you suffer."

I was not listening. I was searching for some logic in my dark, dark despair. For some guidance. "And she will help you in your career? Will she put in what I apparently did not?"

A faint smile flickered over Nathan's lips. "Oh, yes."

"Minty's very ambitious, you know. For herself."

"Minty is strong, energetic and free. It makes me feel that I can be the same."

"And she has style. It takes style to steal her boss's husband and her job in the same breath. Economy and thrift, too."

Nathan looked at me with a kind, caring look that suggested he did not expect anything else from me. I felt sick with humiliation. "Go away," I ordered him, "before I say something really awful."

He turned for the door, halted and pulled an envelope from his pocket. "I nearly forgot, Rose. Here's a check for the time being, to see you through until things are sorted out."

"I don't want it."

"I expected you to be stubborn." He tucked it behind the vase on the mantelpiece that had belonged to his mother. It was a dreadful thing, early Rockingham, I think, stuck all over with china flowers that trapped dust, but Nathan cherished it.

"Take the check back," I said.

"No." He started when he spotted my wedding ring on the shelf, then picked up his mother's vase. "If you don't mind, I'll take this with me."

At the front door, he placed a hand on the latch and pulled it down. "Rose, I know Hal was hanging around at our wedding. I saw him."

I swallowed, and the burden of the past sat heavy on my shoulders. "He came to say goodbye, Nathan."

Having no experience of what to do next after a husband has walked out finally (leaving a thoughtful check to cover contingencies) I wondered if Flora Madder had received a check when Charles Madder departed for the mistress with exotic tastes. Perhaps being paid off was the final straw that made her search for the rope and a revenge with a long tail that, for years to come, would lash at those left behind.

It was silent in the bedroom. The newly liberated Nathan had not bothered to shut the wardrobe door or close the drawers in the chest we shared. This was a piece of sentimentality left over from the early cash-strapped days when we had had no money and limited furniture. The symbolism of having our underwear so close together amused us, and we had retained the habit.

The drawers were half empty. Reasoning that it was wise to embark on an unavoidable painful process sooner rather than later, I shifted a folded nightdress into Nathan's vacated half. The movement dislodged the lavender bags I kept tucked into the corners, releasing a spicy fragrance.

But even smells were a problem—too spicy, too evocative, too sickly—and I dropped everything, went downstairs and phoned Maeve.

"Hi," I said. "I just wanted to know how things were."

"Oh, Rose," she said, as if she was trying to place me— remember me, even. "How are you?"

"Not terrific. I just wanted to touch base. See how you were. Perhaps have lunch. I owe you one and it would be on me. We could meet somewhere neutral."

"Things are very busy," she said quickly. "Timon is putting on pressure. We don't have a moment to call our own. I suppose you want to know how Minty's doing."

The trouble was, I did.

"Early days there." Maeve was guarded. "Look, I would like to have lunch . . . sometime, but I'm too busy at the moment to make any plans. The one free day I can see in the near future I've earmarked for the hairdresser. I must go. I need to get the gray hairs seen to." She gave a short laugh. "I *daren't* let them show. But, Rose, do keep in touch."

As usual, everyone's coats were jumbled on the pegs by the back door. I shrugged on my old gray mac, which had seen many years' tramping the cliffs in Cornwall, tied the belt round my waist and left the house. It was raining, a fine, penetrating drizzle that crept down my neck and back in a V of damp.

Panting a little, stomach growling, as it did these days, I walked across the park, stopping every so often because I felt so shaky, and plunged through the doorway of St. Benedicta's.

The nave and transepts were empty but there had been a wedding or a christening recently, because vases of white lilies had been placed on the font, on the altar, and in tiny bunches at the ends of the pews. Only one candle burned under the Madonna whose pinkness glistened like the makeup of an ageing actress.

I had no idea what I was doing there, or what I hoped to find.

I extracted a candle from the pile, lit it and wedged it into the iron claw.

How was I going to get through this? Had I deluded myself that if and when the difficult times arrived I would cope? Now, at this moment, I possessed nowhere near the required reserves, or the courage. Search as I might for the brave face, I could not find it.

The candle guttered, flamed up, resumed burning.

When it was halfway down, I got up, brushed at the damp on my mac and walked back along the aisle. As usual, the table was littered with the hymnbooks and pamphlets. I did not think anyone would mind if I tidied them up.

Chapter 12

"You don't want to go there," said Ianthe, when I announced I was going to try for a place to read English at Oxford. Her lips pursed and her eyes grew cloudy with distress, as they frequently did the older and more independent I grew. She scented a dash for freedom. The Oxford idea presented a more serious, realizable threat than dreams of traveling through the Patagonian wilderness and deserts. "You don't want to go there," she repeated. "Anyway, they don't like girls, whatever Mr. Rollinson tells you." She thought a bit further. "He shouldn't put ideas into your head. They don't take people like us."

"He's giving me special classes. He thinks they'll offer me a place."

"And what sort of job will you get at the end of it?"

At that moment I hated my mother, who was, as always,

adept at slipping a knife under my shaky confidence and prising it loose. But I toughed it out. "Watch me," I said.

I was eighteen, so very *nearly* nineteen. On the first day of term, of my first year, Ianthe accompanied me on the coach, and we found ourselves by mistake outside Christ Church, not St. Hilda's. At the entrance, Ianthe took one look at the enfilade of courtyards and the confident architecture, and slapped down the cheap suitcase. "I'll say goodbye here," she said. "You make your own way there. It's best."

As I kissed her, I tasted salt tears and caught the faint, elusive reminder of her lavender cologne. Ianthe grabbed me by the arm and, for a second or two longer, held me close. Then she pushed me away. "Go on," she said. "Enjoy your new life."

What did my mother feel as she climbed back onto the coach and began the journey back to Pankhurst Parade, to issuing tickets and timetables in the travel agent's? She left me with the burden of her apprehension and disapproval, but I often think about that neat, stubborn, retreating figure in the tweed coat. She might have believed that she had been shucked off like a nutshell. The womanly role finished. Or, maybe, she was free to retreat into her unhappiness, to explore it more fully.

"My God," Hal Thorne was reported by Mazarine to have said when, a month later, he knocked me off my bicycle in the high street, "I've killed her."

She also told me that Hal had behaved impeccably, placing me in the recovery position, summoning the police, detailing Mazarine, his passenger, to take the names of any witnesses. He was heroic in his actions and his guilt, she said, and knew it. The last was said with the light, glinting irony that Mazarine commanded.

Hal was a rotten driver, but not bad enough to kill me. I had not been aware of his white van snouting up behind me, and I did not hear the screech of the brakes, but even now I am plagued by a memory of throwing up my arms to defend myself before I plunged down.

There was another memory . . . of Hal sitting beside the gurney, rolling my tights into a ball, and of the low autumn sun, which shone through the window and invested him with a halo of light. Memory informs me that he placed the tights beside the neatly stacked pages of my essay on Donne and the bicycle lights, which had been retrieved from the accident.

Past and present swirled helplessly in my shocked, puzzled mind and I imagined I was back in the square at the via Elisabetta in Rome . . . for the strange, fair-haired man, so absorbed in tidying my possessions, seemed to my unreliable vision to possess the perfection of the stone youth who guarded the Barberini fountain.

I must have shifted, and my shocked bones cracked against each other. This made me groan and his head flicked up. "Hi." He leaned over and took my hand gently, as if he knew how to handle people who were hurting. "I should be shot. It was my fault, and I'm afraid your bicycle is a write-off. You nearly were, too."

I registered that his accent was American and I made the mistake of frowning, which hurt. I whimpered, and he was quick with reassurance. "You have a cut on your head but it's above the hairline, thank God, and you're massively bruised. They've x-rayed you and nothing's broken." His smile was clever, confident and enigmatic. "I haven't destroyed your beauty, for which I would never have forgiven myself."

Still only half conscious, I was bothered more by the idea of

Death having brushed past me than any destruction of my possible beauty.

"Are you an angel?" It seemed sensible to check that I was not being addressed by one, preparatory to being ushered into a nether region.

"If you want me to be one, I will be."

"Not yet, I hope."

I fixed on the movement of his lips, the inclination of his head. Those figures in the fountains had brought with them the blare of tropical sun, the whiplash of polar cold, the rustle of savannah grasses and the silence of the desert—and one was here, holding my hand.

It began then.

Each day for a week, Hal visited me in hospital. A Rhodes scholar from the American Midwest studying archaeology and anthropology, he imported objects for me to look at as far removed from the trolleys and sluices of the Annie Brewer women's ward as it was possible to be. A Tuareg blanket, a Naudet photograph of a nude woman as plump and pearly-skinned as a corn-fed chicken—all part of a strange convalescence.

On the last day I was in hospital, he arrived dressed in khaki fatigues with a red scarf wrapped round his neck and held up a piece of barbed wire. "An early example used by the American pioneers. It's a collector's item."

My face was still bruised and swollen, and it hurt to talk. "People collect barbed wire?"

"There's a museum of it." He pressed it into my hands and the barbs, which had an unfamiliar configuration, bit into me. "The pioneers developed it to mark out the boundaries of the homesteads and farms."

I imagined coils of barbed wire looping over the dry dust

terrain. Inside the pale, there was a cackle of geese and hens, dogs, children, the smell of home baking, women in dusty pink prints and sunbonnets, rough wooden furniture and a stoop of water. Outside in the wilderness were the watchful Red Indian, the buffalo, the slinking coyote and the prairie dog.

"Don't you mean defend? It's an aggressive thing. That's its point."

"Very funny," said Hal, and retrieved it. He paused. "Of course, property is theft."

I lay back on the pillows. "You stole that line."

With a swift movement, he bent down and smoothed the hot tangle of my hair. "Of course I did. We steal from each other all the time."

Apparently Hal lived in a small, unheated house (the *ferenghi* ghetto), in the part of Oxford called Jericho, which he shared with two other Rhodes scholars and a couple of foreign-language students, one of whom was Mazarine. ("Very chic, very BCBG," Hal said, in his amused way, "and I, on other the hand, am just a redneck hick." I had no idea what he was talking about, only that his knowledge and self-assurance were way beyond mine.)

The house was crowded, badly maintained by the landlord, uncomfortable—and magic. After the doctors released me from hospital, with the advice to keep out of the way of mad drivers, Hal collected me in the white van and we stopped there briefly before he took me out to dinner. "I want you to meet Mazarine. You will like her."

How right he was. He had spotted that we were of a kind.

Hal kept a permanently packed rucksack in his room: water-bottle, day sack, all-seasons sleeping-bag, lightweight walking trousers and water-purifying tablets. He explained that it was ready to grab at a moment's notice, when he could not bear being confined any longer. It was, he explained, necessary to him to have that readied rucksack.

He spoke rapidly, carelessly, with the confidence I craved for myself. Had he suckled it from his mother? *"There, my golden-haired baby," she would have said, kissing him frantically, "no awkwardness for you. No doubts, no blunderings. Not if I can protect you."* Or had Hal worked at it, chiseling away at the lumpen miseries of growing up?

Mazarine listened in to the rucksack explanation. Dressed in a black skirt and slenderly cut jumper, she was a great deal more knowing and sophisticated than any of the girls I had met in college. In heavily accented English, she said, "I should point out that he employs others to wash his socks . . . Don't let him keep you up too late, you must be still weak."

Hal bore me off to a Moroccan restaurant, which had recently opened on the outskirts of the city and, a novelty, was extremely popular. "It's a very small way of saying sorry," he said, as he ushered me inside. It was crowded with students cherishing their drinks and rolling their own fags but, to my dazzled eyes, Hal stood out like a beacon.

He sat down opposite me, placed his hands on the Formica tabletop and studied me. "I could have done a lot worse. I like the blouse. Young ravishing beauty versus old clothes. Guess who comes off best in the contest. Even with bruises." He touched the one on my cheek.

I felt color sneak into my face and fiddled with the lace on my cuff. Money was so short that I dressed more or less entirely in second-hand-shop pickings, and I was wearing a muslin blouse trimmed with lace. It was worn and soft, and held the faint suggestion of other lives. "If I had been an old lady, would I not have got dinner?"

"Probably not. A nice bunch of carnations instead."

"I don't like carnations."

"Pity. They have an interesting history. The name derives from the Arabic *qaranful,* a clove, by way of the Greek *karpy-hillon,* the Latin *caryophyllus,* the Italian *garofolo* and the French *giroflée* but they are very English. You should like them."

This was the first of many teases, but I was not going to let the point slide. I was still so unsure, so raw, so shakily unconfident, but I summoned my wits. "I wish to defend elderly ladies. You are discriminating on the grounds of age, which is no basis."

The transformation from tease to steely seriousness was instant. "On the contrary. On the basis that anything, money, good luck, space on this planet, is finite you could argue that the old lady has had her share of fateful or important encounters and must not be greedy. On the other hand, by virtue of your age, you have not."

Shocked, I stared at him, only to be transfixed by the blue eyes. They reminded me of gentians in an alpine meadow, the rich blue of an Italian nobleman's surcoat in a painting, the pure glassy resonance of a sapphire. "You don't really believe that?"

"What do you think?"

I swallowed. "I demand to be greedy."

"Luckily it's a long time, Rose, before you will be old. And me. But we must cultivate the right attitude to keep age at bay. Travel. Keep on the move."

"Poor old lady," I said, my heart as light and dancing as a feather. "Poor dinnerless old lady."

"As it happens, she is done out of her dinner because you are here." Once again, that confident gentle hand traced the outline of my bruise. "Thank goodness."

The helpless, unstoppable feelings that had been gathering inside me as I lay in hospital fused, ignited and burst into flame. Tentatively, I put up my hand. Our fingers met and the beat of my heart was as loud as a drum.

Hal dropped his and picked up the menu. "Chicken tagine?" He made it sound impossibly exotic.

Halfway through the meal, he put down his knife and fork. "I'm falling in love with you, Rose. Isn't that funny?"

I shivered.

Hal was often away on a dig and, with her firm intellectual grasp on life, Mazarine approved. "Pain is essential," she argued, "or how do we recognize the opposite?"

It was, I pointed out, a position argued from innocence, for at that point no pain had touched the clever and lovely Mazarine. Surely the validity of the argument rested in the experience of it. "Poof," she said.

Apart from a troubling stiffness in one hip, I recovered quickly from the accident. The addition of love and adrenaline to the blood coursing through the veins proved a great healer. In one respect, the stiff hip was a godsend, for I had plenty of time to work during the next two terms. "This is a student knocking at the door of a first," wrote my happy tutor at the end of the summer term. "Let us see if she can knock it down."

Hal was so considerate about my injuries. He fussed over them, called taxis, kept me warm, and made me feel that no other woman existed on this earth. "I'll will you better," he said. "Then we can concentrate on us."

That was in character. He never asked questions—he was not interested in my past. Nor was he interested in telling me his. It doesn't matter who or what we have been, he said, it's the now that matters.

How true that was. The sun had never been so bright, the sky so blue. My body was weightless, throbbing, never satiated. I was filled with insane joy and thankfulness, touched with awe that this had happened to me.

He was the stranger who came from other lands; he was the other for whom I had been searching.

On the last day of the summer term, we walked by the river in the botanical gardens; its watery rush sounded above the traffic. The sky had thrown off a half-veil of cloud and the smell of earth after rain pricked sweetly at my nostrils. I pinched a stalk of lavender in the flowerbed between my fingers.

Hal grinned. "*Lavandus,*" he said wickedly, "from the Latin, to be washed. The Romans washed in it."

I seized his hand and plunged it into the purple-blue blooms, and the leaves released their fragrance. I pressed his fingers to my face and inhaled. "I am bathed in you."

Abruptly, he pulled me to him and kissed me. "Lovely Rose," he murmured. "What would I do without you?"

The next day when I had packed and was ready to leave, I phoned the house. "Darling," Mazarine sounded concerned, "he's left this morning, with the rucksack."

I felt a chill go through me. "Is there any message?"

"No. I thought you would know."

"See?" said Ianthe, when I arrived back at Pankhurst Parade, shaking and tearstained. "I told you that you would come to no good."

Hal was gone for three weeks, during which I was driven to

the edge, and went over and over what had gone wrong. Why? I questioned everything: my mind, my body, my sexual inexperience, which Hal had thought so touching. I tried to identify where I had failed him, *where I had failed,* where I had erred and why he would leave me without a word.

Three weeks later, I opened the front door and there was Hal. He looked tanned and fit, but in need of a shower and with every finger wrapped in Band-Aids. "Get your boots on, we're off to Cornwall."

Between speechlessness and laughter, I demanded, "Where've you been? I had no—"

He was genuinely surprised. "Didn't I tell you? I was on a dig up north. Roman."

I felt myself turning white with rage. "No, you did not. Why didn't you tell me?"

"I'm here now so it's all right, isn't it?"

"Go away."

He inserted a foot into the door. "I've bought you a rucksack. A good one."

Despite his winningly phrased plea that, as an ignorant American, he wanted to see as much as possible of this island and only Rose could show him, Ianthe disapproved of his carrying me off. Girls did not go jaunting around the countryside as if they were already married. But I was past caring, and I left her standing on the doorstep with a face like thunder.

When I returned, I had a pink glow in my cheeks, my feet had toughened, my hip had healed and I had grown used to the sound of the sea. I told Ianthe of Penzance, Marazion, Helston, St. Mawes . . . of how we walked the coastal path, observing how the rockscape changed from granite to slate, and how, in the evenings, we sat in pubs, drank beer and cider and ate fish and chips. Of course I did not tell her of the nights, white and violet nights, when I unwrapped the Band-Aids from his battered fingers and, one by one, kissed the wounds made by the hammer and chisel. Or of how he turned me this way and that until I thought I would die, not of pleasure but of love.

It was not a light thing. I was not reinventing myself as the good-time liberated girl. I wanted to step into something serious. I did not want those extraordinary feelings to come and go, like birds wheeling and taking flight over a cornfield. I wanted Hal to imprint himself on me, and I on him. I wanted our affair to have weight and depth, and I wanted to move knowingly from a state of innocence into the unfamiliar abandon that surged through every nerve end, powered every heartbeat.

At Fowey, we had turned onto the Saint's Way, which went up to Padstow, a cross-country route of thirty miles or so. "The route of the Bronze Age traders and missionaries from Wales and Ireland."

We looked at the churches with their gray headstones, the epitaphs to drownings, plagues and early death, and I thought, We should not be deceived: the Celt still rules here and this is a country of fire and passion.

At Port Isaac, the route took us north and the terrain became more demanding. Every so often, Hal called a halt to rub my back where the straps bit into it, but we made good progress. At last, we rounded the corner and stopped.

The sea roared below us, and seagulls coasted on thermals. Before us rose monumental black cliffs and, high up on them, the remnants of salt-lashed walls. These were the ruins of Tintagel.

I slipped off my rucksack and sank down. The turf was hard and springy, my lips and skin were salty and I was tired. Hal hunkered down beside me. "This is the first of many journeys, I hope."

"So do I," I said.

Hal folded his arms around his bent knees and talked about climbing mountains, traversing deserts and finding the valley where hard apricots were harvested and soaked in spring water.

The sea ran up the beach, indifferent and careless. Suddenly I was cold. I thought of Ianthe's scones on a blue and white plate and of a fire burning in a grate and how far they would be from the valley where the hard apricots grew.

Later, huddled behind a rock on the beach, we ate our sandwiches and told stories about the castle.

Treading carefully over the slate and past the rock pools, the pregnant Queen Ygrayne would have wrapped her furlined cloak around her swollen body and entered Tintagel, the door clanging shut behind her. As she went upstairs and prepared to give birth to a son called Arthur, she would have given thanks for refuge from the violence that had killed her husband.

And here, too, at another time, high up where the seagulls flew past the arched windows, King Mark installed his wife, Iseult, of the hand's-span waist, to reign over the cliff and the sea. Here, too, a young knight halted to pay homage to the king. His name was Tristan.

"These are not happy stories," I pointed out to Hal. "A mother left alone. A husband abandoned. Lovers who die."

Hal's arms tightened around me. Through his jacket, I could hear his heart beating.

Chapter 13

When I was pregnant with Sam, I swallowed iron pills, poured milk down my throat and avoided wine, coffee and curry. I slept in the afternoons, visited the dentist for regular check-ups and every week I consulted the manual as to what had happened to the bundle of cells, then the miniature footballer, that I carried. I told it that I was doing my very best to give it a sporting chance, that, however tedious, I realized my relinquishing of favorite foods and other little adaptations of behavior were vital to its future. And how time spun itself out. How each week dragged its feet into the next.

Time dragged now. March limped away. April and May were slow, oh, so slow. June came, and my hard gestation of grief showed no sign of ending.

The oldest memories are so much sharper and clearer than the near past and, thinking over this hypothesis, I could see that this was—partly—what Nathan had battled against when meeting Minty had forced him to take stock. He chose to believe that those sharp old memories meant more than the blurred, tumbled, frantic moments of our family life. He feared that my sweet, vivid awakening into sexual passion and love with Hal had greater staying power than my years with him.

Robert Dodd, the solicitor, and I stitched up the final strands of my severance package and I signed a document agreeing that I would not take up a similar job within six months. The trade-off was a reasonable, but not generous, sum of money.

"Must be nice to have six months." Robert allowed himself to show a glimmer of frank envy.

"I might be back," I told him, "for the divorce. But I hope not. I hope Nathan and I can work through this."

He smiled with professional detachment that suggested experience had taught him otherwise then showed me out.

Sam made a point of coming up at weekends, and for the May bank holiday he brought Alice with him. I slapped on lashings of red lipstick, too much, and made them a supper of chicken breasts seethed with garlic and fennel, and pushed a piece around my own plate.

Apart from pointing out that I should try to eat more and drink less, Sam was quiet, but Alice made up for it. Smart as paint in a gray suit and gold jewelery, she questioned me closely as to what had happened at work. "I hope you made them squeal," she said at last, fiddling with her bracelet. She had painted her nails with a shiny, clear gloss, which made her hands look efficient. Then she asked which I minded more: losing my job, or my salary, and it struck me that, on this subject, Alice was vulnerable. It was also a good question. "It must be difficult," she said, "not to have a financial base. If you have no money you have no power, and it is others who drive the negotiations."

"Experience counts for something," I pointed out.

She smiled disbelievingly. "Not enough." I liked Alice better for her honesty, but she was straying close to the bone. I tried to change the subject and asked her if she had seen Spielberg's latest film.

"Alice couldn't possibly spare the time." When he wished, Sam had his own brand of irony. "Her power base demands all her attention."

Displaying her efficient nails, Alice raised her wineglass to her lips. "Jealous, Sam?"

Yet when we said goodbye Alice surprised me by giving me a kiss: brief and businesslike, but a kiss all the same. "I shall think of you, Rose," she said. "I really will. I'm sorry about . . . Nathan." She meant it, and I found myself kissing her back.

Unlike Alice, I had plenty of spare time at my disposal and, a past master at tweaking my conscience, Mr. Sears made use of it.

Apart from taking him Sunday lunch, my charity consisted of tossing coins into hats held out in the streets and responding irritably to telephone requests for donations, but the image of Mr. Sears sitting each day in his fuggy, dingy room was not easily dismissed. Cross and snippy as he could be, his right to more pricked away at me like a thorn. In the end, I told him I was taking him out. "Don't mind if I do," he said, which, considering he had not left the house for three years, was pretty cool. Somehow, I bullied the reluctant social services into providing a wheelchair and a carer for a few extra hours. "Call this a bus?" he said, when the single-decker drew up. She and I manhandled him onto the number eighty-eight, where he was completely happy. The three of us did a double run, which took most of the day, and he sat by the window, treating us to a running commentary on a cityscape in which familiar landmarks, mostly pubs, had been transmogrified into bars and grills. "What's wrong with a pub? If you wanted a cup of coffee you nipped up to the Kardomah."

It was not beyond the bounds of possibility that Mr. Sears concluded, given the treacherous pace of change, he was better off in his room.

The second that finals were over, Poppy materialized at Lakey Street and unloaded her possessions all over the house. In a lightning procedure, she repacked her suitcase, kissed me good-bye and demanded money for a taxi to the airport. "I forbid you to worry," she said. "Worrying is for wimps."

That weekend I bought a copy of the papers and the Digest. Until then, I had not touched it, but I wanted to see the worst for myself. I carried it into the park and walked up and down, gathering sufficient resolve.

Whatever else she might be, Minty was professional. The pages were different but fine: more celebrities, more photographs, and more books covering a younger age group. Yet I had not been entirely obliterated, for Minty had built on what had been there, but my ideas no longer held the center stage. It was a kind of compromise, a nod to the relationship we had once shared.

Astonishingly, as I read on, I felt not jealousy but a growing detachment from that which had previously absorbed me. A small Martian in a shiny helmet and kneepads streaked along the path, followed by a puffing adult. I followed their progress, feeling that on this subject I could breathe more easily, and I seemed to have been granted a respite from professional rivalry. It was not that I did not care, but I did not care so *very* much any more.

I turned to the other sections. "Where Will Our Staff Be Heading This Summer?" ran one feature under a shrunken map of the world. The city editor was going to Martha's Vineyard, the features editor to Tuscany (naturally) and the books editor was planning two weeks on a remote Greek island. The article included a photo of Minty dressed in a scoop-necked top and skimpy skirt. "Kea is really hot and secluded," she was reported as saying. "Nothing but sea and sand."

I reread that bit twice. Minty was not aware, or had not troubled to find out, that Nathan hated heat and would almost certainly be extremely bad-tempered on a tiny Greek island.

A breeze gave the pages in my hands a life of their own. A woman now struggled along the path with two children in a double buggy. A dog ran past with the anxious loping gait that suggested it had lost its owner.

Poor Nathan.

I checked myself. There was a sad little law that applied to abandoned wives: if they were not careful, they fed with appetite on their usurper's mistakes and shortfalls. *Her taste is vulgar . . . she poisoned the guests . . . she's nasty to the children.* I had seen it operate through Vee and now I spotted the early signs in myself. Not—as Poppy had a habit of saying.

I dropped the papers into the nearest litter-bin and continued on my way. In future, I would not bother with it.

Recent rain had turned the grass boggy. Over by the river, a maple had shaken out its new foliage and under it bloomed a clump of late tulips. I bent down and examined the nearest. Its stamens were swollen and sticky, and greenfly had taken shelter inside on the smooth, convex curve. Insects and bell-shaped petals appeared so still, so set, like a piece of Rockingham china. Like Nathan's vase.

My calm vanished. It never took much, just a nudge, a glancing allusion, and I was plunged back to picking myself up when Nathan had left.

Longing for an away-day from myself, I turned for home. The breeze had freshened, and I pulled my sweater down over my hands. Then I heard it. *Click. Click.* For a second or two, my mind slipped free of the net in which it was caught and I glimpsed the prospect of release, a future where I would be empty and clean. It was the cool, fresh wind blowing through a sickroom. The promise of rain over a parched landscape. The splash of a fountain. It was only for a moment and then I was back, plodding with muddy shoes over the wet grass.

When I woke on Monday morning Parsley was not on the bed. I went in search of her and found her stretched out on the blue chair. "Parsley?" She did not respond. She smelled odd, and her flanks were laboring. With a shock, I realized she was in pain. "Parsley . . ."

On my last visit to the vet, Keith had warned me, "You can't expect miracles at her age." But I had. I did.

I stroked one of her paws. I knew her well enough to understand that she would not want me to interfere, and she would wish to handle her diminution and death in her own cat terms. I knew, too, it was useless to imagine that behind the green eyes lay an emotion as deep for me as mine for her. I tried again. "Parsley."

My voice penetrated her shadowy limbo. With an obvious effort, she raised her head and looked at me, the one who loved her most.

When he saw me with the basket in the waiting room, Keith's eyebrows climbed toward the haircut that the family swore was based on Henry V's portrait. It is the type of haircut that people, having spent their youth being disgusting, adopt when excess has become too exhausting. Keith had the perfect look for a vet whose functional, clinical rooms sheltered the love, nonsense and wild feelings between humans and their animals.

I coaxed Parsley out of the basket. Keith placed a bony hand on my shoulder. "You know what I'm going to say, Rose. I could pump her full of vitamins and antibiotics, which would boost her for a day or two. But that's all you can steal at her age."

He pressed my shoulder and I turned away. *Where were the family?*

"Do it now," Sam would be likely to say.

"No, *not* yet. We have no right to intervene in a natural process." That would be Poppy.

Nathan would ask, "*Exactly* how long does Keith think he can keep her alive?"

"All right," I said to Keith. "But quickly, because she's frightened being here."

As gently as we could manage, we wrapped Parsley in a towel. She struggled briefly and Keith shaved a patch off her front paw, bent his Henry V head and kissed her. "Ready?"

I would never be ready but I held my cherished cat as the needle slipped in. That much I owed her. I owed her far more but there was nothing I could do to pay the debt. Parsley was the companion to maternity, noise, children: a silent, sensuous, feminine commentator. A witness to a heated, physical, domestic world.

Almost immediately, her head sank back against my shoulder. The green eyes widened, let in the light, then dimmed, shuttered, and Parsley went into the night.

Keith stood back and I cradled her until the final rill of pulse fluttered to a standstill.

Back home, I carried Parsley into the garden and laid her under the lilac tree beside the black hellebores and double anemones. Then I went upstairs to Poppy's room and searched in the chest for the white wool shawl in which I had wrapped my shouting babies and walked them up and down to hush them.

I fetched the spade and fork and dug into the knotty, insect-ridden, bindweed-infested earth. The fork tines severed white, stringy roots and drove the insects from their subterranean refuges.

A fine and private place, Parsley.

Forget the *click* in my mind, the cool promise of the future. I had had enough. I wanted my grief dead, my longings finished, my body shrouded from the gaze of others.

I dug on.

I was burying a past, a marriage, a job. That funny, ex-hausted, desperate slice of my life when Parsley slunk beside me on paws that clicked on the stone and wooden floors and kept me company through the night when the children cried and Nathan slept.

When the hole was large enough, I laid Parsley in it, and I fussed over the ends of the shawl, wrapping it round until I was satisfied. The wool was soft, the texture of much washed baby clothes, and still retained that faint, oh-so-suggestive smell of yeasty, milky children.

I threw in a spadeful of earth, then a second.

Parsley's grave did not take long to fill in.

I told myself I should eat something, but I had lost the habit of regular meals. Anyway, my fingers were stiff and ice cold. I poured myself a large slug of whiskey, which finished the bottle, and dragged myself upstairs to bed.

During the night, I was violently sick. Panting and covered in sweat, I sat back on my heels. I was burning, burning up. In my haste, I had blundered from my bed into the bathroom with-out switching on the light and the neon glimmer from the street painted the porcelain a thin, unappealing orange. I pressed my hands to my face.

I was slipping. Where had I read that women who were slipping drank too much, wept too much, wore too much lipstick, dealt with their solitariness in empty neon-lit rooms?

At dawn I was sick again, and a pain in my stomach took up residence. By morning, I had a raging temperature and I spent the day huddled in bed. On the second day, my temperature rose even higher and I floated through the fever, in and out of heavy but fitful sleep. I could feel my heart thudding and banging in my chest. Was I dying from grief? Was I dying because I had been discarded? From time to time, I imagined the telephone rang—but it was the church bell tolling for my father's funeral.

Nathan materialized in my dreams. Tall and drivingly ambitious. "I am going to leave you, Rose," he said. I told him that he already had. *But it's not that easy, Rose.*

During this exchange I appeared to have grown a pair of wings and rose above Nathan, who vanished into a dot.

Now Minty poked and tugged at me. She seemed unsettled. "What do you think of me, Rose? What do you think of your former friend?"

"If you must know, I think you're ignorant," I replied, adding kindly, "but it's not your fault. Wait until you are older."

Big tears splashed down her face. "I refuse to get older. I shall always wear tiny tops and short skirts." I shook my head, and she wailed, like a child, "It's so unfair."

With a mighty beat of my excellent wings, I soared up into the sky, which had replaced the bedroom ceiling. Far below, Minty's wet, upturned face was as flat and featureless as a swamp.

"Rose . . ."

Nathan was bending over me and I blinked. My tongue had

turned into felt, and my lips were so cracked that I tasted blood, and it seemed to be evening. "What are you doing here, Nathan?"

"You look *awful.*" His eye lit on the thermometer by the bed. "Here, stick this in."

I tried to raise my head. "Can't."

He took a step back. Nathan was one of those men who hated anyone to be ill except himself, and he was never at his best in these situations—"You're not that bad," he would protest, if I dared to mention that I was not feeling up to scratch, and assume his suffering expression. For a day or two, there were sighs and looks that meant, *I am carrying this family entirely on my shoulders.* Pretty soon after that, he developed identical symptoms, which were *worse, much worse than yours, Rosie.* As a result, I rarely took to my bed. Anyway, mothers do not have time to be ill.

"We're on our way to dinner with Timon and I thought I'd just check as I've been ringing and ringing."

"I've been ill," I pointed out helpfully.

"Hang on," he said. "I'd better get some help." He disappeared and, a few minutes later, reappeared with Minty.

I was too weak to feel rage, too distanced to care that she was there. They conferred in the doorway . . . temperature . . . awful . . . doctor. Minty shifted from foot to foot and threw me pointed glances from those slanting eyes.

I made a huge effort. "Nathan, could you get me some water?"

It was always a smart move to give a Nathan a task. It settled him.

While he was gone, Minty maintained her distance. "I wasn't going to come in," she confessed. "Nathan made me. But I wouldn't have done . . ."

I closed my eyes. "I don't care what you do."

She was silent. I opened my eyes. She was examining the room—a glimpse of Nathan's remaining clothes through the partially open door of the cupboard, a photo of Sam and Poppy, taken in a rare moment when they were enjoying each other's company, a stack of books on Nathan's side of the bed. There was a hungry, siphoning look on her face, and I knew she was trawling for the clues she needed to understand Nathan.

It was then I realized how deadly intent on Nathan she was, how elated by the task of making it work but also secretly terrified at how little she knew.

I could not blame her for wanting Nathan. How could I? I wanted him, too.

But this was the Minty who had said, "Commitment? Don't make me laugh."

She must have read my mind. "People do change, Rose, particularly if someone like Nathan is involved." She fussed with her jumper, a low-cut blue mohair that only just reached her waist. Every time she moved a little flesh was revealed. You can look at me, she was saying, my beauty and ripeness, and you may envy and desire. "I'm twenty-nine," she said, in a wondering voice.

With a huge effort, I turned on my side and blotted out the sight of her.

"You're very thin." She bent over and smoothed the damp sheets with a proprietorial gesture. "You should take more care of yourself."

I was almost choked by fever and hatred. "If you have any shred of compassion, go."

Her heels *clip-clopped* down the passage, leaving me to reflect tiredly on the objectives that Minty had once professed to despise. Years of marriage—the sporadic wars, ententes and a deep, protective peace. Nathan had married a girl in jeans who turned into a mother, who turned into a career woman who wore trouser suits, carried a book bag and read office memos. From time to time, this woman had congratulated herself on juggling these various states and emerging sane and optimistic.

Quite soon after our marriage, Nathan had abandoned the safari jacket for double-breasted office suits, the trouser buttons gradually let out. Some days he arrived home whistling under his breath, a sign that he felt happy and confident in his decisions. On others, I caught him staring out of his study window as he puzzled over problems. Sometimes he worried about money and we made lists of how to economize. A few of those were still stuck up on the fridge with magnets, turning yellow. In the summer, he sat in a chair in the garden and watched me at work. In winter, he begged me to make shepherd's pie and chocolate pudding. *To keep me going, Rosie.* (More letting out of waistbands.) We ate at the table in the kitchen, discussed our children, discussed our ambitions. As the children grew up, we had more energy, talked less of domestic matters and more of politics, newspapers and the troubled state of the world—a regular airing of each other's mental geography, which had seemed right, natural and happy.

"Here we are. I've made some toast, and got you some aspirins." Nathan set down a jug on the bedside table. "Should I feed Parsley?"

The mention of her name brought instant tears. Nathan knelt down beside the bed. "Rosie, what is it? Are you in pain?"

I told him and he said, "Poor old Parsley," and stroked my cheek.

"Will you do something for me?"

"If I can."

"Brush my hair. It feels dreadful."

Nathan reached for the hairbrush, propped me up and settled me back against his shoulder. The bristles scraped through
hair as lank as tow. "She had a good innings, Rosie."

I wiped my face with the sheet. "That makes it worse. I assumed she'd be around forever."

"Do you remember when she went missing and I found her
in that strange house, the one with the creeper growing over the
windows?"

"I found her," I murmured. "You were at work."

"No, it was me." He paused. "You're pinching *my* memories."

I twisted my head to look up at him. "So I am. But you
pinch mine."

He bent over and his cheek rested against mine. "So I do."

"Nathan?" Minty called from downstairs. Nathan stopped
brushing but I allowed myself to relax against his shoulder.

"Nathan . . ." Minty materialized at the door, and the dark
eyes narrowed angrily. Perhaps she was looking through a tunnel
to the light at the end, which shone on the past, against which
she must compete. "Nathan, we'll be late for Timon." As she
turned to go, the blue jumper rode up over the taut stomach.

Instantly Nathan disengaged himself and stood up, my tall,
driven, ambitious husband, who knew what he wanted, who
until this point had been sane and predictable. I turned away my
face because I could not bear to see the change in him.

"Coming," he said.

Chapter 14

It took me a little time to get back on my feet. Not only was I weak but, without the routines of work and play, the days felt soft-set, like underdone eggs. I was used to them being quite different, all neatly stacked up and filed.

The garden told me that summer was here: a languid seraglio, swooning with scent and covered in foaming, lacy white. When I felt up to it, I pushed open the French windows and stepped outside. I knew it so well. Each brick in the wall. The hole in the lawn dug by the squirrel. The intersection where the fence had rotted. When the children were small they had demanded grass to play football and French cricket on, but as they grew older, like the Dutchman claiming the polders, I snatched back my flowerbeds.

The olive in its pot was sway-backed and gray-green. It meant peace. It meant home. It meant green oil smelling of thyme and marjoram into which to dip a crust of bread. It meant good things.

Hal had given me the olive after our second expedition together, walking through the Mani peninsula. Thin, dirty, dusty, happy, we were on our way home. In Kieros we sat under a clump of olive trees and waited for the bus to take us north to Athens, and ate bread and feta cheese. The sun blazed and dry harvest dust drifted in the hot air. Up in the valley, laden donkeys toiled up the slope and poppies bloomed at the edges of the fields and by the road. I leaned back on my rucksack and thought that I had never seen anywhere so harshly beautiful: gray-green olives, stony scrub, scarlet poppies and the blue of the sky. He chose that beautiful, wonderful, hot moment to tell me that he planned to stay in England for the time being. Why? I asked. He got out his penknife and scrambled to his feet. You know why, he said, with his back turned.

He excised a twig with a wedge of bark at the end and presented it to me. Cosseted in dampened tissue, it lay hidden in my rucksack until we got home. I mixed earth and compost in one of Ianthe's pots, but not too rich for a tree that likes heat and dust, and planted it. Olive trees didn't grow in this climate—Ianthe was suspicious and unhelpful—hadn't I noticed?

But I persevered and, one day, two buds were pushing through.

Now I pinched a leaf between my fingers. A breeze had sprung up and, depleted by illness, it made me shiver.

As I paced the garden, depression settled over me like a cold fog. In the absence of my care, the Iceberg had grown thin and attenuated. The Buff Beauty was half buried by the *Solanum* and I had failed to go to its rescue. My roses were unused to neglect and poured over their stems, feeding on the infant buds, was an undulating sheath of greenfly. I stopped, seized a branch of "Is-pahan" and, not caring that the thorns drove into me, ran my finger and thumb down it. *That* was the way to kill greenfly.

A yellow and green stain flared over my fingers. I bent down and wiped them on the grass. Then I went indoors, closed and locked the French windows behind me.

I did not want to go back into the garden. I cannot explain, but I felt it had let me down.

Ianthe made her weekly call. "Have you talked to Nathan? *Have you?*"

Robert Dodd rang (calls charged at twenty pounds). Nathan had asked him to discuss the separation details with me, the set-tlement of which was going to be expensive.

Poppy rang from God knew where to report that she was alive.

Mazarine rang from Paris. "You must come."

"I can't," I said. "I don't want to go anywhere." I looked out of the window at the street, which appeared unimaginably wide, and felt my knees tremble. The more time went by, the less I felt capable of negotiating the outside. "I'm finding it difficult to leave the house."

"Listen to me. You can. It will help you to forget the terri-ble Nathan and your little job."

"It was not a *little* job."

"If you say so, *chère.*"

Curator of a left-bank art gallery, Mazarine still cherished her high intellectual standards and the tussle between her exact-ing vision and my populist leanings had given us much pleasure over the years. According to the flyer she sent over, the current show was a deconstruction of the mythology of underwear.

I made a huge effort and pulled myself together. "How are the knickers?"

"Stop it," she hissed down the phone. "I will expect you next Thursday."

Nathan did not like Mazarine. At least, not in the days before I went to work when Mazarine and I spoke so often and were so close. "Not my type," he said, which was nonsense, for Mazarine had brains, looks and the kind of outlook Nathan relished in women. His dislike was because Mazarine was associated with Oxford and Hal, the bit of my life he had had nothing to do with.

Nathan's dislike did not stop us making regular trips to Paris to stay with her. (After Nathan was promoted, we opted to stay in hotels, which steadily became more luxurious.) In the Mazarine days, we piled the children into the back of the car. They punctuated the journey with cries of "Are we there yet?" When the questions turned to wails, which they always did, I executed a precarious maneuver into the back and sat between them in a rubble of toys and biscuits, holding them close and shouting to Nathan above their noise and that of the engine.

One particular trip we left the children—Sam, thirteen, Poppy, eleven—with Ianthe. The car sped south down the autoroute from Calais and, in the adult peace, I brought up the subject of returning to work.

The effect on Nathan was instant. He frowned, hunched over the wheel, did his disappearing act into himself. "Why? Aren't you happy?" He glared ahead. "You wanted the children so badly. Why not look after them? We're managing."

"You wanted them, too."

I sensed his struggle, against what I was not sure. "My mother looked after me," he said at last.

My mother-in-law was not a subject I wished—ever—to

pursue. "And mine did, too, just as well, only she combined it with work."

He transferred his attention to overtaking a lorry loaded with livestock. "An alternative would to be work from home. Would you consider that?"

I was puzzled. "How strange, Nathan. I had no idea that you would be opposed. I thought you would encourage me."

The suggestion of any shortfall angered him. "I know that plenty of mothers work. I'm not against. Far from it. But should *you*? We're talking about us. The older they grow, the more the children will need you."

"Oh, for God's sake," I snapped. "There is a compromise. If you feel so strongly, you look after them." He did not reply. "Ah. Not so keen to do that, are you?"

"It's not you working," he repeated, "of course not. It's the children I'm thinking about."

"And me?" But Nathan had shaken me. I had considered every angle of working in a rational manner, and it stung that Nathan assumed I had not thought of the children first.

"Why do you feel the need? Are you missing something?"

The flat reaches of the Pas de Calais flashed by. "Isn't that rather an odd question? Can you imagine not having your work? Nathan, *I'm* getting older, too, not just the children, and if I'm not careful it will be too late. Is that so very selfish?"

"No," he answered, the closed look in place. "Of course not. It's just that I thought we were happy as we are."

"But we are," I cried. "Nothing alters that."

He asked me what I was thinking of doing, and I told him that I had ambitions to be a books editor on a paper. "If I work my way up."

"Bloody hell," he said. "That's not a job. No, I don't mean that—I don't know what I mean."

I shouted "Bloody hell" back and ordered him to stop the car at the next lay-by, which he did. I wrenched open the door and got out. A family was sitting at one of the benches the French are so good at supplying, eating a midday picnic. A stream skirted the edge of the area, flanked by a sward of grass. I walked down to it and stood looking at the water. Someone had thrown in a child's disposable diaper and the white plastic eddied dismally in the current.

Nathan came up behind me. "I didn't mean it about it not being a job. Of course it is."

"I wish you wouldn't patronize me."

"I'm not," he was genuinely bewildered, "but you have to consider who is to look after the children and if all the upheaval would be worth it."

I was icy with rage. "I'm so angry with you—I can't remember when I've been so angry. We might as well go home. *Now*," I added.

Nathan ran his hand over his hair and scratched the back of his neck. "It's taken me by surprise, that's all. I don't like surprises."

"It's not *so* surprising."

"It's just that we seemed so settled, and it was working." With his hands he mimed the shape of a box. "We all fitted in so well."

I moved away toward a group of poplar trees that soared skyward and shouted at him, furiously, "I'm allowed to change. Everyone changes. Even you."

Nathan threw back his head and roared with laughter. The French family stopped eating to watch the roadside drama. "You look so funny."

"Oh, do I? And what do you suppose *you* look like?"

He smiled and, as usual, it transformed his face and leached the tension. "Just as silly." He came over and took my hand. "Don't change too much, will you?"

Still angry, I disengaged mine. "I'll see."

We got back into the car and drove for the next hour, mostly in silence. As we drew nearer to Paris, the traffic intensified and Nathan was forced to concentrate. It was not until we had passed the turning to Senlis that he resumed the discussion. "Of course," he said, "I could ask around the group. That way I could keep an eye on you."

Then I understood part of the problem. Nathan was worried that I would push open the door and hop out of the cage. He was frightened that I would spread my wings and soar away.

But I wanted to do no such thing.

Wearing a tightly fitting short-sleeved scarlet jacket and skirt with spiky black heels, Mazarine was waiting at the Gare du Nord, which smelled of French tobacco and heated croissants. My spirits lifted just a fraction. To be back in Paris.

"You look awful." She gave me a kiss, which confirmed the verdict for she did not often demonstrate open affection. "And what is that?" She indicated my linen trouser suit.

I tucked my hand under her sharp, creamed elbow. "It's a very nice suit but, I admit, a bit hot. I'd forgotten how hot Paris can be."

"It's a terrible cut," she said. "Unflattering." However left-bank her intellectual interests, a late, childless marriage to a businessman confirmed Mazarine as a chic Parisienne who favored silk scarves, monogrammed handbags, slim skirts and high heels.

She bundled me into a taxi, which dropped us outside Mimi's, a restaurant with a blue and gold striped awning. My heart sank. "I can't eat much at the moment," I confessed.

"I can see that, but part of the point is being here. Just enjoy. Good restaurants are therapy."

I laughed. "Clever Mazarine."

I knew that she would not ask for intimate details about Nathan and his departure. She would stick to the overview, and to the elegant theories that made her strong. No ifs, buts and messy reminiscences, certainly not for Xavier, her dead husband, who had been several years older.

"So . . . are you going to kill him?" Mazarine arranged her napkin on her scarlet lap.

I concentrated on my stuffed chicory, and its thin, bitter taste. "No. I could do more damage by killing myself."

"If you are thinking of doing so, tell me, and I won't take you shopping as it would be a waste."

I told Mazarine about the minister's wife. Mazarine sighed. "What did she expect? All pleasure and no pain?"

"She got too much pain, and probably too little pleasure."

She considered. "Do you think there is any sign of Nathan coming to his senses?"

"He's been gone a while. Since February." I looked up at Mazarine. "Since February. A lifetime. And that makes it more difficult to repair, should he want to do so. He wanted a change. He wanted a fantasy before it was too late. He didn't believe in me any more. Also, and this is strange, I think Hal came into it."

"*That* old story. How peculiar."

"Anyway . . ." I remembered how Nathan leaped to his feet when Minty called to him, and the soft, sleek gleam ". . . Nathan is besotted with Minty."

Mazarine cut me short. "The young and pretty can be pretty wicked, and Minty will get away with it—for the time being."

The bright cosmopolitan setting seemed to go dark. "It's

what you feel after a death . . . you would know. But there is no body to mourn."

Mazarine adjusted her earring, and it struck me that she looked uncharacteristically hesitant and uncertain. "I hope you made endless big scenes."

"Not really. Now, of course, I rather wish I had."

"Of course. The English take not only their pleasures but their sorrows sadly." I let this one pass. Mazarine poked at her shellfish, and her lipsticked mouth was drawn into a cynical expression. "We never do know, do we, what our so-called loved ones plan to surprise us with?" The pause was a fraction overlong. "When Xavier died, I had to go through the papers. Of course. And I found something I would never, ever have expected." Another pause. "Going through a dead person's effects gives you an advantage you don't necessarily want . . ."

A waiter came with the plates on which halibut had been exquisitely arranged with green beans. Mazarine regarded it without her usual critical sharpness.

"When Xavier died two years ago, he had numerous business interests, the bakery, property and everything. And, it seems, a house—as it happens a beautiful house in the sixteenth."

I was puzzled. A beautiful house in the sixteenth must qualify as one of the better surprises. I put my hand on hers, which was trembling. "Mazarine?"

"It turns out that this is a house for *poules de luxes*. Very expensive and exclusive. Now do you see?"

The halibut had grown cold. The clatter of expensive lunch being expensively served continued around us. The heat, the stiff napery, the casually chic clothes of the other diners, the sun spilling over the blue and gold awning reminded me of the arthouse films Mazarine and I had gone to see in Oxford and, as often as not, failed to understand.

She said again, "It's a beautiful house, full of beautiful things, and I'm told that Xavier took immense pains over the furnishings and arrangements. And the women are beautiful. Apparently quite a few make good marriages and go on to have good careers. Cancer specialists and television producers." She looked at me bleakly. "The old fool. He could have told me . . . I would have made a big scene, I tell you, but we would have shared it."

"Are you going to live there?"

"*Live* there? No, I shall sell it and get a good price."

I did my best. "Xavier didn't expect to die, Mazarine. He wouldn't have done this to you willingly. He would have told you sometime."

Mazarine looked everywhere but at me. The waiter slid tiny coffee cups onto the table and left a pot of coffee between us. I poured it and gave her a cup. It was all too complicated and painful.

Mazarine shaded her eyes. "How silly I am. Nearly as silly as you."

I gave her a shaky smile. "Okay. Let's tot up the loyalty bonuses. Your reward for being a good and lovely wife is a brothel which, I must point out, is infinitely more exciting than being replaced with a younger woman."

After lunch, Mazarine took me shopping. "This trip is to get you sorted out," she said. "I think you must face facts and pay attention to your appearance."

"Do I look so bad?"

"Yes."

"Shopping will sort me out?"

She shrugged. "It is a duty."

Our first stop was La Belle Dame Sans Merci, a boutique specializing in underwear. There was a poster advertising Mazarine's exhibition in the window. "No jokes, Rose." Once inside, she submitted me to the attentions of an exquisite-looking youth. "Not interested in women," she murmured.

I observed myself in the mirror. "That's lucky."

While he measured and prodded, I gazed awkwardly at the knots of cream satin ribbon that tethered the curtains. Mazarine and the youth conferred and pushed me this way and that, as if I was weightless.

A full-length mirror reconfirmed my thinness but it did not please me as it might have done. Who was this person in the mirror, without presence, without bearing?

"Pay attention, Rose, and try this on." Mazarine handed me the first of many garments.

I obeyed and felt my flesh settle into lace and wire.

"There," she said, a magician happy with her work. "Good."

For anyone's information, the healing quotient of getting without difficulty into a black lace body embroidered with tiny butterflies is high.

"How are the finances?" Mazarine inquired, a little late in the day, as we carried expensive-looking bags out of the boutique.

"I have six months' salary. Or I did until an hour ago."

Mazarine looked smug. "This is an investment in your future."

"I'm not looking for a husband replacement."

"Who said that you were?"

Our next stop was Zou Zou, whose proprietor, a slender, chic woman, appeared to be on the best of terms with Mazarine. The two women conferred fast and emphatically with many a gesture in my direction, and I got the impression that they considered I did not possess a rag worthy to sit on my back. They hustled me into a cubicle and practically ripped off my clothes.

Hands and voices fussed and chattered and pinned on alterations.

I found myself in a sleeveless linen dress cut in the oh-so-French manner. But, dear me, the buttons were not, apparently, in sympathy with my bustline. I confess to being enchanted with this notion. So much in life is wasted or lost—supermarket packaging, emotion, methane gas from cows, years of building up a marriage—but this particular art of placement was the one area in which nothing was overlooked. Buttons sympathetic to the precise line of nipples were there to help salve the wounds of time and love that had gaped open and bloody after one short sentence had been uttered: *I've found someone else.*

Chapter 15

The Rose in the mirror had undergone a metamorphosis worked by Mazarine's intervention. Breast, waist and leg were cradled by lace, wire, linen and silk: no longer was I the neutral, unremarked shadow I imagined I had become—the shadow who slipped through streets alongside hundreds of other neutral, unremarked women, whose hearts beat, as mine did, with rage that they had arrived at this point. More than that, I had stepped over fear and habit and kicked them away. That's why I looked different.

"Hallo, Rose," I said softly.

The figure in the mirror moved, and the delicate, expensive materials cradled curves, accentuated the swoop of bone under the flesh. No, certainly not a ghost. Certainly not insubstantial. Mazarine gave me a little pat and I was filled with gratitude to the friend who countered whatever life threw at her with elegant theories and shopping. "Hurry up," she said, "we'll be late for the *salon de beauté*."

Two hours later, smarting from the toughest depilation I had ever endured and glowing after a mud pack culled from a prehistoric spring, I sat down in a pink silk chair and presented my hands and feet for the final lap.

A girl sat on a stool in front of me and a pair of thin white hands kidnapped mine. The rest of her was thin, too, and she went to work abstractedly in a way that suggested that, if her body was present, her mind ranged elsewhere. Eventually she spoke. "Madame has not been taking care of her nails."

This was indisputable.

She examined my right hand. "If you cultivate the habit, you can train them."

The grit in the oyster, I sat in the luxurious room while layers of cream, powder and varnish were applied to turn me into a pearl. The girl proceeded to tackle a cuticle, which certainly had not acquired the habit, and the discomfort was such that I decided to defend myself. "But I will be acquiring the habit," I said. "Definitely."

As a philosophy it had limitations, but it would do.

Because I was curious, Mazarine took me to see the house in the fashionable sixteenth and, in an area that grew beautiful houses like mushrooms, it *was* beautiful. Built of dazzling white stone, many-windowed, it exuded poise, certainty and memories of a civilized history.

"About 1730," Mazarine whispered, as we peered, like children, through the wrought-iron gates into the courtyard.

"Why are we whispering?"

"I don't know." Mazarine adjusted her voice to normal. "It belonged at one time to the Duc de Sully. We won't go in but it's kept in immaculate order. Not a thing out of place. White muslin, bleached wood, that sort of thing. Huge beds. The housekeeper is a fiend at her job and lectured me on how get to rid of silverfish."

A couple of the windows had been opened, and there was a flutter of white muslin. "Not a home, then," I said. No shelter for a sobbing child, exhausted adolescent or hurt adult, even. Just a place where desire was kept artificially in a state of permanent expectation.

"Let's go. I hate it." Mazarine was stiff with tension.

A girl went through the gate as we were leaving, *taptapping* on high, spindle heels. She was slender, dark and expensive-looking. She paused to adjust the gold chain that anchored her handbag to her shoulder, caught my gaze and sent me a small, hard smile.

A flower seller was positioned by the entrance to the Métro, with a mass of starved-looking lilies and roses in buckets. The lily petals had retracted like claws and the roses looked bruised. Beside them was another bucket, stuffed with harsh orange gerberas. Ugly but alive. On an impulse I bought a bunch.

Back in her apartment, Mazarine arranged the gerberas in a vase. The corners of her lips were turned down. "Xavier *should* have told me." The mouth became more tragic.

I arrived back at Lakey Street on a warm Sunday afternoon and the post was splattered all over the floor. I picked it up and sorted it into piles. Bills, circulars, a postcard from Poppy, another from Sam. Both informed me that they were well and happy, and I was not to worry.

Warmed by my children, I moved round the house opening

windows, letting in fresh air, and phoned Ianthe, who was coming over for supper. Next I checked up on Mr. Sears.

"Didn't notice you'd gone," he said, as I placed in his lap the box of chocolates I had brought for him.

"Glad you've missed me."

"I've been counting my blessings. It takes me all day."

I laughed. "Actually, I've been counting mine."

Back home, I made a macaroni cheese and laid the table in the kitchen. My mother had never lost her taste for good, heavy, plain food.

On the dot, Ianthe arrived looking her usual neat self in a soft blue cardigan and flowered cotton dress with a full skirt, but a little pale. She noted the laid table. "Can't we have supper in the garden? It's a shame to be inside."

I did not attempt to explain my neglect of the garden. I pulled out a tray and piled onto it the cutlery and china.

Ianthe watched me. "Any new developments?"

"Not as far as I'm aware."

She sighed, the blocked, irritable sound of a parent pinned against a brick wall. "I don't know what your father would have thought."

"Dad was very practical, Mum. I'm sure he would have understood. I feel . . . well, it's gone too far for retrieval. I have to face the fact that Nathan has decided to go. I can't undo that. I know he wouldn't have done anything so final unless he meant it, and it's not as simple as saying forgive and forget."

"Yes, it is, if you decide it is."

"Mum, believe me . . ." Ianthe's stricken expression forced me to change tack. "Since we're on the subject, you've never really explained why you didn't get married again."

"I didn't find the right person."

It was my turn to sigh. "Nonsense. There was Jimmy Beestwick. He hung around for years. Or the nice Neil . . . so why? You would have been much more comfortable. Less lonely. All that." Ianthe's gaze fell away. "Go on, tell me."

The admission was slow in coming. "Your dad was everything. I wasn't sure I could do it twice. Have the luck, I mean."

"So it's *not* that simple. It's magic, witchery and good timing."

Ianthe picked up the tray. "Sometimes, Rose, I think you're being deliberately stupid. It's common sense and being unselfish. But I'm not sure anyone sees it like that anymore."

"You're contradicting yourself, Mum. Admit."

Defeated, she shrugged. "I can't explain."

This year I had not exhumed the chairs from the garden shed, so I fetched a couple from the kitchen. Ianthe sat down heavily in hers.

Macaroni cheese is comforting, and we ate in silence. Afterwards, Ianthe said, "Your father was a wonderfully secure person to live with, and he made people around him *feel* secure. That's why I could never get over the will business. It was so unlike him."

To my horror, her eyes filled with tears. "Oh, Mum, don't. Please don't."

Ianthe extracted a neatly ironed handkerchief from her cardigan sleeve and pressed it to her eyes. "It's nothing . . . I'm all right . . . Actually, there is something. It's just that I have to have some tests and I haven't been sleeping that well." Her pause was more alarming than anything she said. "Nothing serious, you know."

I pulled my chair closer to hers. "No, I don't know, Mum. You'd better tell me."

Ianthe gave the irritating laugh she reserved for social occasions when she felt out of depth. "Just a lump. The doctor says it's more likely than not to be a cyst." She tapped her chest.

I thought rapidly. "When are the tests and where?"

"That's just it. There's a bit of a wait."

I started up. "I'll ring Nathan. You're on his insurance."

Minty's phone number was still stored on the phone's menu in the sitting room and, with the flick of a button, I was talking to Nathan. "Nathan, Ianthe has to have some urgent tests. I wanted to check it's okay to go ahead and use the insurance."

Nathan cleared his throat. Always a bad sign. "I've been meaning to get in touch about this. I've had to take both your names off."

"I see." Pause. "Or, rather, I don't." But I did. "Is this because you *had* to put Minty on instead?"

"That's right."

"Couldn't you have told me?"

"I should have done, but it slipped my mind. I'll explain why one day, but it was necessary. Don't worry, I haven't made any other alterations."

"Let me get this straight. Ianthe can't use the insurance for urgent tests, but we can summon the gasman to mend the boiler. We can die safely in a heated house." I struggled to keep calm. After all, what else should I expect? I said, more to myself than to Nathan, "What am I going to do about Ianthe?"

"I . . ." I heard Minty make a comment in the background and Nathan covered the receiver with his hand. There was a muffled and, judging by Minty's tone, rather heated exchange. "Rose," Nathan came back on the line, "if you want some help . . ."

"It's fine, Nathan, don't bother."

I put down the phone and looked at my feet. Ianthe always said that she could not go on forever but I expected her to. The room grew chilly, and I with it. I shook a little, whether from anger or fear I wasn't sure. One thing was certain, however: I was on my own.

I lied, and told Ianthe that everything was arranged, and she was to have the bill sent to Lakey Street so that I could check it out before forwarding it to Nathan.

She seemed reassured and insisted in her quiet way that she wished to look at the garden and led me down the path, stopping frequently to assess a plant. I followed reluctantly. "You've been neglecting it," she scolded. "What a shame."

"I haven't been out in it much."

"You should." She bent down to examine a clematis and her flowered dress made a graceful waterfall. "This has got wilt, Rose. If you cut it right back, you might save it." She looked at me severely, questioningly. "You've been letting things go. Whatever has happened, you must not give up. Others depend on you, and you must set an example to the children, and to me. We all depend on you." Lecture delivered, she pinched an olive leaf between her fingers. "I never thought you'd grow," she told it.

Smarting as I was, I laughed all the same. "I never thought I'd see you talking to it. Give it a few more years and you won't recognize it."

Ianthe turned away. I could almost taste her fear and anxiety and I could have bitten out my tongue. *Maybe I don't have any more years* hung unspoken between us.

"Mum . . ." I thought rapidly. "Mum, I was going to ask you to help with the fountain. I need an extra hand."

At once her face cleared. "Of course."

I fetched the trug, the trowel and the bucket, and began to clear the debris that had accumulated. Even in water, leaves do not rot very quickly and those I extracted from it retained their shapes. We worked together, not saying much. Ianthe peeled back the wire covering the motor and held it, while I inserted my finger into the mechanism and scooped out the body of a dead tadpole and clods of mud. "Okay, Mum," and she eased the wire back into place. I switched on the mechanism and the water dribbled, then flowed down into the cleansed pool. I made a few extra adjustments to the larger stones Poppy, Sam and I had collected years ago at Hastings, and stood back to admire our handiwork.

Ianthe brushed down the front of her dress, which was spattered by stagnant water. "I'm glad we did that."

When Nathan's mother died he said he wanted to remember her as she had once been, before the illness took a grip, and that I should, too. It was a good, helpful thought, and typical of Nathan. There and then, I resolved that that was how I would think of him when I went back over the memories. The man who took trouble with his mother-in-law and spent time helping her with tax and pensions. Not, perhaps, how he wished to occupy his spare time, but he did it. The man who had told me privately that some people were damn ignorant about how the world functioned, but did his utmost to help all the same.

The following evening the doorbell went unexpectedly. It was Vee, flushed and panting. "Transport's terrible round here," she said.

"Always was," I said.

I kissed her, and took her into the sitting room. "I've just come to check I haven't a suicide on my hands." Vee plumped down in the blue chair, and I knew she must have been talking to Mazarine. The knowledge that they were watching over me made me feel better.

"Children okay?"

"Sam comes up a lot and Poppy writes me postcards telling me not to worry."

Vee smiled. "They're the best."

Hearing my children praised never failed. Vee leaned back in the chair and closed her eyes. "I am *absolutely* exhausted. Completely, *utterly* drained. Why did I do it?"

I handed her a glass of white wine. I did not need to ask what she meant. "Drink this."

"All I dream about is being alone, completely alone. And sleeping." As she spoke, her features slackened, her skin paled, and Vee fell asleep, just like that. Sipping my wine, I sat and looked peacefully out of the window. After ten minutes or so, she woke. "Oh, God, Rose. Why did you let me do that? It's dreadful. I do it all over the place. I'm terrified I'll fall asleep in a meeting."

"As long as you're not speaking, no one will notice."

"Beast."

We laughed comfortably. She poked at her bag, *her* book bag. "Apart from the pleasure of seeing you, I want to use you. One of my reviewers has become temperamental so I sacked him yesterday, which leaves me without my round-up of travel books for the summer." Vee's eyes opened wide. "Knowing your *histoire,* knowing you had plenty of time, I thought of you. You haven't been gagged by the heavies? It's not full-time employment. I'll pay top whack . . . The thing is, you have only two days." She swallowed. "And one of the books is . . ."

I said it for her. "By Hal."

"Yup."

Tears suddenly rained down my cheeks, an unstoppable release of emotion, and I was helpless. Vee leaped up and dabbed at my face with a tissue. *"Stupid."*

My long-term habits are, so to speak, ingrained in my blood and bone and I have to dig deep to break them. *A Thousand Olive Trees* wasted an hour or two of valuable time lying on the kitchen table before I stretched out my hand and, for a second time, picked it up.

It described the journey he had made on foot through Italy. "A journey," he wrote in the preface, "marked by a succession of painful blisters, a common affliction, which has more effect on history and war than might be supposed."

He began in the Veneto and picked his way south, along an ancient route taken by the merchants. "Those who embark on these old paths are normally looking for secular rewards, the benefit of exercise, the charm of unfamiliar surroundings, a sense of achievement—but are often taken by surprise when they experience a feeling that might be called spiritual."

Hal's language was as unfamiliar to me as Nathan's had become and, if I was not mistaken, he was less golden-tongued, and that made me smile. But I could picture his walk, an impatient quick-march that used to leave me gasping. I, too, hefted my rucksack and placed my feet in his footprints and slithered down the stony scree, up the winding path into the hills, through a maquis of wild herbs, so bruised in passing that their aroma scented the hot air.

Blisters forced him to a halt in the village of Santa Maria, which fitted into a curve of the hillside among the olive groves in Umbria. And there he had discovered an olive farm that required an owner. The second half of the book was his account of buying it and settling down to learning about olive-tree cultivation.

I wrote the review, paying *A Thousand Olive Trees* no more and no less attention than I gave to the others in the round-up. I said that it was a book for dreamers.

Chapter 16

I sent in the review by e-mail, and sat back in my chair, hands clasped behind my head.

Definitely there was a plus to having done some work. A step forward: and I was the better for having given my brain a workout. In the peace and silence of my study, being on my own did not seem to be quite so drastic a fate. I was even beginning to suspect that it had one or two compensations. Had we ever confessed, Vee, Mazarine and I, how exhausting marriage could be? Good management in a marriage was not merely a question of being one step ahead of one's spouse, but two. And it had been Nathan who taught me that good, competent management is the key to comfort and efficiency, which, if as a principle it lacked poetry, had the merit of being honest.

Did he feel, on his side, I wondered, that he had had to manage me as well as himself? What we had not managed was familiarity. I saw that now. Mark Twain had been right after all. Familiarity is edged with the danger of tedium.

Sun flooded the landing, and I felt the house settle around me, my warm, companionable, familiar setting. The carpet under the window had been stained by damp and the sash window— probably—required replacing. Idly I added it to the list of the must-do and, as idly, flicked into my e-mail in box. There was one. It was headed SURPRISE, SURPRISE.

Darling Mum. This is the biggest surprise.

Rashly, it crossed my mind that our nagging had paid off and Poppy had done well in her finals.

We are on Koi Sumui. It is the best. I have never been anywhere so lovely. It's so unspoiled. You would love it. I love the East. So cool, so into different things. But, hold your breath. Richard and I have got married. On the beach, and it was beautiful. It was quite wild and I am so happy. Please tell Dad. I will ring you. I love you. Poppy. PS I got a 2:2.

I picked up my bag and ran out to the car.

"My dad," Poppy was also overheard confiding to her friend Emily at the ninth birthday party, "loves me the best."

On more than one occasion, I explained to Poppy that this was not the case. Both of us loved both her and Sam equally. But Poppy, who was never in the least bit interested in the level playing field, merely giggled naughtily and held up her arms to be cuddled. Clever, instinctive Poppy knew that the conspiracy to present life as fair and equal was just that.

Outside Minty's flat, I held my finger on the bell. The door jerked open to reveal Minty, with a half made-up face, wearing a satin teddy underneath a white toweling dressing-gown. "What on earth—?" She frowned. "Rose, have you gone mad?"

"I'd like to speak to Nathan."

She hesitated. "I'll see if he's free."

"Just get him. On second thoughts." I elbowed Minty aside and stepped into a diminutive hall, made even less negotiable by two large suitcases, which I recognized as Nathan's, propped against the wall. "Nathan?"

There was the sound of running water from the bathroom, which stopped, and Nathan emerged, also wearing a snowy white toweling dressing gown. Its unfamiliarity brought me up short.

"Rose, what's the matter?" He looked alarmed. "Is it Ianthe?"

"No, not life and death but a bit of a shock. Nathan, Poppy has just e-mailed to say she and Richard have got married." I paused. "She sounded happy."

"You're joking," Nathan said quietly.

"Good grief," said Minty.

He led the way into a tiny sitting room, cluttered with newspapers, books and unwashed coffee mugs. An overlarge sofa and one chair made it even more cramped. Nathan dropped down on the sofa and put his head in hands. He was shaking. "I don't know what to say except that I'll kill him."

I sat down beside him. "She's only a baby, whatever she thinks."

"So were you," Minty pointed out.

"But that was different." Nathan addressed me, not Minty.

"No, it isn't." Minty regarded the pair of us sourly. "For God's sake, Poppy's twenty-two."

We ignored her. Nathan sought my hand. "Did you have any idea? Did we miss something?"

"How could we possibly have known? Poppy never gave a hint."

Nathan grasped at a straw. "Wait a minute. It might have been one of those potty ceremonies that aren't legal."

Minty tied the belt of her dressing gown tight around her slender waist and looked superior. "Nathan, Poppy is an adult, and free to make her own choices. The fact that she did not involve you is sad, but not the end of the world." She had succeeded in capturing his attention. "Does it occur to you that Poppy went off precisely because she did not wish you to interfere?"

"I bet that man pushed her into it." Nathan shaded his eyes with his hand.

Minty raised her eyes to the ceiling. "Don't be so Victorian. Poppy wasn't pushed into it, she made the choice for herself. You can't start huffing and puffing and indulging in conspiracy theories because you don't happen to like what's she's done."

In one sense Minty was correct. But in another she was quite wrong and she did not—could not—understand. "You don't have children," I told her.

There was silence in the slightly frowsty room.

Nathan and Minty exchanged a look. Minty stacked a couple of the books that littered the low glass coffee table on top of one another. "Having children doesn't make you Mastermind, Rose. I *am* closer in age to Poppy." She slapped another book on to the pile. "Having children doesn't put you into a superior category of the human race. You don't have a monopoly on experience and judgment. We lesser mortals have one or two things to say that matter, too."

"Minty," Nathan said warningly, "I think—"

"It's fine, Nathan." Minty had reminded me of what I had—those long, interesting, love-filled years that nothing and no one would ever take away.

Minty scuffed the carpet with her foot. "Sorry."

Nathan blew his nose. "I don't even know Richard's surname."

"You do. It's Lockhead," I said.

Nathan stood up and went over to the ungenerous window that overlooked the terrace opposite, which had been built in depressing red brick. He seemed far too big for the room's meager proportions. "What do we do?"

Minty said impatiently, "For a start, I'll finish dressing—and so should you, Nathan. Otherwise we'll be late."

The bedroom door banged and Nathan turned to me. "Don't go quite yet."

When Minty reappeared in a leather skirt and a stretch purple top, beneath which her nipples were outlined, we were still deep in discussion. Nathan was all for flying out to Thailand and dragging Poppy home. He had also been honest enough to say, "How could she have done this to us?"

Hand on hip, Minty listened. "I can't believe I'm hearing this rubbish. Could I point out that Poppy is now a married woman? You'd make yourself look ridiculous by scurrying out there."

I sneaked a look at Nathan. His reaction had been more subdued than I had envisaged, and that was worrying. He was hurt, bitterly so, at Poppy's cruelty in leaving us out of such a momentous event.

Minty ploughed on. (She did not know of the filing cabinet in Nathan's study that contained notional budgets for the wedding he had planned to give Poppy.) "Shouldn't you be relieved that Poppy's safe, well, happy? She hasn't developed leprosy or anything." She pursed her lips. "After all, Nathan, you sprang your surprises, why shouldn't Poppy? She probably felt she was paying you back."

This angered Nathan sufficiently to snap him out of his distress. Icily cold, he said, "Okay. You've made your point."

I jumped up and grabbed my bag. "I'm going. If you want to discuss Poppy you know where to find me."

"Rose, let's talk this over tomorrow when I'll have thought it over." Nathan swung his attention back to me. Funnily enough, he was much more in control when he was angry than when he was sad, which, I think, was why he allowed himself to be angry over quite a few things, and, if you did not know him, subtracted from his sweetness at other times. It was a fascinating, wayward combination and I was used to it. Minty was not. She turned on her heel and left the room. The bathroom door banged.

I sat in the car for five or ten minutes, endeavoring to pull my thoughts together. How very like Poppy it would be to pay back Nathan and me in our own coin. Or had she been so shaken by our break-up that she had fled elsewhere for security? Oh, God, without realizing what she was doing.

I inserted the key in the ignition and the door to Minty's flat opened. Nathan and Minty walked rapidly toward his car, talking hard. Minty was clutching a short magenta jacket over her leather skirt, and she was scowling. In a dark suit and blue silk tie, Nathan looked thunderous. He got into the driver's seat, slammed the door and did not wait for Minty to get in before he started the engine.

Frantic e-mails went to and from Thailand. "Why the fuss?" wrote Poppy. "Why aren't you happy for me? What's Dad playing at? We're going to honeymoon up-country and plan to come back at the end of July. Out of touch till then."

With that, we had to be content.

Ianthe's stay in hospital had involved waiting in virtually every department but, as a grand mistress of the art, she coped with her usual grace. When I went to fetch her, she was ensconced in a sitting area at the end of the ward, watching the fish in the tank, which had been chosen for their ability to look dispirited. On the table were piled ancient, dismembered magazines. Nurses squeaked over the linoleum in rubber-soled shoes and a telephone rang incessantly in the background.

"There you are, Rose."

I sat down beside her and we discussed how she was feeling. Then I said, "Mum, I'd better tell you. We've heard from Poppy."

"Dear little thing. How is she?"

"The dear little thing has gone and got married on a Thai beach. To Richard Lockhead."

"Oh." Ianthe fiddled with the pearl button on her cuff. "How disappointing. None of us was there." She fiddled some more. "Does this mean . . . she's pregnant?"

"Not as far as I know. Anyway, I don't think Poppy's generation get married because they're pregnant." I picked up Ianthe's suitcase. "It's been a bit of a shock," I said fiercely, "but I'm determined to look on it as exciting. We'll have to give a party for them when they come home. When has the doctor asked to see you again?"

"In a couple of weeks when the final tests come through. Let's not think about *that*."

She seemed so determined not to talk about it that I did not question her further. We drove back to Pankhurst Parade through a city that was emptying of traffic for the summer. From time to time, I glanced at her. Her color seemed good and the lipstick was as bright as ever, and I felt nothing but pride for my brave mother who had taught herself to grapple with loneliness and little money.

Poppy's news stirred up Ianthe's memories. "When your father proposed he took me up the beck to the trout pool. The daffodils and catkins were out and it was so pretty and peaceful, but all I could think about was that my hair was frizzing in the damp. It was drizzling a bit. I hadn't had time to change my blouse and I was worried that I smelled . . . well . . . sweaty because I'd had to run for the bus." She smiled. "He looked so sweet and earnest in his tweed jacket and there I was in a state because I didn't think I looked my best, and I wanted the moment to be perfect."

"You were perfect at the wedding," I reminded her. "You looked lovely in the photograph."

"It rained then, too, would you believe?"

"I wish he'd lived longer," I cried. "I wish you hadn't had to suffer."

"There's nothing special about suffering, Rose. It's as common as hair growing. We just have to deal with it, and get on."

Number fourteen was like a hothouse and I went round opening windows while Ianthe made tea. "One of the nurses would insist on calling it 'Mr Comforter.' I ask you."

Afterward, I helped her to unpack. I had not been in Ianthe's bedroom for a long time. A photograph of the three of us, taken outside Medlars Cottage when I was eight, was displayed prominently on the bedside table. A pot of Nivea face cream and a bottle of natural-colored nail polish stood on the dressing table beside her silver-backed brush, so old that many of the bristles were missing. The wardrobe contained six pairs of neatly stowed shoes, her herringbone winter coat and dresses bagged up on hangers. Ianthe watched me inspecting them. "As you grow older, Rose, you need fewer clothes."

"How depressing."

I opened a drawer to put away her clean nightdress and was choked by a familiar smell. "The lavender. It's so strong."

"That reminds me . . ." Ianthe searched on the shelf in the wardrobe. "I bought a couple of bags for you at the fête."

Wordlessly, I held them in my hands, assaulted by the charged, never-to-be forgotten nostalgia of lavender.

Vee had not finished with me. The invitation to the summer gala dinner to celebrate the year's best books arrived in the post. For years I had hosted a table—the guests and seating had occupied much time and debate. Scrawled on the back of Vee's invitation was: "*I* have a table. *You* are on it."

I propped it up on the desk in my study. This was a novel situation for me, and I felt an eddy of excitement and nerves in the pit of my stomach, even of curiosity to see what would happen and how I would react. Admittedly, during the past weeks, I had not thought much about my business world and it had grown distant. On cue, the phone rang.

"No ifs and buts," said Vee. "I know it's last-minute but you're under orders to show up. And, Rose, treat yourself to the hairdresser."

I was proud of myself as I got ready. Without a moment's hesitation I pulled the black sleeveless dress out of the wardrobe and selected the outrageously stylish shoes I had bought in Paris. I applied foundation, brushed on gray eye shadow, drew a scarlet line around my lips and filled it in.

"There," I addressed the resulting construct in the mirror,

"not bad." I placed a hand on my stomach, which felt delightfully flat. My lips gleamed, my dress flowed over my hips and my feet arched in the high heels. To complete the vision, I emptied the contents of my handbag on to the bed, threw away crumpled tissues, picked out the fluff from my hairbrush and put it with my lipstick and keys into a witty bag in the shape of a flowerpot.

When I arrived at the hotel, a stream of men and women, dressed predominantly in black, flowed toward the room where the drinks were being served. A strange girl poked at my bag. "Safe," she said.

Someone else said, "Hi, Rose. Long time . . . let's keep in touch . . ." and drifted past.

Wearing a pair of large, flashy earrings, Vee materialized out of the mass and waved me over. "You look fabulous. Not even a hint of the wronged wife. Introductions," she cried. "This is Rose."

I was introduced to a distinguished theater critic, who had written a book on Whither the Theater?, currently receiving a lot of attention, a man dressed from head to toe in leather and a cross-looking female novelist in a full skirt, a wide belt and a waterfall of necklaces. The theater critic turned his attention to Leather Man and I was left to struggle with the novelist, who wrote under the name of Angelica Browne.

"You've just published a new novel, I gather?"

Her crossness intensified. "It's doing well and I'm rather proud of it except . . . I've had some nasty reviews. Critics, you know."

"I do know about critics."

Anxious as writers always were, she pressed on. "I was writing about a design fault in nature. Young females are flooded with estrogen and oxytocin, hormones that make them broody.

Young men are flooded with testosterone, which tugs them in a different direction. In middle age, when male testosterone levels begin to fall, females lose their estrogen and start producing testosterone and off they go, just as the men are happy to play golf and win prizes for their lawns. Fictionally speaking, it's the stuff of tragedy."

"I suppose it is. Do male and female ever balance?"

She shrugged impatiently. "That's the point."

"Angelica," Vee shepherded us into a huge dining room, which had revolving glass balls in the ceiling, "gender is dated. Gender is out. We don't think about it any more."

I found myself seated between the theater critic, whose name was Lawrence, and Leather Man, a printer from Essex, who leaned over and unfolded my napkin. "Let's get stuck into the wine," he said hopefully.

I was getting along famously with Lawrence, who was in fine, spitting form, until I made the mistake of looking across our table to the next. Nathan was sitting there with his back to me. A seat away from him was Minty, whose profile I could observe—if I cared to. Their table was made up of senior exec-utives, including Timon, from the Vistemax Group, with their wives—including the Good Wife, Carolyne Shaker—and a cou-ple of big authors and their companions. Among them, Minty stood out like a sore thumb. She had chosen a dress in a dull green that was too low-cut and did not flatter her. Her contri-bution to the conversation appeared minimal.

Vee made desperate faces at me across our table. *Sorry, sorry.*

Ridiculously, it was Nathan's obliviousness to my presence that upset me most. It brought back the terror that I was dissolv-ing, becoming invisible, melting into the walls and carpet. It re-opened the question: who was Rose?

I concentrated on summoning the figure in the mirror in

Paris—the interesting, exquisitely dressed one who had something to say, who had managed motherhood, a career, a home,
who had loved her husband, her children, food, wine, the sea . . .
her garden. Little by little, the panic dissolved and I could
breathe more easily. I looked down and discovered that I had
shredded the roll on my sideplate into pellets and arranged them
into a pattern, the smaller ones in the middle, the larger ones in a
circle round the edge of the plate.

Under the cover of listening to Lawrence's diatribe on the
modern theater—too expensive, no sense of adventure,
mediocre—I studied Nathan. He seemed different. Looser and
less contained. Less poured into a mold that had settled around
him after he had been promoted to deputy editor. A colleague
passed by the table, greeted him, and Nathan replied—easy and
charming amid the clutter of candles and glasses. Smiling
through the ease and affluence.

My breath quickened: leaving me had made him look
like that.

Minty fumbled in her handbag and applied another layer of
lipstick; her mouth was like a scarlet gash below the slanting
eyes. Carolyne lifted her glass to her lips and sent me a nod of
solidarity. The beef arrived, too spicy and fussy. I left most of it.

"Not hungry?" inquired Leather Man. With relief, I turned
to talk to him.

I did not register much about the speeches. The lights
dimmed, the globes flashed and, no doubt, the winners were
modest. Eventually, the audience clapped for the final time and
the evening began to break up. A hand descended on my shoulder. "Hallo, Rose, I've been searching for you," said Monty
Chavet. "You look like a gorgeous flower. Can I put you in my
vase?"

He propelled me through the crush and tapped a male back,

whose owner swung round. "Hallo, Monty," said Timon, all af-
fability until he saw me.

"Look here, Timon," Monty was at his loudest, which was
pretty loud and I was touched by his chivalry, "you've made a
mistake getting rid of this girl. She was the best in town. You
should think again."

Timon did not miss a beat. "Rose did a brilliant job, didn't
she? I'm glad you think as highly of her as we do." He draped
his arm across Monty's shoulders. "A little bird tells me you
have a book coming out in the autumn. You must be sure that
we have a look at it. Send it to me."

The battle taking place in Monty's breast was probably a sin-
cere, well-fought one, but doomed. "Sure." He gave a tiny shrug
and I smiled at him to show there were no hard feelings.

Timon drew him away. "There's someone I want you to
meet."

There was a polite touch on my elbow. "Hallo," said Neil
Skinner, the junior minister. "I thought there was a chance you
might be here." He looked marginally less fraught than when I
had met him in February. "The whisper is that I might gets arts
in the next reshuffle, so I wangled an invite here." He eyed me
up approvingly, which was infinitely cheering.

"I thought about our conversation a lot after Flora Madder
killed herself," I told him.

Neil frowned. "Yes, that was awful. Of course, it was a well-
known secret that she was a manic depressive and had been
threatening suicide for years. Charles had been trying to keep
the show on the road, terrified that she'd kill herself, but it was
only a matter of time."

"I'm sorry." I thought this over. How stupid I'd been to forget that the press only deals with the appearance of something.
"Even so, the papers must bear some responsibility."

Again, he touched my arm. "You're still in the nasty trade?"

"I was sacked, but I'll be looking for another job."

"Keep in touch, won't you?" It was with pleasure that I said I would.

On the way to collect my coat, I spotted Minty. She was attempting to negotiate the stairs up to the cloakroom in her tight dress and awkward heels and, at the same time, to hold a conversation with Peter Shaker. She moved stiffly and I knew she was not enjoying herself.

At the top of the stairs, she turned. Her eyes widened and I caught . . . what was it? A hint of panic and . . . fury. Whatever Minty had promised herself had not materialized.

The moment passed, and she shook herself back into the recognizable Minty. She leaned toward Peter, touched his arm and he redoubled his attention. Bitterness rose sharp and acid in me, and I struggled with it. It was not so much that life had proved itself unfair—it was not as simple as that. Life *was* unfair and a quicksand. It was more that Nathan's departure had taught me I had not come to terms with that, and my mastery of myself was not complete.

"Rose." The drawl was familiar, yet not. I swung round. "Rose. It is Rose, isn't it?"

Chapter 17

"Hal!"

"It *is* Rose. I wasn't sure."

His hair was longer than in the photograph, and better brushed, but ruined by sun. I don't think either, in the three years I knew him that I had ever seen Hal in a wing collar and a dinner jacket. He looked like a prosperous film producer.

The departing guests flowed around us like the Red Sea. I stood face to face with the person I had once loved more than anything on this earth and time performed one of its somersaults. I was transported back to the hot, airless hotel bedroom in Quetzl where, famished for every scrap of him, I lay on the bed and told him that I had chosen to live a different sort of life from his.

"What are you doing here?" I asked.

It was a silly question. Just as fazed as I, Hal replied, "I'm here as an author."

I recovered my wits. "Of course, and your books are very successful."

There was an awkward silence as we considered where, conversationally speaking, to venture next.

Typically, Hal took charge. "Have you got a minute? I think we need a drink." Without waiting for an answer, he tucked a hand under my elbow and we retraced our steps to the dining room where he cajoled two glasses of brandy from a surly waiter who wanted to go home.

The old confidence was still there, the quick, decided gestures, the impatience and the charm. He handed me a glass. "I read your review of *A Thousand Olive Trees.* Thank you."

We sat down at an empty table. The waiters moved tiredly from one to another, whisking away the debris of wineglasses, crumpled napkins, half-eaten rolls and ice buckets filled with melting ice.

Hal smiled at me. "I'm not sure where we pick up, if that's the right word."

"Probably 'begin' is better."

"Yup, 'begin,'" he agreed. "It was a long time ago." He peered at me. "You don't *look* so different."

"Neither do you." That was not quite true: close up, he was older and there was a scar on his chin that was new to me. I said, as calmly as I could, "I know you've been doing well. One of the most famous travel writers of your generation."

"So they tell me."

He looked well, lean, fit and as if he was enjoying his life. Had he been spoiled? I could not tell but I was amused by my speculation, which was far more interesting than whether his beauty still made me dizzy. When I first met Hal the question of his moral texture was the last thing that interested me. Twenty-five years is such a drop of time—a snap of the fingers—but it is

quite sufficient to have moved from one state to quite another
and I wanted to know which.

He shrugged. "I had a hunch I might bump into you." His
drawl was less marked than I remembered. "No, that's not true. I
asked the publicist if you might be here."

"Are you on a publicity tour?"

He looked at me for a long time. "I settled in the UK," he
said, "after I got married. Amanda put up with me as best she
could, then she pushed me out but I stayed here. I'd gotten used
to being on an island." He tapped his nose. "If I'm honest, it's
nicer being a big fish in a small pond than vice versa. But, yes, I
got what I wanted. I made a life that suited me. And you?"

The brandy glass felt cool in my hot hands. I chose equally
cool and, I hoped, neutral words. "I'm between jobs."

"And?"

There seemed no point in prevaricating. "I'm afraid my husband and I have recently split up. He decided to live with someone else. I'm just getting used to the situation, then I'll think
again."

Hal looked down at the contents of his brandy glass. "Was it
worth it?"

This was an unfair question but it was wise to get it over and
done with. "Yes. Yes, it was."

"So be it," he said.

I steered the conversation onto safer ground. "Where have
you been lately?"

"Supervising the digging of wells in Namibia. There's an
acute water shortage and no funds." He fingered his glass.
"Next, though, is a return to the Yanomami territories. Remember them?"

I stiffened. "Of course."

He leaned forward until our faces almost touched. "One

thing I've always wanted to know. Did you have children in the end, Rose?"

"Two. A son and a daughter. Did you?"

"No, and I can't make up my mind if that's a relief or not."

There was a thoughtful silence and I thought of many possible replies. Again, I chose the most neutral. "You had other things to do, Hal." I began to feel more comfortable with this encounter, and very curious. "Tell me about the olive farm in Italy."

He relaxed in the chair. "At the moment the house is a tip, but the country is beautiful. The trees need a bit of attention, which I'm hoping to give them." He drank some brandy. "Second question. Did that olive cutting ever take?"

"It did. It's in my garden."

We caught each other's eye, and shades of the young Hal and the young me rose between us, impudently demanding readmission. A waiter edged past the table with an armful of tablecloths and I concentrated on that. "Seems odd making small talk with you," I said eventually.

"Okay. Let's move it on. I often wonder . . ."

"Don't." I looked down at my ringless left hand.

Hal followed my train of thought. "You mustn't fret." He spoke in the sweet, disarming way that I had known so well. "I don't. Not a good idea."

This was so Hal, and I laughed. "I knew *you* wouldn't fret. I knew you would be glad, and you were. You were perfectly free to do as you wished."

"Yes and no." He placed his hand on my bare arm and the flesh pricked under his fingers. "I'm not saying I didn't mind, Rose, because I did. But you taught me that you have to move on. You grow out of situations. They don't suit any longer. It happens. Of course I don't know the circumstances but you mustn't castigate yourself." He assessed the remains of the brandy in the glass. "If you can manage it, it's best to see it as an opportunity."

Hal was making it easy and I began to feel ridiculously light-hearted. "You haven't changed a bit. My husband has run off with a *younger* woman and it's opportunity knocking?" I put my glass on the table and noted that it was almost empty. "That's the kind of comment one makes years afterward, when it's all dead and past. But Mazarine—do you remember her?—would agree with you."

"So, you think it's too calculating to view it in that way?"

"Sort of."

"But you made a cold calculation when you left me." He spoke evenly and without malice.

"Not cold, Hal." I looked up at him. "It seemed for the best of reasons at the time."

He rolled the stem of the glass between his fingers. "I'm sorry you've had a bad time." He smiled gently. "Would your husband's leaving have been less awful for you if the woman had been older rather than younger?"

"God knows. Possibly. It's useful having a hate figure, and if she'd been a nice hard-done-by widow, it's possible I might have felt differently." I brushed down the black dress over my knees. "Now the first shock is over I keep thinking about silly things, like how are we going to divide the china and who will take the gumboots? We have an archive of gumboots." I knew perfectly well I was veering from the point. "Actually, the woman, Minty, was my assistant and a friend, and while she was at it she took my job."

He raised an eyebrow. "Go on. We're making interesting small talk."

I took the last sustaining mouthful of brandy. "First I lost

Nathan. That was bad enough. Then it was as if a wand had been waved and I was invisible. From having a settled position, as a wife and all that that meant, I was suddenly the blurred figure in the background of a painting or photograph. You know, one of the nameless ones left behind to sweep up the manure after Napoleon's cavalcade has swept through. The ones who are asked to wait until last to climb on to the life raft. I don't mind being a nameless one—probably very good for the soul—but it was a shock." Emptied of my brandy words, I peered at him. "Hal, am I talking sense? No, I don't think I am, but never mind."

The door to the dining room opened.

"Hal," interrupted a voice, "*there* you are. I've been looking for you."

A publicist I vaguely recognized had stuck her head round the door. "I've got Jayson Verey from Carlton who wants to see you. Can you come?"

The room had grown chilly and, emptied of its glitter, depressing. I hugged my flowerpot handbag. The publicist looked uncertainly between Hal and me. "It's Rose, isn't it?" Her forehead puckered. "I'm sure we've met."

"We have," I said. "You came to a Christmas party last year that I gave at the paper."

"Did I?" Her face cleared. "Oh, of *course*."

Hal got up, kissed my cheek and followed the girl out of the dining room. "I'll see you," he said.

If I was asked to describe my mother I would reply that Ianthe was the kind of person who held vivid pictures in her mind that were no less sharp as she grew older. Young bride, happy wife and mother, the widow whose perpetual grief ratified the above. *Your dad was everything. I don't want to spoil it. I don't want anyone else, Rose.*

At first, I agreed with her position: no one could possibly have occupied my father's chair and I loved to hear that he was irreplaceable and unique. It was only later, when my eye had become beadier, that I saw through it without understanding precisely what hampered my mother. Given Ianthe's innate sympathy and skillful handling of men, her domestic genius and the constant terror of not making the pounds stretch, it was a deliberate waste. And why did she send us into exile down south?

"I thought it would be easier near the big city," she told me. *For you,* she meant, the mother pelican plucking the feathers from her own breast to cushion her young. At the time, she was in the kitchen at Pankhurst Parade, mixing dough for scones. "Any road, home is where you make it." She flipped the scones onto the griddle. The kitchen was instantly flooded with a delectable smell. When they were cooked, she cut them in two, buttered them and slid the blue and white plate over to me.

But for Ianthe, home was not down south. Home was where the drystone walls fanning up the dales resembled fish skeletons, and trees grew so close to the beck that their branches bent over and ruffled the water. When it rained, their bark turned black.

Ianthe could make scones or a steak and kidney pudding in her sleep. Her life of domesticity was as natural as breathing. At Medlars Cottage, she had coaxed vegetables and herbs out of the kitchen garden. The potatoes and carrots bore spots and blemishes, while the peas were tiny and tasted of sugar and earth. In the kitchen, she wore an apron that enveloped her tweed skirts and pastel-colored jumpers and was tied in a bow at the back. At the sound of my father's step in the evening, she whisked it off and ran her hand through her hair. In those days, it was short and permed into a halo.

After my father's death, the log pile diminished, the gutters clogged with leaves, the garden disintegrated and my hands sprouted chilblains. When I spread my fingers, the skin cracked open. More than once, I discovered Ianthe crying over her potatoes, which had developed blight, or the too-fatty scrag end of lamb that Jo at the butcher's had sold her, thinking he could put one over on the widow. He would not have done that when she was a wife. Yet Ianthe accepted these rapidly accumulating limitations, and emulated the images she carried in her mind. Widowhood was pain. It was sacrifice and loss.

During this time, her perm grew out, leaving her hair lank and unlovely with grief and depletion. Settled in Pankhurst Parade, where there was no money to spare for a hairdresser, she gave up cutting it and put it up, which suited her better.

She knew what was what and defended her right to tackle the world with her set of rules. "That woman needs a good smack," she declared darkly, after listening to a production of Ibsen's *A Doll's House* on the radio. "He won't ever settle," she said of Hal, her mouth set in a way that infuriated me. "Men like him don't."

We had quite an argument about it. From her standpoint, Ianthe waxed wrathful and terrible. But it was no use. I was deeply in love, wild with passion and the excitement of the venture into a new world, Hal's world.

And during that third year at Oxford, my energy ran hot and strong and I worked myself into a stupor. "How nice to welcome her back," wrote my tutor. "We thought she had strayed onto other paths." In the spring before finals, I attended interviews for jobs. One was for a junior position in a press association where I was invited to discuss the changing nature of news. I argued that as hard news was now conveyed by radio and television, the papers should mop up other areas of interest. "It's the age of the feature," I concluded, which seemed to go down well as I was offered a job—possibly because no one else would have been foolish enough to accept the meager salary.

Of course Ianthe disapproved. She wanted me to opt for a steadier profession, like teaching. She did not trust or understand the media. At that period, she was the thorn in my flesh that pricked and jabbed, but I paid it no attention.

I got my first.

"Right," said Hal, after the all-night celebration party. "We're going on the Big One. The real expedition." He was feeding me with a hangover cure, teaspoon by teaspoon. Even though my head ached, my stomach heaved and a drum beat the retreat in my head, I watched his every movement with aching love. Above me, there was a blaze of candles, and angels swooped on feathery wings.

The teaspoon was inserted between my lips and I bit it. "Where precisely?"

Hal whipped away the teaspoon and kissed me. "Wait and see." He licked my chin and kissed me again, and we shared the hangover remedy in a very efficient way.

I was thinking about that time, when Nathan rang and asked to meet.

It was a hot, heavy day. I walked across the park to St. Benedicta's and parked myself in front of the Madonna dedicated to victims of violence. Did you overlook me? I interrogated her silently. I know you're busy and death is epidemic but I'm selfish enough to wish you hadn't.

I lit my usual candle and thought about it. But it's fine, I re-assured the wide, painted eyes. I have taken the point. With all the horrors you have to deal with I quite understand that the troubles of one no-longer-*quite*-so-young woman do not matter very much. I can cope.

I took the bus up to Mayfair and met Nathan in a bar just off Berkeley Square. It was an area where shops sold either ex-pensive briefcases and credit-card holders or newspapers in vari-ous languages, but nothing in between.

Nathan was late and arrived with his executive expression pinned into place. He stacked his briefcase under the stool. "Sorry. Budget meetings."

"How's it all going?"

"Fair to middling. The Sunday paper is still in a bit of a dip."

"Are you doing any promotions?"

"Well, that's just . . ." He looked at me sharply. "We didn't come here to discuss the paper."

"No."

"I saw you at the dinner."

"Did you? I didn't think you had." I added, with only the faintest tremor in my voice, "You seemed to be enjoying your-self."

"Did I?" he replied. "Automatic pilot." A second or two elapsed. Nathan blew at the foam on his coffee. It spattered the counter. "Who was the man you were talking to?"

I mopped the counter with a paper napkin. "Lawrence Thurber, the theater critic." I considered my next sentence. "Or do you mean Hal Thorne, who I bumped into afterward?"

Nathan became fixated by a lorry backing up the road. "Hal Thorne." He sighed. "Well, as you said, that was a long time ago." He kept his eye trained on the lorry. "I've been thinking . . ." Another great pause. "Now that I've had a chance to think things over, I can see that I overreacted . . . to him."

This was Nathan at his most disingenuous and I began to tremble. So much time had been wasted on the subject. For nothing. "Oh, Nathan. Do you know what you did? Introducing a great black specter?" My nail dug into my thumb. "Now do you believe me that, very early on, Hal disappeared? He went because I was happy." I peered at him. "With you, Nathan."

He winced. "I could never quite rid myself of the suspicion that your point of reference was not me but him." He stirred his coffee and pushed it away. "That's not true. It was fine to begin with but when you started working I felt you were telling me that you weren't happy."

"Nathan, all I wanted was to use my mind. That was not a criticism of you."

"It was natural, I suppose." He sighed. "Then I began thinking about my own life, and later . . ."

"Later what?"

"I met Minty."

"And she came with no baggage?"

He shrugged. "But why did you talk about him?"

"I didn't."

"You told Minty about him. She told me. That set me off again. Started it all up."

I said furiously, "It didn't occur to you that Minty made a point of telling you? That she meant you to get the wrong idea?"

"No need to lose your temper."

The coffee machine hissed and gushed. Customers drifted in and out of the bar. I dropped my head into my hands. From a minor reference, a light exchange of confidence, something much bigger had—apparently—grown. "Nathan, everyone comes with something from the past."

I raised my head. Nathan was staring at me. Slowly he put out a hand and touched my shoulder, his hand just grazing my breast. It was an old gesture that I loved. "Did he do that to you?"

I turned my face away.

"Rose." Nathan withdrew into his formal office manner. "I'm sorry about the Hal problem. I think it was because I'm so bad at discussing these sort of things, and he seemed convenient and easy to latch on to. I used the idea of him."

I closed my eyes. "How could you?"

"We all do stupid things. Even you, Rose." He reached for his briefcase and produced a sheaf of papers. "I've made some lists . . . about things and how we should divide them. Take them away and see if you agree. I'm open to negotiation. We also have to talk about the house." He pushed the papers over to me. I glanced down but left them on the counter.

I should be saying, *Please, let's think again. Let's try.* In accepting the lists I was accepting that Nathan and I were finished.

"Please look at them," he said coldly.

The balance had altered. Something had been smashed out of existence, and I could not put it back together again. And, yes, I had done a stupid thing. I had not noticed that Nathan and I were drifting. We had been at the stage of taking each other for granted yet we had not reached the stage when we were strong enough that it was no longer dangerous. Our keener edges had blunted, and I had stopped searching to keep us in balance . . . or, rather, I had not made allowances for Nathan changing and, thus, trapped him and denied him air.

I put out my hand and picked up the lists. Chairs and the sofa to him. Mirrors and the blue chair to me. "I'm not sure," I said. "I'll see." I looked up at Nathan. "I'm not ready yet."

He shifted on the stool. "You must take your time, of course."

"Thank you." This small courtesy was comforting, a tiny straw at which to grasp, and I glimpsed a time in the future when it might be possible to face each other peacefully.

Then I spoiled it. The state of Nathan's shirt had been puzzling me—it was not properly ironed. I leaned over and fingered the crumpled collar. "Don't you have an iron at Minty's flat?"

Nathan pulled irritably at it. "Minty is not one of nature's ironers. It was her turn . . . and I tried to show her . . . you know, about shirts."

"Did you? And what did Minty say?"

Nathan seemed baffled. "When I explained that the trick is to iron from the yoke outwards, she threw it back at me."

"Well I never. The free spirit."

He jerked the lock of his briefcase shut. "One minute women are saying one thing, then they're demanding the opposite. They want to be noticed, they demand homage. Then we provide it, and find ourselves accused of rape or of some fearful transgression against their rights. They say they want us to be free, and they want to be free, and, saps that we are, we believe them."

"Oh dear," I said. "It didn't take long."

Angry and hostile, we slid down from our precarious perches on the stools and went our separate ways.

Chapter 18

I knew Nathan would deny it. I knew he would fight against a feeling he would consider wrong and beneath him but, looking back, my job introduced an irritant into our marriage. It was to do with timing, for later on Nathan was fine about it.

I think he felt we had lost an innocence, that an illusion had changed.

Six months after I began work as the assistant in the books department, Sam fell ill. It began with a high fever. "It's just a bug," I assured Nancy, the bright New Zealander who helped out in the afternoons and whom I had had to bribe to stay for the whole day. I grabbed my book bag and headed out of the front door.

On the third day, Sam began to vomit and his temperature was still worryingly high. Nancy rang in at eight o'clock to say she was sorry but she could not miss any more of her college course. I cornered Nathan in his study. Could he take time off? I asked. Being new to my job I did not like to risk cutting corners. Nathan dropped a pile of envelopes into a basket marked BILLS and looked thoughtful. "Not really," he replied, and I had the impression that he had been waiting for a moment such as this. "I can't take a day off at such short notice."

I squared up to him. "Please." If Nathan was in the slightest danger of saying, "I told you so," I knew I would lose my temper.

"I told you so," said Nathan, but in such a way that my anger was stillborn. This was a serious disagreement.

There was an icy silence. "I don't believe you said that."

He had the grace to look uncomfortable. "Sorry. But you know what I feel about you working. This is *exactly* what I predicted would happen. I asked you to wait until the children were older." He turned his back and stapled a couple of documents together. "Do you realize how fortunate you are, Rose, in not having to work?"

"I'll overlook the moral blackmail, Nathan. What's happened to 'I help you, you help me'? Where's that gone?"

"I don't know," he replied.

I grasped the nettle. "You helped me get the job."

"You were set on it."

"Fine," I said. "I'll remember that next time you need support."

I rang Ianthe and begged for help. Delighted to be of use, she arrived bearing an old jigsaw puzzle of the Battle of Marathon that I had played with, plus a copy of *Little House on the Prairie*. I had doubts that Sam would respond to a girl's account of pioneering in the American west, but when I returned in the evening, Poppy was perched on his bed, playing nurse and feeding Sam sips of freshly squeezed orange juice, while he read aloud in a feeble voice from *Little House*. He looked up as I entered the room. "Mum, such a *wicked* story."

It was a soothing, textbook sight.

Ianthe was hemming a skirt. "I think he's a bit better." She bit off the thread, and I breathed a sigh of relief. The needle dived in and out of the flowered material. "Supper's done," she said, "and the washing." She reached for her scissors and a machine bobbin fell out of her basket onto the floor, unraveling white cotton as it rolled. "All under control."

Ianthe had been overly optimistic, and that night Sam was worse. I kept vigil in a room that smelled of sickness and disinfectant. Nathan tiptoed in and out, ignoring me. "Poor old fellow," he told Sam, who was trying to be brave. At one o'clock, Nathan went to bed, leaving our differences to grow colder.

Sam muttered and tossed. Every hour I took his temperature, and at one point I went down to the kitchen and heated water, which I carried back upstairs through the white-tinged darkness and silence. Bit by bit, I washed Sam, his thin white boyish legs, then his arms, his fingers, the white, exhausted face. Please get better, I kept saying to myself. Please, *please,* let there be nothing wrong.

At five-thirty, I managed to get a couple of teaspoons of boiled water down him, and he dozed. I plummeted into sleep.

I was woken by the sound of pitiful, desperate retching and Sam's sobbing. I panicked. "Nathan," I called. "Nathan." He shambled sleepily into the room. "We've got to get him to hospital." Without a second's hesitation, he swung into action.

Together we wrapped Sam in Nathan's old green dressing gown for extra warmth, got him into the car and drove at top speed to St. Thomas's emergency department. There we huddled on chairs for an hour and took it in turns to hold our drooping son upright.

Nathan whispered reassuringly to Sam and kissed the top of his matted hair. He spoke to me only when necessary.

So we sat amid the blood, the noise, the stale air, and battled with our separate thoughts. Sam slid down onto my shoulder. So tired that my eyes burned, I held him close. "Nathan," I whispered. "Please."

He turned and looked at me—at the wreckage of me. "Oh, Rosie," he said. "I'll get you some coffee!" He returned with it, and manhandled my free hand around the polystyrene cup. "Go on, drink it." He stroked my cheek—his way of saying sorry. Gratefully, I looked up into his face, and he smiled down at me. "Go on," he urged. "Drink up."

Sam was admitted to hospital for observation, and improved rapidly. The pediatrician was not sure what was wrong, but was equally sure it was nothing serious. "He may have had some sort of shock, or an allergic reaction, and his system has rebelled. He needs rest, quiet and no upset."

At nine-thirty I rang work and told them I would not be in for a couple of days. I told Sam I would stay with him while he was in hospital. White and frightened, but still trying hard to be brave, he whispered, "I'm glad you're here, Mum."

I slipped my arm around his shoulders. I had been in danger of forgetting the wonder and terror of being a mother.

"Just a bug," I told Hal, after throwing up in the plane to Brazil and then in the hot, noisy hotel by the airport. I lay down on the bed with a handkerchief rinsed in cold water over my eyes.

The sun slatted through my half-closed lids, its light and heat intrusive in a way I had never experienced before. This was the continent of lush harshness, damp, drilling heat and a magisterial river.

It was Hal's surprise trip, his secret expedition. I had hoped we would be going to Morocco and the desert: I longed for somewhere fierce, dry and unequivocal, but Hal was gripped by his passion for ecology. This was a new science, the way forward, etc., etc. Someone had to do it, he said, but I thought it was the romance of the subject that had got to him. Good versus evil. The little guy fighting the big ones. For the past six months, he had been working to acquire financial backing for an expedition to monitor the effects of tree felling on the Yanomami, a people whose territory extended from the Orinoco forests in Venezuela to the northernmost reaches of the Brazilian Amazon basin.

"No wonder you didn't tell me," I said, when he sprang this surprise destination on me. I was packing up my things to leave Oxford for the last time. "I don't want to go there. You should have asked me."

He took from me the pile of clothes I was holding, dumped them on the bed and pulled me into his arms. "You had finals, remember. Listen, these people are under threat. They're down to between ten and fifteen thousand and decreasing rapidly. Logging is destroying their home, and the big companies don't care a toss." He buried his lips in my neck. "We have to take a look and alert the agencies who can do something."

Leaving Oxford was going to be a wrench and I felt weepy and irritable, not like myself. I shook him off and stuffed a pair of socks into my suitcase. "You can't just rely on me dropping everything."

"That's fine," Hal said easily, lightly, in a take-it-or-leave-it voice. "I can find someone else." I whipped round. He lifted his shoulders dismissively. "Not to worry, Rose. I thought you'd like the surprise. Someone else can hop on board. Couldn't be easier."

It was a threat, and I panicked. "No, Hal!" I cried. "It's fine. Of course I'll come. Forget what I said."

Hal was good in triumph: unlike me, he never crowed. "I don't think you'll regret it." He bent over and gave me one of the kisses that reverberated through every nerve. "Next one the desert, okay?" His lips moved on down and, as usual with Hal, I yielded.

I let him mold me, but what did I care? Hal was my poetry and my passion. He was the dreaming youth, the whisper of enchanted lands, the magician that transformed my life.

"There's nothing wrong?" he asked me, a couple of days later.

"No, no, nothing."

"Are you sure?"

"Quite sure."

The study was projected to take four months, and we agreed that I would join him for the first three weeks, then return to England to begin my job. We flew into Brazil and took a connecting flight up to the small town of Quetzl where we met the guide. We spent a week wrestling with the language problem, tying up details and a timetable and working out the supply drops. After that, we loaded up a six-seater plane and took off over the rainforest.

Mile after mile unrolled underneath the plane in a world of unimaginable dimensions. The vegetation was so thick that it was impossible to see the forest floor but here and there a tributary glinted, muddy and sullen. In places, mist lay thickly over the trees.

The plane shuddered in the thin air and the pilot took frequent swigs from a thermos. Hal made a face at me, and I managed a joke. "The Chinese have a curse: may your dreams come true."

The plane lurched, and suddenly my stomach crawled with nausea. The words shriveled on my lips and I bent over to retie a bootlace, knowing that I had lied to Hal. There *was* something wrong, and I had not dealt with it.

God knew how we managed to land on the rudimentary airstrip but we did. The forest rushed up to swallow us, the aircraft ricocheted over the uneven surface and we were there.

The following morning, we trekked up to base camp, which was a deserted Yanomami settlement. Hal went ahead with the guide, keeping up a cracking pace and making light of the obstacles on the path. Behind me, the porters were loaded so heavily I felt embarrassed, but they did not appear to mind.

The forest was like a cage, built of green interlapping plates, some of which did not fit well. After several hours of slogging, I began to miss the sky, as I might a good friend. It was damp underfoot and our feet were sucked into mud of varying consistency. Roots writhed in and out of it, and strange star-shaped bright-colored flowers bloomed among the detritus. It was an alien habitat, whose heat pawed at the skin.

Every so often, Hal turned to wave encouragement. Once he plodded back and retied the bandanna round my neck to catch the sweat. "Good girl, Rose."

"Are you happy?" I asked.

"Very."

Wrapped in mosquito nets, we spent the first night in hammocks strung between trees, and listened to the noises of the rainforest at night. At intervals, a porter got up to tend the fire and patrol our camp. My stomach full and temporarily quiescent, the magic, strangeness and noises of the forest worked on me.

"Tarzan loves Jane," said Hal softly.

I did not reply. In this big, strange world, words were inadequate.

After a second day of hard trekking, we reached the Yanomami settlement, abandoned after a logging company had started operations a mile away. Their huts remained, doughnut-shaped and thatched with palm leaves. Each could accommodate a large number, sometimes as many as two hundred, but every family had a hearth to itself. The central area was set aside for communal activities, such as dancing and singing.

I chose a hearth, and dumped my rucksack on the floor, which was of beaten mud. It had dried unevenly, and its colors shaded from blood to dark crimson. It was alive with insects. Any minute now, the tropical night would descend with the swiftness that took my breath away.

Hal appeared with the rest of our stuff. "Light's going."

"Let's get things sorted."

"Here." He handed me a cotton sleeping bag. I ignored it, clapped my hand to my mouth, ran outside and retched into the undergrowth.

I sensed that Hal was behind me. I stood upright and wrapped my arms across my stomach. "Tell me the truth," he said. "Could you be pregnant?"

"I'm not sure. It's possible," I whispered. *"I don't know."*

"How late?"

"Over three weeks."

His hand closed roughly on my shoulder. "What are you going to do?"

"Don't you mean what are *we* going to do?" I closed my eyes. *It was a question of will, and I would will it not to be so.* "It could be anything. It happens. The system goes haywire and then adjusts."

"I hope so," he said. "Jeez, I hope so."

The first of the two scheduled expeditions from base camp was by boat up to Zaztelal where the logging company had also set up an outpost and where sightings of the Yanomami had been reported.

Hypnotized by the yellow-green mirror over which we paddled, I sat in the back of the boat. Hal was in the prow, taking notes and photographs. After each shot, he recorded the position from the map references. He snapped me, too, or, rather, the hat that shaded my face.

Greedy with love, I feasted on every tiny detail about him. His hair, already bleaching in the sun, his excitement, the long legs braced against the movement of the boat. Just as greedily, I feasted my eyes on a hummingbird, whose plumage was of so iridescent a blue that it almost hurt to look at it, on the strange blooms that hung from the trees and the silent fish shapes in the water. The heat wrapped us in a second skin. Every so often our passage disturbed a pocket of methane gas trapped in the water and the stench filled our nostrils as we glided onward.

At Zaztelal, the villagers came out to meet us. Over a communal meal they told us tales of the Yanomami, who had a reputation for aggression. They also told us of the logging company's riches, which had showered over them, of the strange disease that killed many children, of their shock when the conquistadores moved on after they had plundered the forest.

Hal wrote, "Measles?" in his notebook.

The following morning, we made a preliminary reconnaissance of the logging area, which was roughly ten miles in diameter. Here, severed tree trunks wept sap, the undergrowth had been pulverized, the soil polluted with oil and chemicals, and the sky was all too visible. The guide explained that the forest was renewing itself but not quickly. Normally, if Yanomami were around they would have been cultivating their crops of plantain and cassava. Also, monkey, deer and armadillo would have been in the forest.

We returned via an alternative route, which looped to the north and took us past the northern spur of an oxbow lake. Apparently, otters often chose them to build their dens in and I lingered, fascinated, while Hal loped over the rope bridge to the other side.

"Come on," he said.

Halfway across, I stopped: I had never been good at heights. Drenched in sweat, I clung to the rope. "Come back, Hal," I called.

He walked toward me and the motion of the bridge made me retch. I gazed down at the water. Hot, sluggish, muddy . . . alien. If a fish from it flopped into my lap I would not recognize it. A mistake to think of fish—I was sick.

Hal waited until I had finished, then smoothed my hair back from my wet face. "Oh, Rose," was all he said, impatient to get going.

I took his hand, looked down—and screamed.

Gummed up by debris, forced into pools alongside the bank, the water slowed and eddied. Floating on the surface of one of those pools was a human hand with stiff, splayed fingers.

I pointed. Hal pulled me over the bridge then he and the guide edged down to the water. The guide took his stick and poked hard. There was a hiss, an explosion of bubbles and gas, and a body wallowed to the surface.

The face was decayed, half eaten and terrible.

Together they hooked a rope around one of the legs and tethered it to a root. "We'll return to camp and get help," said Hal, and wrote down the location on the map. "Body here," he wrote. "Time: 14:15."

The next day, we went back to the base camp, and Hal radioed the police in Quetzl.

It was not such a big mystery. Six weeks ago one of the logging firm's European supervisors had gone missing. Apparently he had failed to pay the wages owed to a couple of native employees. They had taken revenge in the manner appropriate to them.

After that I had nightmares. I dreamed of the dead face, of hostile eyes, of being hunted in the strange, dangerous forest . . . and over and over again of Ianthe and me, watching the men *tip-tupp*ing our furniture out of Medlars Cottage.

I grew heavy-eyed and lethargic, and dreaded the nights when I tossed and turned in the hammock, listening to the rustle of insects in the palm roof.

During his convalescence, Sam and I struggled to complete the Battle of Marathon (a thousand pieces), only to discover the last two were missing.

"I *can't* get better, Mum, until we find them." Sam sent me a pale smile.

I believed him and searched the house from top to bottom, for Ianthe swore the jigsaw had been complete when she brought it over.

I discovered the missing pieces, all right. If I had had my wits about me, it would have been the first place to look. The breastplate of the youth who was about to run from the battlefield and into myth was tucked under Sam's pillow, along with a section of the olive tree that grew in the background.

With a tray poised on his knee, Sam sat up in bed and made a small ceremony of dropping those two final bits into place. "I wish you could stay at home," he said.

Chapter 19

I shall will it not to be so.

So I said, so I believed, with the hard confidence and igno-rance of twenty-one. But it was wasted, for I had come up against something stronger than will. I had been beaten by biology.

Deep in the rainforest, I took the plunge. Driven almost mad by hormones, fear and love, I cornered Hal after an evening meal eaten around the fire. "I am pregnant."

He closed his eyes. "I knew it." He opened them. "What are you going to do?"

"Keep it. There's no question. It's our baby." I felt a whisper of excitement, of tenderness. "Our baby, Hal."

"No," he said flatly. "That's not the plan. I don't want chil-dren."

It was dark and I could not see his face clearly. But I sensed that a stubborn, ruthless gleam would have sprung into the blue eyes while mine would be reflecting confusion and anger . . . yes, anger. "Well, we *can't* ignore it. It's not an overdraft or a headache."

"I didn't ask for it."

"You're being outrageous."

"Sure, I am. If being honest is outrageous."

"But it has happened." I reached out to touch him but he moved away. My hand dropped to my side.

"Our plan was to work and travel."

"I know. I wanted to do that, too, but plans change. They have to sometimes. We must make others."

He peered through the dusk at me for a long time, and it was as if he was saying, After all this time, we have not understood one another at all. "But I don't wish to change my plans, Rose."

I could feel his rejection, almost taste it. Snippets from previous conversations rushed through my mind—a lighthearted allusion to "the glorious nomad mentality" and his statement that "The best life, the only life, is unfettered"—which had always persuaded me how intriguing Hal's point of view was, how different he was.

The implications sank in. "Hal, I imagined you would be horrified, angry perhaps, but that in the end you would say, 'It's not what I wanted, but we'll deal with it.'"

That hurt him and he hunkered down beside me. "Have I ever been dishonest with you? Have I promised you anything?" He shook his head. "I can't . . . I know I can't. I'm not cut out . . . I need . . . No, I want to get on with the work I plan to do. Life is short, and I want to be free to concentrate on it. But I'm sorry, Rose, that this has happened."

I looked up at him. "We are responsible for a baby. It has no one else."

"Only if I accept responsibility."

The prospect of being alone with a baby made me panic, and I heard an ignorant, desperate stranger's voice—mine—babbling. It wouldn't make any difference, I argued, and the words poured out of me. It need not alter anything. Babies were hauled around in slings, left in cloakrooms, given to someone else to look after. A baby could be as unobtrusive, and as uneventful, as one wished it to be.

He listened in silence. At last he stirred. "Even I know better."

I bent my head. "Okay," I said. "We won't talk about this again. I will deal with it."

Obviously it was not the end of the discussion, but there was only so much I could take. Anyway, I had to think.

Hal got up to check the fire and to exchange a few words with the guard. I remained where I was. Sweat gathered under my arms and in the dip of my back. But inside I felt cold.

We went to our hammocks in silence. That night, I heard Hal tossing and muttering in his sleep—then, and in the nights that followed, when I lay awake and faced the problem with which I had been presented.

We were polite and solicitous, almost strangers. Ironically, I began to feel better, less sick, and accompanied Hal on the planned trips. It was the closest physically I had ever been to him, but it was the proximity of two people who had elected to be on either side of a divide.

On the Monday of the third week, I woke from my customary uneasy sleep to a heavy cramp in the small of my back. Searching in my rucksack, I found the aspirins and tossed a couple of them down.

During the day, the cramp transferred itself to my stomach. I took yet more aspirins and slogged on. That night, in desperation, I begged for a glass of brandy from the medicinal bottle

in our equipment. Hal peered at me but, with the new polite-
ness, did not inquire further. He said only, "Big day tomorrow." We were scheduled to travel upriver again. "Hope you're
up to it."

I squared up to him. "You're being cruel."

"Yup," he agreed. "I am."

"Hal, it was a mistake."

"I've got the picture. And I *am* behaving badly. But we came
out here to do something else. Let's do it. Then think." He softened a little. "Just let me get used to it, Rose."

When it was time to leave, it was clear that I was incapable
of swinging out of my hammock, let alone paddling upriver.

Hal bent over the hammock where I lay, my face screwed up
with discomfort. His drawl seemed more pronounced. "What
do you want me to do?"

I tried to sit up but failed. "Hal, do you think there's somewhere I can lie down properly? I need firm ground under me."

He stroked my face and, for a minute or two, we were back
to where we had been. "I'll see what we can do. Then we'd better get you out of here."

"I might be losing it," I said. "But I don't want to, Hal. It
has a right to live."

To his credit, Hal did not reply.

He and the guides set about constructing a rough pallet and
they laid me on it. Hal tried to radio Quetzl but a tropical storm
raging in the area made reception impossible, and by the time he
got through, all the available planes had been commandeered.
He managed to consult a doctor, who thought that if I rested
there was a chance that I could stave off a threatened miscar-
riage. He gave Hal some basic instructions and advised him to
get me down to Quetzl as soon as possible. What, he asked Hal,

was I doing in the rainforest pregnant? The worst bit was that he forbade me to take any more aspirin.

Hal bent over me on the pallet. I shifted and felt sweat inch down my legs to the blood-colored mud floor. "Any better?"

"Worse."

"Poor Rose."

I had the strangest sensation that my body was rotting. "Do I smell?"

"No." His lips brushed at my wet cheek. "You look beautiful."

"Light's bad," I said.

Hal postponed the longer trip upriver, but I persuaded him to make an alternative day trek to check out a reported sighting of the Indians. To do him justice, Hal was reluctant, but I knew the form and I made him go. "I can't move yet but I'm not in any danger so go."

He took my hand. "I'm sorry," he said.

It seemed stupid to be angry and distant. "You are my joy, Hal." He caught his breath audibly. "You give me the profoundest joy, the sharpest and the tenderest feelings and there are times . . . when I think we're merged with each other. I just want you to know that."

He stared down at me for a long time. Then, leaving food and water within reach, he briefed the porter who remained to stand guard. Through the opening in the hut I watched him load up and move off.

The day crawled by. I fixed my gaze on a tree framed in the doorway. Its leaves were palmate and shiny, and the bark was fretworked by holes, which revealed fleshcolored pulp. Too late. It reminded me of the dead man in the river.

I studied the map. It was almost noon, and Hal was scheduled to have reached the point where the river curved back on itself, but you could never be sure in the rainforest. At two o'clock he would be heading back.

The map dropped onto the mud floor.

The porter looked in, went away. On the dot, tropical rain drove spears into the clearing then vanished. The leaves steamed with moisture and figures materialized through the steam in the clearing—singing, dancing Yanomami, their feet beating the forest floor into blood-colored mud. I woke. I dreamed. I shifted from one side to the other.

A few hours later, the pain returned with sickening force and then it was all over.

In the descending dark, I fought against my body, which I was unable to control. No angels, no lit candles here.

I must have cried out, for the porter sidled into the hut. He took one look at me and came back with a drink. It tasted disgusting but I was past caring.

As it grew darker, I drifted in and out of sleep. I was drenched in sweat and wet with blood. There was nothing, no one, for my slippery hands to hang on to, nothing except my loss. Nothing except the dark, beating heart of the jungle.

It was not enough that Hal was my profoundest joy. There were other important things in life. I wanted the responsibilities that Hal did not. Above all, I wanted to keep my children. That was my freedom—a little shaky perhaps, a little circumscribed, but possible. My choices were as simple as Hal's, but different.

There was no point in looking for Hal. Not now, *not ever*. He was set on his path, and I did not wish to spend my life loving and waiting and then, as time crawled by, just waiting. Neither was I going to trek along jungle paths and paddle down rivers with this body and its biological design flaw.

The timing was wrong.

I woke with a start as Hal came into the hut, carrying a pot of water. He was very excited. "Rose! We saw them and they stayed long enough to make contact. I got some fantastic shots. It was a good trip, the best trip. Couple of blisters on my feet, which I must see to, but first, I'm going to wash you. It was like nothing I've done before, it was . . ." He peeled back the cotton sleeping bag. Our eyes met.

He tried so hard not to let anything show. But the sudden lightening of the gentian eyes told me how deeply the shadows of what might have been had frightened him.

"Let me wash you, Rose?"

God knows how, but Hal had managed to heat the water. How I had craved the ordinariness of warm water. Carefully, tenderly, he sponged me down and, in my fever state, I imagined that the floor was running red. Without hiding place, without defense, I allowed him to do this for me while I flinched at being so exposed, so female.

Hal kept talking, softly, sweetly: "I'm paying special attention to your feet because feet are important. If they don't feel comfortable, nothing does. That is the first law of the traveler." He prised open the spaces between my toes, the water dripped through them and then he dried them. "Happy feet?"

"My feet are very happy, thank you."

He made me roll over onto my stomach and, miraculously, I began to feel clean. He sponged under my arms. "If you need more padding, I'll tear up a shirt."

He washed me clean and then he kissed me. Weak, frightened and desperate with love, I returned the kiss, but it was a Judas kiss.

A week later, we flew back to Quetzl in the alarming plane and checked into the hotel by the airport.

During the night, I told Hal that I was leaving him, because I loved him, loved him so much that I could not bear us to destroy each other. "I want peace, stability, a family," I told him. "Sooner or later the issues would have had to be dealt with, and we might as well get it over and done with."

Hal was facing me on the pillow and he turned away. He said nothing to change my mind. I had known he wouldn't. He sighed and I tugged at his shoulder to make him turn back. With a shock, I saw that he was crying. "I don't want what you have described," he said, "but that makes it even harder."

In the hotel room the next morning, I woke late. Hot sun slatted into the room and the cheap bedcovering was rough and grimy.

Hal and his rucksack had vanished.

I lay and pictured him walking through the close, crowded streets, stopping for a coffee to clear his head, or to sift through his fingers a pinch of a bright-colored spice on a stall. Already he would be rebuilding the present, talking of the future, anticipating the journey back into the rainforest. He and I knew that he had been released from years of compromise, disagreement, the specter of me waiting.

On the way to the airport I asked the taxi driver to stop. I got out of the car. The heat blasted me like a drill, and the noise and smells slapped my senses. The sky was a vicious, burning, gunmetal gray. Lining the sides of the road were piles of rubbish, figures picking through them, digging with bare hands.

I walked to the nearest and placed my boots on it. Before two seconds had elapsed, someone darted down the heap and seized them.

I got back into the taxi. The town's straggle slipped away, to be replaced by fields and scrub. I did not look back.

Early on in our affair, Hal had lectured me that everyone must travel for it widened the horizon. Uncritical with love, I agreed.

He had been wrong, and how surprised he would have been to be told that. Travel narrowed the horizon. (I think Bernard Shaw wrote that.)

On the flight home, I met Nathan.

Nathan had been fascinated by the story. "Why," he wanted to know, "if you loved the wretched man, did you leave him?"

I tried to explain about not having the courage to face dead bodies in the jungle or rather, what they represented. Neither did I wish to be the one who waited at home. I didn't tell him that I loved Hal so much that, in the end, I did not trust that love.

"But *nothing* would stop me marrying you," Nathan plunged his hands into his pockets, "now that I've met you. I wouldn't care if you lived up a tree."

"Perhaps I haven't explained well enough," I said, and I probably had not, for the subject was unbearably painful to me and muddled.

If Vee or Mazarine had asked me how it felt to meet Hal again, I think I would have replied, "Inevitable."

In one sense Nathan had been right, but not in the way he had feared. Once acquired, the habit of someone does not go away entirely. It goes underground. You may not see them again, or you may, but they are there in situ.

The days were rolling by, and summer was now well advanced. I was still not sleeping well although I was not unhappy, just restless from the aftermath of a great battle to survive that had been waged in me. One hot night I pushed open the French windows and stepped into the mysterious night world of the city.

The air was like velvet, with just a hint of chill. A fox barked three or four gardens up the terrace, and stopped when it scented me. Leaving a tracing of my bare feet in the dew, I trod over the lawn. Cream and white roses glimmered like lamps through the watery dark. In the shadow, I could just make out the dark smudge of curved leaf scimitars and the lax sprawl of the plants.

I was bathed in sweat and my heart pounded, for I was remembering the excitement and strangeness of the rainforest. When I reached the fountain, I sat down on its brick lip. There was a tiny splash. In Parsley's absence, a toad had taken up residence. I had seen it quite a few times. I do not know how long I sat there, but I must have been very still for the toad came creeping out of the water.

Would I have chosen differently in this small history of mine? I do not think so. *Roses are such domesticated flowers, Ianthe always said. Remember that.*

The light was growing stronger. I got up, stretched and sniffed with pleasure at the cool night scents.

Lily beetle watch time. Best done in a nightdress, I found. The Madonnas grew in a group of three pots and I bent down to inspect their foliage. Lily beetles have an amazing capacity to multiply and they were there, tucked up, shiny-backed terrorists with jaws like steel intent on destroying the lily's beauty.

I picked one up between finger and thumb. This one was young, glossy and greedy. A Minty of a beetle that could not help stealing and plundering because it knew no better. Squeamish gardeners are no use and, having been greenly indoctrinated, I did not use sprays. For the good of the world, I employed cruder methods. With only a tiny regret, I dropped the young, glossy, thieving lily beetle on to the stone and crushed it.

I searched for another.

Mazarine had been correct when she argued that we must experience pain, otherwise delight will never have its proper savor, nor pleasure its sweetness, nor love its bittersweet ache—which is what I had wanted from that love's foreign convulsive grip.

But I had learned not to confuse my experience with Hal with the everyday. Real life was different. It was home territory. Having skimmed off a layer of fantasy and yearning, I had been left free to light on moments of pleasure, happiness and affection sandwiched between the routines and the habits. No, looking back, I had sought and accepted the torment and the anguish of Hal in order to remember and store the tenderness, the profound joy, the awe at being so shaken by the exquisiteness of passion.

Of course, I had carried some of those memories, my knowledge, with me to Nathan. That was how it worked.

Meeting Hal again had reminded me.

Chapter 20

My energy returned. I cleaned Lakey Street from top to bottom. I went through my desk on the landing and threw out every bit of unnecessary paper. I climbed into the attic and sorted through a suitcase of my old clothes, scooping up the too-short skirt, the little knitted dress that had to be worn without a bra, the figure-hugging blouse—clothes that belonged to the past—carried them out to the car and drove them to the charity shop.

I even ventured into the garden with the intention of *doing something* and, after a few hours, an old pleasure reclaimed me. The rabbit-out-of-a-hat magic. I was at home here, and the rules did not change. It was too late in the season to do any serious repair work on the uncared-for plants but this was reassuring: "It's good to know you're needed," I informed Vee, "even if it is the garden."

Vee groaned. "What I would do *not* to be needed?"

For twenty-five years high summer had meant Cornwall but not this one. Perhaps never again, because I could not see myself returning without Nathan.

The idea cast a shadow over my present tranquillity—and I was on my guard against shadows—so I phoned Sam and drove down to Bath for a weekend. Alice was away on a brainstorming conference so we took ourselves off into the country and walked. Sam endeavored to explain his frustration and bewilderment at how little progress the affair was making.

After a while, it struck me that Sam still talked about Alice with an unhealthy reverence that I considered should have been leveling out by now. Alice's abilities were, no doubt, awe-inspiring but not superhuman. Then I concluded that he was suffering from an overdose of tragic, courtly love, perhaps *not* so unusual at his age.

I dared to ask, "You don't think it's time to move on?"

He shook his head and—so like his father—his stubborn look closed down his face. "No." We were negotiating a barbed-wire fence. Sam pushed down the top strand and I maneuvered myself over it. "You know, I hate to give up." A thought struck him. "Are you saying you don't *like* Alice?"

"I was just wondering if you'd had enough of feeling miserable about it and if it was time to give yourself a breathing space." Sam's trousers were hooked up on the wire and I bent to free him. "Have you spoken to your father?"

"Dad?"

"Who else is your father?"

"He seemed all right. He was just off to Greece, but he was asking about you."

We slithered down a dry slope to a field at the bottom and filed along the bank of a stream. A clump of chestnuts had

thrown their branches across it, and the water was cool and mys-
teriously dappled. There was the flash of a dragonfly, the undulating flutter of a cabbage white and clouds of flies swarming
over cowpats.

"I think Dad feels cut in half with guilt, and he worries
about you." Sam came to a halt on the stone bridge between
fields and leaned on the parapet.

"Worries about *me*? I'm worried about *him*." I stood beside
him and observed the dragonflies skimming the water. "Sam . . .
it seems wasteful to cause such an upheaval then feel cut up with
guilt."

Sam shot me a look. "I went to see them, you know." He
scratched at a patch of moss on the stone, which made his fin-
gernail black. "I can't help feeling that Dad is busy convincing
himself."

"Don't."

He scratched at more moss, and tiny parings slithered down
the stone. "Sometimes I think I hate her because she has such a
hold on me," he exploded. "Does that make sense?"

He meant Alice. "Perfectly," I said.

We walked back across the field to the car. "Actually, I'm
worried about Ianthe and Poppy. Ianthe is so stubborn sometimes, and she won't tell me what's going on. Except that the
doctor is keeping a weather eye on her."

"Like mother, like daughter," said Sam.

"As for Poppy . . . we don't know anything useful about
Richard or why she suddenly decided to get married," I said.

Sam bent down to pick a blade a grass and sucked at the
pulpy stalk. "Poppy always lands on her feet. When's she due
back?"

"That's just it. I don't know." I bit my lip. "I wish I did. I
wish I knew how she was."

Sam's hand on my shoulder was infinitely comforting.

Just as I was leaving Alice arrived back from her conference. "So sorry I wasn't here," she said, and kissed me, "but I'll make Sam invite you more often." I was surprised because I thought she meant it. Without pausing, she dumped her bag by the door, carried her laptop into the sitting room and unzipped it. "I'm sure you two had a lovely time." She flipped up the screen. "Sorry, just have to do one thing." She looked at me. "Have you got a job yet, Rose?"

Back in London, there was a letter waiting from Neil Skinner, who had, as he predicted, been shifted to the arts ministry, asking me if I was at liberty to do a couple of weeks' research work for him. The PS read, "Not terrific pay, I'm afraid." I contacted him, and he explained that he wanted some facts and figures, plus a toe-in-the-water assessment of how public opinion would react to raising the rates of the Public Lending Right, which was currently under review.

I spent two exhausting but enjoyable weeks trawling through reports and statistics, and making phone calls to people who were always on holiday. One was to Timon—What the hell? I thought—who, to his credit, came on the line. "Ah, Rose," he said. "A bird told me that you're looking well. Are you well?"

I informed Timon that, all things considered, I had never been better, and outlined my questions: did he think there would be support in the press for the case? Would he give it space in the paper? Timon did not hesitate. "I don't think anyone, least of all in the press, would care a monkey's if an author got an extra tenpence on his earnings. Or not. I wouldn't waste more than a paragraph on it."

"So that means the government can do more or less as it likes?"

"Rose, do you imagine that the press has *any* effect on what the government thinks?" We laughed, and he added, "It's not fair that it's not a sexy subject, but there we are."

"That's what I needed to know. Thank you."

"Rose, since we're talking, was it always your decision as to what the lead title should be each week?"

"Of course," I said. "Who else?"

"Have you been keeping an eye on the pages?"

"No, I haven't. Should I? Are they not up to scratch?"

"I'm not going to answer that. But sometimes experience counts."

"Don't tempt me to say something unwise."

"Sounds interesting. Would you like to come and have lunch?"

I was startled. "In the office?"

"Don't be witless. At a restaurant of your choice."

"No, thank you."

Timon chuckled. "See you at the Caprice."

Neil was pleased with the work I submitted and invited me to the House of Commons for dinner. To my astonishment, I enjoyed listening to political gossip and afterward he took me down to the bar for a nightcap. "There's someone here you might like to meet. Charles, can I introduce Rose Lloyd? She's been doing some work for me. Rose, this is Charles Madder."

"This is my wife, Rose," Nathan used to say, keeping his hand lightly and possessively on my arm. After the children had grown up, that is, and he had decided he could be proud of my job. "She's a literary editor."

A tall, dark man was propping up the bar. "Hallo, Neil." He was whippet thin and his face was creased and unutterably sad. It was not the face of a man whom anyone might imagine kept a mistress with exotic tastes. "I'm sorry about your wife," I said.

He examined the contents of his glass. "So am I."

"I hope the children are . . . coping." He looked at me as if to suggest that we might as well dispense with the anodyne comments because only the truth had any point: the children would not cope for a long time. "I've thought about your family for a particular reason," I continued, "because at the time I worked for the Vistemax Group. Many of us felt some responsibility."

The thin nostrils flared with disdain and weariness. "You know that Flora went to them in the first place? That's how they got on to the story."

I looked round the bar. It was a masculine place, with puffed leather furniture, large ashtrays and a miasma of smoke. "I didn't know."

He peered into my face. "You look too nice to have worked for Vistemax."

"It's not a question of niceness. There are a lot of nice, right-thinking people who work for it. For any paper."

"That's a free press."

We were touching on several issues, and here was a man who had been badly hurt in his private and public life. I said gently, "It's a press that relies on personal stories to flesh out its pages. In that respect, they were doing their job."

Neil touched me on the arm. "I'm just going to have a word with someone over there," he said. "Back soon."

I said to Charles Madder, "I sometimes question if the free press results in exactly the opposite because everyone is too frightened of being exposed to do or say anything honestly. Our honest thoughts don't bear examination in the press or they become hostages to fortune. Or the honesty is interpreted so wrongly that it becomes a lie."

Charles Madder lit a cigarette and sucked at it as if he had only just taken up smoking. "The joke is, Flora got the best of them. You've heard of policemen who shoot an armed suspect and it turns out to have been the victim's elaborate method of committing suicide? That was Flora. She provoked the press into pushing her to kill herself." He took another drag. "I know she did." He looked up as the smoke drifted to the ceiling. "She got her wish in almost everything. She died a wronged wife, the object of compassion and pity." He shrugged. "She died." He stopped, then continued. "Flora was clever in that way and disguised quite how *mad* she was, and she saw to it that the press made sure that no one ever realized it."

He meant to jolt me, and he succeeded. I thought about the line stretching between appearance and the truth, and how easily I had tripped over it. "I'm so sorry."

"Are you married?"

"I'm not sure. In between. My husband has left me for a younger woman, but at least it wasn't blazoned all over the papers."

There was a spark of interest in the dark eyes. "Ah, that explains why Neil . . ."

I looked at Charles Madder's hurt, weary face and my sympathy stirred. "Neil is a married minister, with ambitions."

Charles Madder understood perfectly. He smiled at me, and I could see that he had been an attractive man. "So was I, once. So was I."

Hal's publicist rang me. "Is it okay if I give your number to Hal Thorne? He's very insistent but I thought I'd better check." Her tone implied that I would be mad to pass up the opportunity.

"That sounds like Hal."

Her tone altered. "Oh, you *know* him."

I looked out of the window. Summer was on the turn. The evenings were cooler, darker. The garden had lost its airy white innocence, and was now fretted by the orange, red and deep blue of autumn. "Yes, you can give Hal my number," I said slowly.

I decided to make a cake for Mr. Sears. Cake making had not figured in my routine for a long time and, as I struggled to line the tin with greaseproof paper, I remembered why.

When I bore the result over to him, he was listening to football. Routinely I picked my way into the kitchen and began operations on a tomato-ketchup-encrusted plate. I carried tea and cake in to Mr. Sears.

He eyed the vanilla concoction. "You must be perking up."

I passed him a slice. "Have some tea with it. I'll bring you a lasagne tomorrow."

Mr. Sears ate hungrily. "Don't like foreign muck."

I knew this game. "I needn't bring any."

"I didn't say I didn't like your foreign muck."

"That's all right, then."

We drank our tea companionably. Mr. Sears cut a second piece of cake. "What are you going to plant on Parsley's grave?"

There followed a long discussion on what would suit her. Daffodils were too municipal, cyclamen too humble. Roses would not flourish. In the end, we decided on another hellebore and I went back to number seven to fetch a couple of gardening books to show Mr. Sears the illustrations. He pointed to a white one with purple markings. "That's Parsley," he said.

He inserted a finger with a yellow nail into his mouth and rattled it around. "Course," he said, "now you're not a missus any more you'll have plenty more time to come over here."

When I got back to number seven there was a message from

Hal on the answerphone. "Sorry to have missed you. I'm off on a book tour to the States. I'll contact you when I get home. Rose . . . it was good—no, it was lovely to see you."

That night I dreamed in vivid, unnatural color. I was folding clean clothes in the kitchen. Little pairs of trousers. A tiny pink jumper. Socks the size of mushrooms. I was enjoying smoothing them into shape and the clean starchy smell. Yet I could not see any of my own clothes. The stack began to tower above me, and I had enormous difficulty in lifting the basket. I felt it slip between my fingers.

When I woke, I was convinced that I could feel the soft, warm circle of a cat sleeping beside me.

Later in the month, Vee sent over a couple of books for review, which, my finances not being expansive, I welcomed.

One was the autobiography of an actor who received instructions from God before he went on stage. ("Lucky thing," said Vee. "At least he knows what's what.") The second was a handbook on the "amicable" divorce. "Copy date Sept. 30," she had written. "Not a moment later." I was putting the finishing touches to both when I heard the front door flung open and the thump of a bag hitting the floor.

"Mum?" Poppy ricocheted up the stairs to the landing. "Mum, I'm home."

I sprang to my feet so quickly that I knocked over the chair. With a mixture of speechless love, fright and irritation, I flung my arms around her. Birdlike bones, smooth skin, hair that smelled spicy and of the East . . . that was my daughter. I pulled her as close as I could. "Thanks for warning me."

Poppy giggled. "Here I am, a married woman, complete

with ring." She stuck out the relevant finger and there was no ring, only a tattoo. "Fun and longer-lasting than metal, which I think is important, don't you?"

The tattoo was a heartbreakingly wispy line around her finger, barely there. I stroked her hair. "Where's the bridegroom?"

"He's gone north to visit the parents. We like to do things separately."

After a pause, I said, "Really? How sensible."

"Yes, well . . ." Poppy looked down at the carpet, and out of the window. "I wanted to have you to myself, not share you. You do see, don't you?"

"Of course."

She brightened and twirled around so that her muslin skirt floated in a *frou* of color. "I'm so excited. Do you think we can have a party to tell everyone?"

There was something in the way she said it that told me Poppy was not quite as excited as she made out. "Of course. Let's go and open some wine. I want to hear everything."

But Poppy insisted that I give her all the home news first. Obediently, I fed her the latest on Sam and Alice, on Ianthe and Mr. Sears. Of Nathan I said nothing and finished up with, "Jilly has rung a couple of times. She's home from New Zealand and job hunting. Had a fantastic time and demanded to see you the instant you got back. She didn't know your news so I didn't say anything."

In the past, Jilly was always the first person to know anything about Poppy, and normally long before Nathan and I did. "Sure. I might phone. Perhaps tomorrow." She took off her glasses and rubbed at the lenses. "And you, Mum?"

"Fine."

"Oh, yes. My father leaves my mother after twenty-five years and you say you're fine."

"But I am. Not fine-fine, but fine."

"Oh." Poppy seemed upset that I was so calm. Perhaps I should have rocked and wept to reassure a new bride—but I had done all that. "Darling, I'm picking up the pieces. Now, please tell me about you and Richard, the wedding . . ."

Poppy launched into traveler's tales, which culminated in a story of a tropical ceremony where the food had been served on banana leaves, the guests danced on the sand and dived, naked, into the sea. She did not, however, talk much about Richard.

"Dad wouldn't have budgeted for naked guests," I said, thinking of Nathan's plans in the file. Poppy's red mouth tightened, a warning sign, and I changed the subject. "You always said you didn't want to get 'tied up and desperate.' Like me. Darling, are you quite, quite sure that Richard is the man with whom you want to share the rest of your life?"

"Given the situation, isn't the 'rest of your life' bit rather ambitious? After . . . after you and Dad, I don't want to think in *those* terms."

I felt myself flushing. "We nearly made it." I grabbed one of her hands. "Nearly."

Poppy pulled herself free. "You're angry with me. Richard said there'd be a row."

I guessed that Richard had not said anything of the sort. It was Poppy who wanted the row. "I don't mind how you got married," I lied expertly, "as long as you're happy. I can wear the hat to someone's else wedding."

She was not sure if I was teasing or bitter, laughing or crying—I was not sure myself.

Poppy stood behind me and slid her arms round me. "It was so easy, Mum. Thailand is magic and moonlight. It seemed right to go with one's feelings." She was silent. "I got caught up."

"As long as you're both happy."

Poppy's arms tightened around me. "Where's Parsley?"

I told her and she burst into shuddering sobs, which I suspected were only partly for Parsley. Eventually she calmed down and settled back on the sofa, her sweet young face swept of its defenses. "You'll like Richard, really," she said. "You don't know him yet." This was true. "He's *full* of surprises, and Dad got off to a bad start asking him all those questions about jobs. It brought out the worst in him."

"I see. Our fault, then?"

"Got it in one." Poppy grinned, and I felt better.

Chapter 21

The minute he heard the news, Nathan drove over to Lakey Street. I opened the door and almost did not recognize the figure in the crumpled shirt and shorts. In Greece he had obviously got very sunburned and the skin on his face and arms was still peeling.

He surged into the hall and Poppy came tearing down the stairs and flung herself into her father's arms. He hugged her convulsively. "What have you done, my girl?"

She beat his chest with her fist. "What have *you* done?"

This was a private exchange, so I left them to it and went out into the garden.

The fountain splashed contentedly. The delphiniums had shaken out a late and final giddy display of blue and white parasols and the *Ligularia* had put forth garish orange flowers. "Rose?" Nathan had appeared on the patio. There were tears on his cheeks and he wiped them away with the back of his hand, then ran his fingers through his hair. "I can't believe she's married that man. Has he been in touch with you? He hasn't contacted me." His expression was as bleak as I had ever seen it. "Did we go wrong? Or is this Poppy?"

I wanted to pull him close and tell him that, yes, he had been a good father, the best, which was what he was driving at. His own culpability in the situation. "It's not a question of where we've gone wrong. Getting married without us does not make Poppy bad. Or us bad parents. We had got used to thinking of our children as children, not as separate people. Poppy's reminded us, that's all."

Nathan rubbed the burned triangle at his throat. "What's she been living on all these months while she's been floating round the world? We didn't give her much."

The question had crossed my mind. "Presumably she and Richard pooled their resources."

"Richard's resources! He wouldn't recognize a resource if it sat in his lap. That man has welfare dependency written all over him." We had only met Richard three times but Nathan prided himself on his instant character assessment. (To be fair, he was often correct.)

I stared at this crude reincarnation of the Victorian father. "You don't mean that."

"I suppose not." A bundle of bamboo stakes lay on the path. Nathan seized the nearest and drove it savagely into the flowerbed. "I'm damned if I'll give her a party. She can bloody well go to a pub."

Tactfully, I waited until Nathan had hauled out his handkerchief and wiped his face and hands before I said, "We have to accept this marriage, Nathan."

He looked even bleaker as he shifted the options around in his mind. "Are *you* all right?"

"Fine."

He gave the still quivering cane a kick. "While I'm here, Rosie, I have to talk to you about the house."

I stiffened and, because I was frightened at what was coming next, I sounded sharper than I intended. "Don't call me Rosie."

"But . . ." He gave an offended shrug. "If that's what you prefer."

It was ridiculous that we were sparring over a nickname but I asked, as calmly as I could, "What did you want to talk to me about?"

Nathan straightened up and assumed his office voice—always a bad sign. "Please think about what I'm going to say. What if I bought you out of your half of the house?" Then he added, in the same smooth tone, "After it had been valued professionally."

"What?"

Nathan retreated to the garden bench, sat down and patted the space beside him. I ignored the invitation, which meant that he had to look up at me as he put his case.

"It would save money, which you will need. We could do it quickly and without too many middlemen." He faltered at my expression. "We have to be practical."

I said childishly, "I don't have to be. Not any longer."

"Yes, you do, Rosie . . . Rose. Please don't let your anger get in the way of what makes sense."

"I'm not letting Minty set foot in my house."

"*My* house, too."

"But you left it," I blazed at him.

There was a difficult, dangerous silence. This was like being rejected all over again but worse: it made me feel that Nathan had shrunk and his grand gesture of striking out for freedom had not been that at all. I could understand his wild, sweeping decision, his uncharacteristic unpredictability, which at least had been courageous and bold, but not this feeble putt, designed to restore the status quo, except with a different woman.

I turned on my heel and went inside.

"Will you please listen to me?" Nathan hotfooted after me into the sitting room, where I dropped into the blue chair.

I shook my head. "No need. I've got the general idea. I agree to give our house up to you and Minty. It's simple enough and extremely simple for you and your . . . Well, I don't know what term I should use for Minty. There are so many."

"I mean well."

I thought about that one and decided to give him the benefit of the doubt, but I was puzzled. "I thought you wanted to break out."

Wisely, Nathan ignored the comment. "You'll do better out of it." He inspected the catch on the French windows. "This looks dicey. I'd better call Charlie and ask him to come over and mend it."

"If you like."

"As I'm not here to see to things, it would be best." He gave it a final rattle. "I'm glad you see my point of view."

"I don't. No, that's not quite correct. I can quite see how the convenience appeals to you but what I can't understand is how you could possibly suggest such a hurtful arrangement. You know what the house means . . . *our* house, Nathan. At least Henry the eighth beheaded his wives."

"What a ridiculous thing to say." Now Nathan was looking at me as if I was someone at work who needed to be dealt with sharply. "I know it sounds awful but if you allow yourself time to think." He spread his hands in the reasonable, negotiating ges- ture that he had down pat. "You know as well as I do that what appears to be one thing is often different when stock is taken."

Certainly that had been true of Flora Madder. "Can't you see? I don't want to give up my house, though I know I'm going to have to . . . I certainly don't want to give it up to Minty."

There was an audible gasp. Both of us swiveled round. Poppy was in the doorway, her mouth set and white. "Have I gone mad or are you suggesting what I think you're suggesting, Dad?"

Nathan looked thunderstruck, and struggled: "It's between me and your mother."

"No, it isn't." Poppy advanced into the room. "Sam and I have to put up with what you've done, too. It's bad enough that you've left, without turning Mum out like a beggar. I think I have a right to a view on that."

I almost smiled; I almost wept. "Poppy darling, your father and I will sort this out."

"Well, speak up, Mum. Don't let him walk all over you."

"He isn't, Poppy."

"You could have fooled me. Fact: Dad buggers off with an- other woman and, not content with looking a fool—although, I agree, there are lots of other men to keep him company—he wants to turf you out of our home so he can install his trophy woman here without any trouble to him. He won't even have to pack." She turned to Nathan. "Full marks for economy of ef- fort, Dad." Under her onslaught Nathan turned white. "It's true, isn't it, Dad? *Isn't it?*"

Now Nathan was gray. When he had first taken Minty into his arms and helped himself to that glossy body, he could not have imagined for one minute that he would have to endure the lash of his daughter's judgment. "Apologize," he said, through clenched teeth.

"No, I won't. I'm out of the net. I'm an independent woman."

"Well, that's good." Nathan lost the battle with his temper. "I'll stop the allowance. And if you think you're getting a party because you want to celebrate the fact that you married that idiot, you can think again."

I stepped forward and put a hand on his arm. "Nathan, *enough*."

Poppy whipped off her glasses and dropped them on to the table. "Isn't that like you?" she spat back, eyes huge with fury. "'If you don't do what I want . . . ' I thought you were supposed to be my father who supports me. I knew it. I *knew* it. The minute I do something my way . . . Richard warned me."

"And what did Richard say about our family, about which he knows *precisely* nothing?"

"Perhaps that's because you never so much as said good morning to him without making it perfectly plain what you felt." Half blind without the glasses, she thrust her face at Nathan. "You've conveniently abandoned Mum, and now you want to abandon me, and you can't possibly bring yourself to be nice to my husband. Well, *fine*." She fumbled on the table for her glasses and snatched them up. "I'd better warn Sam that he's next."

She ran from the room and up the stairs.

Nathan sat down abruptly. He looked much older, and wretched. "She's right," I said flatly. "You should support her."

Nathan stared at the fountain. "I hate that thing," he said. "Always have."

"I'll turn it off."

Nathan failed to master his feelings, and they spilled over.

"If I had been told only a year ago that I would find myself in this position, Rose, I would have laughed myself sick. I probably wouldn't even have listened. Now, I hate myself. Why? I thought I had it so clear in my head. Minty arrived out of the blue, and I thought I knew why, but I don't think I did. Or do. And I don't have time to sit down and work it out."

"It's too late for explanations." I bit my lip. "But I can't understand why you let it go so far."

"She bewitched me. I was at an age when I wanted to be bewitched. A middle-aged man. The stuff of comedy. Very simple, really."

I caught my breath. *Does she still bewitch you? I wanted to ask him.* "Isn't it curious, Nathan, how much more orderly and loyal children are? Far better behaved than adults, with their affairs, divorces and mayhem."

Nathan's lips twitched. "About the house, Rose. I promise I was thinking of you as well as me. Being able to give you more money, I mean."

Upstairs, Poppy was moving about, drawers opened and shut. There was a blast of pop music. The sounds were upsetting and discordant. Then she ran downstairs into the hall, talking away into her mobile. "You were right . . . He's unreasonable . . . I hate him. My father . . ."

Nathan winced and his face distorted.

Once upon a time, I had imagined that I would die when I left Hal. But I didn't. Instead I grew and, like the green tree in the story, gave forth fruit and flourished. Depending on your point of view, it was a happy ending. But I had learned I was not the kind of woman to whom the Good Fairy automatically gravitated: I had to make my own happy endings. Which brought me back to a question of will.

I planted myself in front of him. "Nathan, I hope Minty and

her bewitchment is worth it. You must *make* it worth it. We can't go through all this only for you to say you don't know why you did it. You can't be fuzzy and undecided while everything is being destroyed."

In response, he dropped his head into his hands. I felt anguished by this exchange, anguished about Poppy. Equally, I knew I would not die from love, abandonment or losing my house. It was no use *thinking* about the pelican plucking out the feathers from her bloody breast to help her young. My downy, precious daughter needed help and some sort of order had to be pulled from this family's chaos.

I closed the sitting-room door. "Now, listen to me. Here's the deal. If you agree to back Poppy and give a party to show the world we're happy and approve, I will sell my half of the house to you." I leaned back against the door. "But I will insist on the full price. As you have pointed out, I must be practical. I also insist that I stay here until at least the spring. You owe me that."

The door handle was smooth and cold under my fingers. I shut my eyes. She had won. Cool, thieving Minty would click through this house on her kitten heels. Invader and plunderer, her hands would touch my things, my shelter, my spaces.

I understood her better now, much better than when she had worked for me. The answers had come to me during the nights, the wakeful ones, the ones without dreams. Minty had become frightened by life hurtling past. She was worried that she had been in the sun too long and was in danger of drying up.

"Nathan, does Minty know of this grand plan?"

He had the grace to look discomforted. "I thought I'd settle it with you first."

What would Minty say? Would it be as straightforward as Nathan had calculated? Probably not, but that was Nathan's business. I said quickly, "If you behave over the party, I'll undertake to deal with the rest of the details as quickly as I can."

Nathan got up and rested his hands on the mantelpiece, sifting over the pros and cons. The money. Could he forgive Poppy? How much longer could he tolerate living in Minty's cramped flat? "You mean it?"

"Yes, I do."

I felt a sudden release. The lance of a boil. I had let go.

Nathan poked at a china saucer and figurine, which was all that remained on the mantelpiece since the removal of his mother's vase, and dislodged my wedding ring, which had remained there ever since I had taken it off all those months ago. He picked it up, frowned, and rolled it between his fingers. "Will you replace Parsley? I mean, of course you can't *replace* . . . but will you get another cat one day?"

"I'd rather replace my cat than replace a wedding ring."

Nathan winced. "I see. Okay." He put down the ring and pulled out his car keys. "It's a deal, then."

Still leaning on the door, I explored the thinner curves of my waist and back, which felt good. "Incidentally, won't this house be too big for you?"

Nathan jingled the keys in a self-conscious manner and I knew that something was coming that had a bearing on the conversation and that should have been mentioned earlier. "Actually, Rose, Minty wants to start a family." Nathan frowned. "She's keen. *Very* keen. It would make sense to be here."

"I think you're mad." Vee dabbed crossly at the peppermint teabags in the mugs.

We were in her rustic kitchen (rustic in *urbs,* that is), to which I had fled. A collection of herbs and saucepans hung from a stainless-steel butcher's rack in the ceiling, and there was an amphora-shaped jar of sun-dried tomatoes in oil by the stove. Vee had been doing her get-ready-for-autumn wash. The whole place smelled of damp pashminas ("too damn expensive to dry-clean them"), which were draped over clothes horses. Our conversation was punctuated by the shrieks of the children, who were in front of the television at one end of the kitchen.

"What are they watching?" I asked.

Vee glanced in the direction of the television. "It's a safety video. It teaches them not to talk to strangers, never to accept sweets, that sort of thing, and to tell an adult if they see anyone hanging around."

Out of the corner of my eye, I caught a frame of a man in a beige raincoat sitting on a park bench and two children running away from him.

Annabel was lying on her stomach and had buried her face in the floor. Mark was fiddling with a brightly colored train, but, every so often, he glanced up at the television with the fascination of a rabbit caught in headlights. "Won't that frighten them, Vee, looking at such stuff? Unnecessarily?"

"But they have to be frightened, Rose. Life is frightening and dangerous. I wouldn't be doing my job if I didn't warn them."

"At this rate they'll never trust anyone."

Vee sat down. "But they shouldn't. Don't you think? They *should* never trust anyone." She shoved a mug at me. "Don't you think you've let that creature walk all over you?"

"I did it for Poppy. I wanted to. I'm perfectly okay about it. No, that's not quite true. I can't believe . . . I can't quite take on board Nathan and *her* trying for a family."

Vee looked as though I'd lost my wits. "Sweetie-pie, you have to get through this and emerge intact. Take it from one who knows." Her expression sharpened. "I was far too nice. That was my vice. It's yours, too."

In her difficult divorce, Vee had won the court case against the erring Robert, which meant he tendered up a large portion of his not-so-fulsome income, plus the house. I was well aware that behind Vee's doe-eyed exterior, lurked considerable strategic powers. "You weren't very nice to Robert."

Vee opened the doe eyes even wider. "Oh, that wasn't *me*. That was the lawyers." She picked up her mug. "She's in your house," she hissed, "poking through all your things. Sleeping in your bed. Hanging her clothes in your cupboard . . ."

I took a mouthful of the peppermint tea. It was sweet and digestible, warming and healthy. "I had thought of that," I said, and smiled.

I was making Poppy a late lunch when Kim Boyle rang up. I sat on the table, put my feet on a chair and prepared to gossip. Kim was an old colleague who had gone off to the rival *Daily Dispatch*. "I'm off to the States tomorrow," he said, "but I want to see you."

"That's nice."

"For your insider knowledge, of course."

"Of course."

"And a possible little job attached to it."

I felt a familiar pricking in my thumbs. "You want to pay me to divulge my Vistemax secrets." I liked the idea of being a woman with desirable secrets.

"We want to know what's going on and we could do with your experience."

I reminded Kim that I was several months out of date, but I knew how they thought. Kim said this was precisely what *he* had thought and, if a job was in the offing and he could sort it out in the next few months, when could I start?

We agreed that January would be as good as a time as any. "By the way," he added, "I'm sorry about you and Nathan."

"Nathan decided on a new lease of life."

Kim clicked his tongue down the phone. "Old dogs and new tricks. I can't make up my mind if it's comic or tragic. Or there-for-the-grace-of-God-go-I."

Chapter 22

However good Nathan was at calling in favors, it was difficult to arrange a party for Poppy and Richard at short notice. In the end, Simon Proffitt offered us his art gallery in Kensington, which had a large conservatory tacked on to its flank. It was a beautiful place, and at night it glittered with candles and tiny white lights. Simon had a theory that people will always buy if their senses are seduced. I saw his point.

The invitations were dispatched for the first week in December.

"I take it that Poppy will be wearing white." Ianthe tackled what was, for her, the important question of color.

"A bit late for that, Mum."

"You wore white," she pointed out.

The party was not to be elaborate but we would serve the best wine we could afford, provide good eats and a decent wedding cake. I had several perfectly polite telephone conversations with Nathan about the details, but he sounded tired and strained.

Poppy remained in Lakey Street and Richard came and went, which did not give me any chance to get to know him. He hated to be pinned down, Poppy explained. When he was staying, I often heard them talking late into the night. Once, I woke and sat bolt upright, for I was sure I had heard Poppy cry out.

Gradually, the spare room filled up with clothes and presents, and the rose painting was obscured by them. But I was happy arranging the party and, best of all, Poppy behaved like a conventional bride. Excited and terrified, she lost weight, groaned over thank-you letters, tried out several hairstyles, made an appointment for contact lenses and bought an extravagantly stylish dress.

The night before the party, Sam arrived from Bath. He kissed Poppy and congratulated her. She kissed him back. "How's Alice?"

Sam tensed. "Fine. She'll be up tomorrow." He took off his jacket and draped it over a kitchen chair. "She's thinking of taking off to America for a year or two. Probably a good thing."

"Yes," Poppy said. "What a good idea."

Sam looked suspicious but let it pass. "Alice thinks this country is dying on its feet. She feels we're a can't society, not a can-do, and it's best to get out."

"She can vote," I said, drily.

Sam shrugged. "Politicians. What can they achieve? The only effective opposition is the press, and God help us there."

I sat down and cupped my cheek in my hand. "Will . . . will you go with her?"

But Sam had got the bit between his teeth. "Rules and regulations are mad, public transport chaotic, the roads impossible. Politicians lie. Look at France, Switzerland. They manage to run themselves. If I rendered to my employer the kind of service that the government gives me in return for my taxes, I would have got the sack long ago." Then he redeemed himself by grinning. "So it's laughter in the dark."

Sam's worldview was decidedly acid. Presumably, this was an accurate reflection of the state of affairs between him and Alice.

Shortly afterward Richard arrived. He had gone up north to escort his parents to London and to settle them into a hotel. Poppy let him in and brought him into the kitchen.

"Hallo, Mother-in-law." Richard kissed my cheek. "I'm sorry I'm late."

I disgraced myself by staring. Gone were Richard's flowing locks, replaced by a haircut that looked, frankly, expensive. Vanished, too, were the Indian garments, usurped by a linen suit that looked designer. The duffer in beads looked sleek, groomed, almost dangerous.

His smile had a mocking edge. "My wedding present to my bride. Like Samson, I have sacrificed my hair to a woman."

"Not . . ." I collected my wits ". . . that you will be enfeebled."

"No, but I might bring the house down."

"I hope you'll spare Lakey Street," I said hastily, poured him a glass of wine and announced that supper was ready.

"Not for me." Richard accepted the wine. "I've eaten."

"Nor me," cried Poppy. "I couldn't eat a thing."

"Sam?"

He shook his head. "I had a huge late lunch."

I surveyed the chicken *chasseur* and *mousse à l'abricot*. "Darling Mum," cried Poppy, grabbing both my hands and looking deep into my eyes, "you needn't have bothered."

The three of them drifted into the sitting room and I could hear them talking. Left in the kitchen, I dismantled the laid places at the walnut table and stowed the food in the freezer. I put away the creamy linen napkins and mats, and replaced the white china bowl in the cupboard.

Quel seesaw, as Mazarine would say. One minute you're needed every minute by your children, the next not.

I ran my hand over the table. Under my fingers, it felt like satin. I opened the store cupboard and sniffed cinnamon and vanilla. Nathan and I should have been spending these final moments before Poppy's send-off in talking over arrangements, fussing about the guests, going over the speech, telling each other that we would be fine. But we were not. All the same, I had a presentiment that Nathan and I would go on insisting that we were rid of each other yet continually be brought up short against the fact that we were not.

Before the guests arrived the family gathered in the gallery. Ianthe had chosen a pistachio-green dress, which was a little startling, but Poppy, eyes huge with the new contact lenses, looked quite different and dazzling in the Vivienne Westwood with cream roses in her hair.

I was wearing my French underwear, of course, a skirt and jacket with a scoop neckline and nipped-in waist that Madame Zou Zou had fitted on me so carefully. I have to say that I took deep delight in its clever and feline artistry. Nathan was in his best dark suit and a silk tie. He kissed everyone and told Poppy she looked magnificent. She hugged him with the old tenderness and pride.

"Goodness," said Ianthe, who, I noticed, had not returned Nathan's kiss, "you do look tired, Nathan."

Nathan frowned. "Work, as ever," he said, and turned to Richard. "Have you any idea where you two are going to live yet?"

"I'm on the case," said the bridegroom. "It should be sorted by the new year."

"What?"

"The flat in Kensington." Richard was cool.

Nathan's patent amazement was not flattering. "Bought? How?"

"The usual way." There was just a hint of danger in Richard's demeanor. "Two bedrooms. It should do us for the time being. I rang my father while we were in Thailand and instructed him."

"Oh, good. I just wondered if I should offer some help . . . but no need."

"No," agreed Richard.

This was certainly not the tree-hugging, spirit-of-earth's sanctity persona to which Nathan and I subscribed. Richard added, "I'll be starting the job in a couple of weeks."

Usually so good on his feet, Nathan only managed. "Where?"

"Arthur Andersen. Have you heard of them?"

"Why didn't you warn me?" Nathan hissed at me as soon as we could exchange a private word. "He's got it all sorted, and there's no need for the heavy-father act."

"Shush." I touched his arm. "The guests are arriving."

The waitresses moved into place and poured champagne with a soft hiss. The massed candles glowed. In the middle of the room, Poppy swirled round and round, gripping Richard's arm, and I caught my breath at the beauty and color.

Nathan was collared by Clive Berry, one of his cousins who lived in Lincolnshire. They launched into the route conversation.

"You came by the A twelve?" Nathan was surprised. "Didn't you barrel through Boston and Eye?"

"Hallo, Clive." We had known each other a long time, and I gave him a kiss. From having been perfectly at ease Clive tensed, for he was not sure how to handle the situation. Taking pity, I tried to defuse it: "Have you seen the bride?"

At that point, Poppy grabbed me, "Oh, hallo, Clive. Nice to see you. Speak later, I must just have a word with Mum," and dragged me over to the comparative privacy of the catering area. "Mum," she said furiously, "who said that woman could come?"

"Which woman?"

"Dad's woman. She's here. How *could* she?" Poppy's mouth was pale and set. "I so wanted it to be just us. I don't want people noticing and talking."

"Minty? Are you quite sure?" I stroked Poppy's cheek to calm her. "Of course she wasn't invited. If she's here, I'll get rid of her."

Rubbing at the tattoo on her finger had become a habit with Poppy and I put my hand over hers. "I wanted it to be as if you and Dad hadn't split up and we could pretend we were a family. I don't like everyone seeing that he's an old goat."

"Rose . . . and the lovely bride." Sally Curry hove into view, trailing in her wake a husband who worked with Nathan on the paper. "Your dress is wonderful, Poppy, and it's such a smart setting. How did you do it?"

"It's easier than arranging a full-scale wedding." My disloyal daughter pulled her hand free and faded expertly away leaving Sally, who rattled with gold jewelery, to focus on me.

"But given everything . . ." she said sympathetically. Sally's husband nudged his wife but she ploughed on: "Miles and I are sorry we haven't been in touch but Miles says," she glanced at the appalled Miles, "Miles says that, in these cases, one has to choose. You can't be friends with both and since Miles . . ."

I did not blame Sally Curry. Loyalty to the side that provides the bread and butter is, perhaps, not the best loyalty but it is sensible. All the same, I took a small revenge. "As we weren't really friends, Sally, that's perfectly all right. It is useful to know where one stands . . ."

They drifted off, leaving me to reflect on the blasted heath of my social life. Sam glanced up from the group centering on Alice, who looked superb in bright red, and came over. I drew him aside. "Sam, Poppy thinks Minty's here. Have you seen here?"

Sam tucked a supportive hand under my elbow. "Poppy's probably fantasizing. She wants even more of a scene than she's getting. Don't worry, Dad wouldn't do that."

"I've just been rude to Sally Curry because she told me that Dad is more useful to her as a friend than I am. She's right."

"That's fine, then." His gaze lingered on Alice, who was now chatting up Nathan's assistant, a handsome, spin-doctor type. The latter reached over and touched her shoulder. Sam flinched and I took action.

"You haven't seen Jilly for ages, have you? Not since she got back from New Zealand. I warn you, the ugly duckling is now a swan."

I dragged Sam off and collared Jilly, who turned a countenance on Sam so radiant with pleasure and admiration that I blinked. "Sam," she said, in her light rapid voice, "I've been *longing* to see you." There was a tender, questing quality about Jilly that was difficult to describe, but quite specific in its effect. Her blond hair brushed her bare brown shoulders, and she looked young and fresh and avid for the next turn of events.

Sam's expression lightened. I left them to it and went in search of Minty. As I saw it, I had two options: one was to kill myself; the other was to devise on the spot an etiquette for dealing with a gate-crashing husband pincher.

I did not have to search for long.

At the other end of the conservatory, framed by one of the illuminated arches, Minty was talking to Clive. She was wearing enormously high heels, which pitched her forward, and a sleeveless black dress. It was the outfit of the Good Wife—but she had got it all wrong: it was too short, too high and too low-cut. She looked both terrible and wonderful, and Clive was hanging on her every word.

At the sight of her my anger, against which I had struggled, sprang to the surface. She had gone too far, presumed too much. As I pushed my way toward her, Minty turned her head and saw me. The dark, slanting eyes widened with . . . what?

I would find out.

Clive was well launched into the science of the wind turbine, his speciality. "Sorry to interrupt." I planted myself in front of them. "Minty, could I have a word?"

Clive merely glanced at me and continued in full flow, blotting me out. In doing that, he caught me savagely on the raw. In that shadowy moment of erasure, I felt the wing tips of my grief brush my spirit, and the rush of hard, bitter hatred, which I hoped I had discarded.

"New technology," Clive said. "Regional rejuvenation . . ."

I opened my mouth to spit out bile and anger, but just then Minty sent me one of her cool, complicit looks, a smile hovering at the back of her eyes. It took me back to the office—the glance exchanged between friends and colleagues. *What a bore,* it said. *Pity me.*

Now that I was close up, I could catalog changes. Small, tense lines had been drawn round Minty's mouth by a light pencil. A suggestion of disappointment? There was a hint of defiance, rancor even, in the way she was holding herself. But, most of all, determination to see through what she had begun.

Minty had no idea of the indescribable pain she had caused—or perhaps she had, and those lines were the result. Even so, I surprised myself by regretting the change to the pretty, greedy face on which shadows had settled.

Again, I cut across the history of the wind turbine. "If you wouldn't mind, Minty."

Clive was arrested midflow. He was about to take the coward's option of slithering away when Minty laid a hand on his arm. She had always possessed excellent fighting instincts. "Of course," she said. "Shall I catch up with you in a moment, Rose?"

"No," I said. *"Now."*

Clive seized his chance and bolted. "So," I said, "what are you doing gate-crashing Poppy's wedding?"

Minty licked her glossed lips. "Pots and kettles," she said.

"And what does that mean?"

But I knew.

I wore white at my wedding to which, in a manner of speaking, Hal came, and for which Nathan's parents paid—tactfully, of course. Thus, I was not married from Pankhurst Parade—no loss there—but in an alien Sussex village with a picturesque church.

I longed to be at Yelland where, at that time of year, the straw would have been baled in the fields. If I closed my eyes, I could see pictures: the wash of soft colors, the umbers, burned yellows, tired greens and the gray-blue sky. Up there, the air would be cool and pure and everything so much simpler. But maybe I was remembering it wrongly, through a childish filter, and I kept my feelings private.

If Nathan was the groom, Hal was the knight who kept vigil through the violet summer night. Somehow he discovered where the wedding was being held. Perhaps Mazarine told him. If she did, she never admitted it.

Hal was the specter at the feast, the beautiful, rackety, solid flesh of love's witchery, the personification of the poet's sweet madness and disordered senses. Nathan was collected, rational, sure and loving. He was the rock that Hal would never be.

I remembered his sureness particularly.

Syringa and lilies perfumed the Saxon church. In the beamed village hall, a cake drowsed in three white boxes of graduated sizes. Covered by a protective sheet, my dress hung in the wardrobe in the hotel bedroom. I laid out tissues, lipstick, scent on the dressing table. The last thing I did before getting into bed was to replace my engagement ring in its leather box.

It was dawn, and someone had moved across the gravel in front of the hotel. Confident and practiced. The tread of a person who was used to darkness and tough terrain. In a second I knew who it was.

I slid out of bed, parted the curtains and saw Hal outlined in the milky gray light. I saw him so clearly. I saw right through him even, with the X-ray vision of my put-aside love and desire.

I pulled on my clothes and slipped down the staircase, which smelled of occupancy and cheap potpourri, and let myself out into the hush where every sound was magnified.

I had loved Hal so much that I couldn't stand it. I knew this love was too ferocious and demanding to have a long life, and I did not trust it. It would burn for those moments when, my feet leaving black smudges on the dewy lawn, I fled toward him on the morning of my wedding and we held each other. Flesh chilled and damp, breath on each other's cheek. Then burning love would consume itself, and the darkness would be the blacker for it.

"You can change your mind," he muttered, covering my face with kisses. "You can, you can."

Shakespeare's Prince Hal renounced the chimes at midnight, the madness and the passion. So did I.

Later, with Nathan resting his hand on my waist at the point where the heavy satin dress curved over my hips, I looked up from cutting the cake and through the window to where Hal was walking down the road. He did not look back.

With a steady hand, I grasped the knife and plunged it down. I loved Nathan, too, and I was quite, quite sure.

Sweet goodbye.

"So you see," Minty pointed out politely, "it is pots and kettles. Nathan guessed it was Hal at the wedding. He told me, when you were cutting the cake . . . He saw him through the window."

"Did he?"

"Yes, he did, and he's never forgotten it."

I stared at the hateful, but now shadowed, face. What had I done in my life? How had I arrived at this point of dismemberment, blown, decaying, finished? Bitterness and despair rose and elbowed aside the peace and stillness I had striven to cultivate. We choose between certain paths we label "good" and "bad," and it is important that we believe in the goodness and badness. Or I think so. What else is there? I had believed in Nathan: he had been good, and so, too, had been what we had made together.

Nothing lasts.

Minty smiled, a smug little flicker of her lips, and it burst from me: "How dare you? How *dare* you come here? You have no sense of compassion. None. Go away and take your curiosity with you."

Under the lash of my words, Minty's eyes narrowed. She

glanced around quickly. "Shush," she muttered, much as Ianthe might have done. "People will hear."

I paid no attention. "Have you no kindness at all, Minty?"

"And you have a monopoly on goodness, I take it? So much so that your lover comes to your wedding. *That's* how you used Nathan."

"It's none of your business."

She shrugged: careless, knowing, triumphant. I took a step toward her and Minty took a step back and the too-tight dress rode up her thigh. "You will never have what I have had with Nathan."

She turned deathly white. "We'll see."

Chapter 23

Vee intervened. She had been observing this exchange and came over to rescue me. "I've been sent to find you by Poppy. Speech time." Ignoring Minty, she slipped an arm round my waist and steered me expertly in the direction of the wedding cake. "Take no notice of her," she hissed. "All red hat and no knickers, as Grandmother would say."

"She's not wearing a red hat."

"She is mentally."

I clutched at Vee. "Until I saw her here I had no idea I was capable of murder."

"Keep it to yourself." Vee changed the subject skillfully by poking me in the flank. "I hate you for being so thin. Picture the scene at home and pity me. Everyone tucking into baked potatoes plastered with butter, and me grazing on a lettuce leaf." She giggled, because she was happy with her lot. "Have you heard from Mazarine?"

"Of course. She couldn't come because of an opening. Apparently another of our national traits is to economize on champagne and she warned me against it."

Vee glanced round the guests. "No fear of that."

The wedding cake was extremely pretty and different— chocolate, iced and decorated in nineteenth-century American fashion with fresh violets, roses and voile ribbon. Pure Louisa Alcott. Hands around each other's waist, Poppy and Richard were poised to cut it.

Applause broke out as they did so and, under its cover, I whispered to Nathan, "Get rid of Minty. That was the deal. She was not to be here."

Nathan looked astonished, then furious. "I didn't know she *was* here." He pulled at his cuffs. "We'll discuss it later." He stepped forward to make the speech.

Poppy's contact lenses were making her blink. The tiny sapphire earrings I had given her swayed above her slender shoulders and she glanced frequently and lovingly at her groom. Certainly, Richard was smiling and revealing, I noticed, well-tended teeth. I had no clue what he was thinking.

Minty was at the back of the room, hugging the outer circles of guests, her dark eyes fixed hungrily on the tableau by the wedding cake.

Who needs a family?

I tried, I tried so hard, but every so often my gaze returned to her and, while Nathan was giving the speech for our daughter, Minty stole my attention and that was, almost, the greatest sin I laid at her door.

But Minty was also watching me. Not Nathan, not Poppy or Richard, but me. Should she not have been considering her lover's pride in his daughter, his tenderness, his public face? His words? Should she not be shuddering inwardly for having over-stepped the mark? At the punishing words we had exchanged?

Should I not be concentrating on the quick rise and fall of Poppy's breath? On the way Richard was holding her hand? Should I not be utterly focused on my daughter's future?

Minty and I had arrived at a point where we were objects of fascination to each other. We had infiltrated each other's bedroom, kitchen, bathroom, and we were the shadows that had been cast, deep and inky, over each other's life.

Nathan made a joke, and the audience laughed. Poppy turned her head, and her earrings sparkled in the soft, radiant light. Richard looked down at her and sent her a private smile. *Here we go,* it said.

Nathan made another joke, and laughter rippled through the audience. The guests shifted. Vee slid her arm round my waist. "Rose, please don't look so sad."

I was conscious of a vast disappointment. Surely after all the suffering, mine and Nathan's, the misunderstandings, the painful decisions, it should add up to something greater than a mundane preoccupation with the other woman.

I closed my eyes. However bloody, however hard, I knew I must pull the darkness and anger out of myself, and toss them away.

Yet as Minty and I covertly watched each other, I experienced a steady creep of pity. We all used others, hurt them badly, betrayed them. More often than not, the struggle to treat the world and others with care just did not succeed. I had been guilty of dark preoccupations, and I had almost forgotten that there was warmth. Passion, too, for life, food, sun, knowledge and other landscapes through which to travel.

My thumbnail bit into my finger. At twenty I could not

have stood here and reflected in such a manner, nor at thirty. I would not have possessed the words. But today? In the presence of my children, it seemed the only thing left was to be generous with love and pity. To struggle to be generous.

Exhausted, I turned my attention to Nathan. He was funny and brief, and avoided the obvious pitfall of mentioning our marriage. Conjuring the best of himself for his daughter, the gestures, the timed pauses, the smiles were perfect. They were meant for Poppy, there was no doubt about that, and I melted at the tributes he paid her.

"Such a good speaker," murmured a guest. "So sweet about the couple."

Nathan wound up. "'There is no more lovely, friendly, charming relationship, communion or company than a good marriage.' Ladies and gentlemen, I don't know who said that but it doesn't matter. What matters is the sentiment. Let us raise our glasses . . ."

There was applause and, tearstained and electric, Poppy whirled toward her father. Looking a lot less fresh, less crisp, than when they arrived, the guests shifted, reformed and continued to drink enormous quantities of champagne until it was time to leave, when they were effusive with their praise.

"Such a happy party," said one and, impulsively, I leaned forward and kissed her. She smelled of champagne.

"Thank you," I said. "I think it was."

Poppy and Richard were still at the center of a joshing group. They were due to leave for a hotel for the night, then a two-day break in Bath, and a car was waiting. Richard was talking emphatically, but Poppy had gone quiet, and her mouth was white and set. She looked round for me. "Mum? Where are you? *Mum?*"

As I made my way over to her, she pulled free the rose that was pinned to her dress and sent it soaring in an arc toward me.

The catering staff was clearing up. Plates were stacked and glasses shot back into the honeycomb of the cardboard boxes. The waiters exchanged information on jobs and tips. The fairy lights winked down at bare tables, stacked chairs and filled ash-trays. The place echoed with goodbyes.

"Such a pretty bride . . ."

"Such a nice speech . . ."

I smiled. Early on, when it was clear that Nathan's ambitions were going to be realized, he had practiced a lot on me. We saved up, and Nathan took lessons in public speaking, the deal being that he passed on to me what he had been taught. I got used to statesmanlike policy declarations, the beer-and-sandwich bluff and, in the days of intense union uncertainty, the Henry V rallying cry to the troops. Today it had worked beautifully.

Except for an obstinate cluster by the door, everyone had gone and it was safe to take off my shoes. Just for a second. The beginnings of a headache pounded above my left eye and I rubbed it. A touch on my shoulder made me turn round.

"Had we finished our conversation?" Minty was clutching a handbag in the shape of a flowerpot.

I opened my mouth to say something but a voice cut in; "Rose darling," said my cousin Henry, "thank you so much. You are, as always, a celestial hostess and you look stunning." He bent over to kiss me. "And damn Nathan."

"This is Minty," I informed Henry, "whom Nathan hopes to marry."

Minty paled. Henry raised an eyebrow. "Goodness," he said,

and turned his back on Minty. "But, as they say, goodness has nothing to do with it. Goodbye, Rose."

Minty hitched her dress down. "Brilliant. The first Mrs. de Winter to the life. Admit it, Rose, of all the roles, it's a good one."

"You forget I'm not dead."

Her mouth set in a bitter line and she scratched her arm viciously. The nails impressed white streaks into the flesh, the flesh Nathan preferred. "I don't know what you thought you were doing by gate-crashing, but Nathan wasn't pleased and you've made your point. I'm not angry any more, but it's better that you go."

She looked thoughtfully at my naked feet. "Are they hurting?"

"As it happens, yes."

She smiled and the old sympathy crackled. "So are mine." Her smile vanished. "I . . . shouldn't have come," she admitted. "Nathan will be livid."

"Bad luck." Both of us contemplated the prospect of Nathan in a rage. "Wasn't it a risk, Minty, coming here?"

"I was curious," she said simply. "I didn't know why I should be made to skulk at home, and I wanted to see this side of Nathan. The side you have, Rose, and I don't."

"You don't like families."

"Well, as you would say, a girl must make a virtue of necessity. Mine all sugared off at the slightest excuse."

"I'm sorry about that." And I was. "But not sorry enough to say, 'Help yourself. Don't mind me. Make off with my husband.' Certainly not sorry enough to want you at Poppy's party."

The dark eyes regarded me steadily. "I suppose not. But, in the end, does it matter very much? A lot of people made it their business to ignore me. Quite a few of the men pawed at me because I'm that sort of girl and, please don't forget, I have the dubious distinction of now knowing more than anyone in the room about the workings of the wind turbine."

I gave an unwilling snort of laughter. "Serves you right."

At that moment, Ianthe rode in. Crocodile handbag with its large gold clasp, bought at a jumble sale, hooked over her arm, she positioned herself beside me. Because she had cried, there was a narrow black runnel of mascara drifting under one eye. "Rose, I'm going to collapse if I don't get home." Then she realized to whom I was talking. "You," she uttered, in thrilling tones. "What are *you* doing here?"

Out of the corner of my eye, I spotted Sam alongside Jilly, talking to a final guest. I gestured frantically.

Ianthe was enjoying her opportunity to run up her flag and to display her colors on the mast. "You should be ashamed."

Under the onslaught, Minty exuded contempt and defiance, but she had turned even paler and I took pity. "Mum, don't." I pulled Ianthe to one side. "No scenes. Look, Sam's here. He's going to put you into a taxi, aren't you, Sam?"

Ianthe kissed me crossly. "I know that it's not permitted, these days, to say what you think when your husband leaves you for another woman. You may feel that you must be all woolly and forgiving, but *I don't*."

Sam stepped into the breach and bore her away. For the merest fraction of a second, Minty and I exchanged a look. "See what I mean?" she murmured, and I read disappointment, regret and a new, more savage element to her humor.

"You'd better go, Minty."

"I want to say something, Rose." She straightened up wearily on those impossible heels. "I owe it to you."

I considered walking away but she gave the short, breathy laugh I knew so well and, I suppose, habit and curiosity triumphed. "What?"

"It isn't plain sailing. Not at all."

In the end, things were funny rather than sad. I put my hand on my hip. "Any more thoughts of the floozy to the discarded middle-aged wife?"

"None," she admitted, "and there's the tragedy." There was a pause. "I'm sorry, Rose, I hope I didn't spoil it for you."

I considered, and the image of the Madonna raising her too-pink hands over the terror and waste flashed through my mind. "No," I said. "You didn't spoil it."

The dark eyes widened, softened, said—I think—"Thank you."

I bent down to put on my shoes, and when I straightened up, Minty had drifted away. Yet the irony had struck home. In that curious, careless way life has of tossing in coincidences and convergences, it was apparent that Minty and I shared more than divided us.

"And there it is. The story of the floozy and the wronged wife . . . and the surprising son-in-law," I said to Charles Madder, after I had described the events of the wedding party. "How is . . . what the paper called your mistress, by the way?"

Charles had surprised me by ringing me up and suggesting a drink. It was not often that one had a chance to make new friends, he pointed out. Certainly not in my position. Why not? I thought, and we were now settled in the House of Commons bar with two bowls of peanuts through which Charles was steadily working.

"My mistress? The one with the exotic sexual tastes? You wouldn't believe how far from the truth that was. It was Flora's doing, of course. Her vile lies. Kate is as normal as anyone and her life has been hell ever since the article." Charles looked both defeated and baffled. "We'll probably get married, but it's changed. Exposure to the white heat of publicity that depicts the reverse of what you are does things to a person."

"I'm sorry about Kate."

He stuck a cigarette in his mouth and lit it. "It's nice to talk to someone who means what they say. Most people . . ." he glanced round the smoke-wreathed bar ". . . don't mean a word they say. How do I know? Because I used to be the same. So it's nice to hear a genuine voice."

"Thank you."

Charles insisted I have a second drink and we made easy conversation as if we had known each other for a long time.

When I got home to Lakey Street, pleasantly warmed by the wine and the prospect of a new friendship, there was a message on the answerphone. "I'm back in the country," said Hal's voice. "When can I see you?"

"Hey," he said, when I phoned him, "I have a window, as the publicist would put it. Can we meet for a meal, or something?"

There was no reason not to see Hal and more than one reason to see him. We agreed he would come over for supper, and I swooped into the old routines of putting together a meal and laying the table. The house was filled with flowers from Poppy's party, and I spent time pulling out dying roses and refilling vases. He caught me with my hands full of spent blooms.

"Hi," said Hal, and proffered a huge bunch of . . . roses. "Bull's-eye, I see," he said drily.

In the kitchen, he made me put down the flowers so that he could look at me properly. "I didn't get a chance to study you at that dinner, so do you mind if I do so now?"

I did a bit of my own scrutiny back. I wanted to catalog the changes and to pinpoint the exact shades of disparity between my idea of him and the man who stood so solidly in my kitchen.

"It's very interesting," said Hal. "You haven't turned out as I expected."

"Oh, yes?"

"You were quite shy in the old days. I thought you might grow into a quiet person, an academic perhaps, someone who preferred the country. You're much smarter and more metropolitan than I pictured you would be."

So, the seven-year brain-cycle theory did hold water. "In that case, I've changed more than you. You look much the same." But Hal seemed indifferent as to whether he had changed or not, which was perfectly in character as he had never been much interested in poking around in the psyche. I gave him a glass of wine. "How was the book tour?"

"Fine, if you like that kind of thing. It went on and on. But I've trained myself to do it gracefully. Why not? I want people to read my books and I'm grateful when they do." He shot me a look. "I know what you might say."

"And what might I say?"

"That's a new one. In the past, I never did what anyone wanted." I found myself grinning, for that was exactly what I had been thinking. He continued, "And since I was over there, I took the chance to go and visit the relations, which only confirmed that I'm neither fish nor fowl, neither an American anymore, nor British. It's a bit of an uneasy place to be. But exile is always good for copy."

There was a silence in which I discovered that sharing a past with someone is deceptive. You think you know everything important about them and, deep down, you do, for the strands of a past history are thick and knotty with issues that require airing and tying up properly. Yet when it came to the give and take of conversation, the little negotiations around the gaps that would initiate this process, I found I did not know enough. "Where *do* we begin?" I asked.

He grinned. "With supper? I'm hungry."

So was I.

By mutual consent, we discussed issues that required no more than the exchange of information. We talked about Hal's journeys, his future projects, the olive farm in Umbria. "Nothing special, as I told you," he said. "Except it's very special because the village has allowed me to slip into their lives. There are times when I almost feel I'm not a stranger, and you can't ask for more than that."

"So you're putting down roots?"

"I suppose so. I'm back on my ecological path. There's a battle going on between traditional methods and the new intensive practices, and I want to be there."

"Do you speak Italian?"

"I've learned the dialect."

Over coffee, he asked about my interests and I told him of my passion for the garden, which he had initiated, about my career and its temporary suspension and the new job. But my sacking had yielded pluses, I was astonished to find myself admitting. "I didn't realize I was in a straitjacket until it wasn't there."

Hal lounged back in his chair. "It's an ill wind," he said comfortably. "There must be other things you want to do."

"Yes, indeed, but I've not had time to think about them."

"Now you have."

"The other shock is to discover how quickly I've forgotten about the actual process of being at work. The getting up and going, the coming back at night. I spent ten years doing the job I most wanted to do, it meant a huge amount, I minded most dreadfully when I lost it. But the funny thing is, after a week or so, I forgot about its routines. I know that I was plunged into turmoil over Nathan but not having a job doesn't worry me too much. It is not engrained. How worrying is that? Forgetting something that took up so much of your life, so easily."

"How worrying *is* that?" He spoke seriously but the blue eyes were smiling.

Hal and I stared at each other. It was not an important or significant look, just a relaxed exchange of thoughts—a clearing of the ground—but, suddenly, I was convinced that it would be possible to be happy and whole again.

"If I'm truthful, Hal, I miss Parsley, my cat, more than the job. She was put down earlier in the year and I think of her most days. Sometimes I wake up and imagine she's on the bed." I looked down at my ringless hand, a gesture that was becoming a habit. "She symbolized such a lot of things." I looked up at him. "Like the rucksack you used to keep in your room."

At midnight, Hal got up to go. "That was very nice," he said. "Can we repeat it?" He bent to kiss my cheek, and there was a second's anticipation—*what next?* "We are friends, you know. We go back a long time."

Was that true? Hal and I had not been friends but lovers, and we had failed each other at a crucial point. Then there had been neither time nor room for friendship. But "friends" was a good word. It evoked the loyalty of old acquaintanceship and knowledge. I liked it. It could be carried into my new life.

"Shall I phone?" Again Hal bent and kissed me. A warm, careful touch on my cheek of which I approved, but my flesh, assuming an independent life, had other ideas and responded with a ripple of gooseflesh. His finger brushed my chin. "Since we have begun nicely, shall I ring?"

When you toss a seed into ground primed with rich compost and watered, it will grow. Usually, unless attended by bad luck, it will grow.

"Yes."

Chapter 24

I thought a lot about the house I would lose. The shell and what was in it. "Simple. Buy another one, start again. The house is not the most important thing," argued Hal, when I told him of my feeling for number seven. But he would.

I thought of the hours, the years, I had spent on it, happily and inventively, its spaces, its corners, the places where the sun spilled into the interiors and over its objects. My hands bore a reminder of hours of polishing and brushing, my back the burden of carrying my children up and down its stairs, the king-size double bed the two dents where Nathan and I had slept for so long.

I thought of my garden, of the tiny pointed buds of spring and the mass cull of autumn, the cycle of growth and death. In the past, I had struggled to put house and garden into order, to render clean and fresh my family's dwelling place. I had struggled to put myself into order. Perhaps there is nothing quite so strong as sublimated passion, the one forced underground, which pulses with secret life.

Richard and Poppy planned to remain at Lakey Street until the New Year and ended up staying well beyond that. Apparently the Kensington flat required repairs and it was easier if they were with me while these were done. Richard had started his job; he left the house early and returned late, the deal being that the still jobless Poppy would supervise the move, and repaint the kitchen and bathroom in their flat.

Christmas came and went, a subdued, different but peaceful Christmas, and nothing had been achieved in the packing department, still less in the job-hunting one. "I'm not cut out for DIY," protested Poppy, when I tackled her. "Anyway, paint gets over my glasses and I can't do it in the lenses."

Both she and I knew that these were excuses. The radiant vision that had burst on me from Thailand had vanished. Its replacement trailed around the house, stuffing objects into plastic bags in a vague, unfocused manner, and spent a lot of time on the phone to Jilly. Jilly who, I pointed out, had got herself a job. How irritating of her, Poppy flashed back. *She would*.

I consulted Sam about Poppy's state of mind. Sam, who was sounding a great deal more relaxed, happy, even, these days, laughed and said it was prewedding nerves. Only, Poppy being Poppy, she had got the timing wrong.

By mid-January, however, Richard had developed the habit of shutting the front door behind him with a bang when he left in the morning and I considered it was time to take action.

I chivvied Poppy upstairs to the spare room and made her begin to pack up the presents. Sniffing a little, she drifted around, picking up clothes and throwing them down. The once immaculate room looked as if a storm had burst through the door and out through the window.

"Can you remember when you moved to Lakey Street?" Poppy abandoned any attempt at packing.

"I do. After living in a flat Dad and I were so pleased to have stairs that we raced up and down them."

"Being an adult . . . it's tricky." Poppy hunched on the bed. "Isn't it? Adults are so wicked and destructive."

"You always said you couldn't wait to grow up."

Poppy pleated the hem of her cardigan. "I wasn't to know adulthood takes a running jump and hangs on your back for the rest of your life."

I took this to mean that Poppy wished she was still in Thailand. You could never be quite sure what Poppy was driving at, but the lateral approach tended to be more productive. "Don't you like your flat?"

"I didn't choose it. But that doesn't matter." She twisted the flesh of her wedding finger so hard that I reached over and stopped her. She looked up at me. "Last night I dreamed I was a little girl again. In the silly bed, you know, the one with the sides that let down. In the dream, I tried to make sure that my room remained the same, but someone kept changing it round."

So Sam had been correct about the prewedding nerves. I moved over to the chest and wrapped up a wineglass. "Where's the girl who had so many plans?"

Poppy stood up. "Where *is* that bed, Mum?"

"In the attic."

She brightened. "Can I take it with me?" She surveyed the stack of salt and pepper mills, tablecloths, decanters and a toast rack in the shape of the Millennium Dome. "Do you want any of this? I don't think I can cope with it all."

"As an act of charity, I'll take the Dome."

Poppy shoved it in my direction. "It's obscene being showered with all this stuff. I should never have allowed it. What will I do with it?"

"The usual."

"That's it. I'll have to use it and put it away tidily. Polish things. Clean them. Take control."

"You're lucky, Poppy," I interposed, gently.

"I *know* I'm lucky, so don't start up about refugees and all that."

I tugged at a strand of her hair. "Stage fright, darling?"

Seizing a modern cut-glass decanter from the clutter, Poppy held it out to me. Reflected in its curve were two distorted faces, preternaturally round and smooth. "You take this."

"No." I was sharper than I intended. "Mazarine sent it over from Paris." My lips twitched. "Apparently, it's a modern classic."

Poppy peered at it. "*That's* what it is."

There was a pause. "If you weren't sure about Richard, why did you marry him?"

Both irritated and amused, she snapped back, "You sound just like Granny."

"So I do. And a mother's place is always in the wrong."

"So *sad,* Mum." She rolled the decanter stopper restlessly between her fingers. "It isn't Richard. It's the set-up."

I reached for another glass. "You're right about one thing. Richard's full of surprises."

Immediately Poppy went all dreamy. "Yes, he is."

"That's the main thing," I said. "The rest can fall in behind it."

There was another long silence, but not a good one. Eventually, Poppy burst out, "I hope you haven't been too nice to Dad.

Have you? Richard says it's only sensible he gets the house, but I can't see it like that."

"I wasn't pushed into it, if that's what you mean." I passed Poppy some tissue paper. "Could you wrap the decanter?"

She muttered, "What about *your* pride, Mum?"

Aha. That was the crux of the matter, and I had to tiptoe across crushed glass. "The textbook doesn't always apply."

"Rubbish. That's an excuse."

I abandoned the third wineglass and seized Poppy by the shoulders. "It's true. You can wait years in the queue, patiently shuffling toward the top, then someone overtakes you and administers a hefty kick on the way. You're happily married, and then you're not, and you imagine you're going to die from humiliation and pain." Under my fingers, Poppy's shoulders felt defenseless. "But you don't, not in the obvious way. What's more, you can get your own back—but not in the obvious way. You get your own back by believing that, yes, despite everything you can live as well, perhaps better. Differently, anyway."

Poppy shrugged me off. "Oh, yes?"

Here the seven-year brain-cycle theory would have come in handy, but Poppy was in no mood for evolutionary science. "I've come to the conclusion that pride is too heavy to carry around. And destructive," I said—lightly, but I meant it. Poppy's mouth tightened. "Poppy darling, are you blaming me for what's happened?"

At that she turned on me, a goaded, troubled Fury. "You didn't fight hard enough to keep Dad. *Why* didn't you? Why can't you make him see what a fool he's making of himself? It's as if I'd gone off with a man of his age. Think about *that*. That *Dad* should do such a thing and you should let him."

She glowed with outrage and I caught a glimpse of the Rose of twenty-five years ago, who had searched for order and security amongst the mess and muddle. Conventional wisdom said that youth was adventurous. I wonder. In no way had I been *that* adventurous. Or rather, I had tried to be, then scuttled away when it went wrong. In her way, Poppy was telling me more or less the same thing.

With one of her more dramatic gestures—and she possessed an excellent repertoire—Poppy slipped to her knees. "Mum, *please* try again. Please try to bring Dad back."

I leaned over and cupped her wet face in my hands. My own was wet with tears, too, but I was laughing at her fierceness and indignation, which was unfair. Her skin felt as smooth as that of the tiny baby I had once held so closely. "Shush," I said. "Shush, Poppy."

As promised Kim Boyle contacted me. "Right, my girl, this is the best I can do. Not a full-time job but part-time, to do serial. Will the finances permit? Can I have you next week?"

At six-thirty on January 21, the alarm shrilled. I got dressed in a black felt skirt, a red sweater and a pair of heels as high as I could manage, given that I was going to wear them all day. For breakfast I ate raw porridge oats with a banana, and drank two cups of strong black coffee.

With a lightish heart, I retrieved my book bag from its peg and left the house. The overgrown bay tree brushed wet fingers across my back as I passed, and I was in the office by nine-twenty.

Kim arrived at half-past ten. His assistant, Deirdre, had already installed me at a desk and issued me with security and canteen cards. These slotted back with no trouble into the worn niche in my wallet.

"Good." Kim ran an eye over the bright-eyed bushy-tailed me. "We'll do nicely. I believe in sauce for the feminist goose and her gander, and since I want to see the children in the mornings, you will come in early and I will stay late."

The office was smaller and less architecturally evolved than that of the Vistemax Group, which meant it was nicer to work in. Its smaller size was, however, indicative of the *Daily Dispatch*'s rank in the ratings war. Not a bad thing, for there was a buzz in the office and the distinct sound of warriors buckling on armor.

"Here . . ." Kim tossed me a volume on Handel and a top-secret ghost-written biography of a female pop star. "See what you make of them."

Proust may have had his madeleine, whose taste and scent goaded him into writing his masterpiece of past loves and hates, despairs and longing. My madeleine was more prosaic, less delicately sensuous, but, as surely, as powerfully, the fonts, spines and promise of books pulled me back.

Handel was an interesting man, but the apparent lack of women in his life shocked his biographer. Even so, the female characters in his operas were invariably arresting for he gave them great buffeting passions and the gift of emotional authenticity. Not that the paper would be in the least interested in *that*. However, the story of the female pop star . . .

"Hmm," said Kim, at the end of the day. "Not sure about Handel."

"I didn't think you would be, so I've concentrated on the other."

"You've got the idea quickly." I resisted the temptation to say, "Of course I've got the idea." He leafed through my suggestions and jabbed his pen here and there on the pages—the role I used to have. But I didn't mind. "How does it feel to be back in an office?"

"Bit like pulling on an old but favorite sweater."

Kim shoved the work back at me. "A bit of tinkering's

needed, nothing major, and we'll go for it. I'll let you know the budget." He gathered up his agenda and headed off to a meeting.

I settled down in the office. By the end of the second week Deirdre and I were well on the way to being friends. I had ascertained that she wore a lot of scent, and kept two pairs of shiny high heels in different colors in her desk. She also had a nose for what would work.

"What about this?" I explained that a diet had come in which argued that individuals should eat according to their blood type. You were allowed either proteins or carbohydrates, and only the lucky AB groups ended up with anything approaching normal meals.

"Do you mean to say that the fact that my hips are two sizes too big has nothing to do with the million chocolate bars I've eaten but is down to my blood group?" She leaned over my desk. "Dynamite, Rose. If my blood group's to blame it leaves me free to stuff myself with chocolate. *Run it.*"

Poppy and I finally managed to pack boxes, lock cases and stuff clothes into bags, and a van took them all away. One day Poppy and Richard had filled the house, the next they had gone, leaving behind a snowfall of tissues, discarded labels and dust.

The following day I telephoned estate agents, all of whom promised to send details of the "opportunities" currently on their lists. Sam came up to London and insisted on going through them with me. It took him two minutes to spot the sensible "opportunity" in Clapham. "That one," he said.

We went to view it on Poppy's birthday and were discussing its pros and cons as we arrived at the Kensington flat for a celebration supper. Looking exceptionally smart in a tailored gray suit and gold jewelery, Alice joined us. She offered Sam a cheek to kiss and kept a hand possessively on his arm as she turned to me. "Rose, you're looking better."

Poppy was in one of her floaty muslin numbers, to which she had added a mass of beads. I kissed her but she was preoccupied and, as soon we had settled in the sitting room, disappeared into the kitchen.

Sam and I batted flat talk between each other. "I don't trust you to be sensible," he was saying, as Richard, who had been giving Alice a guided tour of the flat, ushered her back into the room.

"I don't believe Rose is ever not sensible," Richard said, but his expression suggested that he believed exactly the opposite. He was dressed in corduroy trousers, which strained a little to tightly across the buttocks, and Sam and I exchanged undercover grins. The new Richard still required getting used to.

"Does Poppy need any help?"

Richard looked a trifle grim. "Poppy and cooking are combustible. I'd better go and check."

Sam inspected the large, elegant room, which housed a pair of American colonial gilt chairs, a French provincial mirror with the original glass, and an exquisitely inlaid half-moon side table. "Hell," he muttered. "I thought they were into grass skirts, flowers in the hair and that sort of stuff."

"It's lovely." Alice fiddled with her bracelet, a heavy gold chain. Her eyes grazed the room hungrily. "Richard's parents must have been very generous."

"None of your business." Sam was uncharacteristically sharp. I was startled and, if I was not mistaken, so was Alice.

The doorbell rang and Richard went to answer it. "Nathan," we heard him say. "Were we expecting you?"

"I thought I'd just drop this in . . ." In his office suit,

Nathan appeared in the doorway carrying a large, beribboned parcel. He stopped. "I didn't realize you were having a family party," he said, in a cold, hurt way.

I got up and kissed him, for I, of all people, knew how often Nathan had planned surprises for Sam and Poppy, and how much he would mind being sidelined.

"Dad." Sam hugged him.

In a man-to-man gesture that showed a great deal of pride in his son, Nathan rested his hand on Sam's shoulder and ran a fatherly eye over him. "Why are you in town?"

Sam explained that he had come up to help me look for flats and Nathan's smile switched off. "Nice of you, Sam," he said woodenly.

Without warning, the old pain nagged away, and I felt unutterably weary with the process of disconnection from Nathan which, however we handled it, would be prolonged and pitted with obstacles.

Poppy materialized, wild-haired and frantic. She started visibly when she saw her father. "Bit of a crisis in the kitchen. Hallo, Dad. How nice. Ooh, a present. Can you stay for supper? I need two pairs of strong hands."

Sam and Richard obliged, leaving me with Alice and Nathan. Alice hauled out her mobile phone. "Do you mind? I've forgotten something urgent." She proceeded to conduct a conversation to do with deal tunnels, brokerage, leverage and breakfast.

"I didn't know you'd be here," said Nathan.

"Everything all right at work?" I asked.

"Sure, sure," he said, too heartily. "Figures are up. Everyone's behaving. Couldn't be better." He dug his hands into his pockets. "Couldn't be better."

"I'm doing some work for Kim at the *Daily Dispatch*."

"Oh." He looked startled. "Well, that's good."

We lapsed into silence.

"Yes," he repeated. "Everything's absolutely fine."

Poppy did her best to make him stay but Minty was waiting at home and Nathan would not be persuaded. I turned to Alice, who had finished her conversation. "It was nice of you to make the effort for Poppy."

She slid her phone into her bag. "No trouble. I had a meeting and I crave London from time to time." She looked straight past me to Richard. "How's the new job?"

He looked smug. "Not all number-crunching, I'm happy to say. Strategy, no mercy and lots of money."

I found myself staring at Richard, wondering if his cynicism was real or feigned and, if the former, could Poppy be inoculated against it. Or was he conducting a prolonged tease with his parents-in-law? "Tell me more," begged Alice, and I knew then that Bath was never going to be big enough to contain her. "Which are your sectors?"

Richard purred. "Manufacturing bases, specifically textile firms in the Midlands, small family enterprises that have lost crucial contracts. We advise them on cutting the workforce and contracting out East."

"I thought you didn't approve of capitalism," I interjected.

Richard leaned over toward me. "Rose," he said kindly, "these *are* the realities."

At this point, I caught Nathan's eye and we exchanged a tentative private smile.

He tossed down the last of his wine. "I must go." He kissed Poppy and Alice then, after a hesitation, kissed me, too.

The front door closed behind him, and the assembled company relaxed.

"Poor Dad." Poppy had drunk too much wine in the kitchen. She hustled me into a corner and hissed, "He's having a terrible time with Minty's fertility treatment. He's told me all about it. *Horrible*."

Various factors now fell into place. The medical insurance for one. "That's Dad's business. Not for discussion, Poppy."

Poppy ignored me. "They've been at it for months. Dad hates what it involves—imagine, at his age—and Minty is pretty sour at the nonstrike rate. Bet they're sniggering at the paper."

"Shush," I said sharply, because I could not bear to hear any more. I raised my glass. "Happy birthday."

"Thanks, Mum." She rubbed her hand over her face. "With one thing and another, I feel a hundred and ten."

Later that night, I undressed in my solitary bedroom. No one else was running a bath or listening to the radio. There was no Parsley, of course, on the bed. Even the water pipes were silent.

Naked, I stood in front of the mirror. A woman's reflection met me. But which woman? I pinched and patted a fold of flesh on my stomach and flexed my leg in the way Minty did.

Was it possible to find recompense, meaning, connection with others amid the mess and muddle? I had tried to persuade Poppy that it was, but had I been truthful?

In the past, in a crisis, men and women bound up their feet in leather and linen, and set out on a pilgrimage to the tomb of a saint. There they prayed, for health, children or to grab their neighbor's land. They observed the milk of the Virgin, a fragment of the True Cross shimmering with righteousness, a saint's bones, and gave thanks for being vouchsafed such a miracle. Those who survived came home, immeasurably comforted and enriched.

At this point, I began to shiver with cold and felt more than a little ridiculous. I slipped on my nightdress and went to bed.

Before I fell asleep I told myself, Of course you understand who you are and where you are. Or course you do.

Hang on. There isn't a mistake. You are the woman in the mirror, whose name is Rose, who looks fine. Just fine.

Chapter 25

Lakey Street had been valued, and I received a letter from the solicitor outlining the divorce details. "Mr. Lloyd," the letter finished, "would like you to know that he has done the best for you that he possibly can."

I studied those wretched details. It was true: Nathan had been more than generous. "Guilt," said Vee, "and value added," but I could not bring myself to see it like that. I preferred to think that, contained in those careful provisions, was proof that a marriage had once thrived.

Yet again, Sam hightailed up to London and we tramped through the flat in Clapham for a second time. He urged me to put in an offer. "It's got a garden," he said, as the clincher. "You can't live without one."

I put in an offer, which was accepted.

It was Sam who also pointed out that Easter was coming

and, given that our family was not entirely shot to bits, should we have a gathering at Lakey Street?

"That's a tough call." I did not like the idea. "You realize what you're asking?"

Sam was strangely insistent. He placed his hands on my shoulders and said, in his gentle, serious way, "A guaranteed place in heaven, Mum. No questions asked and no previous taken into account. You'll go through without touching the sides."

"You're in the wrong profession." I touched his cheek. "You should have been a diplomat cobbling together continents. If you think this is a good idea, okay, but the condition is, no Minty."

Sam-the-diplomat set about the negotiations and it was settled that we would gather at Lakey Street for dinner on Maundy Thursday. He even arranged to collect Ianthe before whisking off on an errand that he would not specify. "I'll explain later," he promised.

Ianthe had been of two minds as to whether to be present. "I find it hard to talk to Nathan," she confessed, grief etched on her face. I hated seeing it, and Nathan would have, too.

Having been persuaded, and the spring weather being sharp and cold, she arrived in her tweed coat, smelling of mothballs, and bearing industrial quantities of chocolate and nuts.

I hung up the coat in the spare bedroom and unzipped her case. Ianthe sat down at the dressing table. The pistachio-green frock had come out for the occasion and she had cast a bright blue and yellow scarf over her shoulders. The effect was of a crazed but delightful hummingbird. Busy with the unpacking, it was a minute or two before I registered that she had assumed her waiting pose. Instantly I was suspicious. "Is everything all right, Mum?"

She looked down at her folded hands. "I've been meaning to have a word."

I extracted her toiletries bag from the suitcase. "Go on."

"The doctors are very good," she said, and raised her eyes, "and I have every faith. But I'm old, Rose. You know that." She picked up her hairbrush and swiped impatiently at an escapee wisp then reapplied the pink-orange lipstick—of which I had never imagined I would grow so fond. "I'm only telling you, Rose, because I'm going back into hospital for an operation. They did some follow-up tests. But *don't* tell the others."

I sank down on the bed. "Oh, Mum."

"It's all been arranged. The doctor has pushed it through. There's no need to bother Nathan again. I wouldn't like that."

"No."

She gave herself a little shake. "How nice to celebrate Easter." Our eyes met in the mirror. "Coming and going," she said simply. "That's life."

I was back in Medlars Cottage, watching my father tamping his pipe on the stove. Ianthe moved across the room bearing buttered scones on a blue and white plate, her apron tied in a bow at the back. Little sausage curls bounced on her forehead, which was flushed from the heat of baking. In the background, a radio played dance music.

Ianthe might have had reservations about seeing Nathan, but she greeted him politely enough and kissed Poppy and Richard. I had filled the room with flowers and lit a fire, and the room was warm, fragrant and—I considered—beautiful. The atmosphere was not easy, but it was not ominous either. Given that the family had been shaken hard and unexpectedly into a new shape, it was the best we could do.

Nathan occupied himself with the drinks. Richard, it transpired, was well trained in handling elderly ladies and he chatted away to Ianthe. Nathan edged over to me. "I meant to tell you last time I saw you, Rose, that I like the hair. You're thinner, too."

"Thank you. You're looking . . . fine."

He grimaced. "You mean older and tired." I made no comment. Nathan held out his hand, on which bloomed a patch of eczema. I knew it well. *Do something Rose. Can't let this spread.* And I would pat on the cream that I kept specially. *You must relax.*

"There's a tube still in the medicine cabinet if you want to take it," I said, and I knew that Minty must have made a scene about him coming.

He shoved his hand into his pocket. "Thanks."

It unsettled me to be so near to Nathan and I snatched up a dish of nuts, thrust them at Ianthe and hightailed into the kitchen. There were sounds signifying that Sam and—I presumed— Alice had arrived and I went into the little-used terra-cotta-painted dining room to put the finishing touches to the table, which I had laid with translucent white candles, shimmery ribbon, plates of raisins and pink and white sugared almonds, white lilies and white linen.

It was all rather sentimental, and crying into the wind. But I had wanted to put down a marker, a declaration of faith that we would survive, a message, stubborn and optimistic, that we had not been beaten. Anyway, the table looked lovely.

"Mum." A flushed, excited-looking Sam appeared. "I have something to tell you." I swung round, thinking, He is going to marry Alice. But behind Sam lurked a figure in a short red skirt and jacket and it was not Alice. It was Jilly.

"Jilly," shrieked Poppy in the background, "what are you doing here?"

"Mum . . ." Sam took Jilly's hand and pulled her forward. From being quite pale, Jilly turned pink.

I pulled myself together and kissed her. "How lovely."

Poppy kidnapped Jilly. "What *is* this? I didn't know you'd be here."

"No, you wouldn't know, because I didn't tell you."

Ianthe shook out her best clichés, which she kept for eventualities such as this, where no one had any idea of what exactly was going on. "The more the merrier. Jilly, come and sit next to me."

Rather obviously avoiding Poppy's eye, Jilly took her seat— or, rather, Alice's. Sam unfolded his napkin and cleared his throat. "Happy Easter, everyone."

With a lightening of my heart, I knew that something had happened to Sam, which would be for the better.

Jilly asked for water and took a sip. "You will be wondering . . ."

"Yes, you will." Sam placed a hand on Jilly's arm. Poppy rubbed an eye, which made it water. "You'll be wondering why Alice isn't here."

"Don't mind us," said his sister. "Take all night, please."

Sam looked at Jilly, and Jilly looked right back at Sam, a tender and excited look. Sam cleared his throat. "Jilly and I are going to get married."

"Good God." Nathan put down his glass.

"How lovely," Ianthe echoed.

"Jilly and I have been seeing each other since the party. It sort of progressed from there."

A no-doubt foolish but happy smile seeped across my face. I could not help it. Not so Poppy, who was incensed. "I thought we shared everything, Jilly. You never said a word."

"I couldn't. It was . . . private." A shade that might possibly have been guilt crossed Jilly's radiant face, but only a shade. She helped herself to smoked salmon. "I didn't know what was going to happen, and when . . ."

It was Richard, scenting the coup de grâce, who leaned forward and urged softly, "And when?"

". . . we discovered," Jilly cut a huge piece of salmon and speared it on her fork, "I was pregnant."

Sam looked ridiculously complacent and Poppy gasped.

A candle guttered in its confection of ribbon. Cool and collected, Richard nipped the wick between his finger and thumb. "Well done, Jilly. Smart work."

Nathan shot to his feet. "Excuse me," he said, and left the room.

The napkin bunched on my knee. What would happen to the beautiful, implacable, terrible Alice talking away into her mobile phone?

"There's a thing," said Ianthe, with a little smile. She caught my eye. *Coming and going.*

Nathan reappeared and sat down quietly in his chair. "Sorry," he said, avoiding anyone's eye. For a second or two, movement and sound were suspended around my gaudy table. Then it exploded into life. The words "wedding," "baby," "dates" clicked to and fro across the decorations and the wineglasses glittered as we drank to the future.

We ate, we talked, we planned. We conjured up new illusions to take the place of the old ones, which, I realized with a sense of huge gratitude, would do us very well.

I collared Sam in the kitchen over the coffee tray. "What about Alice?"

The wooden look that I had grown to dread snapped back

into place. "I wanted to talk to you, Mum. She's taken it badly, and I don't understand. I thought the whole point was that Alice didn't want me. So I found Jilly. Now Alice says she'll marry me, so I had to tell her about the baby."

Having assumed that two and two would add up to four, and Alice would dematerialize like a conscience when its owner receives something they really want, my innocent son was troubled.

"Oh, *Sam* . . ."

Poppy had also collared Jilly. "I'll phone you first thing in the morning."

"I might be being sick," said Jilly happily, and slipped her arm through Sam's, "but have a go."

When everyone had gone, I moved through the house, tidying and straightening out the mess. Ianthe was upstairs in bed, and I arranged the remains of the supper on a plate to take to Mr. Sears the next morning.

There was a tap on the kitchen door. I opened it. "Can I come in? I waited in the car until the coast was clear." Nathan was hunched inside his coat and looked exhausted.

"It's very late."

"I thought you might say that. At least give me five minutes to discuss our son."

I stood aside and Nathan entered the kitchen with the polite step of a stranger.

He looked round. A couple of rubbish bags were propped against the sink and he picked up one in either hand. "Where do these go?"

"You know."

He hefted them out to the dustbins, came back, shut the door and leaned against it. "How's Ianthe?"

I turned away to stack plates in the cupboard. "I can't talk about Ianthe."

"I see." He digested the implications. "I'm sorry I haven't been any help."

"I don't expect you to be."

"Rose, look at me." Unwillingly I straightened up and turned round. "Could I have a drink? And then I'll go away."

"I think the wine's finished."

"There was a bottle of whiskey in my study."

"I drank that long ago."

He moved quickly and, before I knew it, I was pinioned against the table. It is so true how smells—in this case, Nathan's aftershave—trigger memory and stir the senses. His eyes were hot and despairing as he said, "Whatever I did, Rosie . . . Rose, it was not against you."

"Nathan, I wish you hadn't come. It was a happy evening . . ." I began to feel dizzy with nerves and fatigue. I pushed him away. "This is not the moment. There's no point either. What's done is done."

He sat down with a thump in a chair. "I blame myself. I feel angry with myself . . . for springing everything on the family, for not knowing enough about my children any more . . ."

I filled the kettle and switched it on. "There's no point in either of us blaming anyone. Don't you see? We were both at fault. It wasn't just you. I should have seen that something was wrong and tried to put it right. You shouldn't have been tempted by Minty but you probably wouldn't have been if I'd been quicker to understand that you were restless." He sighed, a despairing sound.

"Why don't we talk about Sam? I'm so pleased for him. Are you? Jilly will suit him, and bring him out of himself."

"I suppose so."

I reached for the teabags. "You don't sound thrilled."

"It came out of the blue."

"No one knew. It wasn't because you were being left out. I certainly didn't spot what was happening. Detective of the Year." I sent him a wintry smile. "Not." I dunked the teabags in the hot water and watched the stain fan through it. "Will you tell Minty about the baby?"

"Not yet. I haven't the energy. It's difficult . . ." He looked up. "It's a bit tricky . . ."

I think he was wanting me to ask questions but I was not going to oblige. The subject was too painful. Whatever he and Minty were planning was for the new Nathan of whom I knew nothing. The bargains and habits of our marriage no longer applied. I placed the tea in front of Nathan who muttered a thank you and reached for the sugar. His hand was poised with the filled spoon over the cup when, with a sad, unpleasant shock, I realized I did not view him as my husband any more.

In a gesture that sent tea flying over the table, he pushed away the cup. "I don't know why mind and body play such tricks but they do. When I left you, I didn't want you very much. Now I think about you all the time."

The tea pooled on the polished walnut. I sat quite still. A pulse beat at the junction of Nathan's neck and shirt collar, and the feather of gray hair above his ears had grown larger and more noticeable. Only six months ago I would have given a year of life to hear Nathan say that. I would have listened humbly and with immense gratitude. But now the words fell on an inner ear that had been deafened by events. There is only so much discordance to which anyone can listen before the notes become unbearable and they tune out. It is, I suppose, a basic survival technique.

"Go on," he urged, and grabbed my hands. "Tell me I'm a fool."

"Let go, please. Either we talk about the children or you go, Nathan."

He released me instantly. "Sorry . . . shaming. Stupid." He picked up the cup, set it down. "Forget it. I'm not thinking straight."

"You almost make me feel sorry for Minty," I whispered. I got up to fetch the cloth and wiped up the spilled tea.

Nathan observed the patch on his hand, which was dark red. "Things are tricky at work and I can't talk to Minty. She sees things from a different point of view. I can only say this to you, Rose, but it's . . . difficult to be eyed up by younger men who can't wait to get their hands on your job. They don't even bother to be civil to your face. God knows what they say behind your back."

I sat down opposite him. "You were just the same—remember?"

"True. But at least I was polite to Rupert while I waited for him to drop off the perch." The familiar strongman smile flashed briefly. "It's different, as you well know, being at the other end of the process."

"Of course. But you have experience, and you're wily."

"But it doesn't make it easier." Nathan searched in the cupboard where we kept the drinks and pulled out a half-full bottle of red wine. He reached for a glass. "There's this consultant. First-class degrees from Oxford and business school sticking out of his ears and he's been released into the organization like a ferret."

"Don't be so jumpy. You're more than capable of outflanking him."

"Do you think so?" he asked. "Really?"

"Yes." It was easy to say.

Nathan stood behind my chair. "I wonder . . ." His hand briefly stroked my hair and came to rest on my shoulder. "I wonder how long it will be before the ax falls."

This was not the Nathan I knew. I covered his hand with mine. "Listen to me. You're not to give in." I removed my hand. "What does Minty say?"

"I don't know, Rose. I just don't know."

My chair scraped along the floor as I stumbled to my feet, "Oh, Nathan, after all this, you *aren't* happy."

He leaned back against the sink and cradled the wineglass. "I want to say that I'm out of my place, out of my depth, but I can't. I can't order time to reverse. I can't say that I want some peace and breathing space, when I chose to pursue precisely the opposite. I can't say to Minty that she shouldn't have a baby because I should be concentrating on grandchildren. I can't turn to you, Rose, and ask, 'What do I do?' I can't ask to come back."

No, it was not possible. Try as I might, I could not slot everything back into place. Leaving a marriage was not as simple as walking out of the door. It destroyed something so deep, so built into the blood and bone: the love that comes after bruising desire has faded, trust, familiarity, the pleasure from commitment, and it could not be rebuilt.

But something might be salvaged . . . with luck. With generosity and pity, too, which both of us must find.

I put my hand over his mouth. "Don't." His lips moved under my fingers. "Listen to me, Nathan. We're already getting used to not being with each other. It will become easier. Anyway, we won't lose each other entirely. How can we?" I slipped my arms around him and held him, as I might have held Sam. "You hurt me so much that I thought I was going to die, but that's over. I've come to see that love flows and adjusts into different shapes at different times. Meeting Hal the other day," Nathan squeezed his eyes shut, "also made me see that the people who matter never leave you." I shook him gently. "Nathan, look at me. Open your eyes. You were right in that respect. They are there."

Nathan whispered, "I made the mistake of thinking sex was something it wasn't." He looked up at me, tired and baffled. "Or perhaps I'll never know why I did what I did."

Perhaps neither of us would ever know. And that was life.

I made the joke—much as the little mermaid, who made her way with bleeding feet toward the man who did not want her, might have made it. "At least you had a good time making the mistake."

"Shut up, Rosie." Nathan held me as if he would never let go, and muttered into my shoulder, "Minty's frightened of living here."

For a second or two, I held the familiar body that was no longer familiar. Then I released him. "Tough."

He dug his hands into his pockets. "And what about you? What have I done to you?"

It was a moment before I managed a reply. "And what did I do to you, Nathan? I thought I had you precisely right and I fitted myself around that strong notion sitting in my head. But I must have missed something, the bit of you that also longed for the green grass on the other side of the fence. To travel, to do something different. I did at twenty, so why not you at fifty? But I had grown used to you being predictable, and why should you have been?" I looked down at my hands, resolving that I must not make this gesture a habit. "Perhaps that's the real trouble with marriage. The groove becomes so worn and so smooth that you forget to think about it. Properly. Painfully. Until it's too late. But you mustn't worry. I'll be all right. So will you."

"Clocks don't turn back?"

I shook my head. "You have Minty to think of."

"So I do." Nathan picked up the wineglass, thought better of it, placed it carefully on the sideboard and began to weep. They were very final tears.

An hour later, Nathan left Lakey Street. By then he was dry-eyed and pale. He kissed me briefly and said, "We'll keep in touch, whatever happens."

"Of course," and I added, "You can move in here as soon I've got the flat sorted out."

"Anything holding you up? Can I help?"

"Only the details."

The front door closed behind him and I was left in the quiet, shadowed, changing house.

Chapter 26

I exchanged contracts on the flat. I did not talk about it much, and Sam and Poppy were forbidden to make any reference to a new life or new beginning—which, of course, it was. Gently, gently to catch the monkey, I instructed them. I was still shaking out my damp, crimped wings, and I wanted this rite of passage to be made without fuss or grand gestures.

I began to pack my half of the house. Soon, the landing was stacked with boxes. My study disappeared and the cream and white order of the kitchen went with it.

In the attic, I stumbled across an old-fashioned attaché suit-case, labeled "Jack's clothes" in Ianthe's handwriting. It was stuffed with baby clothes, the ones I couldn't bring myself to throw away. A tiny smocked dress. Sam's first dungarees. A pair of scuffed red shoes.

The dust made me sneeze—or perhaps I was crying.

Right at the bottom, hidden in tissue paper where it might have been overlooked, was a flat cap made of tweed. My father's.

I buried my face in it. *Where's my little chickaninny?*

I returned the dress, the shoes, the dungarees and the cap to the case, with layers of tissue paper, and lugged it down to the landing.

A quiet spring ticked away, a healing time, punctuated by calls from the solicitor and the estate agent. I continued to work for Kim two days a week. More often than not Vee sent over a book. *If you get any thinner, I'll kill you.* Neil Skinner rang up and booked me in for more research work in June, this time on arts funding. An invitation arrived in the post to the wedding of Charles Madder and Kate Frett. A note was enclosed: could I come to a small lunch party the day before because Charles would particularly like to introduce me to his children?

Poised behind spring was summer, a riot of color and sensual tease.

Along with the garden, I waited, too: I waited to slough off an old skin, for those new wings to dry in the sun, and to step forth clean and newborn. In a manner of speaking, I was on the road again.

Kim and I were discussing the merits and demerits of a book on interior design. Kim was leaning over the desk and his tie was getting in the way. I was slumped in my chair, sipping cappuccino. We were enjoying ourselves arguing over whether purple walls and gilding had mainstream appeal. (Not.) We also talked figures and contracts, publishers and readers. Into this agreeable interlude came Poppy's phone call. "Mum, I need to see you."

After work, I made the detour to Poppy's and rang the bell in what appeared to be a silent flat. Eventually, the door opened, revealing a tearstained Poppy in glasses.

She led me into the kitchen and I almost tripped over a pile of unwashed clothes dumped on the floor. The sink was stacked with china and an astonishing number of wineglasses. Something was boiling in a saucepan on the stove.

"Grief," I said.

Poppy frowned. "I was trying to tidy up. Richard hates mess." She bit her lip. "I had no idea that he was a tidiness fanatic. He was never like that before. Anyway, I can't seem to get it right. Then we quarrel and he comes home even later. I have all the time in the world, Mum, and I do nothing. I don't know where the time goes, and I get cross so I do even less."

I switched off the gas under the saucepan, picked up the rubber gloves and said, in a practical way, "I'll wash up if you get on with the other things."

Poppy did an abrupt volte-face. "Oh, Mum, there's no need to go overboard."

"Wouldn't it help?"

Poppy flung a couple of tea towels on to the floor. "I don't see why I should give in to him. Just because he has a job, he thinks he can come home demanding supper." She raised her eyes to the ceiling. "Wake up, Richard. This isn't the nineteenth century."

I rescued the tea towels and nudged the pile of laundry into a corner. "Darling, it's very hard giving up traveling and freewheeling for domesticity but it can and must be done, by most people anyway." Poppy sniffed skeptically. "If you had a job you might feel better."

"I don't seem to have cracked that either." Poppy had decided to aim for publishing on the editorial side. "Actually, I was offered one as a sales assistant but I thought it would be silly to do something I had no intention of sticking to."

"Wouldn't it have been better to get a foot in the door? Knowing how books sell must be quite useful, Poppy, and if you had a job you would not be dependent on Richard."

Ianthe's voice, loud and strong.

"You're such a dinosaur, Mum. Richard agrees with me that it's no use compromising."

I sighed. "Then why the upset?"

"I don't know." Poppy hunched herself into a small, perplexed ball. "I don't know why I'm behaving so badly."

I gave in to my mothering impulse and snapped on the rubber gloves. I knew what Poppy was talking about—of course, I knew. Olive trees and a wine-dark sea. Fountains in the sunlight. They were enticing, radiant mental wallpaper. I said carefully, "Poppy, you chose to get married."

She exploded out of her torpor. "But I didn't want to become dull and colorless." She aimed a kick in the direction of the laundry. "I can't understand how Richard has changed. He wasn't like this before. It's as if he's been swallowed up and there's an impostor in his place. All this will-you-get-supper-because-I-go-to-work nonsense. I *know* I'm lucky, and I'm not starving and I'm not a refugee and my relatives haven't all been massacred but, I'm sorry, that makes no difference when your spirit is sore."

I pulled her close enough for the rim of her glasses to bite into my cheek. My poor Poppy. She would have to flex and bend. "Mark time, Poppy. For a little while. Then you'll become used to it. Don't muck up and don't give up yet. You'll regret it if you do."

She sighed and snuggled into me. "What do I do, Mum? You know. You've been through it."

"Your father and I were lucky enough that we both knew what we wanted."

In my case, it had not taken rocket science and Nathan had spotted my needs at once. At our fifth meeting, he had sat beside me in a cinema and during the adverts he took my hand. "I want to settle down, Rose, and I think you do." He lifted my hand and kissed my fingers, one by one. "I want to marry you." A little later, he asked, "Take me up to Yelland. I would like to see where you were as a child. Then I shall understand important things about you."

How powerful another's understanding can be. It works miracles. How richly the imagination can build up love with words and images. How grateful I was for it. How I latched on to the promise of order and love that Nathan offered.

I kissed Poppy's tangled hair and repeated, "Don't give up."

Her eyebrows twitched together. "He's a devil. What on earth made me marry him?"

"Am I?" Richard interjected from the doorway, and both Poppy and I started. "You didn't think that before. In fact, I remember quite the reverse in Thailand."

Poppy wrenched herself free from me. "How dare you eavesdrop?"

"If I'd been blind and deaf, I couldn't have missed this touching scene." Clearly very angry, Richard advanced into the kitchen. He was wearing his office suit and some of the old bead-draped Richard was evident in the two missing buttons at the cuff. "I have a perfect right to be in my own home."

I divested myself of the rubber gloves—always a good idea in a fight. "Hallo, Richard."

Richard ignored me and addressed his wife. "I didn't think you were the type that went running to Mummy."

Poppy put her hands behind her back. "I'm not. But if I did choose to do so, you couldn't stop me."

"What about loyalty?" He took a step toward Poppy and she backed away. "Have you ever heard the word?" He wrenched off his suit jacket and draped it over a chair. I caught a glimpse of his hurt, puzzled expression. "Do you think you could leave, Rose?"

Discretion is the better part of valor, and I edged toward the door.

"I forbid you to go," hissed Poppy.

Richard said, "This is none of your mother's business."

"It is if I say so."

Richard grabbed Poppy by the arm. "Do you want your mother to watch this? Are we a spectator sport?"

"Mum stays."

Richard flushed a dangerous red. "I'm out all day earning our bread and I don't appreciate coming home to a tip and I don't appreciate . . ." he shot me a justifiably nasty look ". . . you indulging in a spot of character assassination with your mother."

Richard was right. This was their affair, and private. I picked up my bag and beat my retreat. As I shut the front door behind me, I heard Richard say, "Poppy, that was unforgivable . . . How could you do that to me?" and the sound of her frantic sobbing.

"Richard, I didn't mean it. I didn't mean to hurt you . . ."

Early the next morning Mazarine phoned. "I've sold the house. At a loss. But I couldn't stand it."

It must have taken a great deal for her to part with such a valuable asset, which in the normal course of events she would have so enjoyed. I stifled a small pang of regret that something so beautiful should drop out of her hands. *"Dommage,"* she added.

"You did the best thing."

"Do you think so?"

"Without question."

Mazarine dropped her habitual guard. "Rose, I am glad you are my friend."

"I'm glad you're mine." We pondered on this pleasurable exchange. In the background there was the sound of banging. "Where are you?"

"In the gallery. The boys are setting up the exhibition. You must come. It's on the neuro-linguistic implications of rubbish. You'll love it. You must come and look, really look, and try to understand."

She sounded relieved and lightened of a burden. I promised to come over in June and wrote the date down in my diary. I also told her the news about Sam and Jilly.

"Nature abhors a vacuum," she said.

I had just put down the phone when someone hammered on the front door. To my surprise it was Sam. He was shocked and out of breath. I ushered him in and shut the door. "Mum, thank God you're here. I couldn't think of who else to turn to. I need your help. I've just been phoned by the hospital in Bath. Alice— apparently—I can't believe this—she tried to kill herself. The cleaner found her and rang me."

"I'll pack a bag."

His face cleared. "Would you, Mum? I need moral support."

"Where are her parents?"

"In Australia. Holiday. It'll be a day before they can get

back." He ran his hand through his hair. "I can't bear to think of Alice on her own."

The nurse on duty at the hospital inquired who we were and when we explained fixed on Sam: "I don't think you should see her." However, she was prepared to negotiate with me when I pointed out that there was no one else. "There should be *someone*," I said.

Alice had been isolated at the end of the ward in a single room that managed to be both stuffy and chilly at the same time. It smelled of disinfectant and something else . . . If despair had a physicality, it would have been that.

When I went in she was lying motionless with her face turned to the window. I drew up a hard hospital chair and sat down. "Hallo, Alice." No answer, and I had a vivid mental picture of the golden, glossy Alice breaking up into pieces. She looked thin and the blond hair straggled over the pillowcase, as brittle-looking as driftwood. I tried again. "Alice, it's Rose."

"What on earth made *you* come?" she whispered.

"We've known each other a little while. I thought you should have someone here until your parents arrive."

Her lips barely moved. "Why bother? We don't have anything to do with each other any more."

I took one of her limp hands between mine. "I'm so sorry that you felt so desperate . . ."

"What do you know about it, Rose?"

"I know what it's like to be left. It . . . it sensitizes you to other people in the same boat."

It took so little to destroy someone.

There was another long pause and she seemed to gather herself. "Isn't it funny? It's the decent, kind ones who let you down in the end. You get so used to them being decent and kind that you forget we're all the same underneath. That they'll seize the main chance just like anyone else."

This was not fair on Sam. "He waited a long time, Alice, and I suppose he gave up. Perhaps he felt there's a limit to how long you can love and wait for someone to come to heel. Or cooperate. In the end, he had to get on with his life."

Tears sprang into Alice's eyes and I leaned over and wiped them away. "I feel so bloody tired," she said. "Stupid, too."

"Alice, do your employers know where you are?"

"I don't know."

"Would you like me to deal with them?"

"I don't care," she said. "Do as you wish."

After a few minutes, I left her and went to find Sam.

Between us we concocted a story about flu, and he undertook to deal with that side of things. We agreed that I would remain with Alice until the evening, when he would pick me up.

I returned to the dingy room. After a bit Alice seemed to doze and the afternoon ticked away.

A trolley squelched down the corridor. Phones rang. A nurse popped her head round the door to check on the patient and went away again. Eventually, Alice opened her eyes and looked straight at me. "I thought Sam would be there for ever. He said he would be. I thought I could take my time before . . . well, before I was dragged into being a wife and all that." She frowned. "That was what Sam wanted but why should he have it all his way? I should have known that no one is ever there forever."

I had no answer to that.

A second nurse came in with a tray and we helped Alice to sit upright. I handed her a cup of tea. "Drink," I ordered. She swallowed a few sips and began to look better. I cleared a space on the locker for the cup and saucer.

I felt her eyes burning into my back. "Why didn't I do it properly? Atypical of me. I'm usually so thorough."

"Perhaps you didn't want to." I turned back to face her.

A weak smile touched the pale lips. "Did you think of it at all?"

"No."

Alice was silent, then asked, "What's Jilly like? What's she got that I haven't?"

I chose my words with care. "Jilly is different from you. She's more conventional . . . I think."

"There's no need to go on. I can picture the type." Alice slid back down the pillows. She shielded her eyes with an arm. "Sam deserves someone nice, someone who will put him first. I would have never have done that. I'm not nice enough. I have myself to look after, too. Anyone who says they don't is lying."

Obviously Alice had been admitted in a hurry, and her clothes had been tossed onto a chair over by the window. I picked up her gray flannel trousers. They were stained and smelled of vomit. A black cashmere jumper was just as bad. Alice's beautiful, expensive clothes. I knew she would mind about those. Gently, carefully, I folded them. "I'll get these cleaned and delivered back to you," I said.

She dropped her arm. "Why are you doing all this for me, Rose? You never liked me much."

"I hate to see Sam hurt."

"So why?"

"Because you were always honest," I replied. "You may have hurt Sam but you never led him up the garden path. You never promised anything you wouldn't deliver."

But she and I were linked by an experience we had not sought and, I suspected, Alice would take longer to heal. I brushed back her hair. "Alice, will you promise not to do this again?"

Her color brightened. "Who knows?" she replied, with a touch of her old imperiousness. "I might have got a taste for it."

Alice remained in contact. After she left hospital she was given a month's leave, and because she felt low and desperate she rang me. Clearly she did not have much rapport with her own parents. But I had a brainwave and packed her off to Mazarine in Paris to help with installations.

They got on rather well. "At least," Mazarine reported back, "she is capable of great pain and passion." She added a (rare) compliment: "In that respect she is more French than English. But I shall take her shopping."

Chapter 27

I was kept busy lighting candles around the Madonna in St. Benedicta's: for Poppy and Richard, Sam and Jilly, Nathan, Ianthe, Alice. I also lit one for myself. It seemed appropriate.

In the office Kim piled on the work. On several occasions, I ended up going in early and leaving late. The buzz was that the *Daily Dispatch*'s figures were looking good, and the advertising department went round with a bounce in their step.

But these days I hurried less. There was no need. Today as I crossed the park, I enjoyed the birdsong, a tense exchange between a parent and child, the drone of an aircraft checking into its flightpath. My father had been a good listener. He had liked birds, the sound of water and the rustle of grass. The sounds that I was enjoying were city ones, but they also repaid attention. They were a line into life: ordinary and unremarkable.

Over by the path skirting the river, the buds on the chestnut were swelling nicely. Pink tulips bloomed under a maple and I bent down to examine the nearest. Greenfly swarmed over the concave inner petal fretworked with tiny green veins. That was good: Nature had not given up.

Swinging my book bag, I rounded the corner into Lakey Street and there was Hal. In the back of my mind, I had been expecting him so I was not surprised. It was absolutely in character that he was sprawled comfortably on the front doorstep, reading the evening paper. Beside him was a basket with a hinged lid.

"Have you been waiting long?"

He looked up and sprang to his feet. "That's great. I'd given you twenty more minutes, and then I was going to try again another day."

A scuffle from the basket broke an embarrassed pause. "What have you got there?"

"If you let me in, I'll show you."

In the hall, he put down the basket and opened it. "Come here. It's a present."

I knelt down on the cold tiles, looked inside and felt my heart squeeze: it was a tiny cat, as rippled and tawny as a jungle creature. I put out a finger, touched its head—and once again I was pacing the house, holding my shouting babies, while a cat drowsed on the shelf above the radiator.

"Abandoned," Hal explained. "Amanda, my ex-wife, found it in the road. But I'm afraid its leg has been injured at some point and healed badly, so it's not very mobile."

The cat had allowed me to touch it, but I sensed this was not a compliant spirit. Its yellow-green eyes had the bold stare of a vagrant used to living off its wits. This was an animal that would require time and guile to woo and tame.

I looked up at Hal. "I miss Parsley more than I can say."

"You can have it, if you want it." He hunkered down beside me. "Poor little guy."

We carried it into the half-dismantled kitchen and tried to settle it. Its injury hampered its movements, but after several bouts of spitting and arching its back, it curled up on an old sweater of mine and went to sleep.

Hal put his hand on my shoulder. "Rose?" He was asking permission. To push past the exchange of information to more weighty things? I did not know, and I did not know what I would ask him in return.

His hand tightened on my shoulder. "You look well."

"I am." I noted his expensive-looking trousers and jacket. "And you look prosperous."

"Actually," he said, "I've come to ask you something."

There was a new jar of honey on the table. I picked it up and put it into the cupboard. Suddenly I felt as awkward as a schoolgirl. "Why don't you stay and have some supper? I could do pasta. Then you can ask me."

"I should take you out."

I shut the cupboard door. "I wouldn't have asked you if I didn't mean it."

"Well, then," he said. "I would. But would you mind if I phoned Amanda? She was half expecting me. Don't worry, she won't mind. And her husband certainly won't."

While Hal was phoning, I whisked round the kitchen, making a carbonara sauce, boiling the pasta, laying the table, and I happened to glance up at the garden.

It was far less tidy, with an unfamiliar sprawling and rambling dimension, but the Marie Boisselot had assembled a whole dinner service of white platelike blooms.

"What are you thinking?" Hal had come back into the room.

The lilac blossom was heavy and abandoned-looking, the *Solanum* romped over the trellis and the buds on the Iceberg by the window looked promising. "That I will plant my next garden with a bit more color. I shall do it differently."

Hal peered outside, but he knew nothing of the white period. One day I might tell him. The notion lit a spark of interest, excitement, even. I made him sit down, gave him a glass of wine and hunted around in the half-packed-up kitchen for bowls.

"Amanda's pleased you'll take the cat."

I busied myself draining the pasta and mixing in the sauce. "How long were you married?"

Hal sat down at the table. "Nine years. Amanda's a good, patient person, but even she couldn't take the absences. Anyway, she found Edward and is very happy."

"Did you mind?" I put a plate in front of him, and sat down.

"Yes, I did. Very much." His eyes met mine. "I was a fool."

I concentrated on forking up the pasta. I did not wish to put everything into pigeonholes—good, bad, indifferent—but it was important to me that Hal minded about the failure of his marriage.

"I seem to specialize in being a fool, Rose, don't I?"

My fork assumed a life of its own and clattered back on to the plate. "Meaning?"

Pushing the plate aside, Hal placed his hands on the table. He cleared his throat. "Let's get this over and done with. I haven't ever been able to say sorry that you lost the baby and for the way I treated you. It's something I have wanted to do. Now I can."

At the first turning of the second stair
I turned and saw below
The same shape twisted on the banister . . .

I hesitated to discuss this subject. I could not bear for us to dissect it into the small and tame. "I should never have agreed to go with you, Hal, but I was sick with love, and I didn't think. I didn't know the dangers. I was ignorant."

"At least I should have looked after you better. I shouldn't have left you in Quetzl, however hard you begged. I thought it was the right thing, that it showed we'd taken proper decisions. But it wasn't very adult."

My eyes locked on to his. "At the time it was . . . the solution."

Hal made no effort to touch me, and I think he wanted to bridge the gap between us, but that was right: we needed to air this subject without distraction. "I'm sorry, so very sorry. I've never forgiven myself for leaving you like that. In that scuzzy hotel where you could have picked up a terrible disease. You were sick, and needing attention. But I was so desperate not to . . . determined to do the work on the Yanomami. I couldn't get over the transition from a love affair to something that threatened to pin me down, and I could only think about myself. So I made the choice."

"It was my choice, too," I offered, but my voice was not quite under control.

"Yes, but it's a proper, better life if we can think about ourselves *and* take on board others. Or one other. Am I forgiven?"

The telephone began to ring, but I ignored it. Eventually it gave up and the silence in the kitchen was shattering. I smiled at Hal. "I forgave you years ago. I had to, otherwise I could not have continued to be married to Nathan. I had to be clear of you to live with him. I pushed you to the back of my mind and got on with another life."

"Do you regret it?"

"No. Never. I've been very happy. And I didn't want it to end. But it has."

The answer seemed to please him, and he nodded. The blue eyes were still like gentians, the color of peace and resolution.

He nudged his glass. "Tell me more."

If becoming older meant loss, the loss of childhood, magic and belief, and the first flush of desire and faith, then it also gave back something unexpected. For as Hal and I continued to talk, and shaped the past into comprehensible slabs, desire reignited its lick and burn, and an old hunger and belief stirred. I was not dead. I was not finished. Neither was I invisible, nor beaten. And fresh air was blowing through the habit and expectation.

Sometime later, I do not know how much later, we had talked out what we had done in the past, and what we planned for the future. Hal's took in Namibia (again), the Yanomami (again) and the Umbrian olive farm. Mine was to rebuild my work (on different terms), earn a living and make a new home.

"I must go," he said, at last. "When can I see you again? Why don't you come over to my flat?" He smiled. "There are no ghosts." He shrugged on his jacket. "Or come to the farm before summer takes hold. It's at its best then."

With his hand on the door, he paused. "I'm glad I took the risk and came here."

It took me some time to get to sleep but when I did I dreamed of floating through sunlit air, as light and unfettered as a feather drifting from an angel's wing.

When I made it downstairs the next morning, the cat was still curled on the sweater, but I sensed it was defensive and un-settled. At my entrance, it raised its head, and its fur was as soft and golden as you could wish. I rustled up a cat meal from a packet of Parsley's favorite biscuits, which still lurked in the cupboard, and some warmed-up gravy. I told it that it was a beautiful creature, and it listened.

It went back into the cat basket without too much trouble but protested when I let myself out of the house and down Mr. Sears's steps.

"Is that you, Betty?" he called.

The weather was growing warm, and the room was stuffy. Even so, Mr. Sears had retreated under his rugs. He looked so small and beaten by life and his disabilities, and he was crying, copiously and silently. I knelt beside him and put the basket on the bed.

"Mr. Sears, I've brought you something. A present."

"If it's from the council, send it back."

I opened the basket, and the cat favored me with a green glint. "You be good," I lectured it. "Know which side your bread is buttered."

I eased it out and placed it on Mr. Sears's lap. "A good home is wanted, and I wondered if you would like to give it. It needs a bit of looking after because it's been injured. If you would like it, Mr. Sears, I'll take it to Keith and get him to check it over."

Mr. Sears gave a great cry, and his hands scooted over the rug. The cat tensed, reared its head and transferred its attention from me to the tearstained Mr. Sears.

He extended a finger with its horny nail. "Lie down," he ordered—against every rule of cat training. By some miracle, the cat merely arched its back, adjusted its stiff leg and did as it was told.

Mr. Sears looked triumphant. "Some things never leave you."

I backed into the kitchen. By the time I emerged, the cat

had settled on the bed and it and Mr. Sears were conducting an ongoing conversation in "stomach talk," as the Japanese would have it. They took no notice of me.

I rang Hal. "I've given the cat away," I confessed. "Someone needed it more than I did but also . . ."

"Yes?"

"It would have been a going back. It would be trying to relive a stage that has gone. I'm not sure I can explain it. I'm sorry. I hope you're not offended."

"Very interesting," he said, "and, no, I don't mind." I could tell he meant it.

"Hal, will you come to a party for a friend who's getting married? I think it will amuse you."

"On condition that you come shopping."

"Which first?"

"Shopping."

Which is how it came about that, dressed in my French linen dress and wearing the French underwear, I went with Hal to Charles Madder's lunch party to celebrate his wedding, which was supposed to be secret.

But the press had been working on it. When we left, we ran straight into a phalanx of photographers. The result was a front-page photograph in the next day's paper—of Charles and Kate leaving the restaurant, followed by Hal and me. I was clutching a large carrier bag, which contained the softest, most supple and expensive walking boots Hal could afford, and which he had insisted on buying me.

Poppy came to view the new flat. "I've been ordered to report back to Dad," she said. "And he ordered me not to tell you."

"Well, don't, then."

Poppy poked her head into a kitchen cupboard. "It smells dreadful—of dead insects. I hope you're going to rip it all out and start again."

"There's no need. Underneath the ghastly paint is some lovely wood. It just needs cherishing."

While I made lists, Poppy prowled through the rest of the flat, but I gave up after a bit. I could do everything when I moved in.

"It's OK," said Poppy, but she was doubtful. "And the garden is twee."

"As long as the flat is warm and waterproof."

"So unlike you, Mum. You always took such pains at Lakey Street. You put so much energy into making it nice. Promise me you won't go downhill and not care."

"Do I look riddled with decay?" Poppy rummaged in a smart, expensive-looking handbag shaped like a croissant. "Nice bag," I added.

A funny little look stole over her face. "Isn't it? Richard gave it to me." She fished out makeup and a transparent plastic envelope full of loose change. "Where *is* my mobile?"

I poked at the envelope—not the luminous envelope I used to think about at sixteen but an infinitely more earthbound, practical one. "Why all the change, Poppy?"

"Richard says we have to start saving. Pension and things. Big trees from little acorns grow. So, I'm saving my coins."

This was yet another new light shed on my impulsive, romantic daughter. I snapped my notebook shut and tucked my hand into Poppy's elbow. "How's it going?"

"Well . . . we had a big row the other day. I packed my suitcase, but Richard stopped me at the door."

"Are you speaking or nonspeaking at the moment?"

There was a pause. "Speaking . . . sort of. I've got a job

interview, editorial, and Richard bought me a trouser suit to wear for it, so I have to speak to him."

"Oh, well, then," I said. "It can't be all that bad."

I drove Poppy back to Kensington. "Has Sam mentioned Alice?" I asked her.

"He said she was going to be all right, that he felt terribly guilty, and he'd had no idea she felt about him the way she did."

I skirted an illegally parked lorry. "I liked Alice much better after Sam left her. She's honest."

Poppy made a face. "Jilly's upset. She feels Alice set out to ruin her happiness."

"I don't think Alice would put herself through all that just to get back at Jilly. I think Jilly was irrelevant."

"Well, that will cheer her up." There was just a touch of malice in Poppy's tone. Perhaps she hadn't forgiven Jilly for keeping her in the dark. "But if you think Jilly was irrelevant you're wrong. Jilly took one look at Sam at the party and went for him."

This was a new perspective on the luminous Jilly.

Each of us reflected on the conversation, until we turned into Poppy's street. "You're not planning to get a small dog or take up knitting or anything, Mum, are you?"

Astonished, I glanced at her. "No. Why?"

"Women who retire from the world tend to do that sort of thing."

"Am I retiring from the world?" I shook my head at Poppy. "Not."

She considered my cutting-edge linen trouser suit and high-lighted hair. "No." She smiled. "But some people do. They decide to let go."

"Well, I haven't. I have plenty to do. Plenty to see. And

there's someone I want you to meet. He's an old friend from university and I thought he might interest you."

Her face darkened. "I find that odd to think about, Mum. You with a past. It's not how I see you. But I suppose I'll get used to it. You don't think," she shot out, "you'd ever go back to Dad? He talks about you a lot when Minty's out of earshot."

I did the only thing I could do. I reached over and took her hand, keeping the other on the wheel. Poppy stared straight ahead. After a minute or two, she retracted her hand, took off her glasses and polished them.

Chapter 28

Timon rang. "What's it like to grace the front page? Could you celebrate with a sandwich lunch in the office? I've checked with Jean. Nathan will be out on a brainstorming day in Bournemouth. You won't run into him."

I laughed. "No need for the deep cover. Nathan and I are perfectly polite to each other when we meet."

More out of curiosity than anything, I accepted Timon's invitation but made sure that I was more than five minutes late.

The office block looked the same and, inside, smelled the same, and the same bright pink notepad lay on Timon's desk, flanked by a plate of sandwiches and mineral water.

He held out his hand. "A lot of water has gone under the bridge."

This was so evident that I did not bother to reply. Timon's smile was a trifle grim. "Okay, Rose, let's dispense with the small talk?"

"Okay," I countered, and did a rapid mental review of the figures I had spotted on Kim's desk. "How do you feel about the dip in your figures?"

Competition always sharpened up Timon. "The *Daily Dispatch*'s weren't that brilliant."

"The *Daily Dispatch* wasn't running a couple of promotions."

We gave ourselves time to reflect on the discrepancy in favor of the *Daily Dispatch*. Timon offered me a sandwich and poured out the water. "You haven't lost your wits. I take it Nathan has seen you all right?"

I did not see that details of the divorce were any business of Timon's, but I knew him well enough to understand that the remark had been kindly meant. "Nathan has been more than generous."

"Well, that's Nathan." Timon chewed a chicken and avocado sandwich. "Did you know that Minty's moving to the consumer-affairs section?"

Without a doubt there had been an ulterior motive to this meeting, but I was surprised Timon had revealed it so early. "No, I didn't."

"You have to keep your edge in this game. Keep moving. I'm not sure Minty kept her eye on the ball." A rim of avocado squeezed out between the slices of the bread and he caught it in the nick of time. Wiping his hands, he said, "You and I both know that what happens in business is not personal."

I put down my sandwich, struck by how old-fashioned Timon sounded—a man devoured and obsessed by his work. "That's one way of looking at it."

"The rules of private life don't apply."

In a previous life, I had worked with these nostra. They slid easily off the tongue, were convenient and portable, like lightweight luggage. But I did not have to carry them any longer.

"Yes," Timon raised one eyebrow, which made him look more a caricature than he would have wished, "running a business does not leave much room for scruple." The phone rang and Timon ignored it. This made me sit up: in the past Timon had never ignored phone calls. He went on, "The books pages have been disappointing. I gather Minty has had a few health problems. The sort that do take the eye off the ball."

"So?"

"If I floated the idea past your delightful nose that, possibly, your old job might be in the offing, what would you say?"

I could not deny the full-blooded, deep-bellied satisfaction. I reached for the mineral water and poured myself another glass. I intended that this moment should stretch and stretch. "Give me the details."

"More money. Better contract. Kim is underusing you."

"Kim and I understand each other. He's been very good to me."

Timon shrugged. "Oh, well." He pulled his notebook toward him and fiddled with the spine. "There are others."

As a threat, it did not impress me. "Of course." But I was curious. "Timon, what exactly has Minty not done?"

He filled in the blank page with a huge circle. "I just have a hunch that she's lost it." He looked up. "My instincts are generally right."

An imp, a devil, performed a merry dance in my head. "You put her there, Timon." I picked up my bag. "Thank you for the offer. I'll think about it and let you know." At the door, I paused. We had known each other a long time, and shared not a little. Good times, bad bumps. I turned back. "Funnily enough, it was good to see you." He had already opened a thick file and was riffling through the papers. "I'm sorry Minty didn't work out."

He sent me a little wave and said, "It happens. Some people don't promote well." A corner of his mouth went down. "She's put on weight, too."

"Not worthy of you, Timon," I said, not quite repressively enough.

Poor Minty. She did not mind using her looks for whatever purpose, but she would hate, simply hate, being condemned for the lack of them.

As luck would have it, I bumped into her as I crossed the foyer.

She was heading for the exit, the kitten heels slipping on the polished floor. Her hair was cut shorter, and the glossy skin had a tired, sallow tinge. Timon was right: she had put on weight.

"Minty?"

She stiffened and turned. "Rose. What are you doing here?" Within seconds her busy brain had put two and two together, and the dark, slanting eyes were as hard as agates. "Oh, I see. Vengeance is mine."

A girl in blue passed us and must have recognized me, for she stared at us both. "Not quite." I was in no hurry to give anyone any answers. "I haven't made up my mind."

"The bastard."

"You could make a scene."

She considered. "I'd say the die is cast. You've been there, Rose, you know what it's like."

We fell into step and I asked how Nathan was.

"Obsessed with office politics. But you know the form." She gave a short, unhappy laugh. "How's this? I run off with your husband and he turns into a prize bore. Even funnier, I've become a prize bore, too."

Her lips were chapped and bitten.

"You look a bit run down. Are you okay?"

She patted her stomach. "It hurts, dammit, trying to get pregnant. It's a pretty bloody awful procedure. Apparently I should have taken more care when I was living the good life. But it was fun. I wasn't to know the consequences." The dark eyes did not blink as she looked at me. "The funny ha-ha thing is I told Nathan I didn't come with a past. No ghosts, I said."

"I'm sorry."

"Don't waste your energy."

We came to a halt by the swing doors. As usual, Charlie was behind the entrance desk. When he saw me, he saluted and I smiled back.

"You've done it all correctly, Rose. A nice husband, a nice house, two point four children and a career. But be happy, Rose, you're free now."

I stiffened with dislike. "I think there are a few things you've missed out." What exactly? Humiliation, betrayal and an almost bottomless sense of failure . . . The fear of vanishing. Anger, acid and bitter. Desperation at the idea that I had been weighed and assessed by this woman with my husband's complicity. The death of a marriage.

But the failure had been not so much what had gone wrong in Nathan's and my marriage but what had not been going particularly right. Into that dangerous space, Minty had crept.

Minty scrabbled at my sleeve. "Nathan rants and raves about having some peace and how we can't afford it. But I say that I have my side of the equation to think about. Just because I ran off with him doesn't mean I don't have a voice. I tell him I'm owed that."

I had a vision of Minty and Nathan moving around Lakey Street, occupying separate rooms, separate thoughts, and I could not bear it for him. Perhaps this was the last thing I would do for

Nathan, but I went to his defense: "Nathan will listen. If you don't know that, Minty, then you don't know him." I wanted to say "deserve him." "You told me once he was a nice man, a pussycat."

She bit her lip, and a tiny point of blood welled on it. "That was at the infatuation stage."

I felt as though I had pushed open a door into a room that contained something very unpleasant. "Minty . . ."

She turned on me furiously. "I don't want to live in your house either. I don't want you peering at me from the corners. I don't want your bloody wallpaper."

"Change it."

Her eyes narrowed angrily. "Nathan says we can't afford it."

I took a step toward her. "Listen to me. You helped to destroy a marriage. You got what you wanted. You make it work."

She raised those unblinking eyes to mine, but there was no comfort any more in their dark depth. That had vanished. "The joke is," the words dropped from the chapped lips, "I haven't told Nathan yet but, against the odds—against what I deserve is what the medics mean—I *am* pregnant. The pokings and probings have worked." Fear, triumph and despair did battle on her face. "I'm pregnant with twins. How will Nathan take that?"

I rang Timon the following day and told him I would not accept his offer. He sighed. "You're not doing me any favors but, then, I couldn't expect you to."

I said something that surprised me: "Let's keep in touch."

I told Ianthe about Timon's offer and my reply as I drove her to the hospital. Ianthe clicked her tongue. "Don't you need a proper, settled job?"

"Possibly, but not that one." I glanced sideways. "I wouldn't mind doing some traveling."

"Not *that* again." Ianthe stared straight ahead. "You'll take care, won't you? You won't get in a muddle?"

By "muddle" she meant Hal. "I don't think so. Not this time."

Ianthe was not impressed and tried one last assault. "Are you sure you shouldn't talk to Nathan?"

"Yes."

The hospital came into sight and Ianthe gave a little gasp. "Rose, I don't want to go in. Can we drive round the block again?"

Eventually we went into the car park and slotted into a space. I stopped the engine and we sat still and silent. "I'll come and see you every day, Mum."

"I don't want to be a trouble." Ianthe grasped the crocodile bag on her knee. "You come in when you can. I don't want anybody making a fuss. I don't want anybody fretting."

This was bit like instructing a snowflake not to melt in the sun but I leaned over and kissed her. I summoned every ounce of self-control and said, "It'll go fine, and you'll be out in a trice."

"Your father was hopeless with illness." The dreamy little smile that always appeared when she talked about him played on her lips. "Fancy, for a doctor."

"Doctors know too much."

Ianthe smiled at me. "I'm glad it's you taking me in. He'd have been no good at all."

That was the best compliment my mother could ever have paid me. I swallowed hard. "Mum, you go in, I'll follow with the stuff."

Ianthe got out. I went round to the trunk and pulled out her case. There she was, framed in the hospital doors, which swooshed back. Handbag swinging over her arm, Ianthe stepped inside, and the doors closed behind her.

The streets of the city were filled with young women as I drove back through the warm evening. Bright, glossy, anticipating, they wore short skirts, cropped tops and strappy high heels. They had slender feet and rainbow nails. In the eyes and eager expressions were reflected lust, energy and greed. No grief yet. Or they hid it well. They ranted in groups, or glided singly along the pavements with rustling supermarket bags, rucksacks and shoulder bags. Some sucked bottles of beer, some bottles of water.

The sun dipped in the sky and sweat gathered on my top lip. I thought of bitter black coffee and music. Of reading books and the glimmer of white roses in the dusk. I thought of deep, tearing sorrow, then remembered—and anticipated—the exhaustion after a night of lovemaking. I thought of grief and its fallout, and the beauty of lit candles. I thought of Parsley, and the part of my life that was over. I thought of how it was possible both to shrink and unfold, how I had experienced both, and how the unfolding at forty-eight was both joyous and unexpected. And would continue for a long time.

I thought, most vividly and longingly, of my children. That first glimpse of Sam. Still confused from pain and the outrage of giving birth, I had accepted without interest the bundle placed in my arms. At first, neither of us registered the other. Then, quiet before the adventure of his life got under way, the baby fixed on my face. In those wide, calm eyes were surprise and astonishment at the prospect of the new world he had entered. A gaze that took me back to the beginning, ready to start again.

When I got back to Lakey Street, the answerphone was flashing. "Mum," Sam sounded happy, "can we come over for supper? Jilly and I have sorted our plans and we want to talk them over."

"Rose," Timon clipped in, "I forgot. I owe you lunch at the Caprice . . ."

"Mother," this was an indignant Poppy, "where have you been? I've been calling and calling. I need your advice, so hit the phone."

"Rose," Vee was harassed, "I've got something that needs doing yesterday. Call pronto."

Next was Nathan. He sounded very far away. "Rose, all set for moving next week. There are a couple of things we need to clear up. Could you possibly give me a call in the office? Jean will patch you through."

Finally, there was Hal, sounding much closer: "Rose, there's a return air ticket to Pisa for you in the post. No questions, I'm paying. I owe it to you. I'll meet you there on the Thursday. Good luck with the move."

When I had been packing Lakey Street the last thing I had tackled was a box of discarded books in the cupboard under the stairs. Right at the bottom, covered in dust, was the paperback on South American politics that Nathan had been reading on the plane when I met him.

He had told me then that he didn't rate the author, but when I opened the book, now yellow and brittle, it was covered in ticks as well as notes in his handwriting. I could only conclude that he had lied. Perhaps that tiny white lie had been told to impress me. It had worked: I had been impressed.

I put the book into the shelf in the sitting room where it belonged.

After my belongings had been taken away to Clapham by the moving men, I let myself through the French windows into the garden. The *Solanum* was in danger of throttling the Iceberg, a delphinium required staking and the grass needed a good cut.

I walked round the forty-five feet that had, once, required taming and, no doubt, would need it again in the future. Irrevocably the garden would change. Neither Minty nor Nathan would pay it any attention.

I knelt by the little mound under the lilac and pulled out the tendrils of bindweed that had crept over it. "Sleep well, Parsley."

The olive tree had been taken away, and my last task was to clean out the fountain. One or two leaves had fallen into it, so I sifted them out and dumped them on the compost heap. Then I gave the pump an extra thorough clean, refilled the fountain with fresh water and switched it on to test it.

The water splashed out into the pool. Always changing, yet never changing.

I turned it off, and the fountain was silent.

I went indoors, closed the French windows and locked them behind me.

Three days later, I stepped out of a car on to a hillside and into an explosion of light, warmth and fragrance. Blossom foamed over stones, the olive trees danced and shimmered, and there was a waterfall of leaf and plant—jasmine, roses and lilies. Morning glory, bougainvillaea, geranium and lavender. Colors that, in the sunlight, were bright and strong.

I felt myself swimming up toward the light, a fluid sun-filled moment of release and pleasure.

Get a sneak peek at Elizabeth Buchan's new novel—a compulsively readable, insightful tale about the true meaning of marriage

THE GOOD WIFE
STRIKES
BACK

Coming from Viking in January 2004

Fanny Savage has a nineteen-year record—earned with patience, devotion, and contentment—as the perfect wife to an ambitious, idealistic politician. But, much as she and her husband love each other and their teenage daughter, Fanny senses within herself a creeping restlessness. She has given two decades of her own life to being the Good Wife—was it worth it, after all? Could it be time for . . . a change?

Chapter 1

It is a truth universally acknowledged that one person's happiness is frequently bought at the expense of another's.

My husband Will, a politician to his little toe, did not entirely get the point. He maintained that sacrifices in the cause of the common good were sufficient in themselves to make anyone happy. And since Will had sacrificed a significant slice of his family life to pursue his ambitions as, first, a promising MP, then a member of the Treasury Select Committee, then minister, and—latterly—as one who was tipped to be a possible Chancellor of the Exchequer, it followed that he should have been supremely happy.

I think he was.

But was I?

Not a question, perhaps, that a good wife should ask.

•

On our nineteenth wedding anniversary, Will and I promised each other to be normal. To this end, Will carried me off to the theater, ordered champagne, kissed me lovingly and proposed the toast: "To married life."

The play was Ibsen's *A Doll's House,* and the production had excited attention. Although I could see that he was aching with tiredness, Will sat very still and upright in the seat, not even relaxing when the lights went dim. An upright back was part of the training he had imposed on himself never to let down his guard in public. Although I am better than I used to be, I am still laggardly in that department. It is so tempting to slump, hitch up my skirt and laugh when my sense of the ridiculous is tickled—and there was much in our life that was ridiculous. Politicians, ambassadors, constituents, coffee mornings, chicken suppers, state occasions . . . a wonderful, colorful caboodle replete with the ambitious and the innocent, the failures and the successes.

Of necessity, Will laughed with circumspection—so much so that, once, I accused him of having lost the ability through lack of use. There was only a tiny hint of a smile on his lips when he explained to me that one small error of attention could undo years of work.

I sneaked a look at him from under eyelids that still stung from the morning's regular date with the beauty salon. Dyed eyelashes were a necessity because, when I do laugh, my eyes water. In the early part of Will's career, when I was being scrutinized and weighed and measured from head to foot by sharp eyes in the constituency, Mannochie, Will's watchful and faithful political agent, had been forced to whisper discreetly, "Train tracks, Mrs. S," which meant my mascara had smudged.

There was no option but to laugh off that one and whisk myself to the nearest mirror for a quick repair job. This was part of the bargain struck between Will and me. In short, to look good as the minister's wife was to be good.

Dressed in pale, shimmery blue, Nora made her entrance onto the stage and her husband asked anxiously, "What's happened to my little songbird?"

Will reached over for my hand, the left one, which bore his wedding ring and the modest ruby we had chosen together. It was small because, newly engaged and glowing with love at the prospect of shared happiness and mutual harmony, I had not wished him to spend too much money on me. Hindsight is a great thing, and I have come to the conclusion that modesty is wasted when it comes to jewelry. The touch of his hand was unfamiliar, strange almost, but I had grown used to that, too, and it was not significant. Beneath the unfamiliarity, Will and I were connected by our years of marriage. That was indisputable.

At the end of the play, still in her pale blue, Nora declared, "I don't believe in miracles any longer." The sound of the front door opening and closing as she left the house was made to sound like a prison gate clanging shut.

Someone in the audience gave a little cheer. It echoed above the perfectly groomed heads in the stalls, and there was a rustle of collective embarrassment at this demonstration of female solidarity.

When Parliament sat, Will lived in London during the week, in a mansion block in Westminster and it was London where he did his deals in the Members' tearoom, and struck alliances. In the old days, he came down to Stanwinton at weekends to nurse his constituency and his family, in that order, and I came up to London infrequently. Now that Chloe, our daughter, was eighteen, I was free to come up to London most weeks, but tonight we were driving home.

I watched the cold, eerie city lights give way to the shadows of the suburbs. At home, I often played the game of not-turning-on-the-light-until-the-very-last-minute. I loved that moment of transition between light and dark, and the textures of light and shade. I had learned that if I remained quite still something surprising might swim up out of the spaces in my head. Sometimes only a fleeting thought. Sometimes a revelation or a conclusion. Its chief element was of surprise and I found myself increasingly craving the delight of discovery. It was the moment to consider peace, happiness, expectation, . . . but, lately, I suppose, to reflect on a certain, creeping restlessness and a growing sense that it was time for a change.

Will cleared his throat—I recognized the signal—and began to talk about his project of the moment: the controversial European initiative to tax anyone with a second car. "There's no question, but we have to do something before the world chokes. We can't stand by and do nothing; we must show that we mean what we say." He turned. "Fanny? Are you listening?"

"Of course," I said. "Look at the road, Will, not at me."

"Well?"

But I was thinking of the days when my energy had been devoted to Will's political life and objectives and wondering why I did not feel the same. It was not as though we were old. I still loved Will, although sometimes ripples of irritation and exasperation made me forget I did—but that was marriage. Our life still held many possibilities.

"Fanny . . . ? Do you agree with what I am doing?"

"I don't think it stands much of a chance," I replied. "I don't think people always want to be told what is good for them."

"So I'm on my own on this one?" he said with the tone of one well used to arguing a case. "Fair enough."

An hour or so later, he nosed the car into the drive, un-snapped his seat belt and reached for the red box filled with papers, which required attention, that was never far from a minister's side.

"I hope you enjoyed the evening." He hefted the box onto his knee and added, "We've made it Fanny, haven't we? Nine-teen years . . ."

I felt a sudden, intense disquiet. Or was it bewilderment? Where had those years gone? One of the saints, I think it was Theresa, wrote that the soul has many rooms. So does a life, and a marriage. Motherhood, too, and I had been curious to shine a light into each one. But having struggled through the muffling intimacies of being a wife and a mother, I was now asking: Which room was mine alone? Into which still, private room could I retreat?

I smiled at him. "It was a lovely evening." Then I leaned over and kissed him.

When we let ourselves into the house, I realized that I'd made the mistake, unlike Nora, of continuing to believe in miracles. The commotion that greeted us—Meg shouting and Sacha, her son, cajoling—meant only one thing. Will's sister had been drinking.

"Why?" I murmured. "Why now? She's been off it for months."

Will's face had tightened into the expression of frozen dis-tress that I knew so well and dreaded. "I'll deal," I said. "You go and check on your papers. Otherwise you won't get any sleep." I pushed him gently in the direction of the study. "Go."

I went down the passage that ran the width of the house and waited a moment or two at her door. The noises had stopped.

"Sacha?"

"Upstairs, Fanny."

I found him in Meg's bedroom, manhandling his mother's inert body onto the bed, and hastened to help. Meg was hunched on her side. I smoothed her hair back from her forehead. She was as fair as I was dark, and much smaller boned. "Has she had a lot?"

Sacha arranged her legs into a more comfortable position. "I'm not quite sure." He added with an effort, "Sorry."

"It's not your fault." I bent down to retrieve a whiskey bottle from the floor. It was still three-quarters full. "I don't think she's had that much . . ."

"But enough."

"She's been brilliant lately, and didn't touch a drop while you were away." Sacha's nu-metal band was struggling to get off the ground, and he was frequently away traveling the circuit.

He flinched and I could have kicked myself. "It *isn't* you. It isn't you coming back. . . . It's the time of year, or an unexpected bill or—"

"She rang my father today. He wants to renegotiate the alimony. That's probably it."

"Yes. That's it." Meg had never got over Rob walking out on her when Sacha was tiny. "Talking to your father is always tricky for her."

"I know," he said. He spoke far too wearily for a twenty-four-year-old. I slid my arms around my surrogate son. He smelled so clean. He always did, however many smoky, drink-filled places he'd worked in. "Don't despair."

"I don't," he lied.

"Shall I sit with her?"

Sacha propelled me toward the door. This was between him and his mother and, now that he was older, he tried to keep it that way—because it was so terrible and so intimate.

I turned to look at him. "It *was* only once, remember," I said. "There's been months and months of nothing."

In Meg's kitchen, her lost battle was marked out by a trail of half-empty coffee cups. The one by the phone was still full, and signaled the moment of defeat. "I hate you for knowing when to stop," she had once told me.

I harvested the cups and washed them up, scrubbing angrily at their brown, scummy rims. Through the window, I watched a vixen slide along the darkened flower bed. She was thinner than a London fox. They say that foxes are safest in the city, but I wonder if they are plagued by a genetic memory of the past. Do they miss the smell of corn in high summer, the crispness of frosted grass?

I left the mugs to drain and found Chloe slumped at the kitchen table beside a glass of apple juice. I bent over and kissed her. She smelled of shampoo and her soft cheeks were slippery with face cream.

She rubbed her eyes. "Couldn't really sleep," she said. "Is Aunt Meg OK?"

I trod warily. Will and I had been clever enough to hide the worst of Meg's excesses from our daughter. Chloe was still too young to be told the absolute truth, but too old to be lied to. "Fine."

She looked anxious and a little bewildered. With her fair hair and dark eyes, she was a smaller, infinitely more delicate version of Will. One day she would be beautiful and that promise gave me deep, unqualified pleasure. "Did you and Dad enjoy the play?"

"It was brilliant; we had a lovely evening."

She polished off the apple juice. "It's nice that you two went out together."

"Did you do all your homework?"

She shrugged irritably. "Brigitte stood guard and I told her to get lost . . . but I did it."

Brigitte was our temporary au pair-cum-housekeeper, who took her duties very seriously.

"Tea?"

She shook her head.

"Bed, then." I pulled her to her feet, hustled her upstairs and settled her. I hunkered down beside her and whispered, "Everything's fine."

Chloe closed her eyes. "Do I really have to go to Pearl Veriker's funeral tomorrow?"

"Dad says we must. No argument."

"It's not fair," Chloe hissed. "Just because you have to do all these ghastly things, you make me as well."

"Go to sleep."

I hovered for a minute or two outside her room. Poor Chloe. She would learn that every shared life, every separate life, has bloodstained patches and tattered remnants of compromise. Sometimes, too, the dull ache of small martyrdom.

Will was already in bed and I slid in beside him. "Chloe woke up. I've tucked her back in."

"Good." He hesitated. "Is she . . . is Meg all right?"

"Sleeping."

"What triggered her off do you think?"

I thought about it. "She and Rob talked on the phone about money, but I suspect that it had something to do with our anniversary."

Our conversation went round and round on the subject of Meg. As it always did. Will scratched his head. "I would give much to think that Meg was happy and sorted out." He turned to me. "She has a lot to thank you for, Fanny. So do I."

My feelings for Meg could be ambivalent, but being thanked by Will was sweet.

He stirred restlessly. "What do you think is best, Fanny?" he said. "Do you think we should arrange more help for her? Could you manage to do that?"

"I could, but it might be better if you could talk to her. Maybe she needs a bit of your attention."

He thought about this. "I haven't got the time at the moment. But I will when I can. I promise."

I used to dream of a big, generous, blowsy household where children rustled and murmured in the bedrooms—two, three, even four of them. And every night, I would do the rounds. "This is Millie," I would say, smoothing fair tangles away from her face. "This is Arthur," removing the thumb from his mouth. "And *this* . . . this one is Jamie, the terror."

But it had not happened that way. After Chloe there were no more babies. My body pulled and strained to obey my longings, but it could not do what I asked of it. Sometimes they haunt me, my nonchildren—those warm, sleeping, rosy bodies, the children-who-never-were—and I listen out for them playing under the eaves.

"I don't mind," Will said to me once. "We have Chloe, that's enough. We look after her. I look after you. You look after me, Fanny. *Be content, please.*"

"Don't you mind at all?" I asked.

He touched my cheek. "I mind for you. I mind anything that hurts you."

Yet, as it turned out, my household was full, and we had

been happy. First Chloe was born, and I was catapulted into the terror and mystery and exultation of a love that would never die. Then Meg came to live with us; Sacha too, after his sixteenth birthday. The au pairs came and went; the party workers slipped in and out, each leaving a ghostly imprint on the atmosphere, their rustles and murmurs dissolving into the general murmur of life.

A PENGUIN READERS GUIDE TO

REVENGE OF THE
MIDDLE-AGED WOMAN

Elizabeth Buchan

AN INTRODUCTION TO
Revenge of the Middle-Aged Woman

Revenge of the Middle-Aged Woman is a modern Everywoman's tale. It is the funny, heartfelt, and sad—but definitely not tragic—story about love and how it touched forty-seven-year-old Rose Lloyd. As a college student, Rose fell in love with a man. His name was Hal and he loved her but also wanted to roam the world. Then she met Nathan, who wanted to marry her and raise a family. Rose loved Nathan, too, although for different reasons. She made a decision.

One wedding, two children, and twenty-five years later, Rose is a book editor for a weekly London paper where husband Nathan also works as the deputy editor. Rose is at peace in her life, happy and secure in the knowledge that she has successfully balanced the often conflicting demands of home and career. But when Nathan announces that he is leaving her for another woman, the stability she has always relied upon is unexpectedly gone.

Nathan laments, "I feel imprisoned by the walls I've built around me," just before he tells Rose that he's leaving her for Rose's own trusted twenty-nine-year-old assistant, Minty. Young, attractive, and incredibly ambitious, Minty has designs on more than Rose's husband. The same day that she loses her husband, Rose discovers that she is going to be replaced on the job by none other than Minty, who promises to bring a younger look and tone to the book section.

Out of a job, a marriage, and soon to be ousted from the cozy home and garden she's lavished with care, Rose is suddenly alone with too much time on her hands. While her friends and children rally around her, Rose is dealt a blow by her mother, who implies that it was Rose's selfish decision to work outside of the home that destroyed her marriage. Rose sinks into despondency, begins to drink a little too much, and wonders if her mother is right. But when in the midst of her mourning, her beloved cat, Parsley, dies, Rose realizes, "I had had enough. I wanted my grief dead." She decides to live—and that's when the fun really begins.

With the complacency and safety of her married life and career gone, Rose remembers how a long-ago trip to Rome showed her that most people lived not in the radiant semitransparent envelope that writers described but in a plain brown one with which they had to make do, but which was better than nothing: "I was sixteen . . . and in love for the first time—with being there, out of England. Rome was noisy, filled with smells—coffee, exhaust, sweat, hot buildings—and its flux of life, noise and sensation flowed through me, intensely, luxuriously felt." As Elizabeth Buchan weaves the narrative back and forth between Rose's youth and middle age, we see Rose once again reach out for the meaning in life and to courageously explore the life-altering decision she made long ago. What she discovers is sweet revenge, indeed: the promise of better days ahead, no matter her age.

A Conversation with
Elizabeth Buchan

1. You weave the narrative beautifully between the joys and sorrows of Rose's time with Hal and her marriage to Nathan. Why did you choose to frame the story this way?

One of the points I wanted to explore was about timing. When we make our choices—to marry, to have children, to change jobs, etc.—has a direct bearing on how successful or not our lives will be. Rose knew she wanted children and, however intense and addictive her feelings for Hal, it was not likely to happen with Hal, who wanted different things. Reflecting on her history helps Rose to clarify the muddle and anguish left by the breakdown of her marriage, and also to suggest these ideas to the reader. Amplifying the same point, Nathan chooses to step back out of one cycle that is coming to an end, only to find he is back in the same place, and is now faced at fifty-something with a reduced income, a wife, and twins. More important, perhaps, he has deprived himself of a peace and freedom that he might have expected after the hurly-burly of raising one family.

2. Ianthe has always been completely unsupportive of Rose. To what degree do you think this influenced Rose in the choices she made?

Again, one of the points I thought would be interesting to write about was the connections and the differences among three generations of women: Ianthe, Rose, and Poppy. Ianthe is very much a woman from an older generation. She does support her daughter, but she also holds different views about forgiveness and about the traditional role of women and how they should conduct their lives. She would consider it part of her support, and duty, to speak her mind. To a certain extent, we all shrug off the nostrums and mind-set of the older generation. If Rose does just that with Ianthe, what is Poppy doing with Rose?

3. When Rose is told about the affair, she questions Nathan: "Is it because as we grow older, we grow less confident . . . and we need to reestablish ourselves all over again?" Do you feel this is the reason why most marriages fall apart?

Of course, becoming middle aged is not all plain sailing—there are disappointments and bitter griefs. Women mourn their changing looks and some feel that they have become invisible. Life is more complicated, less straightforward, and less easy to pin down than it appeared to be in the twenties and thirties. As a result, both sexes may, at times, feel a little daunted, which is what Rose is questioning. Here is where the courage and resilience of middle age can be so well deployed. It is probably true to say that in any long-term relationship a fault line will appear at some point as the individuals are bound to change, develop, and reorient themselves. If the partnership is functioning, this will add richness and exhilaration. But if it is not, and the fracture is not dealt with and discussed, undoubtedly it must contribute to the breakdown of a relationship.

4. Mazarine, upon hearing the news that Nathan has left Rose, blithely comments to Rose, referring to the affair as a phase that will ultimately end, "Be practical and wise, it's our role in a crazy world." Could you elaborate on that statement?

As a Frenchwoman, Mazarine is reflecting a culture where affairs are seen in a slightly different light. But she is also expressing a view on sexuality and sexual behaviour that she is considering within a larger context—a philosophy that comes from her worldly experience. She is urging Rose to view Nathan's straying as a blip and not as a finality. What she in effect is saying: marriages are tougher than affairs. These things happen. Ride through it.

5. Some critics have said that Mazarine is so vivid that she deserves her own book. Who is your favorite "minor" character?

I have to confess to having a great fondness for Mazarine. I love her practicality and her elegant theories of life. But I also find Alice very intriguing—a young woman focused on her career who is thrown hard against a brick wall of inconvenient emotion. In her way, Alice is quite brave.

6. Did you write this story to help liberate middle-aged women from those husbands who wish to start new lives with younger women? What inspired the book's amazing title?

I wrote the book because I was interested in the stage of life where it is possible to look both back and forward, and it is a very interesting place to be. Sooner or later, we all get there and the rewards are that patience, observation, and experience yield more subtle and textured pleasures than the ardency and impatience of our younger years. That is the theme. The plot is about the "happily ever after": i.e., what can happen to us after we have settled down with our Prince Charming and it goes wrong—a situation which offers plenty of drama for the novelist. The title just arrived in my head. Bang. It stems from the Spanish proverb, "Living well is the best revenge."

7. The setting and character of your novels are very British yet the book has become a New York Times *bestseller. Has it surprised you how much American audiences have embraced* Revenge?

The response in the U.S. has been fantastic and generous and I confess to being just a little surprised, but hugely delighted. Then again, the breakdown of a marriage is something that happens in many western cultures—thus, in that sense, it is a universal predicament. I also feel that the slightly older woman has been ignored lately in fiction. Her voice should be heard, too!

8. Are you working on anything now?

My next book is *The Good Wife Strikes Back*, which takes a look at marriage. What is it? How does it work? Why does it last? Fanny has been married for twenty years to a politician, a position that requires her to look good but remain silent in public. But she is no fool and, after her daughter leaves home, she begins to question her choices . . . and her future.

QUESTIONS FOR DISCUSSION

1. Do you think the young Rose should have stayed with Hal or did she make the right decision to marry Nathan?

2. How would you describe Minty's relationship with Rose? Were there definite indicators something was amiss that Rose might have noticed sooner?

3. Do you think that Rose was complacent in her marriage and career? What have you learned from her journey toward self-exploration?

4. What do you think of Minty? Did she really want Rose's life all along and just pretended to be independent or do you think something changed her?

5. Rose sought friendship and solace with friends to help her through the depression. Are there other ways she might have helped herself? What would you have done?

6. The novel was written from a wife's point of view. At any time in the novel, did you find yourself sympathizing more with Nathan than with Rose?

7. Which character, if any, in the novel disappointed you most and why? Which character surprised you most and why?

8. How do you think Rose's life choices have influenced her daughter Poppy's life? Do you think Poppy's marriage will last?

9. The novel ends on an ambiguous note. What do you think happens next?

For more information about or to order other Penguin Readers Guides, please e-mail the Penguin Marketing Department at reading@us.penguingroup.com or write to us at:

Penguin Books Marketing Dept.
Readers Guides
375 Hudson Street
New York, NY 10014-3657

Please allow 4–6 weeks for delivery.
To access Penguin Readers Guides online, visit the Penguin Group (USA) Web site at www.penguin.com.